Passion Flowers

BY DAVID RITZ

Novels

Glory
Search for Happiness
The Man Who Brought the Dodgers Back to Brooklyn
Dreams
Blue Notes Under a Green Felt Hat
Barbells and Saxophones
Family Blood
Passion Flowers

Biographies

Brother Ray (with Ray Charles)
Divided Soul: The Life of Marvin Gaye
Smokey: Inside My Life (with Smokey Robinson)
Rhythms and Blues (with Jerry Wexler)

Lyrics

"Sexual Healing" (recorded by Marvin Gaye)
"Love Is the Light" (recorded by Smokey Robinson)
"Brothers in the Night" (theme song of film, *Uncommon Valor*)
"Release Your Love" (recorded by the Isley Brothers)
"Eye On You" (recorded by Howard Hewett)
"Get It While It's Hot" (recorded by Eddie Hendricks and
     Dennis Edwards)
"Power" (recorded by Tramaine Hawkins)
"Velvet Nights" (recorded by Leon Ware)

Passion Flowers

by DAVID RITZ

115319

DONALD I. FINE, INC.
New York

All rights reserved, including the right of reproduction in whole or in part in any form. Published in the United States of America by Donald I. Fine, Inc. and in Canada by General Publishing Company Limited.

Library of Congress Cataloging-in-Publication Data

Ritz, David.
    Passion flowers / by David Ritz.
        p.   cm.
    ISBN 1-55611-283-1
    I. Title.
  PS3568.I828P37   1992
813'.54—dc20   91-58659
                                                CIP

Manufactured in the United States of America

10 9 8 7 6 5 4 3 2 1

Designed by Irving Perkins Associates

Thanks to Don Fine, Aaron Priest, my wife
Roberta, my babies Alison and Jessica, and the rest
of my family and friends who keep me going with
lots of love.

THREE   WOMEN . . .

Months, even years could pass when they didn't see each other. They might be on the other side of town or the other side of the world. There were distractions, obligations, preoccupations. Especially their men. Yet scarcely an hour went by when they didn't cross one another's mind, flickering images from long ago, feelings of comfort, annoyance or wonder. The connection was absolute.

Their huge talents—clashing, complementary—blossomed during three successive epochs:

Georgia, who came of age in the forties and fifties; Chanel, in the sixties and seventies; Marisa, prodigy of the eighties and nineties.

Grandmother, mother, daughter.

Actress, singer, model.

Entertainers whose styles and motivations were similar yet disparate. Longing to be noticed, especially by one another, especially by an audience of millions of adoring fans. Art and ambition fused. The desire for self-expression. The need to succeed, to beat the odds. Sometimes seen as overly aggressive, often perceived as irresistibly charming, the trio knew the value of tenacity—and shock. Their strategies for survival were intuitively, fearlessly dramatic.

Men were drawn to them; men surrounding them, courting them genteelly, pursuing them doggedly, offering them various forms of salvation, offering them the world. Yet the women remained as always—forces of surprising power, resolutely independent, forever joined, forever separate, linked by a love they were unable to define.

Delicate, exotic.

Now gentle, now fierce.

Fragrant mysteries.

Passion flowers.

PART ONE

The Past

1 9 4 5

Georgia took the train to Pasadena, not Los Angeles proper, because she had read that's where the movie stars disembarked, enabling them to avoid the hordes of fans. In Georgia's right hand she carried a worn suitcase, fastened by two leather straps, representing the whole of her possessions; in her left hand she held a copy of Motion Picture magazine from last October with Lena Horne on the cover. Never before had a colored actor or actress been on the cover of a movie magazine. Georgia clutched the fifteen-cent issue as though it were her guaranteed ticket to Hollywood.

It was May and the weather was mild, the air soft. The trip from rural Florida had been long and uncomfortable, the colored-only section crowded, the food tasteless. A drunken man had given Georgia problems, but the porters were quick to intervene on her behalf. She was a nineteen-year-old who looked at least twenty-four. She carried herself with assurance, although the source of such confidence was unclear. She had left Tampa without a single reference. Officials at the orphanage advised her to seek work in Miami but she paid them no mind. With her fine academic record, they urged her to get a teacher's certificate. But what did they know? She'd known those people her whole life. Their vision was narrow; they lacked the least understanding of her ambition. Once she escaped their province, she felt free. And not unafraid.

For four long years she'd been planning this trip. Working on weekends—cooking, serving, cleaning—she'd saved every dime she'd earned, vowing never to cook, serve or clean again. She was better than that. She realized the power of her extraordinary beauty. She appreciated the advantage of her light skin. She had memorized the train schedules. She had dreamt of nothing else but California.

15

Her real name was Mabel Ruth, but no more. Her new name was Georgia Faith. All actresses adopted new names.

Everything in California looked and smelled new. Pasadena looked like heaven: small orange groves and sweet cottages, sun-splashed gardens and a towering mountain in the backdrop. It was a land of flowers and blooming promise. Life already looked like a movie set and she half-expected to see Judy Garland or Mickey Rooney or Clark Gable come bounding around the corner to greet her. The faces of the citizens of Pasadena were friendly but Pasadena wasn't Hollywood. She had to get to Hollywood.

She wound up on Central Avenue in the heart of the colored section of Los Angeles, far from where movies were made. It was not an easy trip. It involved a great deal of walking, a trolley car, a broken-down taxicab and several rejections from seedy hotel managers who asked questions about the color of her skin. "Negro," she would answer defiantly when asked. Any other reply was unthinkable. In her mind's eye, she saw her exotic beauty as being specifically Negro. This was her identity and, ultimately, she reasoned, it would be her advantage. It set her apart.

But along Central Avenue where the nightclubs were plentiful—the Alabam, Down Beat, Lovejoy's, Memo, Last Word, Turban Lounge—she didn't like the looks of some of the people she saw. Many were not, as she had hoped, refined Negroes. She had read of Sugar Hill in Harlem and presumed Los Angeles would have an area of similar distinction. The sounds and sights of Central Avenue, though, were jarring: some of the men were shockingly forward; some of the women blatantly aggressive. There was sex in the air, and it mingled with the music. The street was jumping. Low jive and high art swam in the same river. Art Tatum, the half-blind jazz pianist some critics compared to Artur Rubinstein, played in joints where women could be bought for the price of a few drinks. This was all news to Georgia who, in her Florida fantasies and wide-ranging reading, had imagined a much different big city. She was directed to a boardinghouse catering to a "good class" of people. Its proprietor, Miss Marva Lavastahl, was herself a self-invented personage.

Miss Marva Lavastahl's house was a Victorian affair with gabled roofs and an enormous porch on Fortieth Street just a few blocks down from the Elks Auditorium, a popular venue for big-band dancing.

"I can see you're new and I can see you're pretty," said Miss Marva. "I can also see you're going to need lots of advice because you come from down South—I hear it in your voice—and this here is certainly not the South. This here is California, dear, and the manners are different, the manners are very important."

Georgia was impressed. Manners had always impressed her. She valued them; she saw them as the key to opening doors. She'd had the best manners of any girl at school, which is why she won every prize. The only prize she cared about, though, was a glamorous life in Hollywood. Never in those dreams, however, had she imagined anyone like Miss Marva Lavastahl.

The woman weighed nearly two hundred and fifty pounds and stood over six feet tall. Yet for all her bulk and height, her manner was regal. She wore gowns with fringes, wide-brimmed red hats, an array of shoes in dyed leathers—orange, gold, kelly green—long ostrich feathers, capes, white gloves which extended high above her elbows. Each morning when she came to the breakfast table her appearance was an event. Her outfits amazed Georgia. Miss Marva took a fancy to Georgia. She gave her one of the better rooms, on the third floor, far in the back. There was an oak dresser, a brass bed, even a side chair. Georgia had never had her own room.

"If you leave your windows open at night," said Miss Marva, "you'll hear music from the street. Now when Mr. Duke Ellington and his orchestra is in the city, they'll be staying here, and you'll meet Mr. Ellington, yes you will, you'll meet his vocalist Miss Ivie Anderson, you'll meet all the people who matter because they all come to Miss Marva's, they certainly do, darling, because they know this is a fine house and they appreciate fine food. Mr. Cab Calloway, he loves my peach cobbler, he tells everyone about it, and Miss Hattie McDaniel, why she's been my guest, and Miss Katherine Dunham and Mr. Lionel Hampton and so many others I forget. Mr. Joe Adams, he's the disc jockey on KOWL, and we call him the Mayor of Melody, and he comes by all the time. I have a book downstairs where they sign their names, and I want you to see it, I want you to put your name in it because I have a feeling about you. Even though you're young I have a feeling you've come to the right place, sure enough you have."

Georgia thought she was in heaven, and Miss Marva Lavastahl was her angel-savior.

"Do you sing, darling?" asked Marva.

Not wanting to disappoint, Georgia nodded. After all, she *could* carry a tune.

"I thought you could. Could tell by how you speak with that sweet voice of yours. I heard music in it. My own daughter was a singer, but she's gone, and that's nothing to talk about, nothing I want to think about. But if you're a singer you'll sing in my house because I have a beautiful grand piano downstairs, came all the way from Italy, yes it did, and so many wonderful piano players come through here, dear. Why there's Miss Dorothy Dandridge and Mr. Charles Brown, there's Mr. Nat Cole, he's playing the 331 Club on Eighth Street, and Mr. Earl Hines who has his own orchestra, and maybe you can sing with these people. I'm sure they'd love to hear you because I'll tell them to listen and they always put me at a table right in front of the bandstand, they call me by name, they treat me like family, they live in my house and pay me more money than I even ask for. That's the class of folks I'm catering to. Do you understand Miss Marva? Do you see who the Lord has sent you to?"

Georgia was not a true believer—strict Christianity was a burden rather than a comfort—but surely something good was happening here. Surely she was being moved in the right direction.

Until that first day of reckoning.

It happened in the large living room of Miss Marva's home. The other tenants—two elderly gentlemen, a family from Oakland, a middle-aged woman and her daughter on hand for the funeral of their grandfather—settled in overstuffed couches while Mr. Teddy Wilson, who had starred with the Benny Goodman orchestra and arranged music for Miss Billie Holiday, played piano.

"Mr. Wilson is a musician of international stature," said Miss Marva, "and his father is a distinguished professor in Austin, Texas."

Teddy Wilson asked Georgia what she'd like to sing. She had thought about this moment for days now—Miss Marva had prepared her—and requested "Travelin' All Alone," a song she had heard at school. One of her teachers owned the shellac record. She had memorized the lyrics and when Teddy Wilson began to suggest the melody Georgia followed along. Her interpretation was correct—which was, as far as Mr. Wilson was concerned, the problem. Georgia had proper enunciation and a small fluttering in-tune voice; she was certainly beautiful—no one had seen green eyes like hers before—everything was fine except for one thing: The girl didn't swing. She was stiff. The song never took flight or trembled with emotion. She was on the beat, never off it, never behind or ahead of it. The beat was obeyed, not played with, not taken for granted, never used as a point of departure but rather a safety net. No chances were taken. The song never soared, the story never told. Teddy Wilson wasn't fooled. Miss Marva Lavastahl and her guests were.

"Marvelous, darling!" Miss Marva exclaimed, clapping her hands. The guests were thrilled to be there for such a sterling debut. Mr. Teddy Wilson kept quiet; he was a gentleman; besides, he looked forward to one of Miss Marva's extravagant smothered pepper steak dinners topped off with several portions of peach cobbler.

Encouraged by her good taste in music, her infallible matchmaking among the musical elite, Miss Marva decided to take Georgia to audition for the great Jimmie Lunceford, whose orchestra would be playing this very weekend at the Lincoln Theater.

For the occasion, Marva herself outfitted Georgia. She fixed her hair, applied her makeup, found her a stunning gown with pale yellow lace and puffy sleeves.

"It's a pleasure doing this for someone who can wear this and look like a princess," said Marva. "A princess out of a fairy tale."

Georgia felt elegant. She was full of confidence. Strong confidence was the basis of Georgia's constitution. She spent a week listening to Lunceford's phonograph records, the same week the newspapers and radio reported V-E Day. The war in Europe had been won. Celebration swept through every part of the city. The boys would be coming home. But while others listened to the news, Georgia kept listening to Jimmie Lunceford and memorized all the Lunceford favorites.

At the end of Lunceford's opening night, well past midnight, with a large crowd on hand, Georgia stood in front of the orchestra and sang. Again, she was correct. Again, she didn't swing. Only this time the leader and his musicians let her know it. "She just don't feel it," said the leader himself. He was a professional who spoke his mind. So did several members of the audience. One man booed.

The boo resonated in Georgia's sleep. The boo turned into a nightmare in which she was run out of town and forced back into the orphanage that had become a prison, a torture chamber, a house of horrors from which there was no escape.

The next morning Georgia's sweat had soaked the bed. She was filled with humiliation and the certain realization that she would never be a jazz singer. She said as much to Marva.

"Doesn't matter, honey. Someone beautiful as you is *bound* to do good."

"I never really wanted to sing."

"Then what is it you came here for?"

"To be in pictures."

Marva's eyes flashed. The crevices in her fleshy cheeks were like rivulets. Her smile was radiant. "Why didn't you *say* so, sugar? Of course you want to be pictures. And does Miss Marva know the right people to send you to? She sure does."

The antebellum mansion looked real. The period costumes were lush. The action on the back lot was fast. It all had happened so quickly, Georgia barely had time to absorb the reality of the fantasy.

Only a week ago, Miss Marva Lavastahl had swung into action. She had contacted her friends, actresses Butterfly McQueen and Louise Beavers, who had provided names and numbers leading to a casting director looking for colored actresses for a high-budget film about to go into production.

"That's it!" bellowed Miss Marva. "That's the picture for my Georgia."

The picture was *Moonlight Roses,* a musical set in the deep South. The theme was rivalry among siblings of a rich family. The director, John Nash, was nervous and the writer, Sol Solomon, was on the set doing on-the-spot revisions.

Georgia was playing a maid, which didn't make her very happy. Nor did the fact that her period had started that very morning with an especially heavy flow. Still, this was an actual Technicolor Hollywood movie, people dashing around, dollies and cameras and lighting scaffolds, the shouting and the call for action.

The audition had gone smoothly. The maid, Regina, had a somewhat haughty attitude that suited Georgia. She read through the part —she was always a star reader in school—with ease. She had presence and spark and strong vocal projection. Her physical beauty sealed the deal. Marva beamed. Georgia beamed. The shooting started the next day.

The trouble started in the makeup room. Georgia knew she had to wear powder, but the caked substance looked like blackface, and she told the woman applying the stuff as much.

"No, honey," said the lady, "it's just special ointment."

She kept putting it on and Georgia kept getting darker and angrier. She kept quiet, though, because they were calling her to the set—she was to serve tea to the family—but when she appeared the director thought she was too light and ordered her back to makeup.

"I don't need more makeup," she announced in front of everyone. A long silence.

"She's too light," the director told his makeup artist, not Georgia. "She looks too damn white. A white woman wouldn't be serving this family."

Georgia swallowed hard. Cramps attacked her abdomen. She barely kept from doubling over but managed her way back to makeup, where more of the dark goop was applied to her cheeks, around her eyes, all over her neck. In the mirror, she saw herself as a spook. She returned to the set, prepared to deliver her lines, but before a word left her mouth Nash was shouting, "Too *light*, goddammit. We still got a skin problem."

"Mister," Georgia said, head snapping, "*you're* the one with the problem."

With that, she marched off the set. And, once out of view, she ran to the bathroom.

A half-hour later, still feeling sharp cramps, she traveled by trolley back to Central Avenue. Marva would be anxious to hear the news. Marva wouldn't believe it; Georgia didn't believe it herself.

Had she really done it? Had she really walked off the set the first day of shooting? Who was she, some gal from nowhere, to throw away the opportunity of a lifetime? But who was he, this arrogant bastard, to humiliate her before a group of strangers? He had turned her—and her character—into a joke. She hadn't traveled this far and taken the risks to put up with fools. At least she hadn't cursed him, hadn't lost her dignity.

"Never heard of anyone doing that before," Marva told Georgia after hearing the story. Georgia wasn't sure whether she was referring to Nash's actions or her own. Marva was busy working over a hot stove. It was nearly dinnertime and her boarders were hungry. "Honey," she told Georgia as she spiced the meat with pinches of salt, pepper and paprika, "you're different than any of the young things who come through here. You got a definite attitude."

"Is that good?" Georgia wanted to know.

"Can't say for sure, honey. All I know is you're for sure different. You gonna have trouble with these white men if you don't know how to treat 'em."

"How about the way they treat me, Miss Marva?"

"Come on in and eat something, baby," was all she said. "You'll feel lots better if you eat."

"There's a white man at the door calling for you," said Marva, knocking on the bathroom door. Georgia hadn't been able to eat a bite; the cramps were still painful.

"Who is he?"

"A Jew," Marva told her. "Can tell by the way he looks and the way he talks. Nervous man. Right downstairs in my living room. Says he needs to see you. He's got a big Hudson automobile parked in front. Bright red. You should see it. Says he's with the movies."

Georgia's first reaction was fear. By walking off the set, had she broken some law, some rule? Was she being fined or jailed? But that was ridiculous; it was a free country, so they said. She knew her Constitution, the Bill of Rights, could rattle off the date of the Emancipation Proclamation. No one owned her.

Downstairs a young man in a double-breasted slate-gray suit sat in a club chair as the colored borders eyed him out of the corners of their eyes. He was studying a racing form, making notations with a pencil. Bushy black eyebrows, wild and thick, dominated his face. His nose was broad, his eyes dark, his body full-fleshed. He was in his mid-twenties.

When Georgia entered the room he broke into an easy smile. She saw he had good teeth. He took off his summer straw—his black hair was thick and wavy—and offered his hand. His fingernails were buffed and polished. Words fairly burst from his mouth in a Brooklyn accent that Georgia found fascinating.

"I'm Sol Solomon," he said. "I wrote the movie you walked off today, and I just came over to say that you got guts and I admire guts.

No one's got guts in this town, but you, little lady, you're something."

Georgia didn't know what to say. What was this man after? Marva understood.

"That story," Solomon went on, "is no good anyway. They keep changing it. The director, this Nash, he's a schmuck."

Was he talking a foreign language?

"I told you he was Jewish," Marva whispered in Georgia's ear. "Jews are rich."

Georgia had never met a Jew before. There was none in the school or community she was raised in. She wasn't quite sure what a Jew *was*.

"I got your address from the office," said Solomon, "and I came over to tell you I quit the movie too. Told 'em to find themselves another hack. Not because of you, because the story stinks. I can tell a story—that's what they hire me for—and I can tell when the story starts stinking, believe you me."

There was a long silence, all eyes on Sol Solomon. Then Marva did something she'd never done before: She asked a white man, a virtual stranger, to her table for coffee and dessert. "I hope you like peach cobbler," she said.

"Love it," he assured her.

Georgia joined them at the table, still stunned that this man had sought her out.

"Funny thing," he said, looking around, "is that we once had a house like this in Flatbush. A big one. My father, he was a furrier until the Depression cleaned him out. Then we moved to a little apartment, all of us squeezed in there like sardines."

Georgia smiled at the image. He seemed gruff but gentle. She saw how he couldn't keep his eyes off her.

To him she seemed to have come from another world where women were somehow softer. God, she was a looker. It was crazy that he'd driven down to Central Avenue chasing after a colored extra, he wasn't in his right mind, but then again maybe he was.

A week later—after several proper visits by Mr. Solomon to Miss Marva's boardinghouse—Georgia found herself sitting next to him in his red Hudson. They were driving up the coast. She had not seen the Pacific Ocean before, never known a day this clear, a sky this blue, a sea so green. Seagulls dived and soared through space. Sandpipers skidded along the shore. Sol was talking. It seemed like Sol was always talking, but Georgia didn't mind. His incessant gab somehow relaxed her, took off the pressure; nothing was expected of her. Once in a while he'd glance over, as though to make sure she was still there, to convince himself she was real.

He hadn't taken her to a restaurant and she was glad. She wasn't interested in public scenes. Back in Florida a white man caught with a colored woman had been beaten to death, the woman chased out of town. Things were a little better in California, said Miss Marva, but not much. Marva approved of Sol because "his feelings are sincere," but she knew what he wanted from Georgia. "He knows important people," she told her protégé. "He'll help you. But if you're gonna get, you're gonna have to give."

If he was handsome, it was only in peculiar ways. Georgia found his peculiar ways intriguing. His street accent had the lure of unknown territory—this place called Brooklyn, where Jewish people talked quickly and unceasingly, where rhythms ran fast, emotions ran high and money was always being made.

"I make decent money now," said Sol, "but not like I should be making. Not like I will be making. When I was a kid I told stories and my father said, 'Sol, one day your bullshit will get you in trouble.' He was wrong. My bullshit makes me money. I don't write like a lot of writers where they think it out or plan it out because I don't have it planned out. I don't even type, I don't write nothing down, I just start talking and there's this girl who takes shorthand, Louise, she fixes it up 'cause she's been to college. She makes it read nice, but I tell her, leave it raw because raw sells. The raw action, the twists and turns . . . hell, *I* don't even know what's going to happen next. And that's the fun part, the part that keeps me interested in this job, this job of writing stories because it's the only job I've ever kept. Working in the liquor store, running numbers, driving a hack . . . I was a loser, promise you I was. Maybe you wouldn't believe it looking at me all dressed up like this in fancy duds, but I was a loser till I started living my life like one of my stories, living like I didn't know what was going to happen next. And I still don't. You see what I mean? Tell me—isn't your life like a story where you don't know what's going to happen next?"

Georgia hadn't considered the idea. She was wearing a slim white summer dress and the breeze on her skin was cool and fresh. The seashore air was clean and crisp. Marva had ironed her dress perfectly. She was lucky to have Marva helping her and now here was Sol Solomon. "He's a man who can take you places," Marva had whispered. "Play him smart."

He was taking her to his cottage high up on a hill. It was small and plain, two simple rooms, a space for eating, a bedroom, a tiny bathroom. There were only a few pieces of furniture, an Emerson radio, the Artie Shaw orchestra playing dance music. The outdoor porch overlooked the sand and sea. By now the sky was electric purple, vibrating with streaks of red, slashes of blood orange, a sunset of glory and promise and optimism. They sat in rocking chairs, Sol rocking furiously, Georgia slowly as he talked about plans to buy up the land around his cottage even though everyone said buying land in the country was foolish. But he wanted land, he wanted peace of mind, he wanted to write movies that millions of people would love, not the kind where the directors change everything and nothing is real, stories about real life and the people he knew in Brooklyn with their fights and schemes—some good guys, some real shits, but everyone wanting something bigger and better because that was the American way, wasn't it? Didn't Georgia want something bigger and better too?

She'd been glad he'd asked her nothing about herself, so now she was startled as he asked questions about her past. When she started answering him, though, she surprised herself with the easy flow of invention. She too was a storyteller. Her story was beautiful, he said, the way her father had been a schoolteacher in this little Florida town and her mother a nurse, how they had their own home and car and they were the elite of the colored society and had dinner parties and went to fancy balls and sent Georgia to a fine college. He bought it all, because he wanted to, and because she was a very good storyteller, indeed. Sometimes she believed it all herself.

"I knew you had class," Sol said. "More than me, that's for sure. Class and brains. None of the dames in this town got class *or* brains, especially the ones who get by on their looks. Well, I need more than looks, I need someone to talk to, straight from here"—he put his fist to his heart—"someone with more than big tits and a good ass, pardon my talking raw."

She liked his talking raw. She'd not heard talk quite like that. It was a candor that brought her to a level of intimacy she had never known with a man. The young men she'd known—just one or two—had disappointed her. Sex had been quick and unsatisfying. Their impatience seemed to make them shallow, they couldn't savor the moment. Well, they weren't writers like Sol Solomon. They could never own a house on a hill like him, never cook her juicy hamburgers on a little pit barbecue in the backyard, never wait on her hand and foot. She liked being waited on. She liked that Sol was smitten, praising her looks, so anxious to please her and serve her coffee with cream and a piece of rich cheesecake he'd bought back in the city that far down the coast twinkled now like stars in the night sky. He talked about his brother, who was killed early in the war. His mother had died of grief; Sol was not her favorite son. Sol's father had died in 1939. Sol was alone. So was she, Georgia said. Her parents were killed in a terrible car crash. Their private revelations, shared intimacies, excited them.

Then for a while nothing was said, and in the silence he finally turned and kissed her. She felt his tongue move inside her mouth, and liked it. How eager he was, his need to please, his appreciation of everything about her, the way he pressed himself hard against her leg . . .

A thin chenille spread covered the bed. It felt fuzzy against her body. Moonlight actually bathed the bedroom, like in her storybook fantasies. He was very patient with her, but she felt his nervousness. He fumbled with her clothing. She smiled and he realized his awkwardness was okay. Slowly, she brought her dress over her head. There was a subtlety to the tone of her skin, a smoothness illuminated by the light of the moon that moved him to kiss her neck, her arms, to caress her with a tenderness not typical of his usual behavior with women. He hated fumbling with brassieres—he never could manage undoing the hooks—but she saved him the bother. He sucked on her small dark nipples, making them stiff. She felt the nervousness of him in the nervousness of his lovemaking. He needed to be told, needed to be led. She surprised herself by leading him, working intuitively with information she never knew she possessed. The chemistry between them was right, their passion responding to one another's shapes and needs. When he entered her, that same nervousness filled her with pleasure: his enormous drive, his desire to make her happy. His desperate energy was inside her, and she was able to give him what he wanted, a sense that he brought her past the brink of control. He unlocked her sexual hunger. She moaned and moved with his thrusts, she let herself go as he said her name over and over, "Georgia . . . Georgia . . . Georgia . . ."

A month later he took her to meet Peter Gold.

"Another Jew," said Marva. "There are a lot of Jews in the picture business, baby. And it looks like you're meeting them all."

Sol had brought Georgia a couple of classy dresses, a new hat and an extravagant supply of Max Factor cosmetics, the kind the movie stars used, he told her. She'd spent a weekend at his beach cottage and several nights in the city at his small house north of Sunset Boulevard. But she had yet to meet any of his friends and she understood why. Marva had invited him to the boardinghouse for dinner and afterward the four of them—Georgia, Sol, Marva and one of her boyfriends, Harper Montgomery—went to the Club Diddle Daddle on Central Avenue, a spot where a mixed couple could feel comfortable.

Marva was outfitted from head to toe in kelly green, her earrings clusters of bright Bakelite fruit. Harper Montgomery was a pistol, a short compact man with a big smile, blue velvet sports coat and black patent-leather shoes. He was a celebrity on the street, a successful tap dancer who commanded a ringside table.

"Herb!" Harper yelled at a man with a big-bulbed camera. "Come meet my friends. Herb's my baby brother. He's got the picture-taking concession here. He's only twenty-five and he's already the best cameraman in the city. Cat's also making movies."

"No kidding," said Sol.

Georgia, wearing a pink rhinestone choker on loan from Marva, caught Herb's eye. She noticed he had his brother's good teeth. His skin was darker and he stood a good five inches taller than Harper. He was reed-thin, a bit slouched and serious-looking. Compared to his older brother, his outfit was modest, punctuated only by a brilliant blue bow tie.

"What kind of pictures you make?" Sol wanted to know.

"Colored movies," Herb replied.

"Shorts?"

"Feature length."

"You got distributors?"

"Theaters in the South. Colored theaters. A few screens up north, a few out here."

"Terrific."

"Snap us," Harper suggested as he put his arm around Marva and Georgia.

Sol was left out but said nothing. Out of his element, he was on his best behavior.

The flash exploded. Aware of Sol having been left out, Georgia squeezed his hand.

"May we have a picture?" she asked Herb.

"I'd love to take your picture," Herb said, framing her face and excluding Sol again.

Another flash popped just as Slim Gaillard and his makeshift orchestra, featuring Charlie Parker, Dizzy Gillespie and Jack McVea, hit the downbeat.

Aside from novelty numbers like "Flat Foot Floogie," the music sailed over Sol's head and left Georgia a little bewildered. The melody was scrambled and the rhythm rim-shot scattered. But the ambience, the dressed-up crowd in full-flavored colors was alive; they looked like the music sounded—spontaneous, surprising, surprised.

Georgia heard the band with only half-hearted attention. Her eye followed Herb around the room and once, in a split second, he caught her looking. He was in the process of photographing not a table of patrons but Buddha-faced saxist Charlie Parker, a musician he considered a genius. When Herb's eyes met Georgia's, though, his serious face broke into a smile.

At the end of the evening, after the band had played its second set and Harper and Sol had carried on about the great singers and dancers they had known, after Marva and the men had polished off two bottles of rye and gotten lost in each other's laughter, after Sol had picked up the check and left an extravagant tip, on the way out the door Herb slipped Georgia a card.

"Please call me," it read over his phone number. "I need actresses."

* * *

"Peter Gold needs help," Sol was telling Georgia as he drove her over to Masters Studio a week later. "He needs me. He's a producer who doesn't understand story. That's like a baseball player who doesn't understand bats."

"But you said he's an important moviemaker."

"He is, he's got a big job working over at Masters, he's head of production, he's making all these decisions and he thinks he knows what he's doing 'cause he's been to a fancy college or something. But no one knows what he's talking about half the time except he married the boss's daughter, which is how it works out here. You marry the boss's daughter, you get to pick the movies they're gonna make, especially when the boss just had a stroke and you get to run the joint. Now the only problem is that the boss's daughter Grace is a dog. I mean, she barks. She got hit by the ugly stick and on top of that she's got a personality like some people got bad breath. I'm sorry, but them's the facts. She thinks he's off screwing half the actresses on the lot and she ain't half wrong. So she's got her spies and she drops by unannounced and embarrasses Mr. Big Shot in front of everyone by talking about how her daddy told her this and her daddy told her that. Her daddy, Bob Masters, is one tough son of a bitch who ain't famous for loving Jews and naturally not exactly thrilled his daughter married one. He gave Peter a top job but he treats him like hired help. Anyways, Peter calls me because he's looking for ideas and he knows I got ideas and I got an idea for a comedy and you're part of it, Georgia, you're a big part of it 'cause it's you who gave me the idea—"

"What is it?"

"You'll hear when I tell Gold, you'll love it."

The studio was off Santa Monica Boulevard and the guard reading a newspaper story on Joe Louis wouldn't let Sol through.

"Goddammit," said Sol, "we're here to see Gold. Call Gold's office."

Gold's secretary had no record of the meeting. Looking at Georgia looking at him, Sol was embarrassed as he jumped out of the car and took the phone away from the guard. "Tell him Solomon's here. Tell him Solomon's here and he ain't leaving till he sees Gold."

Gold was on one of the back lots. Sol wangled a drive-on pass and finally caught up with the head of production on a set designed to look like a sidestreet in Paris. The rain machines were running, a dozen umbrella-toting extras scurrying along, the principals—a man and woman—arguing in front of a make-believe Metro station. Standing behind the cameraman and director, his lanky arms crossed, his slim, tall frame erect and proper, Peter Gold scrutinized the action. He was not pleased.

"They sound like stiffs," Gold told the director. "They don't sound natural."

"That's 'cause the script ain't natural," Sol told Gold.

As Peter looked at the writer, Georgia was struck by the differences between the two. Gold's double-breasted tailored suit fit him perfectly; Sol's loud sport shirt didn't match his trousers. Sol was messy, Peter kempt. Gold's features were delicate, proportioned, his thin light-brown hair sheared that very morning. Sol needed a shave. Peter Gold seemed a man in control.

"We were supposed to have a meeting," Solomon told Gold.

"Please," said Peter, placing his finger to his lips, reminding Sol that they were in the midst of shooting a scene.

"You promised me a story meeting. I have an idea—"

"Who's she?" Peter asked, spotting Georgia.

"The idea."

"Let me straighten out this scene, I'll be in my office in a half hour."

Before Georgia moved off the set, though, she noticed a still photographer in the shadows beyond the lights. She thought it was the man she'd met at the Club Diddle Daddle. But what would Herb Montgomery be doing around here?

"Here's the idea," said Sol, gearing up.

Georgia looked about Peter Gold's office. The streamlined mahogany Deco furniture was designed to fit the space, the immense desk with its sweeping curves, the matching torch lamps, the porthole-shaped windows overlooking the sound stages, the Icart etching of Thaïs, consort to Alexander the Great, seductively reclining on a bed of tiger skins while two leopards kept guard, a tall Grecian urn artfully placed by her side. Well, no question, Mr. Gold had taste.

"Georgia plays a woman," Sol said, "who comes to New York from somewhere—Cuba, or maybe Puerto Rico—doesn't matter, some Latin place 'cause she looks Latin, and she's won a beauty contest down there and she's looking to win a beauty contest here, but because she's naïve and doesn't know the language all that good she gets taken in by these two guys planning a heist who use her as a beard while they rob this here rich society matron—"

"Wait a *minute*," said Gold, slowing Solomon down. "This woman is not Latin."

"No, I'm not," said Georgia.

"She's an American Negress and a . . . a beautiful one at that."

"Beautiful is right," said Sol. "Beautiful enough to play a beauty queen."

"Your story sounds, well, contrived," said Peter. His voice was baritone-rich, and the speech rhythm slow, deliberate. Georgia felt his interest in her; she also sensed how this man, so confident, was driving Sol crazy.

"You haven't heard the whole story," said Solomon. "You just heard the set-up—"

"Sol," Gold said, "you're a man of true enthusiasm. And I *appreciate* enthusiasm. On the basis of your enthusiasm I've tried to direct a few assignments your way. So far, though, the results haven't been exactly spectacular."

"What you talking about?"

"I'm *talking* about story structure," said Peter, lighting his briar pipe and filling the office with the aroma of imported blend. "I'm *talking* about a classic sense of story structure."

"My stories are real, I—"

"I suggest your stories need substance."

"I suggest you're full of shit," said Sol, getting out of his seat. "The streets are my school, the streets are the only school I need."

"Look, Sol, you mean well, I know that. If you'd like to help Miss Faith here, contact our casting office. I'll be happy to arrange an audition for her."

"Thank you," said Georgia.

Gold walked around his desk, took her hand and kissed it.

His lips felt warm.

*　*　*

That evening in his little house above Sunset, Sol Solomon saw that Georgia was distracted. He realized he'd made a mistake, but he also knew there was no going back. He bad-mouthed the production VP; he told Georgia the man was a phony, that Hollywood was full of smooth talkers like Peter Gold who, were it not for nepotism, would be selling encyclopedias door-to-door. Georgia nodded but Sol could read her thoughts. She'd seen the size of Gold's office; she'd been exposed to Gold's manners. Peter Gold had put on his nice-guy bullshit routine.

"Gold will promise you the moon," Sol told Georgia, "but don't hold your breath. His casting couch is sagging with broken promises. I tell you the truth . . ."

"He seems refined—"

"It's an act. He ducks, he hides, he's got scams here and scams there—"

"Then why did we go to see him?"

"It's the movie business, baby. They're all sleaze. One's worse than the other. You gotta trust me on this one. I got better guys than him for you to see, guys with the leverage to put you in a movie—"

"And Mr. Gold doesn't have that?"

"He won't, sugar, when his father-in-law gets back to work."

That evening, as he prepared Georgia a steak dinner, Sol worried that her feelings for him were definitely flagging. Even in bed, even when they made love, he heard her mind turning. Maybe she was just too damn gorgeous for him—too bold, too smart—maybe he didn't deserve her. Or maybe it was too crazy to be dating a colored girl. Every time he stepped out with her in public, his stomach got tight. She knew. She was too smart and sensitive not to feel his feelings. If she were a white girl he'd marry her in a second, wouldn't he? But if she were a white girl, she wouldn't look, or smell, or love him the way she did. If he couldn't marry her, at least he could help her. Or hang on. One way or the other, he had to keep her from slipping away from him.

*　*　*

"You have to look at everyone," said Miss Marva Lavastahl. "You have to look at everything."

Back at the boardinghouse, the women were sipping cold lemonade on a boiling July afternoon. Bing Crosby and the Andrews Sisters were singing "Ac´-cent´-chu´-ate the Positive" on the radio. Miss Marva switched the station to Louis Jordan's "Reconversion Blues." The ceiling fan was whirring fast, like Georgia's mind. She told Miss Marva about meeting Gold, describing the tension between Peter Gold and Sol.

"My way," explained the older woman, "is to be friendly to folks who's friendly to me. Simple as that. Now, men . . . they're like shopowners. When it comes to women, they got them an inventory. They like to have a right-ready supply. Only way I ever seen fit to work with that is to do likewise. Keep me my own supply. Short one, tall one, sweet one, sassy one. Different ones for different occasions. Meanwhile, I got my work and my boarders, I got my house to keep up and my meals to prepare so I need not be bothering about no lovesick gents gettin' into my business. No, ma'am. My business is my business and my men, well, I take 'em or leave 'em. That's the only way to stay one step ahead of the boys—believe you *me*."

"You've never been married, Miss Marva?"

"Once. That's where I learned what I learned. Had me a good man —or thought I did. He was a salesman, a smooth operator—Lord, you should have seen him, Georgia, skin like midnight and soft curls all over his head. He had Indian blood and Indian eyes and a smile that'd make you lonely just thinking about him leaving you. He bought me a little diamond ring—a real diamond, mind you—and we married in that church over yonder, the one just down the street. He promised me the moon and swore I was his life and soul and had me serving him hot apple pie in bed, until I learn he's got girls working for him all over this city. He's putting them on the streets, he's sending them to white men's hotel rooms, he's shipping them over to Hollywood, I mean, the man has an assembly line of these gals moving 'round town night and day. 'But none of them is mine personal,' he tells me, 'they just money to me. Don't mean nothing.' 'That ain't the point,' I tell him. 'You hurtin' them worse than if you'd beat them upside the head with a hammer, 'cause you ruining their hearts for the rest of their lives, can't you see that?' He couldn't. He couldn't see past my pocketbook, 'cause I already had a good business here and he wanted it for his own, wanted the whole house for his girls but, no sir, not Miss Marva. Miss Marva might be fooled for a hot minute, honey, but that's it. He opened my nose but I opened my eyes and I chased his slick ass outta here with a butcher knife, better believe I did. He left with a little nick on the side of his cheek, a little love nick I called it, just to remind him not to come calling or crawling 'round here no more. Far as husbands, he's the one-and-only and the never-again."

"What about Harper Montgomery?" Georgia wanted to know.

"Friendly enough man, but I suspect you really ain't asking after him, are you? You're asking after his brother Herb."

"He seems friendly too . . ."

"He's been round here on several occasions when you were out."

"Does he really make movies?"

"Why don't you go see? I'm telling you, girl, you got the class to earn the cash. You do as you please. You need to get out there and see 'bout all these different men. You can't be afraid, can't be no wall-flower. You gotta take the lead, sugar, 'fore these fools start leading you."

Herb Montgomery cupped his hands. "Action!"

The group of colored actors in Griffith Park, deep in the secluded hills of Los Angeles, responded by setting their blankets on a grassy knoll, opening their picnic baskets and spreading out the food, the sandwiches and chicken and ears of corn. They poured soda pop and beer, they chatted and mingled while the lone camera operated by Herb focused on a couple sitting under the shade of a great oak tree. A few feet away an old man played country blues on a beat-up guitar. The solitary notes were sharp and sweet and punctuated the conversation of the young man and woman.

The couple talked about moving out of Mississippi . . . "No future here," she said. " 'Fraid to leave," he said. " 'Fraid where we going ain't no better." "Being afraid is like being in prison," she told him. "Prison of the mind."

From behind the camera Herb smiled. His instincts were right; this Georgia was a natural. She had built-in dignity, poise. Lines flowed from her without calculation or self-consciousness. She was definitely something else. He'd been certain she was born for the part of Jenny —a self-educated small-town Southerner who wanted to move up. More than her fictional boyfriend, Jenny had a vision of the future and the guts to pursue it. Once in Chicago, though, Jenny would be disillusioned by the city and its racism. And this was the crucial scene —Griffith Park substituting for the rural South—where Jenny would find the courage to face up to the future.

Herb had written the film the week after he had met Georgia at Club Diddle Daddle. Somehow she suggested the character of Jenny, and, once invented, Jenny had suggested the story Herb was writing for her. He wanted her. He would get her in one of his shoestring productions where his neighbors volunteered as actors and the crew consisted of Herb plus two cousins.

"Didn't I see you at Masters Studio the other day?" she had asked him the night Miss Marva invited him to dinner at the boarding-house.

"I was shooting stills. I get work all over town, especially the studios. They use my stuff for publicity. You were there with Sol Solomon. He was hustling Peter Gold for work. He's *always* hustling Gold for work. But did he find *you* work?"

"Mr. Gold is setting up an interview with a casting director—"

Herb raised an eyebrow.

"What is *that* supposed to mean? Isn't Mr. Gold a legitimate producer?"

"No one's legit in this town," Herb told her. "It's hustlers hustling hustlers."

"And you?"

"Looking to put a couple of tan faces on the screen. That's *my* hustle. Wouldn't think it'd be too hard, since there are millions of us colored folk out there ready to pay our hard-earned coin for movies. I'm trying to make movies that are at least a *little* real. I want my pictures to have something to do with us, pictures where we're doing something more than scrubbing bathtubs, making dumplings, polishing silverware and flashing our pearly whites."

Georgia had never heard a man talk that way. He spoke plain sense. He seemed to understand *her*. He seemed to know who he was; he just wanted to tell stories about the people he knew best. Why not? She'd seen some of these films in colored theaters in Florida —*Midnight Shadow, Murder in Harlem, The Blood of Jesus, Marching*

On—but didn't like the hokey plots and lousy acting. Herb agreed with her assessment. And his mission—his passion—was to upscale the quality. That's why he was scraping together money to write, produce and direct.

"I've already written something for you," he told Georgia. "If you wouldn't mind . . . I'd like you to read with me."

She agreed. They sat in Miss Marva's living room—Georgia on the couch, Herb in a straight-back chair directly across from her—and entertained the audience of boarders. Georgia was a born sight-reader.

"Dreams," she began as the fictional Jenny, "feed hope. And without hope, souls starve . . ."

"Now the camera and all the paraphernalia, don't even think about it," Herb said. "Forget the camera. Just learn your lines. Take your time, take your character into yourself."

Georgia would try. Georgia was impressed.

"He's been to college," Miss Marva later told Georgia. "Yes, sir. Graduated from a school in Texas. A right fine school. Now Harper, he don't have a mind like his brother Herb. Harper's brains are in his feet. But Herb, he's serious. He'll 'mount to something. His brain's always working. He's got ideas."

For weeks preceding the first day of principal photography on Jenny, Georgia spent all her time taking her lines to heart. She loved memorization, she was so good at it. She was also a little surprised that, for all the close contact, Herb did not make a sexual advance. That relaxed and worried her.

"I *told* you he's different," Miss Marva said. "He ain't like most men out there. He don't think with his weenie."

Sol came calling but Georgia was obliged to put him off. She did it politely—she didn't want to hurt him—but felt devotion to her role as Jenny. At this point Sol seemed a distraction. He said he understood, but of course he didn't . . . didn't see why she'd be more interested in Herb Montgomery's homemade movie for coloreds-only than in letting him help her with white Hollywood, the real place. He also worried that the reading for Gold's casting director, which Georgia claimed went well, would lead to one of those secret apartments Gold kept around the city. But there were no call-backs from Masters Studios, no messages from Peter Gold. The only real action was in the filming of *Jenny*, under Herb's direction, in working with a story that seemed *real* to Georgia, who, as the central character, went crazy at the end.

"I don't like it," she told Herb. "I don't want it to end that way."

"This isn't a greeting card with some sappy message," said Herb the night before the final scenes using downtown L.A. to simulate Chicago. "This is supposed to be real."

"I still don't believe this woman would be reduced to this."

"She's naïve."

"She's strong, Herb. You made her strong."

"*You* made her strong. Maybe too strong."

"She can't be too strong."

"Look, Georgia, Jenny really doesn't know what she's doing. She's a poet, a free spirit who gets caught up with a man who has no respect for anything but good sex. That, along with a bigoted society, brings her down. No one respects or appreciates her—"

"She should find a way out. If she goes crazy it shows she's weak."

"It's part of her character."

"I don't see it."

"Because you don't want to see it. You're thinking of you, Georgia, not Jenny. Stop fighting her. Stop fighting me. Let's just finish the damn picture."

On the day of the bombing of Hiroshima, principal photography for *Jenny* was completed. News of the destruction of the Japanese city didn't reach the leading lady and director of the movie. They were too involved in their own struggle. To the end, Georgia fought against Jenny's madness. Herb managed to guide her back into her character's mental collapse. Georgia lost, but she triumphed; her acting carried the film and brought home Herb's message. When he finally called out "Cut," she couldn't stop crying, even after the camera stopped rolling.

That night the world seemed altered. Georgia was no longer arguing with Herb. Jenny had to go mad; her character couldn't withstand the assaults of cold-blooded Chicago. She had to fall apart. So deep was her identification with Jenny, Georgia herself felt frightened. Not wanting to be left alone, she asked that Herb keep her company. He took her to his one-room flat on South Vermont Avenue.

Herb was honestly moved by her performance. It was almost *too* real, too close to the bone. The extra edition of the evening paper devoted to the atomic explosion over Japan—"a blinding flash," read the account, "many times as brilliant as the midday sun"—hit him hard. But mostly in terms of Georgia. As an actress Georgia was a blinding flash. Now she was asleep on his sofa, exhausted from the day, her delicate features achingly beautiful. For weeks Herb had fought back his personal feelings for the sake of the movie. When it came to films, he was especially hard on himself, dead serious and determined not to mix business and pleasure. But the pleasure of seeing Georgia at rest, the pleasure of her performance, the pleasure of being with a woman as dedicated as she was . . . he couldn't help allowing the palm of his hand to caress her cheek.

She half-opened her eyes, and smiled. In the smoothness of her skin, in the light sea-green color of her eyes, in the still August air, in the distant strains of Hot Lips Page's horn from the next-door radio, Herb felt something new for him. His throat was dry. He heard himself saying something he had never said before. Quietly. "I love you."

She drew him to her.

They made love that quiet evening in August, first gently, then with fewer inhibitions, and finally with unrestrained passion. He was in love, her man, her director, strong and true to what he believed in. He believed in her, she believed in him. And she'd never stop loving him. Never ever.

"We'll never be able to release it," said Herb. They were at Miss Marva's where the news dropped like a bomb.

"What are you talking about?" Georgia asked. A week had passed since the shooting was finished and the cutting had begun.

"The film, the editing. I've been using Masters' facilities. I go over there at night. Been doing it for the past three years. No one minds. I give the security boys a buck or two and that's it. But someone snitched. Got the word all the way up to Gold, and Gold threw a fit. Put the clamps on."

"Can't you do it somewhere else?" asked Miss Marva.

"I can't afford to. Besides, I know those Masters machines like the back of my hand. Masters is where I taught myself to cut film."

"Maybe I could ask Sol to help us," Georgia said.

Herb looked at her. "He's already helped you enough."

"I think he's a friend—"

"He's a good-hearted guy," Miss Marva said.

"We don't need him," replied Herb.

"We don't?" asked Georgia, looking at Herb. "Well, we sure need someone."

Sol Solomon had been relieved to learn Georgia had a colored boyfriend. At least he assumed Herb was her boyfriend. Herb seemed a nice enough guy. The colored should stick together. The colored were better off by themselves. People who argued that the races shouldn't mix were right. Birds of a feather and all that. He'd been crazy to court Georgia. He couldn't even imagine introducing her to his mother in Flatbush. He'd been out of his mind and now he was thinking straight and even though he had a hard time sleeping nights and even though he dreamt about her and even though he drove by Miss Marva's boardinghouse more times than he wanted to remember—hoping Georgia would be sitting on the porch or walking down the street—he thought he was over her, thought his mind was clear and the jealousy all behind him.

Then she called.

"You already made the movie?" he asked her. "The movie with Herb?"

"Yes."

"Is it any good?"

"We want to show it to you."

"We?"

"Me and Herb. It's not edited but you'll be able to see my acting. I want you to see me act."

"And I want to see you," he said, unsuccessfully fighting back his mixed feelings.

"Can you get us a cutting machine somewhere?"

"You don't have an editing machine?"

"No. I need your help, Sol. I feel like I can count on you."

"You can," he said, feeling like a first-class schmuck.

He was still feeling like a schmuck when he met them in the garage of a friend in the Fairfax district. The guy was a cutter with some old equipment to view the raw footage.

Herb was quiet. Herb obviously didn't want Sol there; Sol wished that Georgia had come alone. She was quite a dame, this Florida girl, getting her men in the same room for the same purpose—to push her damn career. Who the hell did she think she was?

She was even wearing a dress Sol had bought her, a pink affair. Sunbeams angling through the smudgy garage windows gave her a special light. The glow from her face, her easy smile, the sweetness and seriousness she approached this project with didn't just move Sol, they unaccountably took him over. She was determined and eager and why the hell shouldn't she be a star?

One look at the movie and she was a star, only no one knew it. Except Sol. And Herb. The story was clumsy but God almighty, this Georgia Faith brought out the soul of her character. Jenny fell apart in front of your eyes. You wanted her to win, and when she lost you couldn't help losing it inside.

"Has Peter Gold seen this?" asked Sol.

"Gold? Are you kidding?" Herb said. "He's the man who shut me down."

"I'd show it to Gold."

"His casting director never called me back," Georgia said.

"The casting director has her head up her ass," Sol said. "I'm telling you—this will knock his socks off. I'd go to Gold."

"I've already seen it," Gold told Sol.

They were in the big office on the back lot where Peter was seated behind his desk.

"I don't get it," said Sol.

"This Montgomery is wasting her talent, I want her to understand that."

"She's good, real good in that role—"

"Why should she be making movies no one will ever see?" asked Gold.

"They play on the colored circuit."

"She's good enough to star in a budgeted feature."

"But your casting gal didn't give her the time of day," said Sol.

"What does that mean? I've been developing a script for her."

"Without me? After I brought her in?"

"Sorry, Sol, but it's not your kind of story."

"What kind of story is it?"

"A story with across-the-board appeal."

"I know her inside out," Solomon said. "No one else could write for her except me."

"Herb Montgomery didn't do a bad job."

"You're having him write the script?"

"Don't be ridiculous. We have to reach a white audience."

"That's the whole thing, that's just what I can do."

"Not with that story you tried to sell me last time."

"I got another."

"Shoot."

"She ain't Latin this time. She's regular a hundred percent American colored. Except she's a dame like Barbara Stanwyck in *Double Indemnity*. A black widow."

"She's too sweet for that."

"It's a stretch, but she'll make it. This dame is tough, believe me. Sweet outside, steel inside. She gets this guy in her web."

"He can't be white. Maybe *he's* Latin."

"A Latin prince. He comes to the States."

"He's looking to buy a business."

"And buys her bullshit instead."

"Her past," Gold said. "She's got to have a murky past."

"A past that catches up with her. She's done in a couple of men."

"How long to get me a treatment?"

"A week."

"I'll give you every consideration, Sol. That's the best I can do."

Sold, thought Sol. Gold was sold. He heard it in Gold's tone, saw it in his eyes. He'd deliver the treatment and he'd deliver a part for Georgia and she'd be back with him because he had the key she was looking for. He had Peter Gold's pecker in his back pocket.

* * *

Georgia liked being back in Sol's pretty red Hudson. It'd been a while. She liked driving up to Sol's little cottage and feeling the clean ocean air. It was good to get out of town on Sunday, even good to get away from Herb, at least for a day, because he was brooding and upset and could do nothing but think about his film. All he did was hunt for post-production facilities, as he called them, that he could use for free. He was getting on her nerves.

Sol, though, seemed carefree, loose. She was happy to be with him and anxious to hear his "good news" about Peter Gold.

"I'll tell you later," he promised her. "Let's just enjoy the ride."

It was a slightly overcast Sunday morning. The clouds gave the ocean an alluring gray light and the beach was not crowded. Sol was singing "On the Atchison, Topeka and the Sante Fe." The melody eluded him but at least he knew the words. He drove with his left hand on the wheel and his right arm draped over the passenger seat. Georgia was munching on a piece of delicious rye bread he had bought that morning. He had also prepared a thermos of hot coffee and several corned-beef-and-mustard sandwiches. She wondered whether what she felt for Sol was more than friendship. He was a dear man, sincere and direct; she liked his rough way of talking, liked the way he seemed to respect her. And in his funny, unguarded way, she found him sort of sexy, especially in his determination to please her.

In Sol's head, he had won her back. He wasn't sure what would happen next but he didn't care. He wanted this gorgeous creature, this Georgia Faith, wanted her in his place, wanted her in his arms, wanted her in the story he was inventing as he looked at her, fixed her iced tea, walked with her down the hill and along the beach, talking a plot about a woman who took over men by the force of her beauty and subtle smile.

"You're like the Mona Lisa," he said. "You know the Mona Lisa? What's behind her smile? I want to know what's behind your smile." Sol had a line, for sure, except in Georgia's case he meant every word.

She was smiling, but that was mostly because the sun had broken through the clouds and the gray day had turned brilliant blue. She was smiling because she had left Florida for California knowing no one, and now she knew Sol Solomon and Herb Montgomery and Miss Marva Lavastahl, all of whom were so interested in helping her.

She was smiling because her confidence in herself was working out. She was special, she could go with her dreams, she could make it in whatever world she found herself. She understood herself, she understood men —at least she was beginning to understand her power over them.

They sat on a sand dune, she and Sol Solomon, and he talked about some of his old girlfriends—men did that—and why the "dames" in Hollywood put him off, they were gold diggers and he didn't trust them. It was easy being with Sol. When he talked about the plot of his new story, he was interested in her reaction, not like Herb who wrote by himself and shut her out. Herb was serious, good, but Sol saw it all as make-believe, a way to entertain himself and make money. When his cheerful face broke down into a smile, she saw real sweetness.

And when they climbed the hill back to his cottage she was nice and easy with the idea of making love to this man. His warmth and affection excited her now as she remembered what they'd had together in his cozy little bedroom.

It was sunset when they did make love, and she kept her eyes open to see the changing colors of the sky, each color seeming to correspond to a deeper level of desire in her: cool blue, burnished yellow, glowing orange, hot pink. Sol was working so hard. He waited so long. He asked her where. He wanted to know if he pleased her. "Yes," she kept telling him, rising to meet him, rising and falling, her eyes on a translucent purple sky with streaks of red, the fire of the universe all inside her now.

She slept there that night, her dreams vivid and happy. Then in the morning, as she and Sol sat at his breakfast table sipping coffee, a car pulled up.

"Jesus," said Sol, responding to the knock at the door. "What are you doing here?"

Peter Gold was wearing a blue flannel blazer over light white wool trousers. He looked, of course, like a million bucks.

"I remembered you said you lived around here," he told Sol. "I spotted your car and thought I'd drop in. I see you have company."

At first Georgia was startled, then relieved that she had at least applied her makeup and gotten dressed. Her pale yellow dress highlighted the light brown hue of her skin. She was pleased with her outfit, pleased that on the table in front of her were Sol's notes for the new script. It was evident that work was being done. Besides, Gold had seen her in Solomon's company before. Gold knew the score.

"Miss Faith," Peter said coolly, "I hope Sol has told you how much I admire your acting. I saw the rushes. I was impressed."

"Thank you, but I noticed you weren't impressed enough to let Herb do his editing."

"Company policy . . . I assure you, though, you have a future at Masters Studio—"

"I was just working on the treatment," said Sol.

"I'd like to see it."

"It ain't quite ready, Herb."

"Well, maybe you could use a little time alone to work. I'd be happy to run Miss Faith back to the city."

"No need," Sol said quickly.

Georgia, on the other hand, was pleased with the offer. "Maybe Mr. Gold is right, Sol. Maybe you should have time to work alone—"

"I don't need to work alone."

"I'll just gather up my things," said Georgia. "I won't be a minute."

"What about your wife?" asked Sol, playing his ace. "She out here with you?"

"Grace is in Geneva taking care of her father. I'm sure you heard about his stroke. I don't expect them back for another month or two."

"But . . . " Sol began, but Georgia had taken over, and after kissing Sol on the cheek was out the door with Gold, whose Bentley was waiting.

The Bentley smelled of leather, a heady fragrance for Georgia. But why was the roadster's steering wheel on the right side? She was going to ask Peter but he spoke up before she got to it. "I bought this beauty in London last month and shipped it over. That's how they make cars over there, don't ask me why. I also bought a few landscapes for my beach house. Do you like landscape paintings, Miss Faith. Georgia . . . ?"

In the orphanage library in Florida there had been one book of paintings that had fascinated her, a book she had looked at for hours. In contained startling images of burning ships by a man who seemed to capture the soul of the sea. What was his name . . . ? "Turner," she finally said.

"Turner!" echoed a surprised Peter "One of the miniatures I bought was a Turner. I'm glad you know his work."

Georgia smiled.

"Let's take a quick turn up to the house so I can show you the Turner," suggested Gold. "That is, if you have the time."

"I'd love to see the painting."

The mountain road was narrow, steep and twisty. At the top of the mountain she could see a house that looked like a castle, complete with turrets and towers and an ornate gate emblazoned with the self-invented Masters family crest.

"My father-in-law's architect went overboard with the English motif," Peter was saying. "I'm in the middle of remodeling, so things are sort of a mess. But nothing can spoil this view."

When they parked in front of the castle Georgia kept silent. Not out of any strategy but because she was truly speechless. Peter Gold's castle was not of this world; it was from a dream, a movie, a fairy tale. Any minute she could expect a fair damsel to appear at the window. Where was Robin Hood? She thought of the Knights of the Round Table she had read about in school. Below her the glittering blue ocean seemed a million miles away, at the foot of the world. The castle commanded the sea and all the world around it, and Georgia was at the top of the world—and no one could touch her here, no one could hurt her, no one could pull her down. This was where she was supposed to be.

Whatever guilt she felt for leaving Sol had vanished. Nothing could or should prevent her from being in this place at this time. Sweet jasmine filled the air as she breathed deeply before entering the estate.

Beyond the vestibule rose a great staircase with extravagantly carved wood. Huge tapestries hung in the long hallways. The living room seemed the size of a football field. The banquet table sat forty. The library held floor-to-ceiling shelves of books, more volumes by far than the little public library Georgia had gone to in Florida. Peter pointed out a collection of first editions, poets she had read in school: Alfred Tennyson, Edgar Allan Poe, Walt Whitman.

Upstairs was a frescoed ballroom, a small gymnasium, eight bedrooms, a flower-filled terrace overlooking the grounds—swimming pool, tennis courts, horse stables.

"Come see Prince," Peter said. Prince turned out to be a pure-white peacock who roamed the gardens. "And now the Turner."

In private quarters separate from the main house Peter had created a combination office and art gallery.

"There it is," he said, pointing to the wall opposite his desk. Hung above a large leafy plant and mounted in an elaborate gold frame was a tiny painting of such fierce intensity Georgia felt her own heartbeat. It was a picture of a fire, but to her it seemed the fire of a soul rather than any inanimate object. The representation was a little ambiguous, the emotions weren't. Hearts were burning.

Georgia's attraction to this man involved more than the physical. He was plainspoken, not especially articulate. Still, in his carefully chosen words George detected a kind of cultivation she liked, responded to. For her, his aphrodisiac was his power—the power to change her life, put her on the screen, make her face known to millions . . . she felt this, didn't need to figure it out.

And when he made his move, she was hardly surprised. Miss Georgia Faith, in love with fantasy, also understood reality. She had understood what was going to happen the moment she left Sol's cottage. ("You can see Sol's place way down there on the side of the hill," Gold had said from the front of his estate. "It looks like a pimple . . .") Still, she surprised herself when in response to Peter's first touch—he stroked her arm—she mentioned Herb.

"No matter what happens, Mr. Gold . . ."

"Please call me Peter."

"Before anything else, Peter, I just want you to know I think Herb Montgomery is a fine moviemaker and that *Jenny* should be finished. I owe it to Herb to help him—and to myself . . ."

"I understand," Peter said, opening the door to a small bedroom to the side of his office. She stopped at the entry. "But what about the script Sol's developing?"

"That's a separate matter," she said, literally standing her ground. "One thing shouldn't depend on the other. I want to count on your friendship, Peter. And as a friend, I do want your word that you'll help Herb finish his picture."

Gold had to smile. This Georgia Faith was a surprise, not what he'd expected. She was shrewder, smarter. There was a lot more there than met the eye. For a colored woman—especially such a beautiful one—to be this complicated was something new for him. He was powerfully intrigued.

"You have my word, Georgia," he said, glad to surrender. "*And* my friendship."

He took her hand, as he had on the first day he met her, and kissed it.

"Maybe we should be going now," she said.

"Of course," he said, knowing enough to play along, and led her from the house to his car.

During the ride back to the city she asked him questions about England and France, artists and actors he had known, knew. His answers seemed to say he knew everyone. And his opinions were direct and firm. Georgia Faith was very pleased to be in Peter Gold's company.

Herb Montgomery was not pleased.

"You let him screw you—"

Georgia's hand across his face made a crack that brought Miss Marva running from her kitchen. "What the hell's going on here?"

Georgia's eyes were clear—there were no tears—and Herb looked shocked. It didn't help to see the butcher knife in Miss Marva's hand.

"You're out there at his Malibu castle," he persisted, "just you and him. You get him to do you all kinds of favors and you still want me to believe that you didn't give something in return?"

"We're *friends*."

Herb shook his head. "You and Gold?"

"Women," Miss Marva announced, "got more ways of working men than from flat on their backs. Women got smarts. And this here young woman uses *all* her smarts *all* the time. Better believe it."

"The important thing, Herb, is that you get to use the editing machine at Masters."

"I know that, they called me at nine this morning, said the facilities were available any evening after six. And that's when I started smelling a skunk."

"Smells real sweet to me," Miss Marva observed.

"What about Solomon?" Herb asked. "How does he figure in all this?"

Georgia didn't mention Sol's new script for Gold—what would be the point?—but she did say the writer helped reintroduce her to Gold.

"What does *that* mean?"

"Sol likes you."

"Sol likes *you.*"

"He likes us both, he's a decent fellow."

"Excuse me, Georgia, but you're his gift to Gold, now Gold will pay him back with an assignment—"

"I'm *nobody's* gift to *anybody*," Georgia let loose. "If anybody's gotten a gift, Mr. Herb Montgomery, it's you. You've got a way to edit your movie, but you're too hardheaded, you're too jealous, too damn shortsighted to at least say thank you. No, you just want to stand there and insult me for helping you. Well, no one insults me and as far as I'm concerned you can burn your damn movie."

With that she walked out of the room.

"Miss Georgia Faith," said Marva, shaking her head. "That girl puts on a hell of a show."

Sol was upset too. The woman he was with did not make him happy. She had full breasts and a nice smile; her backside moved with a languorous motion, and the Royal Palm Club, a hangout on the Strip, was all action. A steak-and-lobster joint, it was a favorite of the show-biz set, guys looking for dolls, and dolls, often for hire, looking for work. Everyone was an actress at the Royal Palm Club, especially the hookers.

"I'm an actress," said Rhonda Cohen.

"You gotta change your name," said Sol. "Besides, you don't even look Jewish."

"I'm not, but my first husband was. I find Jewish men real fascinating."

Sol wasn't fascinated, he knew the routine. For a couple of lobster tails, a bottle of bubbly and a sawbuck the lady was his. Any other time the size of her breasts and contour of her tush would have done the trick. But Georgia had spoiled Sol Solomon. Like Hoagy Carmichael said, Georgia was on his mind.

He hadn't heard from her since she'd gone off with Gold. The rest of that day had been rough, a real kick in the nuts. The idea of Georgia and Peter together had dug at him all afternoon, filled his night, haunted him the rest of the week. He phoned her at Miss Marva's but she wasn't there. He tried with no luck to get a number at Herb Montgomery's. Finally he called Gold, and wished he hadn't.

"That was a rotten thing you did," he told the studio boss.

"What are you talking about?"

"Georgia."

"She's a lovely young woman, Sol. I'm real glad we're developing a script for her."

"Come off it, Pete."

Peter hated being called "Pete." "Is your treatment ready?"

"How could I write when you're off banging her?"

"Sol, Sol . . . if you want to work with this studio you'll have to submit your material on time. All I can do is give you a one-day extension. Remember, Sol, there are other writers with talent who can stick to deadlines. As far as Miss Faith's personal life is concerned, I'd say that's her personal business—" And Gold hung up in Sol's ear . . .

Rhonda Cohen's earlobes were dripping rhinestones.

"So you write for the movies," she said to Sol. "That must be exciting, I mean, making up stories right out of your head. You got yourself a real imagination, huh?"

Right now Sol was imagining Peter fucking Georgia. Georgia was so hot she could even heat up a cold fish like Gold. Somehow, though, he couldn't imagine Gold with a hard-on. In place of a dick he pictured a minnow flopping at Peter's crotch—a minnow or a stack of hundred-dollar bills.

"I've been in a few pictures," said Rhonda. Sol saw it coming . . . the pitch.

After the fish and booze and buttery mashed potatoes she ordered strawberry cheesecake with a scoop of vanilla ice cream on the side. This one could pack it away.

"Tell me about the picture you're writing now," she said between bites.

"I'm stuck," he said truthfully, and as a defense.

"Maybe I could help unstick you," she said, her palm resting on the higher reaches of his right thigh.

Sol sighed. What the hell. It was a long night. Maybe getting his rocks off would help his narrative flow.

Back at his place she came right out of her clothes. No time to think. Good. He didn't want to think. He wanted to get Georgia off his mind. Rhonda was offering, come and get it. He moved in.

Sol appreciated well-trained pussy muscles, and Rhonda had all the moves. She snapped and pulled, tightened and tugged with slippery precision. She complimented his cock and sucked him clean. She took it from the rear; she sat on his smile; she sounded like she came so many times she deserved a fucking Academy Award. Still, at the moment of ejaculation he didn't feel any pleasure or even release. The image of Georgia was there, except she wasn't. And without her, all the moves of Rhonda Cohen were wasted on a man gone crazy with love.

Georgia read the script. She really liked the character of Wilma, liked the idea of a villainess. She could play her soft, so soft the audience would be fooled. That was the point of the story. The innocent wasn't so innocent. *The Lure* was Sol's working title, and to her it looked like he'd done a good job. Peter had been so pleased he called Georgia to his Beverly Hills home to show her the script, sent his car and driver to Miss Lavastahl's boardinghouse to fetch the actress.

"You got 'em coming and going, baby," said Marva. "Never seen nothing like it."

The boarders waved and hooted as Georgia was whisked away in a white limousine.

Gold was by the pool. His city house was smaller than the Malibu castle, but far from modest. The place sat on six acres and the Italianate styling was grand: the backyard was filled with expensive copies of Renaissance sculpture, cherubs, angels, beautiful boys, half-draped women.

Peter got up to meet her wearing a white robe and leather sandals. Georgia was in pale pink.

"If you'd like to take a swim, Georgia, I can loan you a bathing suit."

"No, thank you."

He got the message—for now. "Okay, I've invited you over to read the script," he said, getting to business, and handed her the screenplay. She promptly sat under a yellow patio umbrella and began to speed-read, which she figured would impress him. But as she concentrated she couldn't help hearing him call his wife in Switzerland, who, according to his side of the conversation, wouldn't be back for several more weeks. Then, out of the corner of her eye, Georgia noticed him slipping off his robe and diving into the pool.

"Well?" he asked after she'd finished the script and he'd dried himself with towels brought by a colored valet who looked at Georgia like she was a mistake.

"The climax comes too early," she said. "You don't want to give away Wilma's character until the very end, do you?"

"Good. I had the same reaction. I'm meeting with Sol tomorrow, and I'll tell him just that. Now you really need to get in the pool. It's over ninety today. The bathing suits and robes are in the cabana."

The one-piece outfit she chose was a light lavender. The fit was clinging, the cut flattering. She covered herself with a bathing cap and white terrycloth robe and proceeded to the pool, where she sat in the sun until the heat was too much.

When she dropped the robe she could feel his eyes. His obvious excitement was exciting her. As she sat by the edge of the pool and dipped her toes into the water he came and sat next to her. She lowered herself into the water; he waited only a moment before diving in. Swimming around her, swimming beneath her, under the cool water he touched her smooth legs, her breasts and her buttocks; she didn't move away, allowing his fingers to probe beneath the crotch of her suit. It felt so good, floating on her back and then her stomach, being caressed, the sky clear blue, swimming away, him following, playing a sexual game of seduction-rejection-seduction. And then, winded, she came out of the water and stretched out in a pool-side chair, and he came there and kissed her on the lips, his words soft, quiet . . .

"You're almost too beautiful."

"Is that a fault or a compliment?"

"It's the truth, and you know what it means."

She smiled. "I hope it means I have your help."

"You *have* it."

"But we don't have a director—"

"Once the script is revised I'll show it to directors."

"Herb Montgomery?"

"Oh, come on, Georgia. He finished his movie at the studio. Isn't that enough?"

"Did you see the final version?"

"Yes . . . I can't stop looking at you."

"And did you like it?"

"For what it is, yes. It'll never be seen outside colored theaters in the South, but he got what he wanted." And now, he said to himself, he'd like to get what he wanted.

"He can do more than that, he could direct *The Lure*." She wouldn't back off.

"I doubt it."

"Let me at least show him the script. And then you just listen to his ideas. He's brilliant."

Peter tried to kiss her again, and she turned her face.

When she stripped off her suit in the cabana he stood by the door and watched. She knew it and allowed him to. His watching her excited her. She was wet. She let him kiss her again, this time with his tongue, to touch her moisture and whisper in her ear, but she still refused what he wanted.

"God, you're driving me crazy . . ."

She was feeling what he felt, but she was determined to control herself. Control . . . "I appreciate everything you're doing for me," she said. "You're my friend, Peter, and you're a gentleman. A rarity. And . . . I look forward to being with you again . . . soon. Please, don't ruin it now."

And he did as she said. Georgia over Peter.

Herb half-liked the script for *The Lure* but there were changes he wanted to make, more colored characters, to start.

He and Georgia were back at the Club Diddle Daddle. Miss Marva was with them. Herb's big brother Harper was on stage wearing a black-and-gold blazer and performing a brilliant tap dance as pianist

Dorothy Donegan played stop-time piano—"That Old Black Magic"
—behind him. Harper stepped and smiled, strutted and tipped his
top hat, spun and won the audience. He was a real virtuoso and they
recognized it. Even among the famed hoofers who occasionally still
worked Central Avenue—the Nicholas Brothers, Bill "Bojangles"
Robinson, Bunny Briggs, Baby Laurence—Harper was ranked right
at the top. No one could understand why he hadn't made it into so-
called mainstream movies.

"There's a natural part for Harper in this film," Herb was saying.
He had just snapped a picture of a table of partygoers and pocketed a
whole half-dollar tip. "When the Latin meets Wilma for the first
time, it's in a nightclub. Why can't Harper be dancing?"

On stage, Harper was dancing up a storm—double taps, triple taps,
defying time, suspending time, falling back on the beat with half-
tipsy control, twirling a cane now, parodying Chaplin.

"Not only can he be dancing, he can be Wilma's friend," Herb
persisted. "My brother's a natural actor. I've used him twice, he's
really good. Besides, Wilma needs a confidant. As a colored woman
she's completely isolated. Solomon hasn't given her a companion, a
peer; she has no one to talk to."

"That's part of the mystery," Georgia said as the crowd cheered
Harper into his second encore.

"That's not mystery," said Herb, "that's the white scriptwriter
knowing zero about Negro women."

"I don't think so, Herb. And I don't think I'd be talking about any
changes in the script when you meet with Mr. Gold."

"Your *Mr.* Gold doesn't want an idiot for a director, Georgia. He
wants someone with a brain and an eye and guts."

And no doubt Herb possessed all those, and articulated thoughts
Georgia had had just about ever since she'd begun going to movies as
a child.

"Where are everyday colored people with everyday problems?" he
was saying. "Why don't we ever see them in the movies? No wonder
whites don't understand us. They don't know us. We're jokes. Ridiculous wide-eyed characters filled with fear or superstition or both. If
we go to a white movie we have to sit in the balcony. Well, why don't
we invite the whites to sit up in the balcony to see *my* movies? Why
don't they learn about *our* pain?"

She liked when Herb talked that way—his conviction added to her own confidence—but she also worried about him putting off people, especially white men.

"Say what you want," said Herb, "but I don't believe Gold is serious about using me on this movie."

"You got to edit *Jenny*, didn't you?"

"The white man's guilt only goes so far. Believe me, Peter Gold's high-mindedness has its limits. And when it comes to you, sugar, he's got other motives. Hell, if he don't, he ain't a man."

"He's a gentleman."

Herb laughed. "I'd rather see you cozying up to Solomon. Least he's got a heart."

"But no pull," Georgia said quietly.

Glowing in the spotlight, Harper finished his third encore with a cakewalk slide, walking forward and backward at the same time, kicking high on the final beat, spinning, leaping and landing on his brother's ringside table, where he planted a kiss on Miss Marva's cheek. She smiled broadly and kissed him back.

"You dog," she told him. "You dirty dog."

Before Sol Solomon agreed to help he wanted to know Georgia's "true feelings." He was still her sometime lover, but the "sometime" drove him crazy. He wanted her all the time. He had to believe she appreciated what he did for her—in bed and at the typewriter. They ignited one another, they indulged each other's fantasies, but Sol also had the nagging feeling that somehow he wasn't enough for this girl. He wanted to show her everything. Wanted to get her an apartment near his, wanted to see her every night. But there was Herb . . . why the hell was she always pushing Herb?

"He's talented," she would say. "Look how he worked with me in *Jenny*. He understands women's feelings—leastways my feelings . . . he knows how to bring them out of me—"

"I can do that," said Sol.

"You can and you do," she told him, kissing him on the cheek. "But you're not a director, Sol. I need the right director and he—"

"That's Gold's call. That's not an actress' business."

"I've told Mr. Gold. Now I want you to tell him, Sol. Tell him you believe in Herb like you believe in me."

Jesus, now she was asking him to push a rival. "You'll be lucky if Gold ever makes this movie. You'll be lucky to be in it at all. I say let Lassie direct it if that's who Gold wants. You're pushing him too far. And me too . . . "

"He likes new ideas."

"He likes new gorgeous dames."

"Everyone likes your script, Sol. Now let's just make it perfect by getting the perfect director."

Peter Gold had it planned. According to his calculations he'd been patient enough. He made arrangements for his driver to fetch Georgia at seven-thirty and deliver her at eight o'clock to his Sunset Strip penthouse, an apartment he had recently rented. She arrived on the dot.

He couldn't stop looking at her. Her beauty—that's what it was, plain and simple . . . except this one was hardly plain or simple . . . seemed to blend with the Art Deco appointments as though they'd been designed just for her. Miss Marva had given her hair a series of soft waves above her high forehead; she wore long dangling earrings, emphasizing the contour of her neck. Her lipstick was light pink. Her black dress, a dramatic re-creation of one of Miss Marva's outfits from the thirties (resewn by Miss Marva herself), was sleeveless with a plunging neckline.

He was ready. He had fresh flowers. He had champagne on ice. Bing Crosby was crooning love songs on the Victrola. The candlelight was flickering and the steamed lobster was succulent and neither he nor Georgia talked about business. They talked about the spectacular view of the city, the ebullient mood of the country at the end of the war. He told her stories about Greer Garson, Ingrid Bergman and Gary Cooper.

She sipped the champagne. In only a couple of months this girl from the orphanage had grown accustomed to the delicious dry taste, the delightful high. He told her about Tennessee Williams recent play and how he had plans to turn it into a movie. He would use the Duke Ellington orchestra for the score.

"I put Ellington," he said, "right alongside Ravel."

"Herb loves Ellington," she couldn't help saying. "You and Herb have a lot in common. Really."

"Well," said Peter between puffs of his pipe, "I see no reason not to meet with him about *The Lure*."

"I'm glad." That done, now she could relax.

He filled her champagne glass. The bubbles sparkled against the candlelight. The crystal felt light as a feather. The cook went home. The music became slow, dreamy. He took her out onto the balcony. They danced, they drank, he breathed softly along her neck. The city was at her feet. Her head was somewhere up in the heavens. Earth, a distant concept. Not real. She felt weightless, suspended in space. Out there with the stars, like the song said.

She had never seen satin sheets before, didn't know they existed. To feel them against her skin was a new sensation, and now he was insistent, and now that he had agreed to do what she'd asked, now that he wanted to help . . . help her, help Herb . . . how could she say no? Why should she? Why hadn't anyone ever told her that in the world there were penthouses with satin sheets, satin pillowcases, satin along her skin . . . ?

"I want you to stay here," he told her in the morning. "I want you to move your things over here."

The satin sheets were moist and her memory fuzzy. She had lost control. She wasn't exactly sure what he meant. Was she supposed to be with him for another night, or two . . . ?

"No," said Peter. "I want you to have this apartment. You'll be comfortable here, I promise. And—"

"I'll have to think about it, Peter."

"There's nothing to think about. It's yours."

"Right now my head's hurting . . . I'd like to go back to Miss Marva's. I need to settle down."

"You can tell Herb Montgomery to call me, if that's what you're so worried about."

"I'm not worried," she said. "Just a little dizzy." Which was the truth. She had lost control for a night, and it scared her.

* * *

The days that followed were more dizzying. Herb couldn't believe that he got right through to Gold. He was to meet with the studio boss at week's end. Sol was invited to the same meeting, and the idea of all three men in the same room at the same time startled and excited Georgia. This, after all, was her creation.

She resisted moving into Peter Gold's Sunset Strip penthouse. Miss Marva held forth on the subject: "It would mean you belong to him. That how you feel?"

"It would ruin everything with Herb."

"Herb? Herb wants to make that movie. He's gonna put Harper into it. Harper's gonna dance and he wants to act. Those brothers take care of each other, yes they do. And they both know how to please the public."

"Herb wouldn't be pleased to see me living in another man's apartment."

"Thought you said it was gonna be *your* apartment. You star in your own movie, you should get enough money to pay your own rent. You pay your own rent, you call your own shots."

"It's a beautiful place, though . . . it's like a dream, Miss Marva."

"Ain't no dream, sugar. It's just your story. You're making up your own story. I've been watching you do it. All the good ones do it that way. So go ahead, girl, and don't be afraid whatever you do."

"And Herb?"

"Herb ain't the one. You're the one. You're why they're getting together, you're the one who got them all hot and bothered. They crazy 'bout you. Shoot, they'd be crazy not to be."

Georgia imagined the get-together, the big meeting . . . Herb, the most serious; Peter, the most reserved, watching the other men's reactions; Sol, talking, talking and nervous—part of him wanting to please everyone, part of him wanting the other two to get off the earth. They all felt that way about each other. Yet they were stuck together. And she had stuck them.

"I just don't trust Gold," Herb told her afterward. He had come straight down to Miss Marva's. "I don't think he's really going to make this movie."

"Why do you say that?"

"It was too damn easy. The studio's never used a colored director —never even thought of using one—and here he is, talking like I'm the prime candidate. Doesn't make sense."

"Did he mention Duke Ellington?"

"What does that have to do with anything?"

"He's going to hire Duke Ellington to write the score. He has all these plans. He's not a bigot, Herb. Did you mention Harper?"

"They liked the idea, both Gold and Solomon. They thought a tap dancer was a great idea—"

"Then I'm right."

"We'll see. There are no contracts, there aren't even any budgets. Right now it's just bullshit."

"But it looks good, doesn't it?"

"So do fairy tales, baby, but that doesn't mean they come true."

Well, thought Georgia, mine is going to . . .

"I already met his brother," said Sol. "He was down there at the Club Diddle Daddle. Don't you remember?"

"Sure I do," said Georgia. Sol had called to report on the meeting.

"He'll be great, I'm writing him in. I'm starting tonight, unless you wanna get together. I could grill a couple of steaks . . ."

"Better not. Promised Miss Marva I'd help out here."

"Maybe tomorrow night."

"Maybe so, Sol. Will you call me tomorrow?"

"I'll come by. I want you to see what I do with Harper's character. I want you to read his dialogue. You'll tell me if it's real."

"I know it will be. Everything about you is real, Sol. Say, that's why I love you."

And in her fashion she did.

"Are you ready to move in?" Direct, for a change.

"Not this very night, Peter."

He was sitting on the divan, not happy with her put-off, and began leafing through Vogue magazine. Georgia O'Keeffe's lush illustration of red haliconia flowers graced an advertisement for Dole Pineapples. "Painted in Hawaii," the caption read.

"I'm sure you heard that the meeting went well," he said, not looking up at Georgia seated across from him. A copy of Somerset Maugham's *The Razor's Edge* sat on the coffee table. The penthouse's parquet floors had just been polished. Early evening lights were flickering on all over the city. A juicy roast was in the oven.

"What's the problem, Georgia?"

"Well, shouldn't contracts be drawn?"

"A contract for you to live in this apartment?"

"Contracts for the movie, silly."

"Contracts *will* be drawn. You have my word. I just thought that the sooner you moved up here the happier you'd be. Was I wrong?"

"I have to be certain I can afford it."

"Don't you be silly."

"Peter, I want to be responsible."

He walked over to her in the green leather chesterfield, leaned over and kissed her lips. "I just can't think of anything else except you, and your happiness. And I know you'll be happy here—"

"I'll be happy when we start making the movie, Peter."

"Soon," he promised, exasperated. "Very soon."

Delays. Part of the business. Rewrites, budget managers, scheduling. But always reassurances. Peter promised. Sol gave it his all. Even Herb became more convinced as the meetings became more serious.

Then things started changing.

At first the changes weren't obvious and occurred as the Southern California heat subsided. The fall weather grew a little brisk and Georgia found herself waking up early. She liked spending her mornings with Miss Marva. They drank juice and coffee and chatted in the kitchen about everything under the sun. Miss Marva, always upbeat, was a constant support, and Georgia got into the habit of making the older woman's breakfast and even helping her with the wash, tasks she had avoided at school. Miss Marva had a gift not only for total candor but for untying emotional knots. She especially loved following Georgia's romantic fortunes.

When *Jenny* had opened at the Washington, the colored movie theater in Watts, they went together—Harper, Herb, Georgia and Marva. Georgia had seen previews and hours of edits, but to see herself on the big screen in a theater crowded with soldiers and smooching couples and regular folks from the neighborhood was the charge of a lifetime. She felt real pride not only in her own performance but in the sensitive way Herb had crafted the film. Afterward, people in the audience clustered around her wanting autographs. And smiling to all graciously, she signed her name as though she'd been doing this for years.

The movie was in stark black and white, but that night her dreams were in Technicolor . . . the Peter Gold penthouse took off like an immense airship and traveled around the world, landing first in London, then Paris, then Rome, cities she had always longed to see. And everywhere the fans were waiting . . .

When she woke up she realized she was not in the penthouse, but in Herb's place. And she was relieved. Since Gold's wife and father-in-law had returned from Switzerland he had relaxed the pressure, was no longer after her to move up to Sunset Strip. Which was fine with Georgia, who was busy enough with Herb and Sol collaborating on her next role.

To her surprise, the two men, so different, were effective together. Sol recognized Herb's seriousness and skills as a director; and Herb, at first skeptical, saw that Sol had a real gift for storytelling. Georgia's contribution was in keeping them together and apart at the same time. She also felt grateful to them both. In fact, the trio increasingly became linked by an unspoken understanding—they needed each other.

But above all they needed Peter Gold.

Since his wife had arrived back in the country, Gold was distracted, edgy. He'd moved into the penthouse with considerable baggage; clearly he had now taken it as *his* apartment, his refuge from his wife, and no longer a place where he'd once hoped to house an exotic mistress.

Georgia, needing reassurance, picked up Gold's edginess. Herb's head was more on moviemaking than on Georgia, which for him amounted to the same thing; after all, she *was* his next film.

On the other hand, Sol was completely involved with her happiness and so the first to detect something might be wrong. He got food from an old-fashioned deli in East L.A. where they made authentic egg creams and sliced lean pastrami. He overtalked and overate and made her laugh with stories about his days as a bookie who couldn't count. In his voice she heard the sound and humor of the streets of New York City, which, of course, she had never seen.

"I'll take you there tomorrow," he told her. "On the train I'll teach you to play pinochle. I'll teach you mah-jongg. What do you say, kid?"

"I say it sounds great but I have to stay for the movie, Sol."

The movie—Sol's story, Herb's direction, Peter's production—wouldn't leave her mind, wouldn't leave her alone.

At first she thought her anxieties about the movie were causing the indigestion. Then a few days later she came down with a sore throat, then a cough, then full-blown flu: vomiting, high fever, dizziness.

The illness lingered. After a week she recovered only to find herself, several days later, worn out and debilitated all over again. That was enough for Miss Marva, who called a doctor, whose diagnosis was unambiguous.

"You're pregnant," he said.

The words seemed unreal.

Her periods had always been erratic, so missing two hadn't meant much. Oh, she vaguely considered it, even worried, but things were going too well for anything foolish to interfere. Probably just nerves. She was above this sort of disaster. After all, she was starring right that minute in a movie playing all over the South. She had plans to go back to Florida when it opened in the town where she'd gone to school. Her career was blooming, her possibilities unlimited. Important men were falling all over themselves to help her. It was just a matter of choosing the right course, of selecting the man who made her most comfortable on any given afternoon or evening. She'd become very good at such choices. Each of them cherished his time with her, each understanding there would be no exclusive on her.

Now *this*.

"There are plenty of people to go to, women right in this neighborhood," said Miss Marva, "right around the block, but, look here, I don't want you going to any of 'em. No ma'am. I know too many girls who got themselves hurt that way. One up and died. Ain't clean. Ain't worth the chance."

"But the movie. I have to be ready for the movie—"

"Wouldn't worry too much 'bout that."

"What are you talking about?"

"It's what Harper's talkin' 'bout. Herb told him last night. Gold's daddy is back in charge."

"You mean his father-in-law?"

"The big boss—whoever. Word came down that the old man's back from being sick and he's going 'round screaming 'bout how he ain't making no movies with colored cats behind the cameras and colored dolls kissing on white men."

"That's just not possible—"

"That's real life, baby—that's what that is."

From the top to the bottom, just like that.

Until now her instincts had been on the money, now . . . she no longer knew what to think, what to do. Surely she had to listen to Miss Marva. Nothing could be worse than a botched abortion. She shuddered at the notion, and she shuddered at the idea of giving up the movie, except if Miss Marva was right, there was no movie to give up. Her stomach filled with pain, and there was pain in her head, cramps and nausea, staying in bed with anger and disbelief and confusion about what was real and what wasn't, drifting in and out of dreams before awakening to the nightmare of reality, turning over and over the question of *who* . . . whose baby was she having? Which one could she tell?

Herb was furious when he learned from Sol that the film was kaput.

"If I could change his mind, I would," said Sol, "but it seems Gold got his nuts chopped off and there ain't shit we can do about it. As long as the old man was out of commission, Gold was in charge. When-the-cat's-away kind of thing. But the cat's back, and Gold turned into a mouse and he says no dice no way no hope don't even think about it. Apparently old man Masters threw a fit, screaming and carrying on while Grace—Gold's old lady—was scared the geezer would get another stroke so Peter promised he'd scrap the project, no colored movie stars at Masters, not now, not ever."

"What the hell is the guy made of? Where's his goddamn back-bone?"

"In his father-in-law's checkbook. I tried to tell Georgia. I explained it to her months ago—"

"But you went ahead and wrote the thing."

"I thought maybe he had a change of heart. And besides, who knew the old man was going to recover?"

"We still have a screenplay—"

"No studio will touch it with Georgia in the lead. I know that. But if you want the movie on your own, go ahead, Herb. If you think you can do it . . . I'm strapped myself or else . . ."

"I'll have to make some changes in the script, do a lot of cutting, economizing . . ."

"Fine with me. But do you figure Georgia's up for it? She seems way down to me."

"It's still the role of a lifetime," Herb muttered, a man holding onto straws.

"When will I start showing?" Georgia asked Miss Marva.

"Month or two. Have you said anything to anyone?"

"No. Should I?"

"Depends. Depends who you got your sights on. Depends on lots of things, mainly depends on who you want, *and* who you can get. Heard from your good friend Mr. Gold?"

"Not a word. He won't even take my calls. Can you imagine, he won't even talk to me! He dumped me, Miss Marva, plain and sim-ple. I hate him."

"Well, Herb and Sol, they sound ready to make another movie."

"They don't know, but I'll be big as a barn right when they're ready to shoot."

"Maybe they can work that into the story. Those boys are clever."

"But what do I tell them when they want to know about the fa-ther?"

"You tell 'em you asking yourself the same question."

"It's not funny."

"Look, baby, I think it's serious as a heart attack, I really do, but frettin' ain't gonna get you nowhere. 'Sides, Herbie and Sol are crazy about you. Just a matter of which suits you best."

"Which do you think?"

"I ain't the one sleeping with them. Herbie's smart as a whip and no doubt going places. Might take him some time but I 'spect he'll get there. Now Sol, that's a right sweet man, and he's got him some money and I know he's stuck on you. Wherever he's going he's going to get there a lot faster than Herb, but his being white and all . . . well, that ain't gonna be no picnic, baby."

Sol packed the food in a picnic basket and drove Georgia down to Seal Beach, where the coastline was deserted and the sea early-winter calm. The world felt fresh but inside Georgia felt stale.

"You lost something," said Sol. "I can feel it. It's Gold, I think. We trusted him and he screwed us. I ain't surprised, but you, you're the trusting kind, Georgia. You believed the bum. Here, eat this apple. I cut it up in pieces. Dip it in honey for good luck."

She held his hand and thought of telling him, but couldn't do it. After all, she no longer knew what *he* felt.

"I'll do it," Sol told her. "I'll write another script that another studio will buy. Promise. Everything's going to be fine. They can't stop you, Georgia, you're too good."

Good and pregnant, she thought.

"Nothing's easy for us," said Herb. "Never has been. Never will be. But you gotta believe this thing will be right, baby. You just gotta believe."

He kissed Georgia on the forehead and put his arm around her as they walked on down Central Avenue on a Saturday night with the sounds of the jazz and blues blowing out of the clubs. Oscar Pettiford's booming bass was at the Turban Lounge and there was Johnny Otis' big band and Lucky Thompson and Sonny Criss at the Down Beat. Harper was dancing at Lovejoy's and they were on their way to see him when a couple of tipsy sailors bumped into Herb and eyed Georgia's legs and said something lewd and Herb threw them both

down into the gutter like they were garbage. They were too drunk to
fight. There was too much booze on Central Avenue, thought Georgia, too much brawling and too much whoring and pimping for anybody's peace of mind. She wanted to say something to Herb but she
knew how much he liked Central Avenue and loved his brother and,
besides, Miss Marva would be there.

On the walk to Lovejoy's Herb kept up the positive chatter . . .
he was going to do it, he was going to make a movie from Sol's script,
he'd find the money, he'd do a film that could play in white theaters
as well as colored. Georgia wanted to believe him, wanted to believe
he was one in a million, a pioneer who could break barriers and take
her with him. She wanted to trust him with her secret, tell him the
truth, ask that they live together, marry, anything to solve her awful
problem. But Herb and Harper, now appearing on stage in a black
velvet tux and shiny red shoes, were brothers in the neighborhood,
and Miss Marva, bless her soul, was right there beside them, cheering
them both on. Yes, Georgia pictured them in the neighborhood for
the rest of their lives. Did she want to be part of that picture . . . ?

The night lingered. The spirit of Harper's dance was infectious; he
was a sparkplug, an elf, a miracle of motion, his spins and flips and
sandy stop-time taps. But even his rhythms couldn't help Georgia,
feeling deep-down sad and trapped. In a few weeks her condition
would start showing. How would she explain? What would she say?

"Let's go back to my place," Herb suggested afterward.

"I'll think I'll go to Miss Marva's," Georgia said. "I said I'd help
her with some things in the morning." . . .

But in the morning Miss Marva wasn't there. She had spent the
night with Harper. No one was there, in fact, to answer a loud knock
on the door except for a still sleepy Georgia.

"Miss Faith?" asked a uniformed chauffeur.

"Yes."

"This is for you. I've been told to wait for you."

He handed her a note.

Please meet me *now*. I must see you immediately. It's *urgent*.

Yours, Peter.

Georgia had the chauffeur wait a full hour while she dressed, applied makeup and arranged her hair. Her heart was furious but her

head was curious. She was determined to look absolutely beautiful for this meeting. Never mind why he wanted to see her; this man had wronged her and she intended to face him down.

It was afternoon before she arrived at the Sunset Strip penthouse.

"Please," he said, "let's sit and talk."

"What's there to talk about? I'm surprised you even took a chance to send your man for me. What if someone were looking? What if someone had seen me riding up in the elevator?"

"I understand that you're angry." He stood on one side of the living room, she stood on the other. His face was lined.

"No, you *don't* understand, Mr. Peter Gold, you don't understand what it feels like to be used, lied to and dumped. It feels cheap—that's what it feels like. And I'll tell you something, Mr. Peter Gold, I never want to feel cheap. *Never!*"

"I've been wanting to call," he said. "I've started and then I've stopped and the reason I've stopped is because I wanted to be absolutely clear and honest about my intentions. If you'll listen to me for a minute, Georgia, I'll try to explain. I didn't anticipate my father-in-law coming back into the business. The fact is, even before his illness the business had become mine. Now all that's changed. He's changed. It seems his recovery has turned him into a different person, far more dominating and difficult than before. Your project was one of many he cancelled—and all over my objections. He scrapped practically everything I had in development. I can't work for him anymore . . . I've quit."

"Oh? And what about your wife?"

"Ours has been a marriage in name only for years. I've told you that."

"You want me to feel sorry for you?"

"I want you to believe me. There's so much going on now—so many changes—I've had to make a lot of quick decisions. First, I'm leaving the country. I'm giving up everything here and setting up an office in London. With the war over, there should be plenty of opportunities. I'll produce films with a group of English investors who seem to have faith in my ability."

"That's real fine, but—"

"Hear me out, Georgia . . . I want you to go with me. I'm leaving on the Twentieth Century Limited tomorrow and I've bought first-class tickets for both of us. From New York we'll be sailing the *Queen Mary* first-cabin to Southampton. In England, we'll be together—that's all I can say. There's still the matter of my divorce, but the lawyers are already drawing up papers. I've got to concentrate on building a studio in a foreign country. London has been devastated by the war, but the English are resilient and the mood's upbeat. You'll like the English, Georgia. And we'll be spending time in Paris, where Negroes are welcomed and appreciated—especially Negro artists. It'll be good for both of us to leave America. It'll be good for your career, good for me. I can't help you here. There, well, the possibilities are terrific. Please, Georgia, come with me. I'm miserable when I'm not with you. Please say yes."

Georgia didn't know what to say. She was stunned. She wanted to tell him the truth about herself—but the words wouldn't come. How would he react? And what was the point? He wanted her, *that* was the point. But was he being sincere or working her over? What was he really offering? She could be his live-in mistress in England. That was the deal. Europe. All right, she'd fantasized about Europe for years, but going there in this condition—secretly pregnant, father unknown, girlfriend to an expatriate white executive . . . ?

"I have to think," she said. "I need time—"

"My man will help you pack."

"I need more time than that."

"We leave tomorrow."

"Why so soon?"

"I can't afford to hesitate. I'm afraid to. I don't want to look back. There's nothing here for me. Thanks to my goddamn father-in-law, I've become a joke here. If I'm going to prove myself it has to be out of the country. Same goes for you, Georgia. Believe me . . ."

The chauffeur took her back to Miss Marva—Miss Marva, the one person on earth she could talk honestly to. She'd know what to do. Even though Miss Marva liked Sol and Herb, she'd understand the problem. She was on her side, she wanted what was best for her. Miss Marva was the only one in the world who knew she was pregnant and knew that any one of three men could be responsible. Miss Marva . . . honest, wise, her best friend . . .

"*Miss Marva's dead* !" A neighbor, an elderly woman standing on the front porch, was screaming out the terrible news.

"*What*!"

"They just took her away in an ambulance. She'd just gotten home when she fell down dead. I came over to borrow some sugar and found her in the kitchen. Seen it with my own eyes. She's gone—that's what the men in the white coats said. Her eyes all bulging out and open. Wide open. Thought she was looking at me but she wasn't looking at no one." . . .

Georgia had Gold's driver take her to the hospital. Miss Marva *couldn't* be dead, Georgia was sure there was some mistake. Strong, vital, Miss Marva didn't just up and die. It must have been a fainting spell, a temporary seizure, something she'd get over.

In a hall in the hospital Georgia found Miss Marva on a stretcher. A sheet covered her body. Georgia lifted the sheet and saw that her eyes were open. So was her mouth. Her dark, empty stare was the awful stare of death. Her skin was cold.

"Cerebral hemorrhage," said a doctor. "Are you her daughter?"

Georgia shook her head, tears running down her cheeks, sobbing. Harper had to be told, Herb had to be called, but Georgia could think of nothing except that now there was no one to talk to, no advice from Miss Marva, no comfort from the woman who never held malice or jealousy, who lived life with an open, generous heart . . . except now that heart had quit and all Georgia could do was stare into blank space seeing the death in Miss Marva's eyes, this loving Miss Marva, dead and gone and unable to say what Georgia should do and what Georgia needed to know, she needed Miss Marva, please help me, Miss Marva, say something because I have to know, I have to do something, I have to decide . . . please tell me what to do . . .

Miss Marva stared back at her without a word.

The little girl watched from the bedroom. She was supposed to be asleep; she knew Mama would be furious to find her awake but she couldn't resist opening the door a crack and taking a peep at the activity in the dining room. The apartment she shared with Mama in Paris was filled with antiques and bric-a-brac not designed for the pleasure of a five-year-old. The American school she attended as a first grader was serious-minded and small. As the only black child, Chanel felt strange and out of place. Having moved from London earlier in the year, she hadn't picked up the strange new language. The simple act of buying candy was an exercise in frustration. She often cried. She wet her bed. She provoked her mother, who was preoccupied, by making impossible demands. Lonely and friendless, she spent her afternoons looking at picture books borrowed from school—fairy tales about fair-haired princesses and blue-eyed princes on white horses.

When her mother was gone making a movie, time moved especially slowly. Little Chanel was left to the care of an Irish nanny, a plump middle-aged woman who chain-smoked foul-smelling cigarettes and complained about the French. When her mother returned after a week or so, Chanel was overjoyed, although she knew it wouldn't be long before Uncle Peter would join them. When Uncle Peter came—like tonight, dining with Mama—Chanel was sent to her room.

Oh, yes, Uncle Peter would always bring a gift, but Chanel well understood that the gift was a bribe. "Now go play with your little toy," Mama would always say. Uncle Peter's best gift came the first day they arrived in Paris: a doll with bright curly red hair nearly as tall as Chanel herself.

69

Chanel began to talk to the doll as though she were real. She named her Margaret after her best friend in London, Margaret Glasgow, a red-headed girl who couldn't get over the dark color of Chanel's skin. "Your skin *shines*," she said in her proper English accent. "Actually it's quite beautiful." Chanel missed Margaret very much. The other children were not nearly as kind. They looked down at her. They were mean. Although she was born in London, Chanel never took on the local speech patterns; she learned to talk by imitating her mother, whose own speech was formed in the American South.

One of Chanel's worst moments was at age four watching her mother being murdered in a movie called *No Escape*. The director, Nino Praz, shot the film in Ireland, and Georgia played a gypsy. Her lover was a Spanish actor who at the film's end slit her throat. Watching that, Chanel could only scream in holy terror.

"It's make-believe, baby," said Georgia, taking the child in her arms. "Mama's right here."

Mama wasn't always right there. The year before she had spent six weeks in Rome working on another film by Praz, who was obsessed with Georgia's face. Chanel was left with a tall woman from Wales, Peter Gold's secretary, who taught her nursery rhymes and made her shepherd's pie. She hated it. Georgia would call several times a week but the connections from Italy were bad and her voice was fuzzy. Chanel was left to encounter her mother in dark and frightening nightmares.

Early on, the child realized her mother was special. Mama's light-skinned beauty and dramatic way of talking set her apart from other women. As she and her daughter motored through postwar London, passing bombed-out buildings on their way to chic shopping sections that had survived the Nazi assault, Chanel felt like a stranger, like she didn't belong here or anywhere. Which was true for most of her childhood. The most acceptance and warmth she got often were associated, though, with buying clothes, and Chanel especially did love Harrod's department store, with its wonderful fragrances and flowery chiffon and lace gowns. It seemed as though Mama could buy whatever she pleased—for herself and Chanel. These were the times the child cherished most, being in stores with Mama, picking out dresses, trying on fancy pinafores and soft sweaters.

There were differences in taste, though, even at Chanel's early age. Georgia liked muted tones; Chanel liked bright, blaring, brassy colors. Georgia preferred loose-fitting garments; Chanel liked things tight. Everything seemed to add to Georgia's beauty—a simple scarf, a white silk blouse—while her daughter never felt pretty. She was, in fact, a chubby child often scolded for overeating. "Keep it up," warned Mama, "and you'll end up a tub of lard."

Now, watching Mama eating with Uncle Peter at the dining room table, Chanel noticed how her mother took a long time between bites. She herself had a habit of wolfing down her food. She watched as Uncle Peter poured Mama a glass of dark red wine. And she listened.

"I'm not happy," Georgia was saying.

"Not happy with the apartment?"

"The apartment's beautiful, Peter."

"And Paris?"

"Paris is a dream."

"Paris will treat you well, Georgia. Paris adores Marian Anderson, they adore Josephine Baker and there's no reason in the world they won't adore Georgia Faith."

"No one here knows my movies."

"The short we made last week will get a lot of attention. And *No Escape* had a strong run here."

"Please, Peter, be honest. *No Escape* didn't have a strong run *anywhere*. Nino has a wonderful eye but half the time the cast didn't know what he was talking about."

"It's an artistic piece . . ."

"Is that the only kind of movie you're going to make —the kind no one sees—the kind you've been making for the past four years?"

Peter lit his pipe. Little Chanel watched the smoke swirl around the room. "European film people," he said, "are different from American. These people are *serious*. Besides, these films have shown a small profit—every single one—on account of low production costs."

"But you keep saying it's industrial films that are paying the bills, Peter."

"They're the reason the English office is stable, but this new office on the Continent will help us grow. I understand that the limited run of these films is frustrating you, Georgia, but the fact that you're making movies at all—"

"I know, I owe it all to you. Isn't that what you want to hear . . . ? Well, I want to be in movies that'll be shown in America. *I'm* an American."

"I have projects in development with French investors. The first feature is yours and the budget is considerable. It takes place in Paris. This is the story we've talked about, where you'll play an American dancer trapped here during the war. You wind up helping the Resistance. It's a wonderful part, and I'm sure the film will find an audience in the U.S."

"I want to believe you, Peter."

"You've no reason not to. I've read the treatment. The writer is Walt Kahn, an American who left Hollywood because of the political heat. He's living in Dublin and should be through with a first draft by next month."

"Before Christmas?"

"It'll be your Christmas present."

"And in the meantime?"

"Why don't you take French lessons?"

"Why do you insist on taking a separate apartment? Why can't we be together? What's the point of the charade?"

Peter paused a long while before replying. "Appearances are important, Georgia. I have to conduct business with all sorts of people. My investors are conservative—"

"That was your excuse in England. I thought the Parisians were different. This is France, land of free love."

"Nothing's completely free, my love." He was rather pleased with the locution.

Georgia was not, but knew when to stop; the man could be pushed only so far. After Peter's divorce she'd entertained the notion of marriage but quickly saw he had no interest. His commitment went just so far. He had featured her in films, found her European directors and challenging parts; he had even hired a publicist who managed to arrange a profile on Georgia in a New York magazine. ("The expatriate Negro actress," it read, "is a woman of extraordinary beauty and sophistication.") He had housed her and her child in comfort. Yet for all the exciting parties he took her to, for all the famous painters, musicians and poets she met, for all the *culture*, she never lost sight of that well-defined line which, it was silently understood, she could not cross. She could not marry him. She could not share his home. Above all, she could not have his name.

On the other hand, he praised her continually. He had seen her potential. He was proud of her, determined to establish her as a film star in Europe before bringing her—and himself as a major producer —back to Hollywood. His humiliating dismissal at the hands of his ex-father-in-law still bothered him. One way or the other he was going to reestablish himself as a force in the industry. It would take time and patience but it would happen. Georgia Faith was a jewel. *His* jewel.

And she did accept the situation. After all, she was living the good life. She was in the movies . . . and still she couldn't help but feel . . . used? Compromised? She well remembered Peter's reaction when just after arriving in London she told him she was pregnant. At first he was furious, then quickly calmed down. He assessed the situation. It was he, after all, who had insisted Georgia come here with him. He had wanted her so badly . . . He even apologized for his reaction, and asked not a word about the father. He understood she didn't know. And he didn't want to know. After all, the child could have been his.

When Chanel was born Georgia did know. The child's dark skin and features were unmistakable links to Herb Montgomery. Peter was relieved, although there was jealousy over what she had shared with another man. A colored man, at that.

More and more, Chanel could sense Uncle Peter's ambivalence. He liked her, and he didn't. Sometimes he paid attention to her; often he ignored her. Underneath it all, she felt his resentment. Finally she didn't really understand who he was. She knew he was not her real uncle. He was not her father. Her father, according to Mama, had been an artist who died of a mysterious disease. He was a genius. "What's a genius?" Chanel wanted to know. "A rare and wonderful human being," said Georgia. Chanel looked and looked but couldn't see the person Mama was talking about.

Georgia often thought about Herb Montgomery—and Sol Solomon. Both good men, and she missed them. Did they know about her child? How could they? If they had seen her movies—as she hoped they had—there were no clues. Her body had returned to form. They had both believed in her. Were they pleased she'd found work in Europe? Were they angry she'd gone off with Peter Gold?

They hadn't tried to contact her; she hadn't contacted them. Still, she suspected they'd both be far closer to her daughter than Peter, perhaps Sol more than the father, Herb . . .

Herb, after all, had never even mentioned children. Like Peter he was all in his work. Georgia had respected his work, especially his commitment to telling stories of his own people. She'd tried to help him and when she went off to Europe it was not without some twinges of guilt. On the other hand, at that moment she had no way in the world of knowing Herb's reaction to her pregnancy or the birth of an extremely light-skinned child. Sol's reaction was equally unpredictable—especially if the child's complexion were dark. And Miss Marva's sudden, shocking death had thrown Georgia into even deeper confusion. Peter Gold was the only one who offered a solution: escape. That's what he was doing, and the temptation to go along with him was irresistible.

Europe, with its castles and museums, seemed an ideal place of escape. Georgia felt lost and found all at the same time. She was more than the mistress of a cultivated white man; she was a working actress who, although still hungering for across-the-board success, at least had the satisfaction of seeing herself on the big screen, playing the parts of women who excited her imagination. And Georgia's imagination was the key: She never ceased to imagine herself as one of the major film stars of the day.

Peter had to wonder where her ambition came from, but he admired it, even encouraged it. And along the way he felt he was falling in love with this woman. He often noted with pleasure how American film people gossiped about him: a man making movies in Europe, a man carrying on with an alluring Negress star. He relished the likely reaction of his ex-wife and father-in-law. No doubt they were shocked. Without the support of Masters Studio they had expected him to fail. Instead he found partners in Europe, financial institutions that had stashed away money during the war and were willing to invest in an entertainment executive from America.

But all little Chanel knew was that Uncle Peter monopolized her mother's time. And on a night like this, sent to bed early and told not to leave her room, she felt especially alone and unhappy. She sang songs to her doll Margaret; she ate fudge cookies she kept hidden in a secret place. Mesmerized, afraid to take her eyes off her mother and Uncle Peter, afraid they'd disappear or leave the apartment without her forever, Chanel watched them as they sipped brandy from strange-shaped glasses. When they moved to the living room her eye followed them to the couch, where the talking stopped and Uncle Peter began kissing Mama. Uncle Peter never kissed her. He patted her head or gave her stiff-armed half-hugs. Standing on a chair so she could peer through the crack in her door over the back of the couch, she saw his tongue dart out of his mouth, she saw her mother's mouth open, heard her mother make funny sounds, moans, the heavy breathing. Was he hurting her? But if he was, why was she taking his hand and leading him into the bedroom?

When her mother's bedroom door closed, Chanel's slowly opened. She knew Mama would be furious if she found out, but still she moved forward, tiptoed across the apartment heavy with the aroma of lemon, broiled fish and pipe tobacco. The floors were ice-cold marble but the sewn-on booties of her flannel pajamas protected her feet. As she stood in front of her mother's door her eyes came to the keyhole and she caught glimpses of bare legs, arms, breasts, Uncle Peter's back, buttocks . . . confusing images. What were they doing? The sounds from her mother scared her so she couldn't help herself—she banged on the door, banged with both her fists, shouting, "Mama! Mama! Mama!"

Peter's first reaction was anger as he pulled himself from Georgia and off the bed . . . and then came a sudden pain, shooting through his arm. His chest felt all afire. He couldn't breathe. Georgia was scrambling for her robe, afraid the child would walk in on her, and didn't notice Peter's convulsion. By the time she had covered herself and looked to see whether Peter had on his trousers, he had crumpled to the floor. Her child still screaming, Georgia didn't know whom to tend to first. Before Georgia had a chance to act, the door opened. Chanel was standing there, looking at her mother, looking at Uncle Peter. The child was hysterical; the mother took her in her arms, ran to the phone, trying in pidgin French to explain the emergency, but she knew it didn't matter, she saw by his cold eyes the same look as in Miss Marva's. It was too late.

Word spread quickly. *Daily Variety* reported the news. Louella Parsons was the first to mention Georgia: "Former Masters studio boss Peter

Gold," she wrote, "died of a massive heart attack in the Parisian apartment of his protégée, actress Georgia Faith. Mr. Gold was forty-one."

Matters were taken out of Georgia's hands. His body was flown back to Boston, where relatives arranged the funeral. She was not invited. She knew Peter owed her money for her work in his previous film but had no idea how to get it. When she contacted the one investment partner she had met, the Englishman was not encouraging. "There are debts," he told her. "Considerable debts. We will suffer a substantial loss." His point was plain—no money for Georgia.

Her head hurt with contradictory emotions—guilt, regret, fear. Why didn't Peter say he had a bad heart? Why hadn't he told her he was in debt? Why hadn't she gotten an accounting of her salary? Peter had paid for everything out of his pocket, doling out her living expenses on a weekly basis. He had provided a housekeeper and nanny for Chanel, but now there was no money to pay them. There was not even any money for rent. She was alone in Paris with her daughter, unable to speak the language, not a franc to her name.

The scene in the bedroom had traumatized mother and daughter. The little girl was terrified that somehow she had killed the man—or her mother had killed him for what he was trying to do to her. The sirens, the ambulance, the men in white coats carrying him away, Mama's frantic phone calls, Mama taking her along to strange offices during the day, Mama being cross and angry with her. Yes, Georgia's facade was cracking, and the child felt the panic.

The train ride to Ireland was long, boring. The rain never stopped. When they got to Dublin a man met them at the train. He was drunk and he stayed drunk.

"This is Mr. Walt Kahn," Georgia said to Chanel. "He's writing a movie for Mama."

But Walt Kahn hadn't written a comma. During lunch his eyes teared over as he spoke about his wife and children back in America, about how he hated Dublin, Dublin was dirty and smelly and he couldn't think in Dublin, couldn't write, couldn't do anything but drink. Even worse, he said, he was dead broke.

"But what about the movie Peter had planned?"

"A pipe dream."

A week later, back in Paris, through an American broker Georgia sold everything in her apartment plus all the jewelry. The money was just enough to book passage for two to Rome, with a little left over.

"Coming to Italy," she telegraphed director Nino Praz. "Need your help."

On the overnight train mother and daughter stayed up until dawn. As the sky faded from black to muddy gray, as morning broke cold and hard, Georgia held Chanel in her arms. "Italy is the friendliest, most beautiful country in the whole world," she told her child. "Everyone will love you in Italy. Nino Praz is a very important director and he'll give us whatever help we need."

Chanel did not see Nino Praz at the train station. Her mother had an address and number for him but the public phones required a special coin that got stuck in the box. Finally Georgia gave up and found a porter who carried her trunk to a cab. Outside the mid-morning sun had broken through the winter mist, and to Chanel, Rome looked full of people in a hurry, people shouting, motorbikes belching smoke, bombed-out buildings under noisy reconstruction, old people on bicycles. She and Mama climbed into a taxi that sped around a square place and then into narrow back alleys and cobble-stoned streets. It all was so strange, nothing looked real.

They stopped in front of an apartment house that looked a thousand years old. The name Praz was written under one of the door-bells. While the cab driver was unloading the trunk, Georgia pressed the buzzer. Coming to Italy, she realized, was an act of guts and desperation. Praz liked her, he admired her acting—he had told her so many times—but she had no idea if or how he would help her.

She did not recognize the older woman who came to the door.

"I am Nino's sister," she said.

Thank God she knew English. "Did you get my telegram?"

"Yes, but I am afraid my brother is away."

"Where?"

"Morocco."

"Oh, God."

"He'll be back next week. If you like, there's a decent *pensione* just down the street. I'll take you there.". . .

For a week they took walks. Chanel held her doll Margaret in her arm and tightly gripped her mother's hand as they surveyed the city's fountains and plazas. The weather was chilly but their coats were warm and the food—the noodles and meats and crusty bread—was really delicious. For Chanel, it was a treat to be with her mother so much. For the first time she could remember, she was her mother's constant and only companion as they waited for the arrival of the great director . . .

To Chanel, Nino Praz looked like a frog. An old man with pop eyes, a small body and a twitch in his left shoulder. When he arrived at the *pensione* he kissed Georgia on both cheeks before bending down and kissing the top of Chanel's head. Words poured out of him, punctuated by busy hands, with an accent thicker than his sister's, and a quick smile. The little girl hardly understood a word he said and Georgia often asked him to repeat himself. But through his fractured English it became increasingly clear that he wanted to help— "Terreeefic," he kept saying, "you are terreeefic actress"—but he really couldn't do much. He was in the middle of his newest movie, cast long ago, but maybe his producer could help. Please call his producer.

She tried the production offices but few people spoke English and even when they did they were no help.

She went back to Nino Praz and told the truth: "I'm dead broke, Nino."

He loaned her enough money to live for another month, but he did so secretively, and soon it became clear why: One day Georgia saw Nino with a very young woman, a blond-haired Dane whom he introduced as his wife. Before he had told her he wasn't married. "She lives in Copenhagen," he told Georgia this time. "Now she comes to live in Rome."

How convenient.

To Chanel, time was suspended. She was glad to be pulled out of school, but without the routine of a classroom her world was out of whack. She watched and waited to see what her mother would do next.

Finally, a call from a production office. There was a part in some comedy that called for an American woman. It was a small role but it didn't matter. Georgia would take it, you bet. When she arrived at the studio, Chanel in hand, Georgia introduced herself to the man in charge and saw right away that he was shocked that she was colored. Praz had forgotten to mention it.

"You haven't seen the two movies I made with Nino?" asked Georgia.

The producer understood no English and his secretary, trying to translate, knew little more. The conversation was a mess but it didn't matter. No work for Georgia. Somehow she wasn't the right type.

And no work this week, no work next week. Christmas came. Georgia put red ribbons in Chanel's hair and took her to the Vatican, where they stood among the massive crowd in St. Peter's Square to watch the Pope bless the world. "Bless me," Georgia silently prayed. Her money was nearly gone. "Bless me in a hurry."

The winter turned wet and cold. The *pensione* had poor heating and cold marble floors. Georgia and Chanel slept in the same bed, huddled together. On New Year's Eve the Romans threw old furniture onto the streets, and a rickety chair barely missed Georgia's head. During the first week of the new year, she swallowed down her pride and tried making two transatlantic calls—one to Sol Solomon, another to Herb Montgomery. Both their numbers, though, had been long disconnected. She had no idea where they'd gone. She had no idea what she was going to do.

Then she saw the poster.

A troupe of American tap dancers touring in Europe were making a stop in Rome. And, wonderfully, included was Harper Montgomery. The evening of the show, Georgia left Chanel with Nino's sister. The performance left Georgia terribly homesick. The Italians looked on the dancers as an exotic novelty, but to Georgia they brought back memories of Central Avenue and the Club Diddle Daddle. Watching the dancers spin and leap, hearing the dazzling rhythms of their metal taps, seeing them turn time into a fabulous playtoy, she felt renewed. But it was Harper who especially got to her with his irresistible smile, Harper who won the hearts of the crowd, stepping out in a dazzling white tux and tails, his body a study in balance and joy.

Backstage, he embraced Georgia, his body soaked with perspiration.

"Girl," he said, "you are the *last* person in the world I would expect to see in Rome. This is just too strange. Where you been hiding?"

"I was living in London, then Paris . . ."

"After Marva died, you just up and disappeared. We missed you something awful. Herb was talkin' 'bout you and some white producer."

"Peter Gold."

"Did he get you in the movies?" asked Harper.

"He did."

"Well, I tell you, sugar, when you left, baby brother was crushed . . ."

"I wanted to write, I wanted to explain . . ."

"Never thought he'd get over it. But you know Herb, Georgia, he keeps on making those pictures."

"Tell me."

"Well, the boy's still at it. And . . . well, a year or so back he married Honey Lincoln, the actress. Put her in some of his movies. You know Honey, don't you?"

"No, I don't." Georgia's heart was at her feet.

"Gorgeous gal. Pretty good lil' actress too. She's been in the last couple of things Herb did. Baby bro' ain't getting rich, mind you, but now he owns four or five movie cameras. He puts those movies together with spit and Scotch tape but he do put 'em together."

"That's wonderful . . ."

"Him and Honey, they living not far from where Miss Marva's house used to be. They and their little twin babies."

"Twin babies . . ." Georgia repeated numbly.

"Girl and a boy. Girl looks like his mama, boy's the picture of Herb . . . Well, say, looks to me like you're doing right fine for yourself, Georgia. You look beautiful, baby, looks like you found a real home."

She didn't have the heart to deny it. She didn't want to go into what had happened to Peter; and she sure didn't want even to mention Chanel, especially now that she knew Herb had kids and a wife.

"We're going out to get some pizza. Man, I ain't leaving Rome without getting me some pizza. Why don't you come along, sugar?"

"I'd love to, Harper, but I've got an early morning call tomorrow. You understand."

"Sure I do . . ."

"Please send my love to Herb. Please tell him . . . tell him I'm really happy for him, and his family."

She kissed Harper quickly on the cheek and left in a hurry. She didn't want him to see her crying.

Walking then through the dark alleyways of the ancient city, Georgia was losing control. She hadn't felt this way since she first learned Miss Marva had died. That was a kick in the stomach. Now this. Herb married. With twin babies. With a beautiful wife, another actress, making movies with another woman, her replacement. Herb . . . father of her child . . .

Georgia realized she had no rights in that . . . after all, she had left *him*.

She'd come close to asking Harper for help—for a handout, even for some work with his dance troupe. But her pride wouldn't let her. She didn't want Harper—and she especially didn't want Herb—to know the truth. How had it happened? How had she been so misled —or had she misled herself? She went back to Miss Marva . . . with Miss Marva's advice all decisions seemed so logical and easy. But without her, she felt lost. Still, wouldn't Miss Marva have approved of her going off with Peter? Wasn't that the most practical thing to do?

Practical, yes, she thought to herself as she walked through Piazza Navona, moonlight glistening off Bernini's fountain of the Four Rivers. The sight of the open space, the ancient church and the starlit sky was too powerful to pass by or ignore. Georgia had to stop, try to turn off the voices inside her head. She sat on a stone bench to take in the silent beauty. Until now, her own beauty had seemed to insure her survival. Well, that had its limits. Love had its limits. Learn, girl, she could hear Miss Marva saying. Why the tears? Why the ache in her heart for a man with his head in the clouds? Because Herb Montgomery had a wife, two children and a home. He was a steady and strong man she had passed over for a so-called practical adventure gone wrong. She was unemployed and broke in a country whose language she didn't speak. She was a single mother whose only skill was acting.

In the orphanage in Florida she had imagined the great things that would happen to her once she was on her own. Well, some *had* happened . . . she had gone to California, she had come to Europe, she had met and loved powerful men, she had acted in movies. And all of

it before she was twenty-five. Yet sitting in the center of the magnificent piazza she felt nearly paralyzed—no money, no prospects, no
plans. A few yards away she watched a hard-looking woman approach
a man, and after a few moments of negotiations they went off together past the ornate fountains into the dark streets. Rock-bottom
. . . the ultimate sell-out. No matter what, she could never sell herself like that . . .

The church in the piazza had been here for centuries. Its beauty
endured. True beauty endured, she told herself . . . like she had
endured her orphaned childhood, because of . . . of something
deep inside her. She walked closer to the church, looked up at the
weather-worn sculpture, the heavenly figures that adorned the
facade, the strength of their character, the faith of the artist who gave
them life. In spite of her gloom Georgia felt something strong inside.
Because at her core was raw optimism.

Suddenly a flashbulb went off in her face.

"That face," said a male voice behind the blinding flash.

At first she was frightened, until she realized it was nothing more
than a camera.

"You and the night and the music," crooned the gentleman in a
silky-soft American accent. Under the pale streetlight he appeared
like some kind of phantom—ashen-skinned, thin blond hair, a short,
slight figure in a flowing black cape, circling around her against the
backdrop of the piazza, looking for angles.

"I don't hear any music," she told the man.

"Shut your eyes and you will."

She shut her eyes as he snapped another photo.

"You create the music," he told her. "You, my dear, are music."

It was a line, she was sure, but she couldn't help responding . . .
"What are you?" she managed to get out.

"I am lucky, blessed to find you here. I intended to photograph an
empty piazza. Instead I find a woman who highlights her surroundings the way the sun highlights the heavens. I am blinded."

She had to smile. Line or not, it made her feel better. "My name is
Georgia Faith." She held out her hand. "I am an actress."

"If I'm not mistaken you were in Praz's *No Escape*."

"You're not mistaken . . ."

"A beautiful film, Nino's a friend of mine."

"I'm here in Rome because of him."

"Making a movie?"

"In between movies."

"So much the better for me. I'm Noel Radison, a soul in search of beauty. Miss Faith, you should forgive my florid speech. But you . . . you are more beauty than I thought possible. Please indulge me for a few minutes . . ."

"Are these pictures for you or—"

"I could never be so selfish. Why deprive the world? Sorry, there I go again, but I am sincere."

"You will publish them?"

"Only with your approval."

"What I'm asking, Mr. Radison," getting down to it, "is whether this involves money."

"When it comes to beauty, Miss Faith, money never stands in my way. As an artist, I need your help. If you need mine, well, it would be my pleasure to accommodate you."

Chanel was eating candy and playing with her doll Margaret on the balcony. It was an unseasonably warm winter day, the sun shining brightly on the red tile roofs of the city. The clouds were cotton-candy puffy and the sounds of the streets muffled below. Georgia had brought her daughter to this sprawling apartment in an old palace with huge chandeliers and gold-leafed mirrors. The place belonged to Noel Radison, whom Chanel liked right away because he was silly. He wore a floppy green hat and never stopped chattering. The moment he saw Chanel, he picked her up and gave her a big kiss, telling her she looked like his favorite treat, an M&M candy. He said he had to take her picture—he had to do it right away—because she was too cute to resist. He ran off and ran back with a camera and a bunch of M&Ms and told her to make a funny face. Chanel stuck out her tongue and he said, *"Perfect,* what a lovely pink tongue," and snapped the shutter.

Noel lived with Harold, a painter with an enormous belly, curly gray hair, a thick English accent and a voice like a foghorn. He was fond of Chanel too. He carried a table with paper and crayons out to the balcony, where they drew zebras in the zoo and kids at the beach.

He asked Chanel to draw a picture of him and she did, making him a laughing Santa Claus.

"But I have no beard," Harold said.

"Now you do," precocious Chanel said, and added a purple beard.

Harold sketched Chanel in charcoal, making her eyes bigger than they really were and planting a wide enormous smile on her face. Noel and Harold made Chanel feel good; she was crazy about them. She loved watching then run around their enormous apartment snapping pictures, making drawings and telling Georgia and Chanel how gorgeous they were. After the last weeks, their words of praise had a healing effect.

While Chanel was on the balcony drawing a bird perched on the roof across the alley, Georgia was being photographed by Noel in the living room. The door was shut and locked. The photographer had spun a white silk turban around her head and applied black cream to her lips. Aside from the turban, she was naked. At first she had refused to do it, but Noel convinced her it was art for art's sake. After all, it wasn't sex, and he and Harold had inheritances so that neither of them cared two flips for money. He was preparing a book of photographs of extraordinary women, and she *had* to be in it. More, he was happy to pay her a modeling fee, whatever she needed to get back on her feet. The one condition was nudity. This was, after all, a book of nude photos.

Four separate heating units warmed the room, and surely there was nothing cheap or salacious about the situation. Georgia had identified with the lovely Icart etching she had seen in Peter Gold's office years before. But unlike Icart's model, her pose was not provocative. Noel was interested in juxtapositions: she sat in an Empire chair, her legs crossed; she stood in front of an ornate Edwardian mirror, arms folded in front of her chest. In Noel's words, these were "ironic portraits."

"I can assure you," he told Georgia, "I detest pornography."

Actually, revealing her body had never been a problem for Georgia. Total nudity, though, was something else. But as Noel said, this was for art. Lust wasn't in the picture. Noel and Harold lived with art. The apartment was filled with rare antiques; they had first editions of Aubrey Beardsley's illustrated volumes: Oscar Wilde's *Salome*, Alexander Pope's *Rape of the Lock*, Ben Jonson's *Volpone* and Aristophanes' *Lysistrata*. As a photographer Noel was intrigued by forms, whether the stiff stamen of an orchid or the smooth curve of a female breast.

In fact, he had published a book of natural formations—rocks, shells, driftwood—all photographed in grainy black-and-white. He had a keen eye for texture and a deep appreciation of unspoiled beauty. That's why he'd insisted on no makeup for Georgia except the stark black lipstick.

During the hour-long session her major feeling was one of pride. She wanted to show her body; after all, she had no blemishes or scars; her skin was creamy; her breasts weren't large but beautifully proportioned, as were her thighs and buttocks. Standing in front of a portrait of Queen Victoria, she regarded the camera composedly, self-assuredly. The setting was perfect, fitting her best fantasy . . .

" 'She's stunning'—that's what he said," Noel announced.

A week had passed since the photo session.

"You showed him the pictures without my permission—"

"My dear," countered Noel, "this is the largest manufacturer of perfumes in all of Europe. Jacques Dufour is one of my closest friends, and if he decided to feature you in his advertisements, why, the advertisements will be as much for you as for his fragrance."

"Will you do the photography?"

"Of course."

"And the advertisements will appear in America?"

"In all the top magazines."

"Well . . ."

Noel took Georgia to Venice—exotic, mysterious Venice was the setting for the perfume ads. When she was told she was to be left alone with Harold, Chanel cried bitterly, but quickly was assuaged when Harold showed up with a puppy named Matisse. By then Georgia and Chanel had moved into the spare bedroom in the back of the gentlemen's apartment and, for the first time during any of her mother's absences, Chanel did not feel anxious. Harold taught her to blow up balloons and twist them into giraffes; he cooked her spaghetti with loads of butter and cheese and escorted her to his favorite cafe, where they made the best chocolate cake in the world. He also took her to visit an English-speaking school, housed in an old monastery, where the headmaster was a schoolmate of Harold's from Oxford.

"Once your Mama finds a flat for you and her here in Rome," Harold told Chanel, "this is the school you'll be going to."

"How do you know my Mama wants to live in Rome?"

"She and Noel are working so well together, I think they'll continue."

"My Mama's always moving," said Chanel.

"Well, maybe this time she's found a home."

Walking hand-in-hand through the Villa Borghese, Harold told Chanel a little about his childhood—what it was like going from London to India when he was a small boy. His father was a colonel in the British army and moved the family nearly every year. Just when Harold made a friend, it was time to move on. Chanel understood that. Hugging her doll, she talked about Margaret, her best friend back in London. Harold understood that.

When they returned from their walk, Georgia was home, wearing a tailored black wool suit and a spectacular circular red felt hat. She had fabulous stories about the canals and gondolas of Venice. Best of all, she had a blown-glass angel from the island of Murano. "This is for my baby," she said. "This is for my Chanel."

When Noel developed the photographs, everyone was impressed. Even little Chanel felt the impact of her mother's beauty against the backdrop of a city shrouded in mystery and fog. In the center of Piazza San Marco, before the Palazzo Ducale, standing on the Bridge of Sighs, her face tilted, grand and aloof, she appeared stately as the monuments surrounding her—regal, radiant, a distant romantic figure.

"These photographs," promised Noel, "will make fashion history."

Georgia believed it.

"He's not using the photographs."

"What!"

Chanel was back in the bedroom, half-asleep, when she heard

Georgia cry out as though she'd been struck. Chanel ran quickly to the door and cracked it open so she could hear the conversation.

"Jacques says he doesn't like the poses," said Noel.

"That's *impossible*," Harold said, furious. "The poses are the essence of what he's trying to sell—sophistication."

"He knew I was colored, didn't he?" asked Georgia.

"How could he not know? He saw the nudes."

"Then what's the matter?"

"In the Venetian light he claims your skin-tone photographs too dark."

"That's *crap*," snapped Georgia, flashing back to her first experience on a film set in Los Angeles.

"I told Jacques as much, my dear. I screamed bloody murder."

"*You* screamed bloody murder," screamed Georgia, "well, wait till he hears *me* scream. I'm not standing for this, Noel, I promise you I'm not. This will not happen to me, not now. I need those ads to get my career back—"

"There are other ways . . ." Harold began to say.

"*No!*" Georgia let loose. "*I'm fed up with this goddamn hypocrisy!* I will not stand another humiliation—"

"I'm afraid—"

"Well, I'm *not* afraid. I'm calling up your friend Jacques and telling him what the hell I think of him."

"Perhaps we can shoot the photos again," suggested Noel, "and make the skin-tone a bit brighter—"

"You mean *lighter*—no, the skin-tone will not be lighter. The skin-tone is whatever the hell it is. This is *my* skin-tone, and I will not—do you hear me, *not*—be insulted again by being asked to change it. I'm fed up, sick and tired of being turned out for reasons that have nothing to do with talent."

"I quite agree."

"Then, for God's sake, Noel, get your friend to agree."

"I've tried, Georgia, believe me I have. The best we can hope for is a reshoot."

"Then forget it. Forget this whole thing. Forget Europe, forget the perfume and the ads, forget everything. I know you two have tried to help, and I appreciate what you've done, but this is too much. I'm taking my baby and getting out. It's worse here than back home."

"I don't think so," said Harold.

"*Well, I do*," Georgia snapped. "All this culture, all these centuries of culture and art all boil down to the same crap. I've had it. I'm tired of losing out through no fault of my own."

She ran back to the bedroom, and hearing her footsteps, Chanel hurried back to bed and pretended to be asleep. She didn't want Mama to know that she heard her crying. She could hardly remember her mother crying before, but now Mama shook and wept for nearly a half-hour while Chanel's heart beat like crazy. She wanted to reach out for her mother, she needed to be comforted by her, but it was her mother who most needed comforting. Afraid, upset, Chanel kept quiet, unhappy for Mama, but mostly confused. What would happen to her now?

"I don't want to leave!" Now it was Chanel doing the crying. It was the following morning and Georgia, Noel, Harold and Chanel were seated around the breakfast table. Georgia had just informed her daughter that they were going to America. She was using the money from the perfume ads, a generous fee paid in spite of the photos having been rejected. Noel and Harold saw there was no way of convincing Georgia to stay.

"Europe is making me crazy," she told them. "Europe is getting me nowhere. It's suffocating me. It's not working. Every part of me says go home. Go back to Hollywood."

"No!" Chanel protested. "I wanna stay with Matisse. I wanna stay with Harold . . ."

"We'll visit you, sweetheart," promised Harold, "and we'll take good care of Matisse."

"No! I'm not going, I don't want to go—"

"You've never been to America," said Georgia. "America's our home."

"I hate America. I hate you!"

"You don't mean that," said Noel.

"I do! I hate her! I hate her and I hate all her stupid movies and all her stupid pictures and the way she kisses all the men with her tongue and—"

Georgia smacked Chanel across the face.

"*I hate you*!" the little girl screamed even louder.

Georgia grabbed her by the arm and pulled her over to the couch where she turned her over and tried to spank her bottom. Yelling and writhing, Chanel was impossible to pin down. Kicking wildly, her left foot struck her mother in the eye. Infuriated, Georgia pounded the child's backside until Noel and Harold came over to separate them.

"Do not touch me!" Georgia told them.

They backed off as she continued to spank her daughter. Afterward, Chanel ran back to the bedroom, her backside burning, and threw the blown-glass angel her mother had brought her from Murano against the wall, smashing the figurine to bits. . . .

A week later, their trunk packed and a taxi waiting, Chanel hid in the corner of a closet. It took Georgia, Noel and Harold nearly a half-hour just to find her. When she was finally discovered she again refused to leave. More hysteria. The two men had to carry her kicking and crying all the way to the street. "Let me stay with you," she begged them. "Let me live here!" . . .

On the ship Georgia took stock of her career, of the next move, whom she would call as soon as she arrived in America. She tried to convince herself she was heading in the right direction. Forget the disappointments and failures abroad. She had now worked in films in both America and Europe, she had experience, she knew what she wanted, and more than ever she was determined to get it.

For her part, Chanel became sick and threw up twice, once on the cabin floor, once in her mother's lap.

When the Italian liner dropped anchor in New York, the year was 1951 and Georgia's intention was to head straight to California. But Noel Radison had contacted a friend who was directing a play in the Village, and though the part wasn't big Georgia was intrigued by it. The storyline was American expatriates in Rome. Georgia played a South Carolinian schoolteacher, a poet unrecognized in her own country. She was thrilled just to be working again, not to mention the parallels with her own life. When the play closed after four months she found work in experimental theaters in and around the Village. She and Chanel lived in a tiny apartment on lower Fifth Avenue.

Chanel disliked the city. She couldn't stand the progressive school off Washington Square and hated the teacher, an effusive woman who wore bright orange lipstick and twisted metal jewelry and gave off body odor. The other children stayed in their cliques; Chanel didn't feel welcome. New York was full of noise. The streets smelled of garbage. The apartment had roaches. The subways were dirty and scary and, worst of all, her mother was back to being gone most of the time.

"Live theater," Chanel heard her mother say on the phone, "is where I've always belonged."

Georgia was excited by what she saw as the city's sophistication. She became friends with actors and dancers, several of whom knew the films she'd made with Peter Gold. When Noel Radison's book of nude photographs was published it made a splash in certain circles, especially the shot of Georgia seated in Noel's Roman study. Georgia felt no shame whatsoever; she enjoyed the notoriety. And her life in Europe seemed to impress people in America. After all, she could tell stories about Jean Cocteau and Edith Piaf. She'd been to the South of France. She'd met Picasso. Of course, like all good storytellers, Georgia embellished. She was especially comfortable around a group of Negro playwrights working on creating drama about the black experience. And it was from one Byron James, a black writer, that she learned news of Herb Montgomery.

"He's a successful cameraman, one of the first colored ones to be working on big features. He was here in New York with Billy Wilder. You just missed them. They were shooting a new Marilyn Monroe movie, *The Seven-Year Itch*. Now Herb's supposed to be working with Charles Laughton on a film with Robert Mitchum and Shelley Winters."

"What about his own movies?"

"He ran out of financing. In this country who the hell's interested in financing films about colored folk?"

"He'd been trying for so long . . ."

"Well, he finally woke up."

Georgia's feelings for him hadn't gone away, and, practical as always, she wondered whether he could now help her professionally. After all his attempts at independence, he had gone Hollywood. Surely he was frustrated, but just as surely his contacts had to be major. He had established himself and was working with top producers and directors. Even if they weren't his own films, they were the kind that most interested Georgia. She appreciated the life of Greenwich Village, but she'd never lost sight of her true goal.

She asked about Herb's wife, Honey Lincoln, and their kids, but no one had details. Georgia managed to get Herb's number in Los Angeles, but when she called there was no answer. She left her name at several production offices where Herb had worked but never heard back. Well, *she* had left *him*. He was probably still sore and who could blame him? He had moved on . . . and so had she, hadn't she?

She had developed a small circle of admirers in Manhattan, people who provided her with steady work in various productions. Her reputation as an actress was growing, but her bank account was not. Only once had she earned decent money, and that was for only a month. That time was the high point of her life in New York City—she'd reached Broadway.

It was 1953 and the play was called *Weeping Willows*, about a family of blacks who left Mississippi for Cleveland. It was a theme and a setting Georgia had played too often, but this time there was a difference. The playwright was not only black but female, and the point of view different from anything Georgia had read before. Action was seen through a woman's eyes, emotions felt in a woman's skin. Georgia had the lead and the notices were raves. This had to be her ticket back to Hollywood.

Wrong.

In spite of the critical raves, the audience didn't respond. Ticket sales slid and a closing date was posted. Georgia had convinced herself that her experiences in Europe and New York had been building to this climax, that the disappointments would only serve to make her stronger, to pave the way to her inevitable triumph. *Weeping Willows* had to be her breakthrough. So when the play crashed, so did Georgia.

Men, of course, were still there—painters and directors, actors and producers, white and black. Her beauty attracted male companionship whenever she wanted it. And, even with her strong physical desires, she was very selective. Since coming to New York she had taken only one lover, Byron James, a man, it turned out, who so disliked children she couldn't bring him to the apartment.

Chanel, smart as a whip and with her mother's dramatic flair, could not be controlled. She overate and overslept. She never cleaned up after herself. In spite of her mother's solicitous care, Chanel felt

Georgia—increasingly she thought of her as "Georgia," not Mama or even Mother—somehow resented her, just went through the motions of being a mother, really resented her for cramping her lifestyle.

On the closing night of *Weeping Willows*, Georgia felt she had no lifestyle, no life, although, of course, her young daughter couldn't really understand that. Once again, Georgia was broke. And down. The audience for her final performance filled only a third of the theater. There was no party, no last-night celebration, not even a consolation visit from the producers.

Only a knock on her dressing room door.

Sol Solomon had gained weight.

His wavy black hair had thinned and, maybe because he was here in New York, his Brooklyn accent sounded thicker. The twinkle in his eye was still there.

"What a doll," he told her. "What an actress!"

She hugged him for a long, long while, clinging to him. Tears came into his eyes. Her eyes stayed dry.

"I've missed you something awful," he said.

"I didn't know how to find you," she told him. "Are you living here?"

"I've been here."

"I didn't know, I wish I'd known . . ."

"How long you been back?"

"Almost three years."

"Here in Manhattan the whole time?"

"The whole time."

"I can't believe it. All this time I've been sitting across the river over in Brooklyn, knocking my head against the wall trying to write a novel—"

"Did you write it?"

He handed her a book, *Kings and Con Men*.

"Sol," she said, "this is wonderful."

"This is your copy. I want you to read it."

"Of course."

"I read some things about you, Georgia, but I couldn't fit the pieces together. When I heard about Peter Gold I tried to get in touch with you, I did my best, I swear . . ."

"You have nothing to apologize about, Sol. I'm the one who ran off."

"It hurt like hell, I can't lie to you, baby. I was sick over it. I figured you were pissed because I never proposed. And Peter, it looked like he had the connections. That was it, wasn't it?"

"I don't know what it was. Miss Marva's death . . ."

"You had to deal with a lot of shit . . ."

"Sol, let's talk about you," she said, taking hold of his hand. "Tell me about your book. What's it about?"

"Gangsters. Hoods I knew when I was a kid. The old neighborhood."

"Well, you always said you were getting out of Hollywood and you did it."

"You too."

Georgia smiled weakly.

"You want to go back to the Coast?" Sol asked. "You still want to make those big movies?"

Georgia smiled again. More than ever, her beauty got to Sol. It had been several years since he had seen her and now, at twenty-seven, her face had somehow gained a deeper impact . . . the fineness of her features, the extraordinary hue of her green eyes, the luster of her skin . . . Poor Sol, smitten all over again.

Georgia, not exactly a sentimentalist, was happy to be with someone who could read her feelings. She wanted to tell him the truth about why she had left, wanted to tell him about Chanel . . .

"Will you have supper with me?" he asked. "You can tell this Brooklyn boy all about Europe."

You bet she would. At Patsy's Italian Restaurant on Fifty-sixth Street she managed to have Sol do most of the talking. Which wasn't hard. He was proud of having stuck with it; he had, after all, written a novel. Hollywood had spit him out. "They didn't want me. So I said fuck you—pardon my French—and I came home."

"That took guts, Sol."

"Hell, you've been living alone overseas. *That's* guts."

She took his hand again. Thinking about the Village bohemians, the avant-garde types, she realized how much more relaxed she felt with Sol Solomon. He ate an enormous bowl of spaghetti and talked like a cab driver, but she felt she could trust every word he said. Sauce splattered over his plaid tie that clashed with his striped shirt; he talked with his mouth full. He sure as hell didn't carry on about existentialism, didn't know the works of Ralph Ellison or W. E. B.

Du Bois, hot tickets among the Negro intellectuals she'd been around. Because Georgia was bright, she liked smart men, but those men had a way of being wrapped up in their own egos. They loved to hear themselves talk. Sure, they stimulated her, and surely Sol was no intellectual. He didn't talk ideas, he told stories. He wore his heart all over his sleeve. He said what he felt, he felt what he said.

"Those schmucks over there," he said, pointing to a couple of guys staring at him and Georgia, obviously upset at the sight of a racially mixed couple, "if they keep looking over I'm gonna belt 'em."

"I'm used to it," she said. "Even in Europe . . ."

"Let's just get out of here . . . can I walk you home?"

"My apartment is so small . . ." Georgia had already called the babysitter to say she'd be late.

"We could go over to Brooklyn, but my place is a mess."

"I don't mind, Sol." She remembered how hard Sol had always tried to satisfy her sexually. The man had powerful energy that went with his need, his desire, to please. He *gave.*

"Look," he said, "my book's in the stores and I'm celebrating and you've been in this Broadway play and, well, why don't I just get a suite at the St. Regis so we can celebrate right?"

Georgia gave herself over to the moment—to the luxurious suite, the champagne, to Sol's ability to give her everything she wanted at this time and in this place . . . his urgency, his mouth on her mouth and his mouth on her sex, kissing her and licking, opening her lips with his tongue, flicking his tongue against her clitoris until she demanded that he come inside and ride her, just slide easy then strong, fast and hard, filling her with more pleasure than she had felt in years, because she knew and trusted him, his thrusts, his sounds, his need to know she was enjoying him, feeling him, feeling right, getting enough of his honest love.

Afterward, the sheets soaked with their perspiration, her eyes half-open, she listened to the muffled sounds from the streets below; on the radio by the side of the bed Julius LaRosa sang "Anywhere I Wander." Relaxed, feeling secure, Georgia felt she could tell him anything . . .

"Sol, I have a child," she said quietly as he caressed her thighs.

Sol looked at her. "That's okay. I have a wife."

Georgia took the news stoically. What, after all, could she say? Was Sol supposed to have waited around for her? He asked her child's gender and name, and was careful not to ask about her father.

His wife's name was Rhonda, an extra out in California, who now worked at Minsky's in Newark.

"What's Minsky's?"

"A strip joint. I know what you're thinking," he said, "but she's sort of nuts about me, a really good broad. Fact is, I couldn't have written my novel without her. If I needed her home she'd be home. If I wanted to be alone she'd leave me alone. Plus, she types. She's no Einstein but I got tired of playing the field, Georgia, I was worn out. Plus, I wasn't making any real money. I had to sell both those houses on the Coast and live on my piddling savings that didn't last. Minsky's pays real good. And Rhonda only has to work three nights a week . . ."

In the cab home, Georgia's mood got darker and darker. The more she thought about what had happened, the angrier she became. She did not intend to carry on with a married man no matter how strongly he felt for her. Also, if Sol was so goddamn honest why hadn't he told her about Rhonda before booking the suite at the St. Regis—not afterward? Okay, she had an effect on him, and she couldn't deny the pleasure he gave her. That part had been great. But it'd been short-lived and ended in another depression.

She spent the next day reading *Kings and Con Men*. It was no *Invisible Man*—the last novel she'd read—and the narrator, a character named Sam, was obviously an alter ego for Sol. But Sam was a great bullshit blower; the book, no surprise considering its author, had great sex. She was sure it would sell and she was right. A few weeks later, with Georgia still out of work, the book hit the bestseller lists.

"I'm sorry," she told Sol, who'd been calling every day to get back together. "I have some very mixed feelings about us."

"I understand, but I really want to see you again, Georgia."

"I don't want to get into that, Sol, I really don't. Let's stay friends. That's enough. And as a friend I have to swallow my pride and say it plainly. I'm out of work. I need help. I need a job."

It had come to that. Her artistic contacts had done nothing. Her critical raves brought no money. Her third-rank agent couldn't connect her with anything that paid. She went out on auditions, on cold readings and cattle calls. Nothing. Even for supposedly tough-skinned Georgia Faith, enough was fucking enough.

Fascinated, Chanel watched her mother apply makeup to other women's faces. She did it skillfully and afterward almost always made a sale. It was in the center of the cosmetics area of Lord & Taylor department store on Fifth Avenue during the busy Christmas season. Chanel loved the festive decorations—the holly, the wreaths, the silver-foil angels—and especially the perfume, the wondrous scents. This was where Chanel learned she was named after a woman of fashion who had invented a fragrance that, naturally, became the girl's favorite.

When Sol's show business contacts hadn't come through, Georgia had no choice but to work the want ads. A sales clerk at Lord & Taylor wasn't exactly what she had in mind . . . one day acting on Broadway, the next selling rouge and lipstick . . . but it was real and she had no other real choices.

After a while, though, something strange happened: Georgia discovered she didn't dislike the job. She was the best one in her department. Her singular looks, her ability to sell, brought her to the boss's attention. She was made assistant department head, and while the commission was slight her sales meant she made good money. For the first time since she was a schoolgirl in Florida working odd jobs, she began to save. And just as her goal as a child had been to get enough money to get to Hollywood, her goal as an adult was the same —sales, by God, however unplanned, would be her ticket back to sunny money California.

On Saturdays little Chanel took the bus by herself up Madison Avenue to visit her mother. She loved the window decorations and crowded streets, felt free from school and its boring lessons, bought herself candy with change Georgia gave her, spent hours walking through toy stores and looking at dolls. At Lord & Taylor she felt special because her mother worked there; this was the store where Georgia always bought her beautiful blouses and skirts and bright-colored sweaters.

This particular afternoon, seeing her mother behind the counter,

Chanel waved, and Georgia winked back. She was helping a woman powder her face. The woman was white with dyed red hair, pale skin and a slow Southern accent. She sported earrings and a mink coat draped over her shoulders. She was about to buy a large assortment of cosmetics.

When it looked like the customer was about to pay, a tall man in a Western hat appeared, took one look at Georgia, grabbed the red-haired woman and snarled, "My wife ain't buying a goddamn thing in this store. We don't buy from coons."

Chanel's heart started hammering. She watched her mother's eyes grow narrow and red. She watched as Georgia took a fluffy powder puff and, as if it were the most natural thing in the world, patted white powder to the man's forehead, nose and cheeks. He started coughing and for a few moments Chanel thought he was going to hit her mother. But a burst of laughter from customers standing around the counter undid the man. And Chanel, maybe for the first time, understood her mother's courage and felt proud. Georgia made the man look like a fool. Storming off with his wife, he yelled, "I'm getting your black ass fired!"

Georgia was not fired. She worked at Lord & Taylor for a year before getting a better job at Saks Fifth Avenue, where she became a department head and was able to save even more money. She also joined several actors' workshops that met at night; she performed in three different off-Broadway plays; she pursued movie agents operating out of Manhattan but without success. From time to time she allowed Sol Solomon to take her to lunch or dinner, but never to bed.

"I'd give up Rhonda for you," he told her.

"Look, Sol, your marriage has nothing to do with me. If it's good, keep it. If it isn't, end it. I'm not getting in the middle."

"You sound cold."

"I don't feel cold and you know it. But I won't be used, Sol. No more. No way."

"I want to help you," he said. "I've hit the jackpot with *Kings and Con Men*—"

"I don't want your money, Sol. I'm making money on my own."

"They're talking about making a movie out of my novel—"

"Great, but there's only one Negro character—a man."

"I could suggest another part, I could change the story."

"And I could play Juliet to Laurence Olivier's Romeo, but I'm not holding my breath."

"It ain't like that . . ."

"Dammit, Sol, it *is* like that—and you know it."

Sol never got to know Chanel. Georgia never invited him to the apartment, never could bring herself to introduce him to her daughter, Herb's daughter.

Meanwhile, Chanel was curious about the men in Georgia's life, and her questions grew bolder by the day.

"Tell me about my daddy," she would say. "Where did he come from?"

"California."

"Was he handsome?"

"Very."

"What was his job?"

"He was a painter and a poet."

"Can I read his poems?"

"I don't have any."

"Why don't you have his picture?"

"I lost everything when we moved to Europe."

"Did he like kids?"

"Of course . . ."

"Was he big and tall?"

"Yes.

"How tall?"

"Very tall."

"I want to see his picture."

"I don't *have* any."

"I don't believe you."

"Please, honey . . ."

"I want to know what my daddy looked like."

"Well, let's see . . . he had fine features and nice brown eyes. He was very graceful and light on his feet. His brother was a dancer. In fact, he came from a family of dancers and artists—"

"Do I look like him?"

"I think you do."

"Why did he get sick?"

"No one knows why, darling. It just happened."

"Why did he have to die?"

"I wish I could tell you. I wish I knew."

"I want to see his picture! I want to see what my daddy looked like!"

Taking Chanel in her arms, Georgia dried her tears with a linen handkerchief and kissed her forehead, whispering into her ear, "We're managing just fine, honey. It's important to learn how to manage without a man . . . important to be strong on our own . . . and you're strong, baby . . . yes, you are . . . my baby is very strong . . ."

1 9 5 7

California had been kinder this time. Georgia settled in with ease. When she had run from L.A. a dozen years earlier she had gone in a panic. The memories were painful. When she remembered her state of mind—the confused state of an ambitious nineteen-year-old—she still felt anger and some shame. No matter. She had learned. Dear God, had she learned! She returned to the sprawling city with both eyes wide open. Her ambition still burned, but she was another person. She was ready to compromise, do anything, except play a cook.

The show was "Meet the Morgans," a situation comedy about a white family relocated in the suburbs. Georgia had told her agent that she wouldn't take the role. But when it became clear that the market for Negro actresses was practically nonexistent, and when the agent mentioned a salary far greater than Georgia had made for any movie, she reconsidered. She and Chanel were living in a one-bedroom apartment off Fairfax Avenue and barely getting by.

As cook to the Morgans, Georgia was Rowena, who had answers to the family's problems both practical and philosophical. The problem, of course, was that Rowena had no life of her own—no husband, no boyfriend, no wardrobe except for a white ruffled apron over a black dress with short sleeves. But because of the exposure and the steady pay, Georgia controlled herself—at least somewhat—in dealing with the producers and writers. Eventually, though, she opened her mouth.

"What does this woman do when she isn't cooking?" she asked the chief writer. "Does she have a family or friends or is she just on this earth to make life easier for the people she waits on?"

Unaccustomed as he was to actresses who talked back—especially black actresses—the writer was at first surprised but later decided Georgia had a point.

"You're right," the writer told Georgia a few weeks later. "We're giving you a niece, a colored girl who comes to visit you for a few episodes."

"I have the perfect child for the role," she said. "She's a natural."

Chanel was thrilled. The eleven-year-old was starved for attention and more than ready to step into the spotlight. Not to mention it meant spending more time with Georgia.

"You're going to have to lose weight," Georgia told her. "You're going to have to go on a diet."

Chanel grimaced and tried. She cut down on sweets, no use. Chubbiness was as much a part of her as her spunky personality.

"I'll put you in dresses that hide," her mother promised. "I'll do my best to get you through this."

The executive producer was charmed. The little girl had boundless energy. Having practiced the lines with her mother, she read for the part confidently and won the role hands down.

She hardly slept the night before the first day of filming. Something great was happening to her; finally she could feel good being her mother's daughter.

In the opening scene she came whirling into the kitchen like a tornado.

"*Auntie Rowena!*"

"Easy, baby," Georgia said, stopping the action. "Not so loud."

"Leave her alone," the director told Georgia. "She's doing fine."

"She's throwing me off balance . . ."

"You'll adjust, let her go."

In nothing flat Chanel stole the scene. She worked against her mother's slow, steady rhythms; her speech was lightning-fast. She played up her punch lines, showed a sense of timing only the observant child of an actress could manage at her age.

Afterward, Georgia felt exhausted.

"I can't keep up with her," she told the crew. "She's really something, isn't she?"

And for three consecutive episodes she and Chanel worked together. No question the child was talented. She'd inherited her mother's flair, but Georgia worried that the pressure and excitement might be too much for her daughter. Besides, the fictional set-up—

that Rowena was burdened with the discipline of her spirited niece—was a bit too close to the bone. At home, overstimulated by her performance, overwhelmed by seeing herself on television, Chanel was more difficult than ever. So when the producer suggested that Rowena's niece be used in several more episodes, Georgia opposed it.

"I'm afraid the experience is having a bad effect on Chanel," she said. "Maybe it'd be better to drop the character . . ."

Chanel protested. "You don't want me on the show, you don't want me because everyone likes me and you don't like me and you don't want anyone to like me because then they'll like me better than they like you—"

"Nonsense," countered Georgia, "it's just that you're missing school and your lessons and—"

"And I hate you!"

"You don't mean it—"

"I do!"

"Get in your room, Chanel, and stay there before I wash out your mouth with soap."

"I *hate* you—"

Georgia slapped her across the mouth, but the child wouldn't give her mother the satisfaction of crying. Instead, she ran to her room and slammed the door.

Chanel hurt all over. For a brief moment she'd been a star, felt important, someone whom the other kids recognized. None of *them* had been on TV. Now, with the show taken from her, she was back to having no identity except being a colored girl in a predominantly white school. Was that all she was? She'd moved from London to Paris to Rome, from New York to Los Angeles, felt disoriented, confused. Her mother was an actress, but what was she?

Georgia was determined to parlay her TV role into something bigger, and spent most of her time at home calling contacts, looking for feature film roles, changing agents. Chanel listened but for the most part, as always, remained alone.

When "Meet the Morgans" was picked up for a second season, guaranteeing Georgia another year of work, she and Chanel moved to a larger apartment, this one on the eastern edge of Beverly Hills off Pico. Georgia told everyone how happy she was to be living in Beverly Hills. "It's so quiet, so peaceful." To Chanel, it was so boring. Beverly Hills—at least the Beverly Hills here they lived—wasn't even hilly; it was just another L.A. neighborhood with low-rise apartments and plain bungalows. The only change was the school—even whiter than the last one ("I feel like a raisin in a bowl of milk," said Chanel)—and the housekeeper Georgia hired to clean once a week.

Her name was Ruth, conscientious, God-fearing, and she took an immediate liking to Chanel. In fact it was Ruth who first took Chanel to the Full Gospel Church of the Living Christ on Central Avenue not far from the house where Georgia had come to live when she had first arrived in Los Angeles in 1945.

It happened soon after Chanel turned twelve. Her figure had blossomed, her breasts and hips were fully developed. She was still heavy but no longer a chubby child. She had the body of a woman.

Ruth had early sensed Chanel's loneliness, and over a Labor Day weekend, when Georgia was rehearsing the show, she asked Chanel to come home with her to meet the family.

"I have daughters her age," Ruth told Georgia. "I think they'll all get along real nice."

They didn't.

Ruth's daughters were aloof, they were jealous of Chanel's fancy dresses and besides, they had boyfriends and girlfriends of their own. Ruth couldn't get them to pay much attention to Chanel and, in fact, on Sunday morning when it was time to go to church, the daughters were still asleep. Chanel went with Ruth and her husband Henry.

The church had once been a Jewish synagogue. Gold Hebrew lettering and menorahs still adorned the facade, and the Ten Commandments, also in Hebrew, were inscribed in a marble scroll above the altar. The walls were paneled in rich mahogany, and while the sanctuary needed refurbishing, its sturdy elegance was intact.

"If you love the Lord," said the preacher, a short man with a wide face, thick mustache and a voice cracking like thunder, "I say, if you love the Lord, let me hear you say amen."

The church said amen.

The church was all colored people, and it was the first such situation for Chanel. She felt immediately comfortable, as though she'd been here before. It was relief from the white world of her school, her neighborhood and her mother's work. The women wore beautiful hats in festive colors—pink, purple, mint green. The men wore fresh-pressed suits and ties and shoes with mirror shines. Children were everywhere. Chanel felt *accepted*, not different, not fat, not odd. The mood was warm, friendly, and when the music started, when the organist hit a chord and the drummer kicked in and the forty-member choir, in their chocolate-brown robes with white piping, sang "Praise Him, praise Him, go on and praise Him," Chanel's heart started thumping. She just couldn't stop smiling.

"Are we going to have church this morning?" asked the preacher.

"Yes!" answered the church.

"I mean," he repeated, "are we going to have *church*?"

"Oh yes, we are!"

Soon Ruth was waving and rocking; everyone in the congregation was swaying to the rhythm of the sermon, the rhythm of the morning's music, the music that crept under Chanel's skin and all up in her body, the music that had her happy and feeling good for no real reason except the music was "go on and praise Him, go on and give Him the praise," and Chanel did that, she followed the others, she stood and waved and she even danced—women were dancing in the aisles, little steps, small but animated shuffles—and she sang along as if she knew the hymns, because somehow the melodies were already inside her head, her heart expanding with the music, the organist, the drummer, the choir, the soloists soaring up and out of the synagogue church, their voices skyward all the way up to high heaven and God, because God, said the preacher, was in the house, God was in their souls, God was giving out blessings, God was goodness, God was grace, God was suddenly all over Chanel Faith until she found herself singing louder, singing all alone, and the choir had stopped and everyone turned and heard the voice that was so powerfully clear, perfectly true, the voice of a believer singing, "Praise, praise, all I want to do is praise . . ."

Chanel had left herself. She didn't understand what had happened but whatever it was, was nothing short of transcendental. Never had she known such a feeling. She'd been out of control yet her voice was in control. Her voice was an instrument of power. She was exhilarated, far more than when she had acted on her mother's show. Here there was no script, no rehearsal. Nothing had been planned. Her cheeks were streaked with tears. She'd never felt so *relieved*, startled by her own strength.

"The choir director wants to see you," Ruth said after the service.

"God has blessed you with a magnificent voice," she told Chanel. "We want you to sing with us every Sunday. Will you do that?"

"Chanel," said Ruth, introducing her to the choir director, "this is Honey Lincoln Montgomery. And this is her husband Herb."

Herb Montgomery tossed and turned in bed. He couldn't sleep. Thoughts buzzed his mind like gnats. His wife Honey was sleeping, in her eighth month, a condition causing them both a lot of discomfort. She wasn't especially happy about the fact—and neither was Herb. At eight years old, the twins were handfuls enough. Besides, Honey had just been getting back into her career when the doctor gave her the news. The pregnancy had been rough—morning sickness and fatigue. It wasn't until Sunday morning when Honey heard Chanel sing that her spirit turned around.

It took Herb only a few minutes to realize whose looks he'd seen in Chanel—his own, *and* Georgia's. At first he pushed aside the first impression. The child hadn't given her last name. She couldn't be Georgia's child. His child. Georgia had been out of his life so long she was only a memory. That memory, though, had seeped deep into a dozen years of dreams, some bittersweet, some erotic. Of course, he knew about her movies with Gold; he had read about Gold's death and Georgia's work in New York. He'd seen her on "Meet the Morgans" and was angry to see her playing a *cook*. More than once he had been tempted to contact her. But he'd been unsure. No woman before or after Georgia Faith had had such an impact on him.

Honey had turned out to be a loving wife. She was religious, which he wasn't, but he respected her devotion. Once in a while he'd go with her to services, mostly to hear the music. Honey was a choir director, a good actress *and* mother, but . . . well, she wasn't Georgia. Mostly she lacked Georgia's passion. Sex for Herb and his wife had cooled, and now that Honey had reached the end of her pregnancy, sex was out.

Five A.M., and Herb was still awake. Outside, dark night had lightened to murky gray. He couldn't stop thinking about Georgia. If that girl was really her daughter, the girl sure had inherited her mother's style and flair. Her musical sense was something else. But if she *were* his daughter, wouldn't Georgia have told him? Maybe. Maybe not. Maybe that's why she'd run off. Maybe she hadn't known *who* the father was and had run off with the man with the money. Who could blame her? Really.

Money—Herb's recurring headache . . . he'd lost all his money on his independent films, none of which ever made a thin dime. Well, not everyone could be a writer or a director. And who could say that being a black cameraman in the white world of Hollywood wasn't an accomplishment? But the cold fact remained: Herb was no longer making his own movies, telling his own stories. Herb's stories, like his thoughts of Georgia, were locked away in a secret place of frustration. He tried not to think about that, just as he tried not to visualize Georgia's naked body on the first night they had made love.

Chanel was thrilled. She had found something her mother could neither disturb nor duplicate; she'd discovered her voice. But when she described the experience, Georgia appeared indifferent.

"That's very nice."

"But the people, the people were so excited they came up to me afterwards, even the choir director, and all the ladies, they were telling me—"

"In that kind of country church," said Georgia, "people are . . . overstimulated, honey. It sounds like Ruth belongs to a real old-fashioned church . . ."

Chanel didn't know what her mother was talking about. This was the only church she had ever gone to. "Why is it old-fashioned?"

"There's nothing wrong with being old-fashioned," said Georgia. "It's just not very . . . well, sophisticated."

"What's sophisticated?"

"Well, *you*, honey, are sophisticated. You've lived in London and Paris and Rome. You've lived in New York City. For a young woman you've seen a lot of the world. You know that carrying on in church—screaming and yelling and dancing in the aisles—is a little . . . silly."

"I think it's fun. They want me back, they want me in the choir."

"Out of the question."

"Why?"

"Because they asked you to join so I'll give money—"

"They don't even *know* about you. They don't *care* about you."

"The answer is no."

"I'm going anyway.

"We'll discuss this some other time. I have lines to memorize—"

"I want to go to that church, I want to sing there."

"There will be opportunities for you to sing in better settings than some neighborhood church—"

"I *like* the church, Mother. I like how the people there make me feel. Ruth says she'll take me back there . . ."

But by then Georgia was no longer listening to her daughter, her mind was moving over next week's script and thinking of ways she could maximize the few moments the writers had given Rowena.

There was a scary wonderful moment in the midst of her singing when Chanel was sure God was inside her. Maybe it was the congregation—"Go *on*, girl, go on and sing." Maybe it was the powerful backing of the choir. Maybe it was the smile of approval on Honey Montgomery's face, a woman about to have a baby. None of those things, though, could explain how, when Chanel reached for a note she knew was impossible, the note was not only there but other notes —higher and stronger notes—were also hers for the taking. It seemed like a miracle. Her voice was opening up right there in the church, in a way that overwhelmed her. It was . . . power. Chanel, a young girl, had *power*. She could make people—grown women, grown men, little children—scream and wave their arms. She could improvise on the standard melodies, not even knowing she was improvising, by just following her feelings. As she changed the melodies and invented new ones, the original melodies grew more elaborate, more beautiful. But mostly she could feel something moving inside her, freeing her mind, entering her . . . soul?

At Ruth's urging, she decided to be baptized, which was when Georgia fired Ruth.

Chanel became hysterical. "I *love* Ruth."

"That's because she lets you eat whatever you want."

Food had always been . . . still was . . . a push-and-pull thing between mother and daughter.

"At least," said Chanel, "Ruth cooks for me. You've never cooked for me."

"You don't exactly fit the picture of an undernourished child."

"You never cook anything I like."

"I've tried to teach you moderation—"

"I want to go to Ruth's church."

"No."

"You always ruin *everything*!"

"Your religious training is my responsibility and no one else's—"

"I wanna sing in church."

"Singing is one thing—being baptized another."

"What's wrong with being baptized?"

"We are *not* members of that congregation. If I were going to join a church—and I most certainly am not—it wouldn't be some storefront operation on Central Avenue."

"You haven't even seen the church, you don't even know what it looks like."

"I'm sick and tired of this church. Ruth has gone too far. I've told her that. I've let her go. Another lady will be coming to clean next week. And *that* is *that*."

Georgia's dream: She was on stage in a Roman amphitheater in front of a tremendous crowd of admirers. The night was spectacular—full moon, floodlights, extravagant costumes. Georgia was dressed in flaming red, and when she stepped forward to deliver her lines, words flowed like honey. The applause was thunderous. Flowers were thrown at her feet, "*Brava! Bravissima!*" echoed. Suddenly from the pit an orchestra slowly ascended on a large lift, all the while playing a complex motif Georgia could not follow. Not jazz, not classical, but something in between. Georgia was supposed to sing, but she couldn't follow the rhythm, didn't know the melody. She was humiliated in front of her public. The booing began way in the back of the vast open theater but soon grew louder, the jeering cruel, relentless until she was forced off stage and woke up, rattled and dazed . . .

During a hot shower she reviewed her dream—the details were

still too fresh—remembering her disastrous audition for Jimmie Lunceford when she'd first arrived in Los Angeles. She was no singer —she realized that—but why, after all these years, was the thought still with her? What difference did it make? She washed and dried her hair, stepped into an easy Sunday cotton dress and went to wake up Chanel. She wanted to take her daughter to Sunday brunch at the Hotel Beverly. The walk down Wilshire Boulevard would do them good.

Chanel's room looked like a tornado had hit. Long ago Georgia had stopped trying to get the child to tidy up. She was impossible. She was also not in her room. Her bed was empty. What was going on? Where could she be at ten on a Sunday morning?

Suddenly it dawned on Georgia: Chanel—stubborn, hard-headed Chanel—had gone to church. No doubt about it. Either Ruth had picked her up or, just as likely, the child had taken the crosstown bus. It was just like Chanel—anything to rile her mother. Well, Mother *was* riled, goddamn good and riled, and she decided once and for all to put her foot down. She was going after Chanel right now; she was pulling her out of that damn country church and bringing the child back to her senses . . .

She found the name of the church scribbled on a piece of paper and immediately recognized the address, smack in the middle of Miss Marva's old neighborhood. Fuming, Georgia started up her blue Impala, the car she'd bought with her first big check from "Meet the Morgans," and headed across town. What a way to spend a Sunday morning.

Central Avenue had changed. Most of the nightclubs from the forties were gone. A kind of sadness seemed to cover the streets. No more hot syncopation, no more bustle and buzz. Miss Marva was much on Georgia's mind—Miss Marva and, of course, the Montgomery brothers, Harper and Herb. She felt funny driving through the neighborhood, a little tempted to stop and see who was living in the old boardinghouse. But when she thought of Chanel carrying on with some holy-roller congregation she fought off the thought and pressed on, pulling into the parking lot marked for members of the Full Gospel Church of the Living Christ.

A woman was talking in tongues, and when she spoke her head snapped back, her eyes closed and her body shivered. As she stopped, another woman started, and then another. One parishioner who fainted was revived by a white-uniformed nurse carrying smelling salts. All the while the preacher called to God, glorifying His name, while Georgia, feeling alienated by the commotion, surveyed the congregation, searching out her daughter.

When she finally did see Chanel, Georgia got angry all over again and began to move toward her—she intended to take her by the hand and lead her out of there—until she noticed the man next to her daughter. At first Georgia thought her eyes were deceiving her. No question, he was more mature, more handsome than the last time she had seen him twelve years ago, but there was no mistaking Herb Montgomery, Chanel's father . . . although neither father nor daughter knew it.

Chanel had gone off to school and Georgia was on the phone to her agent when the doorbell rang. She wondered who would be calling at ten on a Tuesday morning.

The question turned to shock when she saw Honey Lincoln Montgomery standing in front of her—not just because this was the last person in the world she'd expected to see in her home but because the woman looked like she was about to pop a baby right then and there; she was huge and, even in her ninth month of pregnancy, stunningly beautiful.

In church last Sunday Georgia had noticed her directing the choir. She recognized her from the films she'd made with Herb, but when she saw Herb seated next to Chanel, Georgia had decided to leave without making a scene. She waited outside until the service was over, then took Chanel by the hand and avoided Herb's glance.

"What are you doing here?" Chanel had said.

"I came to give you a ride home."

"That's all?"

"I wanted to see the church for myself."

"Did you hear me sing?"

"No . . . I came too late."

Chanel was crushed. "When are you ever going to hear me sing?"

"Soon," promised Georgia, her mind still trying to absorb the jolt of having seen Herb Montgomery . . .

Now Honey Lincoln was telling Georgia, "I saw you in church last Sunday and I wanted to talk to you."

"Come on in and sit down. You're out of breath."

Honey wobbled inside and plopped on the couch. "This conversation is long overdue," she said.

"Looks like the only thing that's overdue is right there," Georgia said, pointing to Honey's stomach.

"I didn't know Chanel is your daughter."

Georgia waited to see if Honey was going to mention Herb, and was relieved when she didn't. "And I didn't know you were the choir director."

"She told me that you don't want her to sing in the church and I came to ask you to let her. The child has a real gift—"

"I know she's talented but I'm afraid we're not much on churchgoing."

"She wants to sing," Honey said, "and I feel like God *wants* her to sing."

Georgia fought to keep down her temper.

"Naturally I know about you and Herb," Honey went on. "I've seen the movies he made with you, and I know how much he thinks of you. I also want to say that I think you're a fine actress."

"Thank you." Georgia did not return the compliment.

"Sometimes I think he never got over you."

"That was a long, long time ago, Mrs. Montgomery . . ."

"Please call me Honey."

"Herb and I have been out of touch for many years."

"You didn't even say hello to him in church."

"I was so surprised to see him." Why was she defending herself?

"To be honest, I was scared when I saw you. I thought you'd come for Herb."

Georgia smiled. "I had no idea he'd be there. I don't exactly associate Herb with the church."

"Well, he only goes there on account of me."

"And I only went because of Chanel. You'll never see me or her there again."

"I hate to lose Chanel."

"Look, Mrs. Montgomery, I appreciate the interest you've taken in my daughter, but when all's said and done, we'll both feel more comfortable if I could find another place for Chanel to do her singing."

"There's a church on Crenshaw closer to your part of town . . ."

"I'm more interested in my daughter using her talent to sing popular music."

"God gave her this gift to glorify Him and spread His word."

"Well, Mrs. Montgomery, I'm pleased to have met you and trust that—"

Which was as far as she got before Honey let loose a groan and was suddenly on the couch, barely able to whisper "I'm sorry, I'm sorry . . ."

Her water had broken. The couch was soaked. "I'm sorry," she kept repeating.

"I'll get you to a hospital, try to hold on, Jesus . . ."

She ran to her phone. No dial tone. For the past few days she'd been having trouble, and now, at the worst possible moment, the thing was dead. She tried her neighbors but no one was home. Back in her apartment she tried moving Honey into her bedroom but the woman was having what looked like convulsions.

"The twins came like this," said Honey. "They came so fast . . ."

Contractions were coming fast, knifelike contractions. Georgia remembered what the nurses had told her in England when she went to a hospital to have Chanel: "Anything can happen in labor, it can take forever," said one of the tough Cockney ladies, "or it can be over clippety-clack, one-two-three."

Nearly an hour later, with the phone still out and the neighbors still gone, Georgia was alone with Honey.

Georgia was furious at this ridiculous piece of circumstance. Here a total stranger, her former lover's wife, the wife of her daughter's father, was screaming and writhing in labor, and Georgia had no help, no choice but to try to comfort the woman by telling her to breathe, by bringing her towels and blankets, by mopping her forehead and removing her panties and seeing that, dear Jesus, dear God, Honey was dilating, Honey seemed nearly fully dilated and no matter how much Georgia cursed the gods of fate, this woman, this Honey Lincoln Montgomery, was about to have her baby right there in Georgia Faith's Beverly Hills apartment . . .

. . . By noon, the cord had been cut, the mother was doing nicely, the infant had been washed and cleaned, the phone was back in order. For what Georgia had been through, she felt entitled to indulge in a small piece of high drama. She did it with one call.

"Herb Montgomery," she said with crystal-clear enunciation.

"Georgia?"

"I'm here with your wife."

"What!"

"She's in my apartment."

"What are you talking about?"

"This morning I delivered your child. It's a boy."

1 9 6 3

On November 22, a few hours after President Kennedy was shot to death in Dallas, Chanel Faith, age seventeen, also gave birth to a baby boy. At the time her mother was in Madrid, working on a movie that was never released, a movie for which she was never paid.

Georgia came back in a rage. The producers had lied to her. Another promise of a starring role had turned sour. A grueling shoot covering three months had come to a halt when the funds had fizzled and the backers backed out.

Because Chanel was normally plump, she had hardly shown at all, and Georgia left the country unaware that her daughter was five-and-a-half months pregnant. Actually she was reluctant about leaving Chanel alone and had arranged for her cleaning woman—the one hired after she had fired Ruth—to sleep at the apartment every night. Two weeks after Georgia had left, Chanel got rid of the woman and brought over her boyfriend, Sonny Wright.

She had met Sonny at Calvary Baptist Church, the congregation she had gone to after Georgia had pulled her away from Herb and Honey Montgomery. Georgia didn't want her in *any* church, but Chanel had defied her. Calvary had the largest and most affluent constituency in the black community, and after Chanel's first solo with the choir she was an instant hit. She also had several suitors among the choir members, the best-looking of whom was eighteen-year-old Sonny, and for the last few years he had been her steady boyfriend, no matter how hard Georgia had tried to keep him away.

"He's beneath you," mother would tell daughter.

"Why do you say that?"

"He's a laborer. So is his father."

"Sonny wants to be a singer. He has a beautiful voice. I think he's beautiful."

"He didn't graduate high school, much less college. You're smart. You want a man with a college education—"

"I don't give a damn about college."

"Well, you better start caring because you're going."

"Sonny and I are going to be married."

"That's crazy talk. What will you live on?"

"I don't care what you say, we're getting married."

"Over my dead body. I'll have it annulled. Besides, if you're so serious about your music, go for it outside the church. You'd benefit from formal training—"

"We're making a record in church. I'm singing three solos."

"That record is going to make you absolutely nothing," said Georgia, who had found only sporadic work on television in spite of her looks and track record.

"I don't care about money," said Chanel.

Georgia laughed. "You don't care as long as I'm the one putting food on the table and keeping a roof over your head."

"Sonny's making money, good money."

"Ten years from now Sonny is going to be doing exactly what he's doing now—pouring concrete."

"He's going to be a singing star and even if he isn't I don't care, I love him—"

"How can someone your age know anything about love?"

"How old were you when you fell in love with my father?"

"Twenty."

"I bet you were younger. Before you said you were only eighteen."

"I should know how old I was, I was *twenty*."

"You know something, Mother, I don't believe you. I don't believe that this mystery father was some painter or poet who died of some rare disease. I think you made him up."

"Don't be ridiculous . . ."

Now, flying back to the United States from Spain, Georgia was thinking that "ridiculous" was just the word to describe her relationship with Herb Montgomery.

For five years, ever since she had first seen him in that church, ever since she had helped his wife Honey give birth to Herb's son, Georgia had been strong enough to stay away. She had no intention of destroying Herb's marriage, although she realized she had that power. He called her often enough. He wrote her notes and letters in which he argued that he just wanted to reestablish their professional relationship, and their friendship. That was all . . . One morning he had even showed up at her door when Chanel was in school.

"Last time a member of your family came over uninvited," Georgia had told him, "she wound up having a baby on my couch."

"What about *our* baby?" he asked her.

"I don't want to confuse her, I don't want to cause her any more pain."

"To tell her she has a father who's alive and well would cause her pain?"

"After years of silence—yes, it would. It would also hurt Honey."

"If I had known—"

"Well, you didn't know, Herb, and now you do, but now you also have a wife and a family and no reason in the world to ruin it all."

"You and I have a child, Georgia. Nothing can change that. I think about her, I think about you, and I can't sleep at night. I want to know her, I want to know *you* again."

"Herb, do you have a happy marriage?"

"What does that have to do with it?"

"Everything. You're looking for an escape. Well, I can't be that escape, Herb. I have my career—"

"I can help you."

"Then *help* me. Get me a good agent. Get me some good auditions. I'm not above your helping me. I never was."

"No, but you thought others could do more. You thought the white man—"

"I don't want to go into it. The white man, the black man, the pink polka-dotted man . . . all men promise more than they deliver."

"You're real bitter, aren't you?"

"I'm realistic—that's what I am. I can't afford to be anything *but* realistic. I've had to support myself and my child . . ."

"If you'd let me—"

"Listen to me, Herb Montgomery, because I'm not going to say it again. I'm going to let you help me any way you can. I'd be a fool not to. Talk to your producers, talk to your directors and your agents. Anything you can do for me will be appreciated. But I intend to keep our relationship strictly professional, because anything else—"

"Anything else would be an honest reflection of our feelings. When I wrote for you . . ."

"The writing was fine, I was the first one to tell you so. But no one saw those movies."

"What are you talking about? *Jenny* played in theaters all over the South."

"To small audiences too poor to support your career or mine. Tell me, who do you work for now? Who are these producers and directors, these friends of yours who can help me? I'll tell you . . . they're white men."

"I've never stopped writing screenplays, I'm still developing my own projects. One is already being considered by—"

"Please, Herb, you're a broken record. You were saying the same thing when I met you in the forties. I don't want to go back."

He placed his hands on top of hers. "We've never stopped loving each other, Georgia. I know it, so do you . . ."

She was not entirely surprised that she allowed him to make love to her that morning. It was raining outside and she was feeling very lonely and down. She hadn't had a man in over a year, and, in spite of her determination to avoid another round of entanglements with Herb Montgomery, her desire defeated good intentions. She marveled at the strong condition of his body; and to Herb, Georgia was more desirable than ever. When he entered her, when she finally opened herself to his insistence, she lost all control, dropping all pretense. Georgia went wild.

But that was only for an hour. When Herb dressed and began talking plans and projects she retreated. She had slipped into a memory of passion, but the rain had stopped and she was back in control . . . or so she told herself.

"Help me any way you can," she told him. "But don't read anything into what just happened. It happened, it's over."

If took Herb years, but he finally was able to influence a producer to cast Georgia in a so-called mainstream movie to be shot in Spain. It wasn't the female lead but it was a supporting role with a lot of on-screen time. Herb was the cinematographer. He was convinced the project was solid. In Madrid the inevitable happened, just as Herb (and perhaps Georgia) knew it would: They slept together, they made love every night. But when the roof caved in, when the producers ran out of money and closed down the set, not even paying the actors' way home, Georgia was furious, angriest at herself for having ignored her own judgment. It didn't help that Herb bought her a ticket back to Los Angeles. She flew alone.

At least she felt alone. She wanted to be alone. She needed to get back her sense of what was real. Herb wasn't real. Herb still had his head miles in the clouds. She was thirty-seven, Herb forty-three, and he still acted like he was twenty-five, still believed that his screenplays and schemes would turn into blockbuster movies. Bullshit. Why hadn't she seen that before she agreed to go to Spain? Why hadn't she demanded—as her agent had advised—her money in advance? Why had she listened to Herb, who swore the project was well financed? Because, she confessed in silence, she probably loved the fool after all, wanted him back, wanted him to be the independent filmmaker he'd always dreamed of being.

Well, damn it, enough. It took these three months to finally cure her of Herb Montgomery. She didn't need a dreamer, she needed a doer; and right now she needed work. Three months and not a dime to show for it. Like the others on the movie, she'd been strung along, payments deferred, promises piled on promises, all broken. As the plane landed in Los Angeles on a mild November afternoon, she had to fight back a rush of despair.

Then, as soon as she entered the terminal, she heard the news. President Kennedy had been shot. It seemed crazy, all wrong, maybe just a wild rumor out of control. But as she stopped in a bar and watched Walter Cronkite on television, there was no doubt. The president was dead. Georgia had liked him, liked his looks, his Boston accent, and especially liked his standing up for the civil rights of Negroes. In a crazy way, it made sense that someone would murder him. He was too good.

Despair was something Georgia Faith had been able to fight off all her life—at the orphanage, during her first days in Hollywood, surviving in postwar Europe, maintaining herself in the fifties. But today despair was all around her, all inside her, the long trip from Spain, the fiasco of the unmade movie, the terrible news from Dallas. She felt herself losing it.

So when the cab dropped her off in front of the apartment complex, when the driver carried her trunk up the walkway, when she reached in her purse for her key and when the door opened before she had a chance to open it herself, when she saw Sonny Wright standing there and behind him her daughter Chanel sitting on the couch while an infant fed from her breast, Georgia's head started whirling, she felt dizzy, faint, on the verge of collapse. Yet, Georgia being Georgia, she reached for the last vestige of composure.

She breathed deeply, aware of her proper posture. Proper posture always helped. Calmly, she walked past Sonny Wright and approached her daughter. Without raising her voice, with perfect drawn-out enunciation, Georgia uttered just one word: "Explain."

"I had a baby."

The suckling infant was chubby and cute.

"I can see that. What are you going to do now?"

"I don't know."

"I don't either," said Georgia, shaking her head in amazement. "I really damn well don't."

1 9 6 7

Bobby Faith was now a beautiful four-year-old boy. He had big brown eyes, a rambunctious spirit and a temperament—not unlike his mother—difficult to control. The child, a whirlwind of energy, understood the advantages of having two mothers. Early on he'd found a way to run in between the two of them. When his mother Chanel was on the road singing with gospel shows, it was his grandmother Georgia who cared for him. When Georgia found occasional work in television shows or commercials, she hired a woman to watch the boy. His father, Sonny Wright, had been something of a presence during the first three years of Bobby's life, but was drafted and sent to Vietnam in 1966, taken prisoner and never heard from again. Even before he was called up, though, Sonny and Chanel had fought. They never married. He thought she should take day jobs so he could concentrate on his own singing. The general consensus, though, was that *she* was the one with the voice; *she* was the one with the future. Chanel agreed. In a rare instance where she and Georgia saw eye-to-eye, Chanel put her career ahead of Sonny's. No surprise, that spelled the end of their relationship.

With Sonny now gone and Georgia working infrequently, Chanel became the breadwinner. At least the gospel circuit provided steady work, and as a soloist Chanel found herself touring with some of the biggest names in the field—Albertina Walker, James Cleveland, Shirley Caesar, the Dixie Hummingbirds, Edwin Hawkins. The tours took her to cities with large black populations—Oakland, Chicago, Detroit, Cleveland, Boston, New York, Philadelphia, Washington, D.C., Atlanta, Dallas, Houston. She missed her son, but the touring allowed her to escape Georgia's domain and made her feel like somebody. At twenty-one, Chanel was making money.

She was also making her mark in gospel music. She had recorded an album of her own that earned little money but added to her reputation. Her other reputation, for being an easy mark for men, was also growing. Georgia had warned her, but Chanel did as she pleased. She was a rebel at home, a rebel on the road. The world of religious music wasn't exactly a haven of puritanical behavior anyway. It was Mahalia Jackson who sang "I'm Going to Live the Life I Sing About in My Song," but not everyone did. After the shows in the wrestling arenas or church auditoriums, gospel folks could party with the best of them. Chanel developed a taste for whiskey and marijuana.

Chanel had never felt pretty. She worried about her weight, had a hard time believing any man could love her for herself, except maybe those earliest days with Sonny, but that seemed a long, long time ago. She thought she had to give something in order to get a man—and that something was usually sex. In an ambience where promiscuity was tolerated, she did not view her own promiscuity as unusual. She looked around and saw women much wilder than she was. At least she had to like a man; she had to be attracted to his looks and his talk and be fairly certain he wasn't crazy or violent. At the same time, she was highly susceptible to flattery.

And one Darryl Booker had flattered her more than any man she had ever met. She had met him after a concert in Memphis. The next day she was due to fly home to Los Angeles. Lonely and road-weary, she'd been gone a month and was more than ready to see her son.

Darryl was a tall man with sculpted cheekbones, slender fingers and the deepest baritone voice Chanel had ever heard. He was a great talker, he loved singing and, even though he was an amateur tunesmith, he couldn't carry a tune. He was a pharmacist by trade and owned a small drugstore in Florence, Alabama. At thirty, he had never married and, right off, he had told her that she would change his life.

"How?" she asked skeptically.

"I want to record you."

"I've already recorded an album."

"I know. I own it. I listen to it and I love it, but it's a gospel album. I hear you differently, I hear you singing the way Aretha Franklin is singing."

Aretha Franklin had just signed with Atlantic Records and recorded "I Never Loved a Man (the Way I Love You)" in Muscle Shoals, Alabama, a big hit across the country.

"Muscle Shoals," said Darryl, "is just across the Tennessee River from Florence. Wilson Pickett cut his hits there. You've heard 'Land of 1000 Dances' and 'Mustang Sally.' Muscle Shoals is where Arthur Conley recorded 'Sweet Soul Music' and Percy Sledge sang 'When a Man Loves a Woman.' I'm telling you, baby, there's something about that part of the country that makes singers sing better. The music is in the earth, it's right there in the red clay."

"I don't sing that kind of music," said Chanel, liking his sweet talk.

"There's not much difference between that music and gospel music."

"My music is God's music," said Chanel.

"All music is God's music. Soul music is spiritual music. It comes from the spirit of our people. You have that spirit—and the only difference between soul music and church music is money. Soul music makes more money. White folks are buying soul music."

"Have you ever made any money in the music business?"

"No, but I'm fixing to. I got me a little recording studio set up above my store. Now all I need is a singer. I want you to drive back to Muscle Shoals with me. I want you to be *my* singer."

"You're sure you want to go to Muscle Shoals?" said Georgia when Chanel arrived in L.A. a few days later.

"Darryl Booker says I could have a hit—"

"*Who* is Darryl Booker?"

"He lives there . . . he owns a drugstore but he's a music-lover—"

"A man who owns a drugstore is advising you about making records? My God, girl."

"He knows all about soul music."

"*Please*, Chanel. Let me find you someone in Los Angeles, a producer who could show you how to sing popular music. Look, I've only said—and I'm saying it now—that there are better places to sing than church. There's more money . . ."

"That's what Darryl Booker said."

"You don't need this Booker character to tell you that. *I've* been saying that for years now, but you wouldn't listen. You had to go touring all over hell and back with your religious fanatics."

"They're my *friends* . . . my *family*—"

"Your *family* is back here. Your family is your mother and your son."

True, Chanel was overjoyed at seeing Bobby. Every time she came home he seemed more handsome. She tried to make up for lost time by taking him to Disneyland the day after she returned. It was there, waiting on line for the Peter Pan ride, that he started talking about Georgia, saying how Grandmama was too strict, how he hated when Mama was gone, how he never wanted Mama to leave again . . .

"Him complaining about *me*?" said Georgia when Chanel confronted her. "You should hear the little devil complain about *you*!"

"He's crazy about me," insisted Chanel. She was wearing bell-bottomed jeans that emphasized her ample figure. Georgia was in a white floral dress.

"He's crazy about us both," said the grandmother. "He knows we adore him. And he knows how to play us like a fiddle. He sets us against each other."

"He's just a little kid, Mother, and you're too hard on him. I see that."

"You don't see anything when you're not here."

"I'd be here if I didn't have to make your rent money."

"How many times have you done that?" asked Georgia. "Once? Twice?"

"At least twice."

"And the other four thousand times, *I've* paid this rent, *I've* bought your clothes and your food, *I've* made sure you had a decent home and a decent education—until you up and quit high school like a fool."

"Quit to make money, money you're not turning down."

"Fine. You go running around the country, you leave your child with me, I care for him night and day. Then you come back and instead of saying thank you to your mother you say I can't wait to leave you, Mother. Well, here's what I say . . . I say that's fine with me because while you're gone my own career, my auditions . . . everything having to do with me and my life gets put on hold."

"How many times have you come to hear me sing?"

"Many times."

"Twice, maybe three times."

"I know you're a wonderful singer," said Georgia, "but I'm not fond of that church music. You know that. You know how I dislike the shouting and the swooning. It gives me a headache."

"My music gives you a headache . . ."

"I didn't say that."

"You never say anything good about my singing . . . ever."

"I just did. The problem is that you need to be praised every damn hour of the day. You need more praise than the Lord Himself. No one should need that much praise. If you just paid a little less attention to yourself and a little bit more attention to your son—"

"Where's Bobby?" Chanel said suddenly, realizing she'd lost track of her son.

"What do you mean? He was back in your room."

"No, he wasn't. He was in the kitchen with you."

"That was an hour ago . . ."

"You were watching him, you were with him this morning."

"This was the morning you were going to take him to the park, don't you remember?"

"Well, where is he?"

"Bobby!" Georgia hollered, looking around the apartment. "Are you hiding?"

"You don't let him out by himself, do you?"

"Of course not. But now that you're back, he feels free to break all my rules. He probably just ran outside—"

"Not in the street . . ."

"Never. He did that once and I whipped his behind so he'd never do it again."

"There's a bunch of kids on the other side of the street," said Chanel, opening the door. "Look. Bobby's over there."

"How did he get across the street alone? Why, that little . . ."

Seeing his mother and grandmother calling for him, Bobby started running down the street in the opposite direction. There was a smile on his face. He loved being defiant. He was also lightning-fast. He wanted to show his friends how fast he was, how he wasn't scared to disobey his Grandmama and Mama. As Chanel and Georgia watched him run away, though, they could see what he couldn't—a big Olds-mobile barreling out of a driveway that Bobby was about to cross. The women shouted even louder, but in Bobby's ears they were shrill, distant sounds to be ignored. His back was turned to them. He was flying. And when the bumper of the Olds caught his legs and threw him to the ground, when the left rear tire crushed his skull, Chanel and Georgia were frozen witnesses to the horror.

The sun was blindingly, cruelly bright. Seated in the back of the limousine, both Chanel and Georgia wore dark glasses. They were speechless, drained. The nights before the funeral had been sleepless. The days had been passed making arrangements. Now their pain had turned physical—cramps, nausea. Their minds flashed from disbelief—it was all a nightmare, soon they'd awake—to raw reality, the church service, the people who would be attending, the condolence calls, the cards, the flowers.

At Calvary Baptist, mother and grandmother sat in the first pew and heard the preacher, who knew Bobby well, describe the child's boundless energy. That only made it worse. Dozens of his friends from school, little boys and girls, had come. As they filed past the small closed casket, their eyes looked confused, frightened. Many of Bobby's teachers were there, their faces streaked with tears. An enormous man named Wilbur Smith, a gym teacher who had been especially fond of Bobby, sobbed unashamedly. Show-business colleagues of Georgia's—actors, actresses, producers, writers—paid their respects, a large white contingency sitting in the back of the black church listening to the preacher say, "God's will cannot always be understood. At times like these, He tests our faith."

Only the sound of a woman singing "Amazing Grace" gave a brief moment of consolation.

At the cemetery, facing the grave, Chanel turned her head and rested it on her mother's shoulder. She couldn't look. Georgia didn't hear the preacher's final words. Walking back to the car, embraced by friends from church and associates from work, the women could only nod, still unable to speak, still in shock. Back in the car, Georgia held her weeping child in her arms and rocked her. "My baby," she said, "my poor sweet baby."

*   *   *

They never discussed the accident. They never openly talked about guilt or blame. In a wordless way, they seemed to forgive each other, even if they didn't forgive themselves. Weeks passed. More than any other time, they got along, respecting each other's privacy, and grief. To Chanel, the world seemed like it was falling apart. Martin Luther King was murdered in April, Bobby Kennedy in June. By July she had decided to move to Muscle Shoals. Georgia didn't argue.

So at twenty-two Chanel was finally on her own. At the same time, she felt safe in Muscle Shoals. Alabama was quiet, laid-back, a distance from the memory that still haunted her, especially at night . . . Bobby running down the street, the car backing out, the impact, the screams, the blood . . .

She still couldn't sleep at night. A part of her soul was dead. But at least the smell of fresh air and the sounds of birds were better than the sirens of L.A. There was something comforting about this four-city area of northern Alabama. On one side of the Tennessee River was Florence; on the other, Muscle Shoals, Tuscumbia and Sheffield, all small towns with a surprising acceptance of blacks. In fact, black music was openly revered and emulated by the white musicians and producers who had turned the area into a mecca for the burgeoning genre known as Soul. "Southern Soul," reported Time magazine, "is the hottest pop music phenomenon in the nation. New York producers are crossing the Mason-Dixon line to capture the feel of its rootsy gospel-based sounds."

And Chanel's sound fit right in. The churchy character of her fiery voice was exactly what was selling. The death of her son seemed to add even more emotion to her delivery; you could hear tragedy in every one of her songs. Bobby's death also meant the loss of her big responsibility. No longer was there any reason to deal with California.

As for Darryl Booker, he was well off by Alabama standards. He had his drugstore and savings. The man was an accredited pharmacist, but his passion was music. An amateur sound engineer, he'd pieced together a studio of sorts above his store and even composed a couple of songs. "Come to Muscle Shoals," he'd begged Chanel. "You'll record for me but I promise I'll find you other work. Good singers like you are working all over town." And Booker paid her way. She presumed—knowing men as she did—that he'd put her in a bedroom in his house, probably his own. She was wrong. Instead she was put up in a small one-bedroom cottage in Sheffield. Her front yard was the Tennessee River, where she loved watching ships and barges drift by. The town had a lazy feel, but the music—there was music everywhere—kept the rhythm right. Music was all that kept Chanel from going crazy from grief. Music was her one and her only release.

When she first arrived, Darryl had played her his songs with two fingers, picking out melodies on an old piano in his living room. Chanel wasn't exactly impressed with his tunes, but she was with his tidiness. She hadn't known a man with such neat habits. They went with his reassuring baritone voice and his optimistic outlook on life. Like Chanel, he believed in God and talked about God's healing powers. He felt her pain and her loss. He was a good man, sensible and strong. Finally, she decided, she had found her man.

"I'm not made that way," was all he said when at an evening's end she kissed him, clearly indicating her willingness.

"What way?"

His eyes studied the floor.

"You'll find your happiness around these parts," Darryl told her. "There are men who will appreciate you, but, well . . ."

This had never happened before, and Chanel thought it was her fault.

"Nothing about you," he said, knowing what she was thinking. "You're a fine woman, it's just that I'm not any good with women . . ."

Chanel wanted to show him he was wrong. She kissed him, gently touching him. He backed away. But she wanted to show her gratitude, she wanted to prove that she could help him get over whatever was wrong. She moved with careful slowness and, much to his surprise, Darryl did respond, let himself be kissed again, opening his mouth to Chanel's tongue, trying to relax until the feel of her fingers gripping him was too much and he ejaculated in her hand.

He was too humiliated to speak.

"You're just too excited, that's all, baby . . ."

She got a towel and cleaned herself off. Darryl didn't want to be touched anymore.

"I don't want this to happen again," he said. "I just want to help you make your music."

The real problem is that his music is awful, thought Chanel a month later as she looked out on a hard rain falling on the Tennessee River outside her bedroom window. Not only did the man have sexual hangups, he just couldn't write a song. The tunes she recorded were lame. She knew it, and so did the local musicians Darryl had hired. Only Darryl didn't know it.

She didn't want to hurt him, couldn't help him and realized he couldn't help her. She'd been persuaded to move to Muscle Shoals by a man whose only real skill was mixing medicines. It was almost funny.

Still, on the plus side, Muscle Shoals was escape and escape was what she'd wanted. She'd gotten out of L.A. And she'd finally gotten out of gospel, something she'd been thinking of doing for years. Besides, she'd quickly attracted other producers and was soon working sessions all over the area. Her talent—the strength of her voice, her ability to sing in-tune and invent on-the-spot harmonies—was recognized.

The majority of the local musicians were white, and Chanel got a kick of how black—how *authentically* black—they played. The town was loaded with brilliant songwriters like Donnie Fritts and Eddie Hinton; piano players like Spooner Oldham and Barry Beckett; drummers like Roger Hawkins; guitarists like Jimmy Johnson; bassists like David Hood. The good ol' boys made Chanel's transition from gospel to soul easy. And she did love their flattery.

"The rednecks are real nice around here," she told Georgia, who finally called after not having heard from Chanel for two months.

"I just hope they can help your career."

"The musician rednecks look like hippies. They're funny. Cool guys."

"Please don't tell me you're getting involved with a hippie."

"They're not just hippies, there are big stars recording down here and I'm meeting them all—Arthur Conley, Percy Sledge . . ."

"Where's *your* record? What about that man . . ."

"Darryl? We recorded something but it didn't work so hot. Never mind, I'm doing okay . . ."

"Well, good . . . by the way, you can see me on TV in 'Julia,' it's a sitcom with Diahann Carroll. When are you coming back?"

"I'm not sure . . ."

Chanel was managing. She kept recording silly songs for Darryl she felt she owed him. With money from studio gigs she paid him rent on his cottage. Soon she found a small house—also overlooking the river —and as time went on she earned a reputation as the area's best background singer. After years of traveling the gospel circuit, she liked having some roots. The place was starting to feel like home— down-home folks, down-home cooking, everything nice and easy.

For the first time in memory, she was even celibate. Until she met a tall white man named Johnny Dodd Huggins. Johnny Dodd was six-foot-six, lean and rangy. When he appeared at Fame Studios with his electric guitar, his rugged smile and his tight jeans, Chanel took note of the firm cheeks of his ass and the swell of his thighs. In his unassuming fashion he was sexy as hell. About her age—twenty-one or twenty-two—Huggins didn't say much. Long wheat-gold hair, light green eyes, gently sloped shoulders, in about that order they came to one's attention as the rest of him quietly slipped into a room. "Not a problem" was his favorite expression. There was a reticence about him that women found fascinating, and the more they tried to know him the more he seemed to draw away. Mystery man.

Chanel took to him right away. He was quietly friendly, unpretentious. It was when he pulled out his guitar, though, and started to pluck that she really took notice. It seemed like he was T-Bone Walker, Muddy Waters and B. B. King all rolled into one. He played, like they said, blacker than midnight, his sound impossible for any white man. Yet there he was with his eyes squinted closed, his hair cascading down his back, his lean fingers picking real-life Mississippi Delta blues as though he were the grandson of a slave, for God's sake.

"You're mean," Chanel told him after a Clarence Carter session. "You play downright nasty and mean."

He smiled. The full-figured black lady was shaking her head from side to side. "Never would believe that a white boy could blow so bad."

"Thank you, ma'am."

"Now listen to this 'ma'am' business." She laughed. "You ain't talkin' to my mama, you're talking to me. Chanel don't need no 'ma'ams.' "

"I heard you singing today," he said.

"And?"

"You're strong."

She smiled. As he packed up his guitar and headed out the door she walked beside him. His pickup truck was parked around back.

"Hope to see you again soon," he said.

"Hope so too," Chanel answered as she watched him climb into his truck. A real nice ass, no question.

The first night they made love in Chanel's cottage by the river, "It's like thunder" blasted over the stereo, "like lightning . . . the way you love me is frightening . . ."

She felt the edge of danger, but more than anything it was purely physical, her body, his body, the way they fit, the curiosity of their shapes, his force, her need to feel him close and bring him inside, letting him know how much she wanted, how much she'd been frustrated these past months—by Darryl, by the isolation, by no loving man. How much she appreciated the touch of him and the way he satisfied her, long into the night . . . When they woke up, Chanel made him coffee and he sat, guitar on his lap, and started to sing.

She couldn't believe it. He sang black as he played. His speaking voice, a soft southern twang, was transformed into a growl, all grits and gravy.

Got loved last night
Like I was never loved before

And this mornin' I'm feeling
Like I need to get loved some more

Morning love is good love
Fresh as morning dew

Morning love is new love
Lemme give my morning love to you

"No arguments here, baby," Chanel said.

Back in bed, bodies aching, they couldn't stop themselves, couldn't resist another ride, couldn't believe it had been so good last night, was so good this morning. . . .

"You make up that song just like that?" asked Chanel when an hour later Johnny Dodd went back to the guitar.

"Ain't nothing."

"Sounds like something to me. Sounds like you can write. And sing."

"You're the singer."

"Well, write me a song, honey. That drugstore man can't write anything but prescriptions."

Johnny Dodd shrugged. "You can sing this here 'Morning Love.' "

"You stay round here, baby, and I'll be singing that shit *every* morning."

He took a while to answer. "Best not be doing that," he finally said.

"You scared?"

"Ain't that, I do as I please. Don't care what other folks think, but I believe in keeping my business to myself."

"What are you going to do then, knock on my front door wearing a mask?"

He reached into his pack of Lucky Strikes, pulled out a neatly rolled joint, lit it, inhaled and passed it to Chanel.

"There's always the back door," he said.

So at the end of the sixties Chanel fell in love hard—first with Johnny Dodd Huggins, then with drugs. Both seemed to ease the pain of losing her son.

She tended to live in a fog, but you wouldn't know it . . . she acted as though things were really just fine.

"They call me the Queen of Muscle Shoals," she'd tell Georgia on the phone. "I'm getting more work than anyone."

And when the inevitable questions came—what about her own record? what about her solo career?—her answers were always optimistic: a New York record company wanted to sign her; an English producer was interested in doing her first album. Georgia heard echoes of her own past, promises by powerful men to make her a star, men who for a world of reasons never ever delivered. The lesson learned early was bitter: smile at everyone; trust no one. "You can only trust yourself," mother would tell daughter.

Chanel didn't dare tell Georgia about Johnny Dodd. To the diva Georgia fancied herself to be, he would seem like nothing more than a poor guitar picker. She also worried about "the racial thing." The affair was kept to after-midnight at Chanel's cottage.

Beyond it all, Johnny Dodd gave more loving than any man she had ever known. He put up with her moods. Because he dealt on the side he had the best weed in town. He piloted her through LSD trips. When he started on cocaine, so did she. She liked the freeze on her gums, the drip in her throat, the pump of adrenalin. She liked the kick of I. W. Harper backed by a couple of cold brews. She liked it all, it all helped. Or seemed to.

She didn't really mind that she and Johnny Dodd Huggins never went out alone. If they did go anywhere in public it was with a group of hip musicians and songwriters, guys who might have guessed what was happening between the black singer and white guitarist but who would guard the secret and not give a damn. Chanel understood the dangerous attention an isolated mixed couple would get in small-town Alabama. The funky music, the clandestine affair, the country food, the imported hippie culture from California and New York City . . . it all made for a heady mix.

Chanel gained weight, grew an Afro, wore wild tie-dyed tops, love beads, antique velvet robes. She had a fluffy gray cat named Willow. She was far off the gospel circuit and happy to be living what seemed a protected existence. Besides, Muscle Shoals was a good jumping-off point. With the national spotlight focused on the small Alabama community, big-time producers like Jerry Wexler and Ahmet Ertegun blew through town for quick sessions, pointing a finger at Chanel and saying, "You're next." Sure.

A year went by. Two. The sessions became more frequent, the drugs grew stronger. For the first time in years she had become a one-woman man. She had not seen her mother since little Bobby's funeral; she had put Georgia and all her disapproval out of her mind. Johnny Dodd Huggins gave her all the approval she needed. He also made her pregnant.

By June of 1970 she had missed her third period and had no doubts. When she told Johnny Dodd he was sitting in a rocking chair, guitar in lap, fingering chords. He took forever to reply.

"Well," he finally said, "I guess it's your decision."

"There ain't no decision," she shot back. "I'd never kill our baby."

The "our" seemed to hit Johnny Dodd hard. She knew he didn't like hearing the word. Well, "our" was the right word.

"It *is* ours, there's nobody else but you, Johnny."

"Well, looks like you done made your decision."

"What about your decision?"

"No problem for me, I ain't going nowhere."

Two weeks later he left for New York City, where within a month he landed a contract with RCA Records, whose publicists were calling him "The Great White Hope . . . the greatest soul singer since the late Otis Redding."

Johnny Dodd Huggins never told Chanel goodbye.

1 9 7 0

When Georgia saw the baby's face—her light brown curls, creamy complexion, luminous green eyes—she melted. The beauty of the child overwhelmed all other feelings, at least for the moment. It suddenly didn't matter that Chanel had waited two months to appear in Los Angeles with her infant. Georgia's first reaction was that the child looked just like her. She was moved to tears by the baby girl's sounds, her small sighs, the way she took Grandmama's finger and squeezed it with her tiny fist.

"I've never seen a baby this gorgeous," she said. "Why didn't you tell me? Why didn't you say a word?"

"Thought you'd rather see than hear," said Chanel.

"I presume the father's white."

Chanel hesitated. "The father . . . well, it doesn't matter about the father."

"Does he know?" Georgia asked, thinking back to her own pregnancy with Chanel.

"He got shipped off to Vietnam."

"You still didn't answer me. Does he know? Does he care?"

"It's my baby. I'll raise this baby. I don't need him for a damn thing."

Georgia nodded. She liked Chanel's independence. Chanel was, after all, her daughter. Holding the baby in her arms, Georgia leaned over and kissed the infant on the forehead.

"Marisa," she said, slowly articulating the child's name. "Pretty. Very pretty."

Chanel couldn't remember the last time her mother had given out compliments.

"You want to leave her here, don't you?" Georgia said.

Chanel began to protest, but what the hell, there was no fooling the old lady. "Just for a little while," she said. "Just till I get back from Europe."

"Europe?"

"Montreux, Switzerland. They want me to play the jazz festival over there. And there's a guy in Paris who wants to make a record with me."

"Is he the father of this baby?" asked Georgia, still remembering her own "escape" to Europe with Peter Gold.

"I've never met the man, but he's heard my tapes and he likes my voice and that's all there is to it. They say in Europe they appreciate the sure-enough blues in a way white folks over here never will."

"You look like you've gained weight," Georgia said. "And what are you doing in those African clothes?"

Chanel knew she had put on some pounds but didn't care. She was proud she had stopped drugging and drinking during her pregnancy. "Let's not start up," she told her mother. "Let's make it right for Marisa."

"You sound like I'm the father of the child," Georgia said. "You came here looking for my sympathy." What else was new?

"I came here with your granddaughter. If you don't want to help look after her . . ."

Both women were thinking of Bobby.

"You trust me?" said Georgia. "You're saying you trust me?"

"I'm saying I need you, Mother. I'm saying, goddamn it, we need each other."

Georgia was dead broke but maintained her front . . . her late-model Cadillac, the Beverly Hills apartment, immaculate and filled with fresh flowers. No one but Chanel knew better. Chanel discounted Georgia's talk about this role being offered and that movie about to begin production. She knew Georgia had always lived above her means. Money, though, was the one thing Chanel did have. Living on very little in Muscle Shoals, she had been able to save. And the record producer in Paris had sent over an advance as earnest payment.

Abandoned by Johnny Dodd, Chanel at least had the comfort of knowing that now her mother needed *her*. Before leaving for Europe, without being asked, she left a check for $3,000 on Georgia's bureau. She bathed Marisa with kisses—she'd taken the last few weeks to wean the baby from breast to bottle—and caught a plane to New York and from there to Geneva, Switzerland, where she rode the train to Montreux. Glistening Lake Geneva took one's breath away—the pristine countryside, the Alps rising to a clear blue sky. No matter how deeply she felt the ache of separation from her baby, Chanel was excited about returning to Europe for the first time as an adult—her own person, about to make her own record.

Georgia Faith and Sol Solomon, each holding a crying infant, meeting by chance in the office of a Beverly Hills pediatrician.

They froze, couldn't believe their eyes. It had been more than ten years since they had seen each other. The initial shock soon turned into laughing smiles. To Sol, Georgia was still the most gorgeous creature on earth, stylish, refined. To Georgia, Sol's warmth got to her still, even if he was wearing a green-and-pink Hawaiian sport shirt.

"Congratulations," he said to her, looking at little Marisa.

"It's my daughter's."

"Georgia Faith a grandma! I can't believe it."

"How about you?" Georgia admired a red-haired baby in Sol's arms. For some unknown mysterious reason, both infants, having noticed one another, stopped crying.

"This is my grandson Jason."

"You're kidding."

"My son's boy . . . my son's gone."

"I didn't know you had a son, Sol."

"Maury. Great kid." Sol choked up for a minute. "He was in the advertising business. A real daredevil. He thought up those car commercials where they put the cars on the top of a mountain and you wonder how in hell they ever got there. He was the one who got them there—Maury and his wife Shirley—they're in the helicopter hauling the cars up there and they're flying over some lake in Louisiana scouting locations for a soda pop commercial, flying in one of those rinkydink planes held together with Scotch tape and glue when they run into a lightning storm—that's it. They found the remains. I had to identify my Maury . . ."

Georgia took Sol's hand. "Sol, I'm so sorry . . . well, Jason is a blessing for you and your wife—"

"What wife? Rhonda? You didn't hear?"

Georgia hadn't heard. She had avoided calling Sol in the thirteen years she'd been living in Los Angeles. She knew he had a house in Bel Air; his name popped up in the trades, but she had been too proud to call. When he called her to arrange for a date, she said no. She knew him. To Sol Solomon a black mistress was a pleasure, a black wife an impossibility. Besides, he had his wife, this Jewish stripper, this Rhonda.

"Rhonda," he was telling her now, "went off year before last with Roger Simms."

"The actor?"

"Half her age."

"I'm sorry, Sol, I really am."

"They're living up in Montreal. When Maury and Shirley were killed and there was no one to take care of Jason, you know what she said? 'You'll make a wonderful home for the boy, Sol. Right now I can't cope with it. Roger and I are trying to keep our thing together . . .' Once this woman, this Minsky's cootchy girl, was my wife. I'm not so smart, Georgia."

"This grandson of yours, I'm sure he'll make you happy, Sol."

"You never knew my son Maury. Also a redhead. This guy here looks just like him."

"How do you like Dr. Krakusin?" asked Georgia.

"Listen to us, talking pediatricians. Who would have ever thought? Have dinner with me, Georgia. I know I hurt you, but let me be your friend. The babies can be friends, and so can we. What do you say?"

Georgia said yes.

After the fourth dinner Georgia was flooded with remembrances of when she was in her teens and Sol was in his twenties and he took her to Malibu to his cottage atop a hill where he made love to her a little awkwardly but respectful of her youth and innocence and so anxious to please . . . Now she was in her forties and Sol was in his fifties and atop that hill in Malibu he had built an enormous house with the royalties from his books. She remembered the spot.

Sol had two houses, this one at the beach and a bigger home in town, but it was in Malibu where a month after they'd met at the pediatrician's office Georgia renewed the affair. She had some qualms, questions for herself, but mainly she had to laugh. What was she doing back in the arms of a lover she had rejected twenty-five years earlier?

Unlike her daughter, Georgia could not give herself easily to men. She was suspicious, cautious. She felt she knew the male species and had too much respect for herself, too much intelligence to buy into small-minded come-ons and sex games. Besides, her initial Hollywood experience with three men—Sol, Peter Gold and Herb Montgomery—had given her all the romantic knowledge she needed. For all their faults these were men who understood her. She judged all other men against them, and all other men fell short.

So when Sol showed up again in her life she found herself in a position not unlike the late forties when she had just arrived in California or the early fifties when Sol had seen her play on Broadway. She still hadn't attained what she thought was rightfully hers—stardom. She still needed help—and money. And sexually she was still starved.

Her orgasms allowed her to sleep that night in Malibu as she had not slept in years. Baby Marisa was being kept, along with baby Jason, by Sol's housekeeper back in Bel Air. When she woke up it was nearly noon. Dark velvet curtains kept her shielded from the sun. Sol was wearing a red terrycloth robe, looking at her as if she were the Queen of the Nile.

"Better than ever, huh?"

"Very good."

"The best?"

"Very good."

"Come on, tell me it's the best."

"I'll tell you you're funny and sweet."

"And the best?"

"Among."

"You drive me crazy."

"Drive me back to Bel Air. I want to see the babies."

On the way back to Bel Air Neil Diamond was singing "I Am . . .

I Said" on the Rolls-Royce radio. "Neil Diamond," said Sol, "is my favorite. Of all the kids singing he's the best."

Georgia was thinking of Sol's 1945 red Hudson, thinking of how, back then, she didn't even know what a Jew was, thinking now she probably knew him as well as anyone she had ever known in her life. The fact that his wife had left him for a younger man certainly brought out his vulnerability, but it didn't change his character. Sol was Sol. And for now, with the California coastline clear and the traffic light, Sol seemed all right.

"Stay for the day," Sol said when they arrived in Bel Air to find the babies crawling around a big playpen.

"I guess not."

"Why not? Where you running off to?"

"I have my home. I have my life."

"Why don't you stay here? Look now nice the babies are together."

"Stay here permanently?"

She knew the question would worry Sol—and it did. "Stay here at least tonight," he said.

Georgia knew. They were back to the beginning, only this time, she thought as she drove herself and her granddaughter back to the middle-class-apartment-house neighborhood of Beverly Hills, this time she was a hell of a lot more realistic.

Sol was a natural-born storyteller, no literary light, no expert on literature, black or white. What you saw was what you got. What he wrote was up-front and terrific narrative. No fancy stuff. Maybe not someone to stimulate the mind, but a friend who at least talked about connecting her to directors and agents, and Georgia didn't doubt his sincerity. He'd do what he could. But there wasn't much he could do. White actresses got roles she knew she could play. It was the old frustration, and Sol was sympathetic but powerless to change that.

As she approached middle age, Georgia wanted something she could *count* on, something to fall back on. Sol had to understand that . . . Driving down Doheny Drive, Georgia noticed a small florist nestled between a grocery store and dry cleaners. She'd always loved flowers, their grace and color, their perfume. What would it take to open a flower shop? Be the owner, in total control of *something* . . . It wasn't exactly a substitute for a good man, but like the song said, a good man was hard to find. She should know.

At the door to her apartment was a package, a cardboard box that contained a record and a note. The record, by Duke Ellington featuring alto saxophonist Johnny Hodges, was called "Passion Flowers," a song written by Billy Strayhorn. The note was from Herb Montgomery, from whom she hadn't heard in years.

" 'Passion Flowers,' " wrote Herb, "reminds me of you."

Passion Flowers, thought Georgia.

An idea.

1 9 7 5

The silence between Chanel and Georgia was thick and intense. A storm neither wanted seemed about to break.

The issue was five-year-old Marisa, napping in the bedroom that had once been Chanel's.

While Chanel had been on the road singing background for people like Elton John and Joe Cocker, Georgia had taken care of her child. But for all Chanel's hard work and admired vocal skills, the so-called big break had eluded her, just as it had eluded Georgia. Soul had given way to disco, a style Chanel disliked. She was a church-rooted blues singer, a rhythm-and-blues singer whose strength of voice, not some repetitive riff, made the song. Chanel had managed to release only one secular album on her own, which did include a minor hit. "Matter of Fact" never made the pop charts and appeared only briefly on the black bestseller list—it was a black song with a black attitude about the here-and-now troubles of a black woman. "Matter of fact, your stories don't ring true . . . matter of fact, baby, I've had it up to here with you." When Chanel sang it she reared back her head, squeezed her eyes closed, belted out the melody and bit into the lyrics like so many salty crackers. But "Matter of Fact," with its sassy point of view, was a soul song, already a relic of the sixties. The new "enhanced" disco sounds were too saccharine for her, the stories too soppy to be gotten across in Chanel's rough-and-tumble manner.

So while she continued to gig in the studios around Muscle Shoals and Memphis, Chanel never made big money, just as her European recordings never sold in great number. All right, she decided, she would go after a major-label deal, keep her house in Alabama, but move to New York—at least for a few trial months—and try the big leagues. Muscle Shoals was comfortable, but comfortable wasn't cutting it.

143

Meanwhile, while Chanel had been traveling all over as a support singer to superstars, her daughter Marisa had been living with Georgia, a situation Chanel now wanted changed as she made up her mind to bring her daughter with her to New York.

"New York might be difficult for the baby," Georgia said to Chanel. "It wasn't easy for you."

Thinking of her New York City childhood, Chanel thought maybe it was those memories that had helped keep her in Muscle Shoals so long. Still . . . "Marisa will manage."

"Children always find a way to manage," Georgia agreed, "but is it good for her, now when she's starting school?"

"Daughters need to be with their mothers."

"I'm glad you said that. I want you here with me . . . to help with my business—"

"What do I know about *flowers?*"

Passion Flowers, Georgia's florist shop on nearby Burton Way in Beverly Hills, was now starting its third year, and Georgia had already paid Sol Solomon back his original investment.

"You can still sing. When I was working at Lord & Taylor and Saks in New York I didn't give up the stage. Acting still comes first with me; in fact, I'm reading for a part later today. The director called me personally. The shop is stability I never had before. It's also given me new connections to the studios and production companies. Some of my best customers are in the music business. These are people who can help you, honey. Now that I have Passion Flowers I want you to share in it—and Marisa too."

"Mother, Marisa is my child, and I've got to be with her, I've got to bring her up my way . . ."

"We'll do it together, we'll work together . . ."

"We can't work together, you know that."

Georgia couldn't really argue with that. "You could stay in Los Angeles. You could record here as easily as New York. I'm just thinking of Marisa . . ."

Who at that moment appeared. She had been listening at the door. The child might be only five, but she had precocious antennas. Mama and Grandmama were about to start one of their arguments— and it excited her to hear her own name mentioned so often, it pleased her to know that her mother and grandmother talked about *her* with so much feeling. She not only sensed but was fascinated by the change in the household whenever the two were together. Of course, when they were she became even more the object of their attention. They both loved her—she'd always sensed that—but in different ways . . . Her grandmother was real proper, kept her emotions under control. Mama was different. In Muscle Shoals everything was more relaxed, Mama was more relaxed. It was a party, lots of good food cooking on the stove, people chattering in the kitchen, lots of music on the stereo and lots of men hanging around. If Grandmama had men friends she must have seen them outside the apartment. But Georgia was good to her. It was fun to listen to her read stories—Grandmama was the best storyteller in the whole world—about princes and castles and witches and knights in faraway lands. And Grandmama wore beautiful clothes, and she bought beautiful clothes for Marisa too. And she brought her over to Jason's house all the time, Jason with his red hair, she liked to play with him because he was real funny and he had a big backyard with swings and a seesaw and a swimming pool with a slide that slid splish-splash right into the water. Next year she was starting first grade, except she wasn't sure whether she'd be staying in California with her grandmother or going with Mama to New York City. Marisa didn't know where she wanted to go, but she knew what she wanted to do right this very instant.

"Shouldn't you be napping?" asked her grandmother, who never could get over Marisa and her deep sea-green eyes, her spring-curled hair, her light, smooth complexion.

"I've been rehearsing."

Chanel laughed. "Rehearsing *what*, baby?"

"My show."

"Oh?"

"I made it up, all by myself."

"That's wonderful, darling," Georgia said. "Let's see."

"Put on that record, please," Marisa told her grandmother.

"Which one?"

"First the one where the lady sings slow, then the one when the lady sings real fast. You know the records."

Georgia did. Having heard the songs on the radio, Marisa pleaded until her grandmother went to the store to buy them. While Georgia looked for the records, Marisa ran into the bedroom.

When the child came back, Diana Ross was singing "Do You Know

Where You're Going To" and Marisa was wearing a long fur wrap that trailed behind her. With lipstick smeared across her face, she mouthed the lyrics, throwing back her head and raising her arms above her head like diva Diana. After her grand finale she blew kisses to her audience with "I love you, I love you all so much." Running back to the bedroom, she reappeared a minute later, this time with a huge red felt hat that covered her eyes and a pleated blue velvet skirt, singing "Love to Love You Baby," lip-synching the Donna Summer song.

Chanel got up and turned off the stereo.

"Now sing it alone," she told her daughter. "Sing it without the music."

And Marisa did. Her high-pitched voice, wavering only slightly, followed the melody—in fact embellished the melody with her startling self-assurance.

"She's a regular female Michael Jackson," Chanel said. "She can really sing."

"More than that," added her grandmother, "she can act."

Delighted to have made both Mama and Grandmama so happy, with the tension between the older women gone, thanks to her, Marisa ran into their arms—first Chanel's, then Georgia's—giving them each a loud kiss.

She was on her way.

Georgia wanted Marisa's tenth birthday party to be special. She also wanted Chanel, due to arrive from Muscle Shoals within the hour to see what a beautiful life her little girl was living in Los Angeles.

The affair was to be at a park in Holmby Hills, one of the city's toniest neighborhoods. Georgia had arranged for an accordionist, a professional Punch and Judy show and actors dressed up as characters from *Alice in Wonderland*—the March Hare, Mad Hatter, Dormouse and Queen of Hearts. At a certain point Marisa would put on a costume and play Alice herself.

Among the guests was one Ted Fairfax, whose child went to the same private school as Marisa. The point for Georgia was that Fairfax produced TV shows and, Georgia had learned, needed a ten-year-old girl for a new comedy about an upper-middle-class black family. If Marisa landed the part it would, of course, mean she would have to stay in Los Angeles, even during the summer.

Georgia and Chanel had an uneasy agreement that was about to collapse. Marisa had been living in Los Angeles during the school year and spending summers with her mother in Muscle Shoals—Chanel had gone back there after not getting the "big break" in New York City. After five years Chanel missed her daughter too much, felt the need for a family member who loved her the way only a daughter could.

In Georgia's view Chanel needed a caretaker—a mother more than a daughter. Chanel wouldn't leave Muscle Shoals, and Georgia couldn't leave California—her prospering shop, her career. The idea of living in Alabama was out of the question anyway. The one time Georgia had visited she found Muscle Shoals backward, boring, not to mention upsetting when Marisa began asking Chanel about her father. Georgia had been outside planting flowers when she heard the voices of her daughter and granddaughter and moved closer to the house . . .

"Why can't I see a picture of my father?" Marisa was asking her mother.

"Because I don't *have* any."

"Why not?"

"Memories were too painful, baby. I was looking at his pictures one day and I was crying so hard I couldn't stop until I threw 'em out."

"Were you drunk, Mama?"

Chanel did a double-take, but realized there was no point getting huffy. Marisa wasn't buying. "Maybe I was, baby."

"And maybe you were smoking your funny cigarettes."

Chanel said nothing.

"What did my daddy look like?" Marisa pressed.

"He was a light-skinned black man or a dark-skinned white man—hard to tell which—but he was a beautiful man, that much I can tell you, beautiful in the face and beautiful in the soul. Like you, baby," she said as she took in her child's prominent cheekbones, her high forehead and fine bone structure.

"What did he do before he went into the war?"

"He was a musician."

"A singer?"

"He played guitar. He was mighty good. A blues player. One of the best, baby."

"Do you have his records?"

"He didn't make any."

"Did he play and you sing?"

"Sometimes."

"Will you teach me to sing blues songs like you sing?"

"Nothing to teach, they're already in you. All you gotta do is follow me. Let me just go out on the back porch where I left my tea. I'll be back in a sec and we'll do some serious singing."

Georgia moved to the side of the house so Chanel wouldn't see her. She knew, though, that her daughter wasn't getting tea; she could hear her sucking on a joint. Georgia knew better than to do anything. This wasn't the time. So she went back to tending the garden in back while the sound of her daughter and granddaughter singing some old blues filled the air. Their voices were strong and true. Alabama was roots country, and Georgia realized that Chanel thrived in the atmosphere. What Chanel did not need, though, were the drugs and the booze that had increasingly become part of her life. Georgia was upset—not only for her daughter but for her granddaughter, whose summers were spent in this environment.

At the end of this particular trip and during phone calls afterward there had been blow-ups—Georgia insisting that Chanel was hooked, Chanel saying she was in complete control and so forth. Georgia planned to confront Chanel tomorrow, but today was Marisa's party, and the party must go on without a hitch. And if Marisa seemed a bit cranky, if she complained about wearing a costume and playing the part of Alice, Georgia told herself that her granddaughter's rebellious streak came from her mother.

"Hurry, darling," she called now to Marisa, who was in her bedroom putting on a white silk dress not unlike the dramatic white silk Georgia wore. "You don't want to be late to your own party."

The 727 was 35,000 feet high above the Arizona desert. Chanel was higher. She was in the toilet snorting cocaine. Spinner Diggs, the provider, was up in first class sipping champagne and playing with his pocket calculator, figuring just how much this Tennessee/California deal would bring him. Spinner wasn't a kingpin, he was a middle man, which was fine by him. He liked the living in slow-and-easy Muscle Shoals, where no one suspected. A run to New York, a run to Chicago, a run out to the Coast—four, five runs a year and he was cool. For the past few months Chanel had been his lady. A big guy who liked calling himself a black Jew—he wore a gold Star of David around his neck—he had a thing for big women. He also had a thing for Chanel's singing and couldn't understand why she wasn't bigger. He knew some music heavyweights in L.A., and had told her while they were there he'd introduce her.

Walking back to her seat, Chanel knew the man was jive. But . . . well, he loved to love her and he loved to party and they were going to party, going to her Marisa's birthday party, and, yes, sir, it was gonna be good to see her baby, good to be tasting this blow and this fine first-class bourbon. Hey, things were good. She had toured Europe all spring and made some good money. Europe was good to her, especially Scandinavia, where they loved their rhythm-and-blues. It was the blues festivals in Europe that had kept her alive.

Chanel was glad to see Spinner nodding off. She wanted time to herself, time to think about how she'd survived the seventies. When it came to her sound Chanel couldn't compromise and wouldn't dilute. No, *sir*. A couple of producers had talked about turning her into a disco diva if she'd lose weight and sing behind souped-up strings. No, *sir*. All her life her mama had tried making her into something she wasn't. If she could stand up to Georgia Faith she could sure as hell stand up to some tin-eared A&R man from Brooklyn telling *her* how to sing. She'd done three or four albums, the way she wanted to do them. Maybe they didn't burn up the charts but she had her fans. She'd found work down south in the upscale black clubs of Atlanta and Birmingham. She was a regular at the Long Beach Blues Festival, and long as she kept expenses down by staying in Muscle Shoals, she was, she felt, in control of things. She also believed in God, God had helped her survive. And yet . . .

Truth be told, she thought as she sipped her bourbon, she was a little pissed. She'd watched white singers with half her voice get twice as far. She knew she had the talent to attract a wider audience, to make more than just a living. What could Tina Turner do that Chanel Faith couldn't? Sure, Tina had that slim body and those long, long legs, and sure, there were times when Chanel had seriously tried to stop drugging and start slimming down, but, well, this wasn't one of those times. She was managing just fine, thank you, and at least, unlike Georgia, she didn't have to sell no goddamn flowers to make her money. She made her money singing. That was something to be proud of, something that made her feel good. And right now, as she spread tiny beads of black caviar across a crisp rye cracker, she was feeling *real* good . . .

Marisa, as she and Georgia were driving over to the park in Holmby Hills, wasn't sure whether she was going to a party or an audition.

"It's both, honey," Chanel had told her. "Just think of the whole afternoon as fun. You'll have fun playing Alice."

Marisa wasn't so sure. She loved performing, always had in front of her grandmother's friends, loved the attention, applause. But auditioning for parts in commercials and television shows was not fun. When they told her yes—that she was the best—she was happy. But most of the time someone else got picked and Marisa felt like it meant something was wrong with her. She *hated* that feeling.

By the time the children and the costumed characters from *Alice in Wonderland* arrived, Marisa's mood had changed. She was excited to see all her friends. This was her day—except Mama was missing.

Marisa hadn't seen Chanel since Christmas when she'd gone to Alabama for a week, and it was more fun there than with her stricter grandmother. Chanel was fun, at least freer than Grandmama. But when she asked her mother why she couldn't live with her all the time the answers were always vague . . . "California has warmer weather . . . I'm so busy working and traveling . . . They have better schools in Los Angeles . . ." The older Marisa became, the clearer the truth—her mother didn't want the responsibility of taking care of her. That made her angry, but she also loved Mama and missed her. It was real important that Mama be there today. She wanted her to meet all her friends and watch her play Alice. She wanted her to be proud.

"Where's Mama?" she kept asking Georgia.

"She's coming from the airport. I gave her directions. But you know your mother. She might have overslept and missed the plane . . ."

Georgia was hoping that Chanel *had* missed her plane. No doubt she'd complain that most of the children and parents were white, she'd want to sing some Baptist hymn, she'd ask everyone to join hands and probably say one of those country prayers. She'd be an embarrassment.

Georgia had carefully drawn up a guest list of her best customers at Passion Flowers, and most of them were on hand, even Brenda Cohen, a writer for the *Hollywood Daily News*, who had promised her a prominent mention. Sol Solomon had arrived with little Jason, whose hair was brighter than the clown's wig. Marisa's schoolmates, dressed up in their designer clothes, were there. As Georgia circulated among the guests, she heard them talking about the presidential primaries— Bush versus Reagan, Ted Kennedy versus Carter. Gently Georgia asked them to congregate in front of the small Punch and Judy theater where a puppeteer from Paris was readying his show.

Georgia stood next to Ted Fairfax, a pudgy man, and his wife Cindy, whose nose had been bobbed, she noted.

"I'm so glad you could come. Marisa is very fond of your Tiffany."

"Beautiful party, Miss Faith," said Fairfax. "I love the Alice characters."

"Why, thank you, I hope you can stay. We'll be having another performance in a few minutes."

The Punch and Judy show was a great success. Marisa was giddy, her head was whirling. The puppet show had everyone giggling, her friends running around in circles, poking at the Alice characters, picking on the pizza, asking when could they eat the cake and ice cream.

"Right after this," said Georgia, who motioned to Marisa to go to the restroom and change into her costume. When she emerged she was wearing an aproned pinafore with puffed sleeves, white stockings and a bright pink bow in her hair. Georgia gathered everyone together.

"My granddaughter would like to entertain her guests on her birthday with a scene from *Alice in Wonderland.*"

A table had been set out under a tree where Marisa and three of the characters—the March Hare, the Mad Hatter and sleepy Dormouse—acted out the famous Mad Tea Party.

The children, most of whom knew the story, seemed to love the performance. Georgia was proud. The child only flubbed once, toward the end—when she looked up and noticed her mother and a man getting out of a big Buick, saw her mother stumble and nearly fall.

"This is the stupidest tea party I ever was at in all my life!" said an exasperated Alice/Marisa, one eye on the March Hare, one eye on Mama, who was fast approaching the makeshift stage.

Over the applause Marisa heard Chanel saying loudly, "What'd I miss? Was my baby good?"

Georgia's heart sank. Chanel was all done up in gold spangles with dangling earrings and shiny pants that advertised her ample backside. The man with her looked like a pimp.

As for Marisa, she could tell her mother was floating, and prayed she wouldn't say anything awful.

"This is my friend Spinner," Chanel said.

"Gorgeous child you have here, baby," he told Chanel.

"And my mother, Georgia. Mother, meet Spinner."

"A real great honor to meet a great lady," said Spinner, trying his best.

"Excuse me," said Ted Fairfax, joining the group.

"How did you like Marisa's Alice?" asked Georgia, figuring that the moment of truth had arrived.

"Enchanting, but I had no idea that Chanel Faith was her mother."

Chanel's eyes, already lit, grew brighter.

"Chanel," Georgia said in a monotone, "this is Mr. Ted Fairfax."

"I have two of your albums," Fairfax told her. "I've been looking for the others. I'm sort of a blues aficionado . . . your daughter seems to have inherited some of your talent. Well, I'm just hoping we're going to hear *your* voice."

"I'm afraid—" Georgia began.

"'Course I'm gonna sing at my baby's birthday party," Chanel broke in.

"There's no accompaniment," Georgia said softly.

"Even better," Chanel shot back, laughing. "That means it's all *me*."

Because of or in spite of what she'd consumed on the plane, Chanel sang with startling intensity. When she sang "Amazing Grace" her voice was so powerful people a full block away opened their doors and windows to hear what was happening. Even the children paid attention.

Looking up at her mother sporting extra-long eyelashes and powder-blue eyeshadow, Marisa decided that Chanel appeared as weird as the Mad Hatter or Queen of Hearts. She was a character out of a storybook. Mostly, though, she was hurt that Mama had missed her performance, and here was Mama putting on her own show.

That night Marisa woke up to the sound of her mother and grandmother arguing. She wanted to hold her hands over her ears, but she also wanted to hear.

"I don't want her back there with you," said Georgia, "not even for the summer. I don't want her around your life, and your pimps—"

"I ain't the one pimping her on her birthday," said Chanel. "I ain't the one trying to sell her to white Hollywood like she's a piece of meat—"

"How *dare* you. Do you know who was at this party? Playwrights, actors, professors—"

"Bullshit. You and your fancy white folks."

"And what about *your* white man? Who ever believed that lie about him dying in Vietnam? Why don't you tell me the truth for once? Tell me, Chanel—what about the father of your child?"

"I'll tell you the day you tell me about my papa. A poet and a painter, you said. Don't make me laugh. You were balling so many cats back then, I'll bet dollars to donuts you don't even know which motherfucker planted the seed."

1 9 8 7

"Let's skip school," Jason urged.

"You're crazy," said Marisa.

"Feel the sun, Risa. Smell the air. This day wasn't made for school. Why fight it?"

She had just slid into his beat-up green English sports car. The paint was chipping, the fenders dented and plastered with Red Hot Chili Peppers stickers, but the top was down and the day was glorious. "We're hitting the beach," he said.

"Who's calling school?"

"Us. You do a perfect imitation of Georgia. I do Sol better than Sol does Sol. So it's settled."

Since they were babies, the bond between Jason and Marisa had been tight. They were each raised by a single grandparent. In different ways they were unique, especially in the private school they attended in Santa Monica. (Marisa was on scholarship; Jason's grandfather was on the board of trustees.) Their relationship had always been more sibling than romantic, and yet . . .

Marisa was excited by Jason's near-manic energy. Plus he had inherited his grandfather's sweetness. He was an experimenter. Marisa was more tolerant of Jason's drugs than, say, her own mother's indulgences. When Chanel got high Marisa got uncomfortable. Recently she had seen Jason through some rocky trips. Most people would have been bored by his verbal excesses, but Marisa liked following the circuitous path of his mind. She liked riding his emotional roller coaster.

As for Jason, he liked everything about Marisa. She was funny. She was a daredevil. She was *naturally* high. She was a nonconformist who wore super-baggy overalls and shiny black workman's boots before it

155

was cool to do so. Her musical tastes were more eclectic than his— Josephine Baker one day, Jimi Hendrix the next. She took him to a black Baptist church, a first for him. He took her to hear the Grateful Dead, a first for her. He became an addict of gospel music; then she became a punk rocker, even sang with a high school punk band. To Georgia's chagrin, Marisa dyed a purple streak through her hair. Jason upset Sol with his dangling earrings and tattoos of William Blake angels. Marisa thought the images were beautiful. To Jason, no one was more beautiful than Marisa.

There wasn't a guy in their school who didn't want to date her— because she was pretty and fun and smart as a whip, because she was a natural-born dancer and singer, a personality. A person. She ran track, she played softball better than a lot of the boys; she had these cool green eyes and this smile and all Jason wanted to do was be with her and make the other guys jealous, make them wonder whether they were lovers or not. They were not. They were both, in fact, intact, virgins. They were best buddies, and Marisa was apprehensive about lousing up their relationship with sex. Jason was ready, pressing the matter. But sex remained untried, a nervous area, and it was comforting for Marisa just to hang out with an old trusted friend and not worry about the big question.

Take today, for instance. On Venice Beach Jason smoked a joint and watched the clouds roll by as Marisa read the *Autobiography of Malcolm X*. Jason's shoulder-length hair was longer than hers; her limbs were more developed than his. The blond muscleheads strutting the beach held no interest for her. She was interested in Jason's funny turn of mind. She read him sections of the book when Malcolm was a hustler. Their own character had been built in large part by abandonment—Jason abandoned by his parents' tragic death, Marisa abandoned by her mother's move to Alabama and the death, according to her mother, of a father she never knew. Not too surprisingly, Jason got along much better with Georgia than Marisa did; and Marisa accepted Sol in ways Jason never could. To her, Sol was a hoot. To Jason, Sol was a schmuck. Conversely, Jason found Georgia charming; Marisa found her overbearing.

The two teenagers could sit on a beach, as they did this morning, and feel at ease in each other's company for hours. They might make up a scenario about the elderly couple strolling along the water's edge—he's a retired Mafia hit man from Buffalo, she's a rich madam from Hungary, they met through a computerized dating service—or they might remind one another of the goofy palm reader they saw last weekend in Hollywood, a wall-eyed woman who told them their fates were entwined and that one day they would strike it rich together.

"If anyone's going to make any money," Jason told Marisa afterward, "it's you."

"Why me?"

"You have talent, Risa. You can sing and dance and play Queen Elizabeth in the school play even though *I* know you're only doing an impression of your grandmother. Me, well, my only talent is going through Grandpa Sol's money."

"You're creative, Jason. You can't argue the fact."

"Who wants to argue?"

Jason and Marisa rarely argued. When they left Venice they headed south and drove to Hermosa Beach, home of Jason's good friend Stan Hirshey, self-published poet. When they arrived Stan was leaving for an overnight trip to Berkeley. "Use my apartment if you want to," said Stan, looking over Marisa. "Just lock up when you leave."

There was a waterbed. There was a stereo with giant speakers aimed at the bed. There was a view of the beach. Outside, beautiful bodies were running, reclining, touching.

"Of course we love each other," she said when he asked the question. "It's just not boyfriend-girlfriend love."

"I know that," Jason said. "I'm not talking about goopy love, TV love or bullshit love. The great thing is that we don't have to pretend. I love you because you're real."

"What does that mean?"

"Don't ask me."

Marisa watched as he rolled around on the waterbed.

"It's fun," he said. "It may make me seasick but it's fun."

"You think everything's fun."

"Lighten up, Risa. Take the plunge."

She did; she jumped in the bed, water sloshing from one side to the other. They were both wearing shorts and T-shirts. For weeks now he had been pleading that lovemaking among friends was only appropriate, but she had refused, saying it seemed wrong. Late this afternoon, though, with the sun melting into the ocean, their arms and legs warmed with a deep tan, their heads swimming with the images of each other's bodies, a day of sensuous bodies everywhere they looked, it seemed, well . . . why not?

They laughed their way through it. It was an act of friendship, an act of trust as much as anything else. They were inept, the pleasure was short-lived, fumblings and missed connections. It happened, just barely, and afterward they were relieved of their burden of virginity.

"We've never discussed something," she said to him.

"What?"

"Are Georgia and Sol—"

"What . . . are they bumping?"

"You put it so delicately. Yes."

"I imagine they've got some kind of arrangement," he told her.

"What does that mean?"

"Like us," he answered. "They're friends."

The psychologist at Barnsdale College outside Boston had a winning, sympathetic manner. Marisa trusted him. He was an Indian from New Delhi, dark-skinned, plump and middle-aged. He had thick graying hair and a soothing accent. Although it took nearly her whole freshman year to bring herself to his office, once he began talking Marisa felt at ease.

"I'm not here to judge you," he told the teenager dressed in cut-off jeans and a wrinkled work shirt. "Mostly I'm here to listen."

"I've never been to a shrink before."

"Most people your age haven't. Talking to a stranger is no easy thing, especially when the talk involves your feelings."

"I've been feeling . . . frightened."

"How long?"

"All semester, ever since I came here. I've kept it in, but sometimes it gets too much and I wake up in the middle of the night, all sweaty. My roommate said I woke up last night screaming. I scared her and I scared myself. That's when I decided I'd better see someone."

"Do you remember any dream?"

"It was about my father. He was in the army and he was coming to kill me. He didn't even know I was his daughter. He thought I was the enemy." Seeing again the image of a man with a bayonet, Marisa squirmed in her chair.

"Tell me about your father."

"I never knew him. He died in Vietnam before I was born. At least that's what my mother says. My grandmother raised me. She's a famous actress. Well, maybe not *that* famous. But well-known, really. And very intelligent. She's read more books than I'll ever read."

159

"And your mother?"

"She's a singer."

"Famous?"

"Like my grandmother, I guess, almost famous. She was here last month. It was her first visit to campus."

"What was that like?"

"Like hell. She never wanted me to go to college in the first place. She just wants me to go out into the world and be a singer like her. I act too—I'm in *The Maids*."

"I haven't had a chance to see it but I've heard good things about it."

"Mama didn't have a clue what it was about. She thought I was wasting my time. She got angry. The next night she took me to Boston to watch *her* perform. That's her way. She was singing on the same bill with the Staple Singers, the gospel group? Mama and the group nearly tore the roof off the place."

"And how did you feel?"

" 'Now *this* is real drama'—that's what Mama said after her show. 'What *you're* doing is bullshit.' "

No comment from the doctor. But he was thinking that they were more rival siblings than mother and daughter.

"Hey, she's probably the greatest singer around, and I don't say that just because she's my mother. I know good singing. But she can't be managed, she can't be told what to do. She tells people off. Her boyfriends . . ." Marisa's voice trailed off.

"Her boyfriends . . . ?"

"It's too much to go into. Except they're losers. Dopers like her."

"I see."

"Now when Grandmama came two weeks ago, she loved the play. She told me that when she lived in Europe she'd actually met the playwright Jean Genet."

"You admire your grandmother."

"I admire both of them. I know they've both been screwed around, they've had it hard. The problem is that when I'm with one for too long, I want to be with the other. Grandmama can be the most controlling bitch in the world. She's a real smart woman but she puts on airs. She plays the diva. My mother loves to shock her by playing the down-and-dirty blues mama. In a way I sort of feel sorry for them both. They've never gotten what they deserved. Both of them . . .

Jesus, they both drive me crazy. They call every night. They worry I'm going to fall into a well or disappear into thin air."

"Do you have siblings?"

"I had a brother who was killed in a car accident before I was born. It's *weird* how I miss him. I miss a person I never even knew—just like I miss my father. I've never said this before, but I love my brother Bobby, I love my father. Or I want to love them and don't know how. I have a feeling of love for them but I don't know where to put it. So many things happened before I was born. Anyway, my brother's name was Bobby and although they've never said it, I know Mama and Grandmama blame themselves for the accident. They were there. They watched it happen but they couldn't yell out to him in time. It must have been horrible. Sometimes I dream of Bobby and we're playing and he's my best friend in the world and he runs away from me into a car and I shout at him but I can't save him. It becomes my fault. In high school I had a friend, Jason, and he was like my brother."

"Was he your boyfriend?"

"Mostly a friend friend."

"How are your mother and grandmother today?"

"I had another dream where they showed up here on campus on the same day. They had a fight in the middle of the quadrangle. Everyone came out of the classrooms and dorms to watch. They had a hair-pulling ass-kicking fistfight in front of the whole college, and when they were through, when they knocked each other out, everyone just looked at me and laughed as though I was the biggest fool in the world. I was humiliated."

"I understand."

"Maybe my fear is that I'll never get over them—never stop hearing from them, never get them out of my head, never stop asking myself what would they think of this, or what would they think of that, never stop dreaming about them yelling at me or at each other, never be free of them."

The psychologist waited for more.

"I want them to make a peace with each other," said Marisa, tired of thinking and talking. "That's all I want."

"They've put you in the middle. That's made it very difficult. To please one is to antagonize the other."

"I always wind up antagonizing them *both*. And they wind up antagonizing me."

"And yet you remain close to both."

"I'm at college. College was supposed to be my getaway. College was supposed to free me up. What's the point of all this *talk*?"

"We can go into it more next time," he said, seeing by his desk clock that time was up. "I'd like to see you again."

But he never did—at least not in his office. Marisa never returned. The only time he saw her again was in the school production of the Genet play. When he left the theater that night he was sure that in spite of her family connections one day she would have her own fame. On stage, this girl was electric.

1 9 9 1

"Dear Grandmama and Mama," wrote Marisa from Barnsdale College shortly before graduation.

I'm writing you together because I want to say the same thing to you both. This is a letter I've been composing in my mind ever since I got to college. Actually I probably started this letter in high school, maybe even before then. It goes way way back. It's a sort of declaration. My declaration of independence, can you stand it? So why does it have to be written down? Why don't I just tell each of you in person? Because in person . . . well, I just can't do it, I've tried it before. I've tried to say, "Look, I understand your lives haven't been easy. I know you both care a lot about me and want me to avoid all the mistakes you've made, but *please* lay off, please leave me alone, keep your advice to yourselves." Those words don't ever come out because once you begin to talk, I begin to listen and in spite of everything, I like what I hear. You're both great talkers. Grandmama's an actress, Mama's a performer, and there I am thinking to myself, *Damn, aren't I lucky to have two such wonderful women in my corner!*

Well, the truth is that *I am* lucky and I am unlucky because I've felt I can stand alone—or act alone—or sing alone—*or do any damn thing alone.* These college productions have helped. The drama coach and the music teachers say I have *it*—whatever *it* is. Sometimes I believe them, sometimes I don't. When each of you came to see me up here I was proud to have you in the audience and of course you were full of encouragement, but you also let me know

163

that this isn't the real world. You kept saying that once I get out of school and start looking for work, casting agents and record producers won't be anything like college teachers. They won't be so nice. I know that.

Well, maybe all I really know is that I have to do it alone. It'd be too easy to have Grandmama as my acting coach, or Mama as my singing coach. I don't want to try to get acting roles in L.A. or singing gigs in Muscle Shoals. That would drive me crazy. If I landed work I'd never know if it was me or my grandmother or my mother.

I'm writing you together for another reason. I want you to know that I'm not joining either of you. I knew if I wrote Grandmama alone she'd think, no matter what I said, that I'd decided to live with Mama—or vice versa. I know how you both think. That's another thing that makes me crazy, but I don't want to go into that now. I have an English final tomorrow and I need to study and sleep but here I am writing because both of you are on my mind so much of the time. I started off telling you about my Declaration of Independence. Okay, here it is. I, Marisa Faith, will go live in New York. Alone. I love you both, but I know this is the only way I'll ever get to know myself. Yes, I want to act and sing, I'd love to make a movie and make a record and be rewarded for whatever talents I've inherited from both of you. If that happens it would be wonderful, but if it happens I also want to know exactly *how* it happened—because of me, not you.

Marisa

PART TWO

The Present

It started during one of those torrential May rainstorms that explode over New York City without warning. Marisa was caught on Madison Avenue without an umbrella.

"Take mine."

"Too late," said Marisa, "I'm already soaked."

"Never too late," said the woman with the large umbrella. "We'll share. Where are you headed?"

"Downtown."

"Here's my car. I'll give you a ride."

The women jumped into the back seat of the metallic blue Mercedes. "I saw you leaving my office. My name's Joan. Joan Winfrey."

"The Winfrey Agency, you're the Winfrey Agency?"

"And you're . . ."

"Marisa. Marisa Faith."

"Lovely name," said Joan. "Lovely face."

Marisa had gone to the Winfrey Agency as a last resort. She'd never seen herself as a model and thought she was wrong for it—which was just what she had been told only a few minutes ago.

"You're an interesting type," one of Joan's assistants had said to the young black woman, "but the look's a bit too . . . unconventional."

There was the matter of her hair—wildly combed, its nappy consistency arranged in a bizarre grouping of curls and braids. A hip-hop hairdo, Marisa called it. Very avant-garde, but to the eyes of Winfrey's assistant, too far-out. The light-green hue of Marisa's eyes, her high cheekbones, full lips, warm smile, light-brown skin, slightly flared nose were all extraordinary. Her teeth were perfect; for years her grandmother had dragged her to the orthodontist. But her body lan-

167

guage and casual outfit—tight jeans, tight white T-shirt revealing no
bra, small breasts and hard nipples—seemed defiant, seemed to de-
clare she didn't want to be there.

"I was just invited out of your office," said Marisa.

"My assistants can be hasty sometimes," Joan said. "Sometimes
they can't see the character of the person for the feathers. I would
have looked at your picture and called you immediately, I assure you.
I look at everything myself. And you, Ms. Marisa Faith, have a *look*
—strong, striking, individual. A look I can market."

Marisa threw back her head, laughing her laugh that started deep
in her flat stomach, traveled to her throat and spilled out of her
mouth in seeming torrents. Well, well, she had finally scored. Tomorrow was her birthday. She was relishing the moment, enjoying the
irony of being rejected and discovered all in a matter of minutes. It
was pouring rain outside, there was thunder and lightning and here
she was inside this plush car with the smell of high-priced leather and
this WASP-looking agent ready to make her a fashion star. At least
that was her reading during the ride. She was laughing because she
had figured that one day it probably would happen like this—even
though she'd been in New York for a year, scuffling and getting
nowhere, running to acting class, taking singing and dancing lessons,
not landing a damn thing. Now, on the eve of her twenty-third birthday, *bingo*!

From the first she had thought of modeling as sort of silly, and had
showed up at Joan Winfrey's with an attitude. Someone had said it
was the toniest agency in town, so she had wiggled into a pair of snug
jeans (she had inherited Chanel's high backside), a plain T-shirt and
a pair of beat-up Nikes. Taking the subway to midtown, she had
flipped through Vanity Fair magazine and listened to Luther Vandross on her Walkman. She adored Luther; Luther was an angel.
More down to earth, the flutter in his voice set off a flutter in the
clitoris. No doubt she was sexually sensitive, receptive, though in the
last twelve months she had slept with only one man. She was choosy
and, as a result, horny. Unfortunately the man she had chosen took
off the next week for Europe to write a novel. No great loss. For all
his brainy talk and bedroom skills, the brother had no sense of humor. Like Winfrey's assistant, who had told Marisa, "Sorry, you're
wrong for us."

"Forget my assistants," Joan was now telling Marisa, "I can work with you. It's just a matter of grooming, management."

"I may be unmanageable," Marisa announced.

"Says who?"

"My mother and grandmother, for starters."

"Maybe they weren't tough enough with you."

Marisa let loose with another laugh.

"Anyway," added the agent, "your relatives aren't professionals."

"The hell they're not." Marisa was about to tell Joan who they were but decided against it. Chances were, the agent hadn't heard of either of them.

"Whoever they are," said Joan, "they're not me."

"Who *are* you?" asked Marisa, squinting her almond-shaped eyes, staring at Joan with mock-serious intent.

Joan Winfrey had ordinary features enhanced by subtle makeup and a chin-length coif. Her hair was blond, her light blue eyes framed by thin tortoise-shell oval frames. Her outfit was all business, a wide-shouldered white linen suit now wrinkled by the rain. Her quick speech went with quick decisions; she could jump on and off the phone a hundred times a day. Her instinct for spotting money in the faces of other women was uncanny, and she had definitely spotted Marisa even in the midst of a rainstorm. Indeed, she thought, Marisa had the best face she'd seen in months—and a body to go with it. Winfrey also sensed this young woman's ambition, her hunger to make it.

"I'm the one who could very well change your life."

"Starting when?"

"Starting now. Come in for a minute."

Next thing Marisa knew, the driver had parked in front of a brownstone on West Tenth Street a few doors off Fifth Avenue. The place was a century old but recently refurbished. The facade was decorated with freshly painted wrought-iron grillwork. The antique brick had been sandblasted, the bay windows trimmed in white.

The driver held an umbrella over the two women as they approached the townhouse, rain still pouring down.

A black maid opened the door and scrutinized Marisa disapprovingly.

"Good evening, Gladys," said Joan. "This is Marisa."

"I'll get y'all some towels," Gladys said, and disappeared.

The place was lean and clean—not much furniture, gleaming hardwood floors, high ceilings, white walls, track lighting, sculpture featuring female bodies, oversized photographs of famous models, all clients. Joan, it seemed, brought her business home, thought Marisa; the brownstone was pretty much an extension of the Winfrey Agency.

"Would you like a drink?" Joan asked. "Hot tea?"

"Yes, thanks."

"Come on into the den, make yourself comfortable. I'm going to change, be back in a sec."

The den had a bubble skylight on which the slackening rain now fell in musical rhythm. An entire wall was given over to a lucite bookcase. Marisa looked at the collection: all fashion—fashion history, fashion models, fashion in Europe, Japan, Thailand, illustrated fashion books in foreign languages. Another wall was devoted to a Bang and Olufsen stereo setup, hardware that looked like modern sculpture. Marisa checked out the CD collection: mainstream stuff, mostly on the square side—Neil Diamond, Barbra Streisand.

"What kind of music do you like?" Joan was suddenly back, now in khaki shorts and a white oxford shirt that revealed the strong-limbed body of, say, a tennis player. She and Marisa sat across from one another on matching slate-gray suede couches.

"I like dance music," Marisa said, tilting her head. "Old music, new music, all music."

"You sing? Dance?"

"Everything."

"You mentioned your mother and grandmother. Are they in the business?"

"Georgia Faith. Chanel Faith. Have you heard of them?"

"Afraid not."

Marisa was pleased and disappointed. It was a relief—after all, the whole point was to make it on her own, to escape those two women, to keep them out of her life—but she also couldn't help feeling sad. As a little girl she was convinced that Georgia and Chanel were the two most famous women in the whole world. And that's when she thought that she too would be famous, that it was inevitable. Disillusionment took a while in coming, the reality of her relatives' marginal celebrity harsh and painful, as though somehow diminishing her too. She worried then, and even more this past year, whether she too was destined to be an almost-ran. In truth, she hadn't even gotten that far. At least they had done something, made some mark. She had nothing to show for all her supposed energy and talent. Whenever she had met up with fans of Mama or Grandmama she had felt excited, renewed. Today, though, for the first time since starring in college productions, she had some news that should excite them.

"It doesn't matter if you don't know their work," said Marisa. "Anyway, one acts, the other sings . . ."

"So you want to do both?"

"I do do both."

"It's cold out there, Marisa. Even for someone as striking as you. Modeling's a great first step. Have you modeled before?"

"Never."

"Well, it's acting, too. It's selling yourself, putting your ass on the line."

"I'm not sure I fit—"

"That's just the point. You can create your own image, make your own mark, go wherever you want to go. But it all starts with the face, with one remarkable face." Joan got up and walked over to Marisa, gently touching her face. It was an odd act, somehow not in keeping with Joan's all-business approach. Marisa was surprised.

Joan went to the stereo and hit a button. Strange that she would play Luther Vandross. "Love Won't Let Me Wait." Luther's seduction as always was subtle. He never failed, making you wait an eternity, strings soaring, soprano sax rising, until he finally approached the microphone, his voice a fluttering reed, his heart right there . . . "I need to have you next to me . . . in more ways than one."

The doorbell interrupted.

"Dr. Clay is here," from Gladys. Standing next to her was a handsome black man in a sports jacket and baggy trousers, with gold-rimmed glasses and beat-up tennis shoes. Kicked-back, casual, intriguing.

"Nelson," said Joan, apparently caught by surprise. "I completely forgot."

"We were going to have dinner at your favorite deli," he reminded her.

"Marisa Faith . . . Nelson Clay," Joan said.

He smiled at Marisa approvingly, she thought. He was attractive,

with a high forehead and clear dark skin. His eyes, she liked his eyes
. . . they seemed to show curiosity and intelligence. She guessed he
was thirty.

"Can I take a raincheck, Nelson? It's been a rough day."

"Sure."

"He's my neighbor," Joan said after Nelson Clay had gone. "Actually, a prominent psychiatrist."

Of course, thought Marisa, he had the rumpled, serious look of a
shrink. A smart man. Smart men—especially very smart men—turned
her on.

Joan took a mini-portable phone out of her pocket, flipping it open
to make a quick call. "Need to check on a shoot over in Jersey.
Hungry? Gladys can whip up something in a sec."

"No, thanks. I'd better be going."

"Not before we make plans."

"For what?"

"The rest of your life."

"Okay," Marisa said, straight-faced. "How 'bout a million before
the end of the year?"

"Give me until the end of next year and you won't be far off."

The thought excited Marisa, even if she didn't really believe it.
"I'm leaving town."

"When?"

"In the morning."

"Where to?"

"L.A."

"I have an office in L.A."

"I have a grandmother in L.A."

"She's sick?"

"Healthy as a horse."

"When will you be back?"

"Soon."

"Leave your numbers. And don't do a *thing* until you hear from me.
Promise?"

"On a stack of unpaid bills."

"Want a ride home?"

"I feel like walking. Besides, I don't want to scare off your driver. I
live on a bad block."

"He doesn't scare easily. Neither do I. I'm signing you, Marisa Faith. I'm giving you fair warning—I'm taking over."

Marisa got off the couch, accepted Joan's strong handshake, and left.

The summer air was clear. The rain had stopped, having washed the city streets clean. Things were changing. Marisa felt good. Damn it, she felt pretty great. She didn't take everything that Joan Winfrey had said as gospel, but finally she had scored, had a promise of a real future and couldn't wait to tell her mother and grandmother. The night was full of the new possibilities, not to mention the delicious smells coming from the corner deli, spicy and inviting.

She glanced in and spotted Nelson Clay at a small table in the back corner. She went to the counter, ordered a sandwich, cream soda and potato salad and headed toward a table close to his. When he invited her over Marisa smiled, nodded, and slid into a chair across from him.

"Joan says you're a psychologist."

"Psychiatrist."

"That means you went to med school."

"Forever."

"Wasn't much fun, huh?"

"Not exactly. Being a model is probably more—"

"I'm not a model. Not really."

"Oh, I thought you were one of Joan's clients."

"It looks like I'm going to be. But I've never modeled before."

"You seem like a natural."

"Thanks, I think. Have you known Joan long?"

"We're neighbors, I know her from our block association."

"You live . . ."

"Right next door."

"Those brownstones are terrific," said Marisa. "They're real old New York."

"I agree . . . do you live around here?"

"Alphabet City. Avenue B."

"Little rough over there, isn't it?"

"Keeps me on my toes. So tell me about being a psychiatrist."

"Well, all the old jokes aside, I suppose it is mostly a matter of listening."

And she found she liked listening to him, to his easy, informal way of speaking . . .

"Just listening?"

"Well, of course, it's how you listen that counts."

"And you never get involved personally? Not like some I hear about."

"Depends what you mean by personally. On one level it's all personal, it's all people. On the other hand boundaries between patients and therapists have to be drawn—and held to. It is pretty serious business."

"Ever fall in love with any of your patients?"

"Come on now."

"Well, do you accept patients you're attracted to?"

"Why do I get this feeling you're a member of the Ethics Board of the American Psychiatric Association?"

"Because you're paranoid."

He laughed. "Okay, if you're not a model, not yet, and not a member of the Ethics Board, how do you make a living?"

"You presume I make a living—your first mistake."

"I stand corrected."

"Back to your patients—"

"Can't discuss them, won't discuss them."

"Then tell me about the process."

"You've never been to a counselor of any sort?"

"Big difference between a shrink and a college counselor."

"Maybe not. Folks hurt and need to talk about it. Where did you go to college?"

"Barnsdale."

"Good school. . . . What was your major?"

"Music and drama."

"Are you an actress, a singer, dancer?"

"All of the above, I think."

"Tough getting work, right?"

"Even tougher if you think you've got the goods but aren't getting anywhere. Going on the cattle calls, seeing your demo tape on a mountain of other tapes in some record producer's office—none of them listened to. I'm sorry, I shouldn't—"

"Rejection," he cut in, "isn't much fun."

"Screw it," she said, eyes sparkling.

"It's probably good you've been able to develop that attitude."

"Mister," she said, "I was *born* with that attitude."

"Inherited from—"

"Are we talking therapy?"

"You're interested in therapy?"

"My mother's been talking about it all the time. Like it's salvation. It's incredible, but Mama has discovered a therapist—a woman, no less—that she adores."

"Wish I could say the same about my mother," he said with a smile.

"She lives here?"

"Newark. Yours?"

"Alabama."

"Are you and she close?"

"Here we go."

"Listen," he said, "we don't have to talk at all. We can walk. It's a beautiful night."

He seemed a nice guy. She liked his style, relaxed, interested, different from most guys she had dated. Not macho, not coming on. He wasn't one of those pumped-up peacocks, arrogant and hung up on themselves.

"I was just going to walk home," she said.

"Mind if I tag along?"

"Not at all . . ."

Summertime in New York could be hell—the sweltering heat, the smell of garbage piled along the streets. But then again, there were times when sweet rain softened the edge of the concrete city, and at least for a brief moment the place radiated magic, like a musical from the forties. Marisa loved those musicals. She was aware of the fact that blacks rarely appeared in them, understood—as her mother and grandmother often pointed out—that racist Hollywood had excluded her people from the so-called mainstream productions. But she still felt attracted to those fantasies where all problems were resolved and all had happy endings. For a moment she could imagine herself and Nelson Clay walking down streets on which the Italian barber, the kosher butcher, the Korean grocer, the Jamaican beautician might at any moment fling open their doors and break into song. She told him so.

"Except I can't sing," he said.

"Well, you can *listen*. It's your specialty, you said."

She told him about the musicals she'd played in in college, including one by Bertolt Brecht and Kurt Weill. "I guess I prefer Gershwin, though. The Germans are so *heavy*."

"I'm afraid I have a tin ear for music," Clay said.

"There's no music I don't like—it's just that some music makes me absolutely crazy."

"In what sense?"

"In the best sense."

"What music is that? I mean that makes you crazy."

"Probably has to do with my mother's music."

"What's it like?"

"Church. Soul. Alabama red-dirt music."

"And that's what you sing?"

"On good days I can sing pretty much any style—at least that's what they tell me. I did a pretty funny bit at college imitating Streisand."

"Let's hear it."

Browsers at a newsstand turned and stared as Marisa broke into a few bars of "People." By the time they arrived at Marisa's apartment building on Avenue B, though, the musical fantasy had ended. The neighborhood had pushers openly dealing drugs.

"You don't mind living over here?"

Marisa didn't want to explain why she was living on Avenue B. To do that would break her mood, get into her defiance of her mother and grandmother. For months now she had refused to take any more money from either of them. She would stick it out on her own. The hell with the occasional rat and stream of roaches, with the crackheads on the corner and the sirens in the night. She was no damn princess. All her life she'd been accused of being spoiled—her mother claimed her grandmother spoiled her and vice versa—and she was here to prove them wrong. She'd tough it out. She had had enough of them fighting over her, fighting each other, driving her up the wall with their bribes for her affection. Mama in the high-rent district of Muscle Shoals, Alabama, and Grandmama in the flats of Beverly Hills—flip sides of the same coin called stranglehold. They just couldn't let go, even for a second. Okay, they meant well, she told herself, but it was baggage that got heavier each year. She wished she could dump it in the East River—

Baggage. Packing. She hadn't packed yet for tomorrow's trip.

A group of teenaged boys were on the stoop of her building, talking and smoking pot. Pumped-up sound from a boom box, the raw rap of Public Enemy blasting out in the night.

"I'll see you to your door," Nelson said.

"They don't bother me," Marisa said.

"I'll walk you up," he said, and followed her to the third floor, apartment 3C. She slid in one key, then another and opened the door. She invited him in.

Marisa liked showing off her apartment, the transformation from what it was when she moved in. She had painted the walls in a series of orange-and-yellow sunbursts and sunflowers. The used wicker furniture gave the place a seashore feeling. From the track lighting hung several pair of big furry dice, the kind that dangled from rearview mirrors of old Thunderbirds. In the corner was a big stuffed whale, a panda bear and a giant Snoopy dressed like the soul singer James Brown. Originally she had hung posters in the bathroom from Georgia's movies and Chanel's concerts, but then she took them down. She didn't need to be reminded. She did need to pack, but her eyes went back to Nelson Clay.

"I can make you coffee or give you some ol' refrigerated wine."

"Coffee," he said. "I like your apartment. Did it yourself?"

"Out of necessity."

The coffee was strong and he drank two cups.

"So now," she said, "if I wanted to be your patient I couldn't."

"Because?"

"Because we're becoming friends."

"Okay by me. I'd rather have a friend than a patient any day. By the way, if you're really interested in therapy I could give you a few names—"

"I'm not really interested," she said. "But I would be interested to hear how you became a shrink."

"Both my parents worked at a hospital—Beth Israel in Newark. Papa was an orderly and Mama worked in the cafeteria. I'd be over there all the time and became fascinated with the operating rooms and the surgical instruments. My folks were always saying, 'You're going to be a doctor.' Starting when I was five, they put away their money and got me through college. In med school I became more and more interested in behavioral science—"

"Is it really a science?"

"No, but it makes us feel better to call it that. Whatever it is, it can never be fully understood, and anything that defies understanding is a mystery that's interesting to me. Sorry, I'm starting to carry on."

She waved it off. "And all this time in in college, in med school . . . no girlfriends, no wives?"

"A couple of girlfriends. Mostly study and surviving the professional jungle."

"Which you've done."

"In a fashion. And with the help of therapy, I should add."

"So shrinks really do get shrunk."

"Many do."

"Which means many are a little crazy."

"Most."

"You don't seem crazy."

"Thanks, but it's early in the evening."

"And early tomorrow morning I'm flying out to L.A."

"Work?"

"My birthday party."

"Congratulations. A big party?"

"Just the three of us—me, Mama and Grandmama."

"That's the family?"

"That's enough, thank you very much."

He was sensitive enough not to ask about men—about her father or grandfathers. "Let me just wish you happy birthday," he said, "and let you pack. It was wonderful meeting you. I mean it."

And the way he said it, she believed him. She also wondered whether he was involved with Joan, or had been. She found herself hoping the answer was no.

After packing a suitcase, taking off her makeup and slipping on a nightgown and climbing into bed, she felt as good as she could remember feeling for a long time. She was happy she had met Joan Winfrey—and Nelson Clay. Excited at the prospect of meeting Chanel and Georgia with her news—that something good was apparently happening to her career. Sleep came only after hours of tossing and turning, and her dream was no match for her waking good feelings . . .

In her dream she missed the plane and wound up hitchhiking. She was picked up by circus performers who took her to Florida and taught her the art of trapeze. Except a hurricane chased them to Key West, where the tents were destroyed, the animals got out of their cages. Her mother's old cat Willow and a full-size tiger were one and the same. The tiger protected her, the tiger saw her through the storm, but when the weather cleared the cat was gone and she was all alone. She got lost in Iowa, in its cornfields, in Colorado, in big parks, in deep canyons and barren deserts. She kept trying to get to California but kept missing buses and trains. No one would pick her up. There was the tingling bell of an ice-cream truck but the man in the white coat wouldn't stop. She was a little girl crying but he didn't hear her. No one did. She took wrong turns and wound up back in Chicago. The airport was a mess—delays, cancellations, fog, storms off Lake Michigan. No way to California. Finally a plane was boarding. She reached into her purse and found nothing but a coupon for Shakey's Pizza. No ticket. She begged them at the boarding gate but they wouldn't let her on. The plane took off without her. From the window she watched the jet ascend before it exploded into a spectacular ball of fire. The sky reddened with blood—

Marisa woke up with a start, relieved she'd just been dreaming. She looked at the clock. She had overslept. She had a half-hour to get to the airport. At least part of her dream was coming true.

It was the day for her daughter and granddaughter to meet Georgia at Passion Flowers. Her morning had been spent at her apartment on Burton Way, where she spent an extra half-hour selecting her outfit. After all, it had been a year since she had seen her family. Silk was her choice. Silk, she felt, always suited her long, slim frame—a sleek turquoise silk dress, a red silk scarf at her neck, tiny jade earrings. At sixty-seven Georgia looked fifty. Some thought she looked younger than her daughter Chanel. Others claimed her granddaughter Marisa was the image of her.

Marisa was much on her mind. Today was Marisa's birthday. Georgia realized Marisa needed direction. The girl was adorable and talented and destined for greatness, but she needed help. Living in New York by herself had been a mistake—a mistake about to be reversed, family relations set back on track. That was the agenda of the day. Georgia Faith knew just what she was doing.

Passion Flowers sat on the eastern edge of Beverly Hills near Cedars-Sinai Hospital, an ideal location. The store was filled with memorabilia from Georgia's past—black-and-white photos from her films in the forties, her roles in fifties TV situation comedies, her occasional appearance on a dramatic series. When business lagged she would invite a television reporter or magazine editor for lunch in the enclosed garden behind the shop. There, with bougainvillea blooming along the white latticed fence, the sound of water cascading from the mouth of a winged cherub carved from gleaming white marble, Georgia would reminisce about the golden days. She would sit so the midday light enhanced the hue of her clear brown skin, her extraordinary green eyes lit with sunshine. She'd talk about Katherine Dunham, Bill Robinson, Dorothy Dandridge, Eddie "Rochester" Anderson, Hazel Scott, Hedy Lamarr, Orson Welles, Ethel Waters. She'd tell stories about taking the Twentieth Century Limited from Grand Central in New York to Pasadena, meetings with Harry Cohn and L. B. Mayer, tiffs with Hedda Hopper and Louella Parsons. She'd exaggerate and imagine, but more often than not, she got away with it. She was, after all, an actress. She understood beauty and its power. And she managed her own beauty, used it to manipulate and control. Her love life was varied and remarkably active for a woman her age. She traded on a calculated mix . . . her looks, the fragrance of the trumpet-shaped freesias, the Christian Dior perfume dabbed behind her ears, her makeup subtle and right. She was a lady, remote when she wanted to be, but accessible when she needed to be.

She worked from a flame-stitched Queen Anne chair in a small office next to the garden. Her desk was English Regency. Mostly she left it to a white man named Stephen to run the store. After all, there was the more pressing matter of her career.

She spent her mornings making calls. There was always another agent—the town was filled with agents—always another casting director, another project in the works, so she said. She was always just about to land a role. A director she had met. A customer who happened to be a producer. A film about to go into production. Looking at her photos from the past, she knew she still had what it took. She had done it before, she'd do it again. It was all a matter of *persistence*—that's what she kept telling her granddaughter Marisa—persistence, patience. Georgia Faith had both.

Chanel's luggage was lost and her top was stained. Some clown on the plane had spilled a drink on her. She wondered whether he'd done it on purpose. She wanted to grab him by the collar and hit him. She was properly pissed . . . to be back in L.A., to be doing her mother's bidding again. Georgia just plain drove her nuts. The less she saw of her the better. Time was she would react like a puppet on a string . . . or at least *felt* that way . . . but it almost did her in. But she was past all that. She'd put away the booze, given up the pot-smoking, the all-night coking, the good-for-nothing men. She'd discovered therapy; she'd found herself a twelve-step program that was working like a motherfucker, forgive her French. Enough, time to chill. All she needed was one good man to satisfy her soul. Hard to find, but things were turning around. She had half a mind to turn around and fly back to Muscle Shoals—and would have, except for Marisa. God, she wanted to see her daughter real bad. She adored her, worried about her.

She understood what the child was going through. She knew what it meant to get away from home, to get away from Georgia. That's what Marisa was doing—escaping her grandmother, no doubt about it. Not that she didn't have her own problems with Marisa, but at least she was starting to understand. It hadn't been easy. When the shrink had asked about her childhood she couldn't help but laugh. Better laugh than cry. Her daughter's childhood hadn't been all roses, she knew that, but at least she'd been a fairly happy little girl, or seemed so when she saw her. Was she a happy young woman? Who could tell? Marisa was staying away, Marisa wasn't calling. That was why she had agreed to come to L.A., in spite of not wanting to go along with Georgia's set-up, for a sit-down family talk. Well, at least she'd get to see her Marisa on her birthday. She'd spent the last week looking for a present and knew Marisa was going to love the CD-set of Bessie Smith classics. Bessie Smith was part of Marisa's legacy, whether she appreciated it or not.

Standing on the curb outside the airport, waiting for a cab, Chanel was hard to miss. Her pants suit was glittery and bold. In spite of her ample figure—or because of it—she wore her clothes snug. She frankly considered her backside her best feature. She walked like she was proud of her extra pounds. And with it all, Chanel was defiantly sexy. Her moon-shaped face was topped by a close-cropped haircut, a natural that followed the curvature of her head. Upkeep was easy. She hated beauty parlors and wigs. Her mother had a wig collection, she said, that wouldn't quit. Indeed, the first time Georgia ever raised a hand to her daughter was when ten-year-old Chanel took a scissors and started clipping her mother's wigs. Chanel hated pretense; she liked it real. Her long, flaming-red polished fingernails were her own. She wore long copper earrings and four strands of multicolored African beads. Silver bracelets jangled from each wrist. She favored blue eyeshadow and never used face powder. Her dark black skin had a radiance. "Soften the shade," Georgia would instruct the teenaged Chanel, handing her makeup. "You want me to look lighter," Chanel would retort, throwing the makeup on the floor. "Well, I won't."

If Georgia's voice suggested the flavor of southern molasses, Chanel was all gravel and grits. "Speak like a lady," mother would advise. "Lower your voice." But Chanel's speaking voice was loud by nature. Her mother considered her daughter's harsh tones a liability; but once she began to sing—sing to God—the harshness turned lyrical.

Chanel's church singing, she came to realize, made her feel that God was on her side. God knew, she needed someone like God to stand up to Georgia. Her powerhouse voice gave her some confidence too. Maybe she never made it big, but she felt that was coming. Blues were back. She had stuck to her guns and it was about to pay off . . . beyond the blues bars, blues clubs, blues festivals. She was about to become more than a cult figure. And she was, finally, sober. People were tired of lip-synched crap. They wanted the real deal . . .

But what Chanel most wanted right now was a nap, except there was no time once she got to the mid-city motel—to hell with those inflated Beverly Hills prices. And staying with Georgia was out of the question. She could not be with her mother at close quarters for any length of time, and besides, she might want company later. For now, though, she had to go over to Beverly Hills in a hurry—Beverly Flats, as she called them, because that was the part of the city, the least expensive part, where her mother lived. She had told Georgia she would arrive by two and it was already three, and now she was in a special hurry because her Marisa would be there.

"Marisa's not here," said Georgia, looking up from her French provincial desk. "I was hoping she'd be with you. Come give your mother a kiss."

Chanel dutifully leaned over and pecked Georgia on the cheek. Georgia remained silent—no hugs; even after a year of separation, no display of emotion. Georgia seemed calm. Her wig, with its soft waves and reddish highlights, flattered her complexion. *Everything* flattered Georgia's complexion, Chanel had to admit. The lady did look great. The shop looked great and it smelled like heaven. Live doves flying around gilded cages. Tall stalks of gladioli and lilies. The little gay guy, Stephen, waiting on Georgia like she was the mother of God.

"You look good, Mother," said Chanel, lighting a cigarillo.

"Thank you, darling," Georgia responded, not returning the compliment. How could she when Chanel was in that vulgar outfit? And she was tempted to say something about her daughter's smoking habit. But why start up? Peace was the strategy of the day.

"Did you get the videotape I sent you?" asked Chanel.

"Which one was that, darling?"

"I only sent you *one*. The documentary on women and the blues. I sing a song over the credits."

"Oh, I'll have to look at it. With all these calls lately from agents and casting directors I've barely had time for the store."

"Something come through?" Knowing it hadn't.

"It's more a question of choosing what's right for me. It's the same problem I've always had. My demand for quality, the lack of decent writing. I have my standards."

"Phone call, Miss Georgia," Stephen announced on the intercom. "Line one."

Georgia picked up the receiver. "Marisa? You sound like you're a thousand miles away."

"I am. I'm on the plane. I missed the first flight but caught another. Mom there?"

"We're both here, sugar. How could you have missed your flight?"
"Bad dreams but good news. Can't wait to tell you."

After the plane had lifted off, cutting through a curtain of rain before
soaring into sunlight, Marisa had closed her eyes and fallen into another dream . . .

She was walking through an unnamed European country, a village,
where she knew no one. She couldn't understand the language,
couldn't make herself understood. Everyone kept pointing toward
the town square. There was a carnival, or a circus. March music, tubas
and glockenspiels. There were clowns and midgets and acrobats.
They thought she was an acrobat. She found herself in leotards
climbing a ladder, walking a tightrope. She wasn't afraid. She could
dance on the tightrope. She could stand on her head. The crowd
cheered from below. Someone started screaming. It was one of the
midgets. He screamed that he was her father, he had the features of a
small and cruel little boy. His blotched skin was peeling from his
face. He screamed that she belonged to him, that all the profits from
her talent were his and his alone. Marisa fell from the tightrope—and
woke up.

She looked out the window and saw a layer of soft white clouds.
Why did she keep seeing herself at a circus? Why in the world was
her father a little boy? She wished she had brought Nelson Clay
along so she could describe the dream to him. After only a few hours,
she already found herself missing him. Strange. Interesting.

Part of her had fought the idea of this trip. Grandmama had, in
effect, ordered the meeting as though Grandmama had the divine
right. Georgia had said it was time to put bad feelings behind them,
time to consider what was right for everyone—by which she meant
what was right for Marisa. Seldom were mother and grandmother
united about anything, especially things about her. When they joined
forces, she pretty much crumbled. She considered that a weakness, a
weakness she'd tried to overcome when she moved to New York.
Still, it was her birthday, and she wanted to be with her family, crazy
as it was. Truth was, of course, she loved both women, loved looking
at them, imitating them, comparing them, and missed them so that
the pain in her heart after a year's absence could no longer be cov-

ered by a lot of derisive laughter or lengthy entries in her journals. No matter what, she wanted to make them proud of her.

She was also curious about her mother's therapy. Who would have thought such a thing even possible? Who would have thought Chanel —stubborn, headstrong, ain't-no-one-gonna-tell-me-how-to-live-my-life Chanel—could ever stop getting high? Now a review she had sent from Chicago said she was singing better than ever. The *review* said it, not Mama.

And Georgia made it sound like things were opening up for her in L.A. She was going to be in a movie, or a TV show, something big. Marisa, who had heard it before, tried to believe it. Hey, these were gifted women, her mother and grandmother, held back through no fault of their own, especially Georgia, born too soon into a society of open racism. Who could deny it? They deserved better.

She called Georgia now from the plane phone, telling her she'd be arriving late. Chanel was already there. Marisa had to smile, picturing the two women preening their feathers, maybe already going at each other. She had to congratulate herself that she had somehow managed to keep both of them from coming to New York. She had even discouraged phone calls, not wanting to hear one bad-mouth the other. That had been their way—Georgia hinting at secrets Chanel was keeping from her daughter, Chanel suggesting Georgia had a mysterious early life that one day Marisa would understand. And meanwhile their pasts were hopelessly muddled in Marisa's mind.

Much of the mystery had to do with men, white men and black men, Europeans and Americans, men in and out of the movie and music business. Marisa had called some "uncle," others by their first names. None were ever "father." Well, they were part of the mess Marisa had left behind, nothing she even wanted to think about. Daydreaming over Palm Springs and clear skies, she thought about modeling for Joan Winfrey, telling her dreams to Nelson Clay . . .

. . . Smog smacked her in her face. Los Angeles International. Inglewood, California. A cigar-smoking cabbie from the Ukraine, a traffic jam on the San Diego Freeway, too much time to think where she was going. And she started feeling like a little girl again. Dirty air burned her eyes, memories burned her brain, and tears, all unaccountably, ran down her cheeks.

*   *   *

The first remark, after many hugs and kisses, was Georgia's about Marisa's hairdo. "It's strange."

"I like it," said Chanel defiantly. "You look just fine, baby."

Marisa wore cut-off jeans marked by a series of calculated rips complemented by a flowery blouse of Chinese silk. Half-funky, half-elegant. Chanel liked the funk; Georgia liked the elegance, what little she detected in her granddaughter's get-up.

"Well, girl," said Chanel, "turn around so we can get a *good* look at you. Oh Lord . . . my child is thin as a rail."

"You can never be too thin," Georgia said. "You look wonderful, dear. Come give me another kiss. Happy birthday, darling."

"Happy birthday, baby," from Chanel.

They were in the patio garden of Passion Flowers. It was late afternoon, the day still warm, the air perfumed; from inside the chattering of customers, the occasional whir of the electronic cash register.

"You gals are looking good," Marisa told them. "Healthy living for everyone, I guess."

Georgia broke the ice. "You said you had good news, honey."

"It can wait," said Marisa, "I'm still coming down from the plane trip. Besides, you sound like you want to say something first."

"I do, I do. Your mother and I have been talking. We're concerned about you, darling. That's why I wanted everyone together today. We have a problem—or rather a challenge—and we need to approach it as a family." Marisa kept a straight face. "Ever since you were a little child you've been special. You were the first in the class to read, you wrote beautifully, your penmanship, your vocabulary—"

"And when it came to running," added Chanel, "you kicked ass. Even whupped the boys. No one could catch my Marisa. Child, you were *lightning*."

Georgia cleared her throat, not liking the interruption. Chanel sat there, barely able to endure Georgia's monologue, trying to keep herself in check. And Marisa sensed her mother's restraint, while she noted that Chanel had gained weight but that her eyes were clear. Maybe Mama really had stopped getting high.

"My Marisa's only got better," Georgia continued, sounding like someone on the old Ralph Edwards "This Is Your Life." "My Marisa went to college and did her grandmother proud. She became the first Faith to do so. And a fine school too—Barnsdale College. She won a scholarship, this brilliant granddaughter of mine. She joined the drama club, she performed in the school musicals—"

"All *right*, Mother," Chanel broke in. "We get the point."

"Please don't interrupt. When Marisa moved to New York after college I tried to explain to her—"

"She don't wanna hear 'bout that," said Chanel, affecting more accent and dialect than was natural to her, mostly to offset Georgia's precise delivery.

"I'm in the midst of an important thought," Georgia declared.

"You ain't on no stage, you know," Chanel snapped back. "You sittin' right here in front of us. Ain't no casting directors 'round here. Ain't no cameras. Just your po' black kinfolk."

"I wasn't happy when you decided to go to New York," said Georgia, turning to Marisa, ignoring Chanel. "I wanted you here in Los Angeles—"

"She hates L.A.," Chanel broke in again. "Hates it worse than I do. Filled with phonies, filled with—"

"Opportunities. That's the point, Marisa. And that's a point that I'd think even you would understand by now, Chanel."

"I understand my daughter, that's one goddamn thing I do understand. You have no idea what this girl is all about. You lived in some fucked-up fantasy world—"

"I have told you before, I will not tolerate vulgarity—"

"Tough shit."

"*Mama*," said Marisa, falling into her old role of reluctant peacemaker.

Chanel tried to remember the purpose of the get-together—helping Marisa.

"I got news for both of you," Marisa finally announced. "I have an agent."

"A theatrical agent?" asked Georgia.

"A modeling agent."

"What sort of modeling?"

"I'm not sure, I think high fashion."

"I suggested that to you years ago," said Georgia. "Modeling was important to me. It saved my life."

"We're not talking about your life, Mother, we're talking about Marisa. I'm not sure whether modeling messed you up more than it helped. But that's history. If modeling helps get my baby's name and face out there, then modeling's a good thing."

"This woman," said Marisa, "this Joan Winfrey wants to put me to work right away."

"I'd like to talk to her," said Georgia.

"Now why is that?" Chanel said.

"I have something of a reputation among fashion photographers—"

"Mother," said Chanel, "you're thinking of twenty, thirty years ago. You're living in a fantasy . . ."

"Don't talk to me about fantasies. I've never known anyone who's been more in a fantasy world than you—fogging your brain with that dope . . ."

"Now *you're* doing it, " Marisa told her grandmother.

"Don't matter none," said Chanel. "I told my therapist, I said to her, 'You wait, I know my mother, she's going to throw it all up in my face just the way she always does.' I told the folks at my AA meeting it's going to be hard seeing the old lady again, hearing the same old crap. It's gonna make me wanna go out there and buy some blow, do whatever to free up my mind, but I know it ain't no freedom—"

"I have *no* idea what you're talking about," said Georgia.

"Ain't surprised," said Chanel. "We talk different languages."

"We're supposed to be talking about Marisa, not you. Is it possible for you to go five minutes without talking about yourself?"

"*Stop it!*" cried Marisa. "*Both of you just stop* it!"

The older women realized Marisa was right. Things were getting out of hand; they needed to adjourn, take a break, collect their cool.

"Stephen will be preparing your birthday dinner tonight," Georgia said. "Eight o'clock."

"Come back to the motel with Mama," Chanel said.

"She'll be more comfortable at my place," Georgia quickly put in. "She'll have her own bedroom . . . you're welcome too, Chanel."

"Won't work," Chanel encountered. "We need our own space. We'll be better off at the motel."

"I'll leave my bag here," said Marisa. "I just want to take a walk."

"I'll walk with you," offered her mother.

"I need to be alone, Mama. Honestly. It's what you just said about space. I'll see y'all at dinner." *If I survive that long. Georgia and Chanel . . . they ought to take it on the road.*

Aside from the Rodeo Drive shopping district, Beverly Hills was no place for walkers. Marisa didn't mind being alone, didn't care that she was the only pedestrian on Burton Way as cars zipped by—jeeps and stretch limos, Hondas and catering vans. The loneliness of the L.A. streets offered relief. Marisa was bone tired, drained by the coast-to-coast flight, Georgia vs. Chanel. Being with the two had her unnerved; she wondered whether it would be the better part of wisdom to go back to the airport and catch the first plane out. No apologies, no calls, just fly away. There was no breeze around here, the air thick with car exhaust. She crossed over to Third Street and found herself standing before a huge shopping mall. At one end the fins of a fifties Cadillac poked through the roof of the Hard Rock Cafe. Trendy America. Inside, though, at least it was air-conditioned and the place might take her mind off her family.

No such luck. Strolling through Bullock's department store, roaming around Banana Republic, window-shopping at Benetton, she couldn't stop thinking about them. The tension between Chanel and Georgia was so great they couldn't concentrate on her good news. Still, they meant well, they wanted to help, she told herself. At Waldenbooks she stopped to leaf through magazines, and in Vogue and Billboard, in Essence and Ebony and People and Cosmopolitan all she seemed to see were pictures of young black women in show business—Vanessa Williams, Anita Baker, Robin Givens, Karyn White, Shanice, Tracie Spencer, Janet Jackson, Jody Watley, Whitney Houston, Jasmine Guy, Anne Marie Johnson—one more gorgeous and successful than the other. She felt glad for them, and also, face it, she felt jealous. They had record deals, movie roles. Why was it taking her so long? Why did she have to put up with the squabbling of her mother and grandmother?

All right, no movie contacts, no record deals, but at least there was this modeling business. She looked at the models in Elle. Aloof, distant, so damned chic. She had to laugh. It was funny—tomboy rough-it-up-with-the-boys Marisa, now a model of quiet dignity on the roster of the Joan Winfrey Agency. Modeling was flying high and getting by on physical appearance. She had never wanted that, never trusted it, knew it had nothing to do with her. But if modeling was the way in, so be it.

Putting down Elle, she noticed Excel, a magazine for black men. The headline read: "Notable Professionals." Flipping pages, she soon saw where her instincts were leading: to a small photo and short paragraph on Dr. Nelson Clay. His eyes were looking straight at her. "Associate Director of the Geriatric Psychiatric Clinic of Beth Israel Hospital in Newark," read the text. "Also enjoys a thriving practice in Manhattan." He hadn't told her that he dealt with problems of the elderly. The idea was sweet, helping old people. "Super-successful," the magazine called him. Why? A six-figure salary? His picture in a magazine? Who the hell was she to be critical. Where was *she*?

That night she hugged her mother and grandmother as though she'd never see them again. She needed them, she couldn't stand them. But God, they looked beautiful—Georgia in a soft peach dress, Chanel in loud pink. Grandmama's pastel apartment was filled with white irises, orange freesia, yellow astromeria, fragrant statice. Stephen served an endive-arugula salad, glazed carrots and mushroom quiche. Georgia drank a single glass of champagne; Chanel stayed off it. Marisa didn't drink, hardly ate, feeling like a little girl all over again. She told them both how much she loved them, how much they meant to her. She let them call her adorable. As a little girl she had no faults; she had disappointed no one. She wanted it always this way, the three of them together, the Faith family, Georgia at the head of the table, Marisa on one side, Chanel on the other.

"Now," said Grandmama after Stephen brought the strawberry tarts and served boysenberry tea, "we're feeling relaxed. We see there's a way for us to work together for Marisa."

"I'm not sure—" Chanel began before Georgia spoke over her.

"I'm sure we agree, your mother and I, that we have to make a plan. Now that you have a modeling agent—"

"Do we have to talk about careers?" asked Marisa.

"Can't you see that you're bothering the girl?" Chanel said.

"We can't avoid the subject any longer. Marisa won't listen to me, and she won't listen to you, Chanel, but maybe she'll listen to the *two* of us if we speak as one."

"Let's just be together," said Marisa. "Please?"

"This agent is not just going to wave a wand," said Grandmama, "and make it all come true for you, darling. It doesn't work that way. That's what I've been trying to tell you. It never comes as easy as we want it to. Your Mama can tell you that."

"Your Mama's doing right well for herself," Chanel spoke up. "Nothing to apologize for. *Especially* to my mother."

"You're starting in again," said Georgia.

"Oh God," moaned Marisa. "Stop it, please just stop it. Both of you."

"We're talking about your future, honey," said Georgia. "We're talking about people here in Hollywood who know me—and respect me, people willing to help you. You need contacts. People at William Morris, ICM, Creative Artists Agency. They're *here*, they call me. They come into my shop and have tea and—"

"And fuck you in the back room if you think it'll get you something."

Georgia slapped Chanel across the face. The smack was hard, the shock was worse. Chanel was out of her seat and about to slap Georgia back when Marisa caught her arm.

"*No*, goddamn it . . ." And she was crying like a little girl as she ran out the door. Chanel followed her.

"Sometimes," Georgia said to Stephen, who had come from the kitchen, "I don't think those two are my flesh and blood. Sometimes I feel as though I have no family."

Stephen kept silent, watching Georgia close her eyes. He knew her moods, how they seemed to come from far back in the deep recesses of her mind. "Take a deep breath and try to relax," he told her.

"Yes," she said. "I must relax. If you'd be kind enough to bring me my coffee, Stephen, I'd be much obliged. And please bring me my photo albums. It always relaxes me to look at my photos . . ."

There were five messages on Marisa's answering machine:

"Just tried to reach you in California," said the voice of Joan Winfrey, "and your mother or grandmother, I'm not sure who, said you were on your way back. Please call me immediately. I think we have an assignment." . . . "Hello, Marisa," said Nelson Clay. "Are you back? If so I'd like to hear from you, hear about your trip." . . . "I know she got my baby upset," Chanel said into the machine, "but don't you worry. I want to come out to New York and talk to you about it. My therapist says it's something I need to do. I do want to make the trip, baby." . . . "Your mother is impossible,"said Georgia in quietly dramatic tones. "I try to be patient and I suppose I could be better at it. But she's a trying woman. You understand, Marisa, you've always been an understanding child. Please call me. I don't like these machines. I don't like speaking into a machine. But I am sorry your birthday was spoiled. I intend to make it up to you, sweetheart." . . .

"Do you recognize this voice out of your past? It's Jason. Jason Solomon. Back from Italy, back from the Venice Film Festival, back from falling in the damned canal and almost drowning, back from hustling my latest project. I've come to New York for a special occasion and I want to share it. How long has it been since I've seen you, Risa? Two, three years? Grandpa Sol gave me your number. He got it from your grandmother. Just one big happy family, just like the old days. In fact Sol's the reason I'm here. They're throwing a wild pub party for his new novel—can you believe this is his tenth?—and he insisted I come. Should be something. They've rented out half of Yankee Stadium because the novel's about baseball, which should be right down your alley, you always could throw a ball better than me. Anyway, it's tomorrow night, Tuesday, and I'm at the Plaza and if you don't call me I'll be crushed and you can't live with that kind of guilt, right?"

Marisa had to smile. Jason always had that effect on her. Last she heard he was living in New Mexico. Jason was someone, like herself, about whom people had these great expectations. They shared common pressures.

"Jason, it's Marisa."

"My God, you're calling me."

"Why so shocked?"

"Last time you saw me I was tripping, I was afraid I'd turned you off forever."

"Forever is beyond me. Anyway, I'm no longer angry."

"Things have changed, Risa. I've changed. I have a documentary about to hit the art-movie house circuit. Can you believe it?"

"Great," she said.

"What's taken you so long to get famous?"

"You sound like Georgia and Chanel . . ."

"Who are, I presume, in good health."

"Physically yes, mentally no."

"They haven't changed?"

"I'm not sure anyone really changes."

"I told you, *I've* changed. You'll see. You'll see my documentary. It's about diners."

"*Diners?*"

"Diners from the thirties, forties and fifties—roadside diners, all along the back roads and big cities of New Jersey and Pennsylvania, diners in the shape of railway cars, old White Tower diners in Illinois, diners with names like Oink's and Curley's, Little Nell's and Stella's and Chappy's. They have real personalities, they practically talk to the camera. When I sit in them stories start coming to me. Meet me at the Empire Diner tomorrow night for dinner. We'll grab the blue plate special and go from there to Sol's party."

"I better catch up with you at the party."

"You've got a dinner date?"

"A meeting that might run late."

"Sounds important."

"Terribly, terribly important," she said with a mock accent.

"Okay then, meet me at home plate."

She did not call back Nelson Clay right away. She wondered why. She wanted to see him again. But he was a psychiatrist, and right now, so soon after her trip, psychiatry wasn't what she wanted. For sure she didn't want to think about Georgia and Chanel, much less analyze her relationships with them. Forget them, take a breather. The pain was too fresh. Jason was just what the doctor ordered—an old friend who understood. Her first man too . . . you never forget.

She called back Joan Winfrey who told her, "Tomorrow afternoon, meet me at four."

Thank God she hadn't lost interest.

Marisa asked about the assignment but Joan said she didn't have time to explain. Marisa also wondered if Nelson had said anything to Winfrey. Interesting, too, was Winfrey's request to see her not in the office but at her brownstone. The whole situation over on Tenth Street was pretty interesting. But all that was tomorrow. Now if she could just get through tonight without dreaming about Mama or Grandmama . . .

It had always been Marisa in the middle, which made her crazy but also reassured her. This, after all, was how her family worked, how they related. Tempestuous ups and downs, highs and lows. She'd hoped they'd be excited by her news, but they'd been too busy going at each other. She was the excuse, but mostly it was about themselves. Which was why she did what she had to do—get the hell out of there, fly home, turn on the answering machine, stick in a pair of earplugs—the city was screaming with sirens—and fight for a night's sleep.

The sleep was deep, lasting until noon. Her dreams, whatever they were, escaped her. She was glad of that. Her body felt heavy and she decided to go to the gym, sweat out some of the California juices.

The gym was a converted loft on lower Broadway with a variety of people in and out of shape, fat and thin, young and middle-aged. No designer leotards for Marisa, she wore baggy sweatpants, an oversized sweatshirt with "Gumby for President" written over an image of the never-say-die green Claymation character. Her hair was gathered up beneath a black kerchief. She wanted to look unappealing, avoid the men who thought the place was a meat market for their pleasure. Creeps. At the same time she couldn't help but be aware of the surrounding body heat, even if the swaggering hunks busting out of their tank tops turned her off.

She mounted the high-tech stair-climbing machine, set it in motion and started pumping. It didn't take long for her legs to begin aching and she thought about lowering the level but hung on. She wanted to sweat, wanted to relieve the pressure. Raising the level, pushing harder, her drive kicked in. She kept on, fought through the pain, with people waiting in line to use this Stairmaster. So here, take it, I'm through, sweat pouring. A half-hour was enough.

She showered and dressed in an outfit likely to surprise Joan Winfrey but one which should play well at Sol Solomon's party: cut-off jeans, a Brooklyn Dodgers T-shirt and New York Yankees baseball cap flipped around so the visor grazed her neck.

She sauntered up Broadway—she wasn't due at Winfrey's for another ninety minutes—sat at a table outside an espresso bar, nibbled on a tuna-stuffed croissant, watched the people pass by.

By the time she arrived at Joan Winfrey's she had centered herself to a reasonable calm—the exercise, the light lunch, the long walk. She was coping again, she felt, with this monster city of monster ambitions.

"It's uncanny," said the agent as Marisa walked through the door.

"What do you mean?"

"Did you talk to anyone in my office?"

"No."

Joan shook her head. "Then you're psychic."

"I don't get it—"

"The NFL, NHL, NBA and major league baseball have hired an ad agency to sell team-labeled merchandise to women. The men's business has been huge, but they've overlooked women—what else is new? Now they're targeting a female market and they want a hip but healthy look. And that's you, Marisa. You're a sexy tomboy who looks like she can play ball with the big boys and doesn't mind mixing it up. I'm putting you on the cover of the catalogue and insisting you be overpaid for a first-time model. I have a contract giving us your representation. I want you to take it home and look it over. Now slip on that Boston Bruins jersey. You can change here."

Marisa went to the bathroom and emerged in the red overblouse. As an assistant snapped Polaroids, Marisa mocked the pose of a hockey fan.

"Marvelous," Joan declared.

The more Marisa cut up, the more huzzahs from Joan and the assistant. In an orange Mets cap tilted over her eyebrows, in a black-and-silver Raiders sweater, in purple Lakers sweatpants she jeered and cheered on the home team—just the look Winfrey wanted.

"You're going to pay me to look the fool?" said Marisa, laughing.

"Foolish, my eye, lady. You've got something most models would kill for. I suggest we celebrate your success over dinner, I know just the place—"

"I'm sorry, Joan, but, believe it or not, I'm off to Yankee Stadium."

"You're going to a ball game?"

"A book party. Ever hear of Sol Solomon?"

"Of course."

"Well, this is his big night, and I'm sort of part of it, from way back . . ."

Marisa spotted Sol standing at second base surrounded by reporters. He had gotten older—that was the first thing she noticed. Hard to believe, but he was in his seventies. His hair was white but still thick, his eyebrows still bushy. He had gained weight but carried it well. Dressed in a blazer, a print shirt and white trousers, he looked more Palm Springs than Manhattan, but what the hell. She began to approach him but a flock of journalists blocked her way, so she went looking for Jason.

The party was popping. The grandstands were dark and eerily empty; all was quiet except for the infield area that was brightly lit and covered with a tarpaulin to protect the surface. Several hundred people milled about, some holding pennants with the title of Sol's novel, *Hit and Run.*

"It's a whodunit with a pennant race," Sol was saying. "I set it back in the fifties when the Giants were at the Polo Grounds and the Dodgers in Ebbets Field because that's when I came home. In the forties I was out in Hollywood and I hated it—I still do. I had to get back to Flatbush to find my roots and the people and stories I know the best."

"Haven't you been living in Hollywood for the past twenty years?" asked a reporter.

"I moved back after my books started selling. But that was later—in the sixties, seventies."

"Now they say your books have stopped selling," said the same reporter.

"This is his best book since *Kings and Con Men*," declared a publicist. "He's found the old fire—"

"That's okay, honey," said Sol. "Actually, the man has a point. I'm just an old-fashioned storyteller. No message, no special effects. Hey, I don't even type, I talk my books out loud, dictate them. For whatever they're worth, my stories are pretty much my life. I stayed too long in California. Anyway, I'm seventy-five and I'm back in Brooklyn. I got a place looking across the river over there in Brooklyn Heights and I told my publisher the least he could do was rebuild Ebbets Field for this party. No respectable Dodger fan should be caught dead in Yankee Stadium, but they said be a good sport, go up to the enemy stadium, so here I am and damned glad to be here . . ."

"I see you really dressed for the occasion."

Marisa turned.

"Jason!"

They met at the shortstop position.

"You look terrific, Risa."

"Thank you, sir. Now where's my hug?"

He hugged her, kissed her and hugged her again, harder. "I've missed you, Risa," he said.

"Missed you too. Hey, have you turned into a Yuppie?"

Jason was wearing a light olive suit and white shirt buttoned to the top with no tie. He wasn't quite as tall as Marisa. His features, with all his freckles, were attractive—slender mouth, strong chin. In contrast to the last time she saw him, his curly red hair was fashionably cut. Last time he hadn't quite grown out of his Beverly Hills renegade hippie mode. But under the lights at Yankee Stadium, holding a glass of white wine and talking about making "good movies, not horseshit," his energy seemed unchanged. He was still going a million miles an hour.

"Still getting high?" she asked.

"Just a little grass, but only for purposes of lewd sex."

Marisa laughed. "You don't look too lewd to me. Sorry, I didn't mean to insult you."

"What about your look?" he asked, flipping around her baseball cap so the visor faced front. "What's this all about?"

"I'm not sure, I think I'm a model."

"Risa, you're an actress, a singer."

"I'm also broke. Look, this Joan Winfrey Agency is a great chance to make some money."

"I understand, last year I cut myself off from Sol. We had a blow-out."

"What about your inheritance?"

"Wasn't that much . . . Have you said hi to the old man?"

"Tried but couldn't get through his handlers."

It took a while to elbow through the crowd but they managed.

"Gramps," shouted Jason. "You got a fan here. First female major leaguer. Hey, she pitches topless. Remember Risa?"

"My God! Look at her! She's gorgeous, an absolute doll, the spitting image of her grandmother. And with a Dodgers shirt, no less."

Sol kissed her and held her hand but before he could ask questions the publicist pulled him away.

"Let's go," Jason urged Marisa. "The old man's too excited to concentrate on anything for more than ten seconds anyway."

In the cab downtown he said, "I'm not crazy about the idea of you as a cover girl, Risa, but in any case you need a good lawyer to go over the deal with Winfrey. I'm going to call my lawyer and tell him to help you. You'll do this modeling for a couple of months and then we'll find an acting job for you."

"Or I'll find modeling work for you. I hear Playgirl's doing a whole spread on flaming red pubic hair."

"You remember."

"An image burned in my brain."

"Jewish men don't get much call for their bods. We're supposed to live by our wits."

At the Empire Diner they talked till three A.M. It had been a long time since Jason had been able to open up, to speak unguardedly to anyone, much less a woman. For Marisa, it felt reassuring to be back with her childhood pal. Jason was thinking of taking the plunge and opening an office in New York to produce his documentaries. "Santa Fe," he said, "is beautiful, but it's sort of a playground. New York is real. If you've got the guts to try to hack it here, Risa, maybe I do too."

Between the two old friends there was still a sexual chemistry. After all, they had been lovers before Marisa backed off, deciding her feelings for Jason were more familial than romantic. He had protested but was smart enough not to risk their friendship. Fact was, he wanted Risa any way he could have her. And hehad never given up hope.

*   *   *

Nelson Clay was listening to her.

"You need to talk more," she told him. "When you don't talk I talk too much."

"Sorry. It's how I make my living." He smiled when he said it.

They were walking through an outdoor art show in the Village. Most of the stuff was pretty bad—seascapes, waiflike kids with big eyes, imitation Monets and Renoirs.

"What I'd really like to see," Marisa said, "is Elvis on purple velvet."

She meant it. She liked Elvis. She liked the sneer, the hair, the movable parts. She realized his rhythms were borrowed from blacks, but that just made him more appealing. The bad white boy.

Nelson Clay, on the other hand, was a million miles away from Elvis and rock 'n' roll. He wore old corduroy trousers and a red flannel shirt, last year's tennis shoes and wire-rim glasses like Geppetto, Pinocchio's father. He scrutinized Marisa carefully—her words, her appearances—but never appeared to be judging.

"What about the place across the street?" he asked.

He pointed to a small Santa Fe-style cafe covered with washed-out pastels and stuffed coyotes. She thought of Jason.

"I like it," said Marisa. "Let's eat."

As he ordered an omelette, she noticed his cap was a little frayed, though it sat on his head at a jaunty angle. She was interested in what was inside that head. Whether out of professional or personal interest, she knew he was going to ask about her trip. He did.

A few minutes later, sipping on freshly squeezed orange juice, she began explaining. No easy thing. How far back should she go? She decided for now she'd give him the bare bones. She described the long-standing tension between her mother and grandmother, but after a few minutes she felt drained.

"Triangles are a tricky business," he said.

"I guess. What I know is, they both drive me crazy."

"They drive you—that's pretty clear. Never mind, eat your waffles, they're getting cold."

"Each one is a star in her own right. Or thinks she is."

"And you're the star in the middle."

"Only to *them*—not to the rest of the world."

"They *are* your world."

"Oh, come on."

"See what happens when I start talking? You get cranky. I should know better. Besides, show business families are outside my field of expertise."

"Unlike geriatric psychiatry? Don't be so sure."

"Did I tell you about that?"

"The article in Excel did. Why old folks?"

"They have special needs."

"Do you have special parents?"

"Not so fast." He smiled. "No turning the tables on me."

"Just trying to get to know you."

"We were talking about your trip to Los Angeles. It sounded . . . frustrating."

"It was."

"Frustration in the arts, it's legendary. Always trying to break down doors. In your grandmother's time, your mother's time, now yours . . . I admire your courage."

"Is that what you call it?"

"I think that's what it is."

"Thanks. That makes me feel better about tomorrow."

"What's tomorrow?"

"My first modeling gig."

"Good. We'll celebrate afterward. Don't shake your head. I won't take no for an answer."

Marisa wasn't crazy about the idea of modeling official team apparel, although she did like the idea of the paycheck. A sports fan, she often watched football on television but found the cheerleaders pathetic. As for the L.A. Laker Girls, the group that spawned rock star Paula Abdul, they were more like the old Playboy bunnies.

When she showed up at the modeling agency, Joan Winfrey assured her sex wasn't the idea of the morning's shoot at all.

"We're shooting for *women*," she said, "not men. Today's going to be fun. I'm taking you over to the studio myself. You'll love Bing."

* * *

"My God!" said Bing Radison, a short blond man in his twenties with dancing blue eyes, a thin mustache and ponytail. "You look so much like a young Georgia Faith."

"That makes sense," said Marisa, "since she's my grandmother."

"*Get outta here*," exclaimed the photographer, who had a light meter around his neck and red velvet monogrammed slippers on his feet.

"Who's Georgia Faith?" asked Joan.

"Pu-leeze," Bing said. "You mean you never saw the photographs of Georgia Faith? They were shot by my great-uncle Noel Radison. They were shot in Rome, weren't they, honey?"

"I believe so," said Marisa, both impressed and annoyed that Georgia, even three thousand miles away, was the center of attention at her first modeling job.

"Of course they were shot in Rome," Bing continued. "Remember the one of Georgia in Trastevere? She was wearing this wonderful wide-brimmed hat. She was pointing to the church of Santa Maria, her arms extended so . . ." He struck the pose. "I have the photograph inside. It's in Gobbi's book. Let me show you."

"Shouldn't we think about getting started?" asked Joan.

"This is too exciting," Bing said. "I want Marisa to sign the photograph for me."

"That's a bit strange . . ."

"My dear, you're a link to history, the history of classic fashion photography—"

"Grandmama was never a model."

"Only once—for Uncle Noel. Which makes her even more special. With the right direction, she *could* have been one of the great models of her time. Anyway, that's what Uncle Noel always said and I believe him. For that matter she could have been *the* actress of her time. God, her work in *Yesterday's Love* should have been nominated for an Oscar. When was that—'51 or '52? And then the TV sitcoms. That was a little sad, wasn't it? But that face, that *face* was so exquisite. She's gotten even more beautiful. Will she be doing any more television? When you speak to her tell her she has a fan—thousands of fans —in New York."

Marisa laughed again. "She knows," she says. "She tells me all the time. But tell me more about her and your uncle."

"We need to get going," Joan urged.

"Uncle Noel was my role model even though he died when I was young. I loved him very much. I inherited his taste. Now I see Georgia's face in your face, and your face is exciting me, it's giving me *chills*. You're more than I could have hoped for. Joan's right, you're perfect for this look. But when we're through with the athletic stuff, I want you for myself—my time, my expense. I want to experiment, I want to make art with you, Marisa."

"Commerce first," said Joan. "Then art."

"You'll melt the lens," Bing Radison said, focusing on Marisa with his naked eye. "You'll *burn* it."

At least the lights were hot enough to burn, Marisa thought. Many of the outfits were winterweight—pullovers and sweaters, thick cotton sweatshirts and sweatpants, each emblazoned with team logos. Bing pulled her through the discomfort and kept her in the mood. He joked and cajoled and charmed. He became the cheerleader, Marisa the fan. He literally cheered her on, at one point kicking off his red velvet slippers.

"Don't think about how you look," he urged, "just let your body lead the way. Get loose, get down!"

She squatted, she twirled, she twisted and jumped, she leaned over and back and found herself playing with the camera like it was an old friend. Surely Bing felt like an old friend.

"What will Grandma think of this?" he wanted to know.

"She's not exactly a sports fan."

"Neither am I, honey," said Bing. "But this isn't about sports. Not anymore. This is about *you* . . ."

"Tell me," said Bing when the session was over, "tell me about your mother."

"Don't tell me you're a Chanel Faith fan too."

"I'm afraid I'm tone deaf, I don't follow music. But I've read she's had her problems, poor thing."

"We all do."

"It hasn't been easy for you, I realize," he said.

Marisa wasn't anxious to open up. The shoot had gone well. Bing Radison was a skilled high-energy photographer; he'd guided her through what could have been an ordeal. On the other hand, she saw him as another queen who reveled in the esoterica of forties nostalgia.

"Can you leave Marisa with me for a while?" Bing asked Joan.

"We have business back at the office," said the agency owner. "Contracts to sign."

"I want to photograph you," Bing Radison whispered to Marisa, "in ways you can't possibly imagine. I can help you, I can put you places where you've never been before. Believe me, honey."

Marisa was pleased.

"It was more fun than I thought it'd be," she admitted to Jason on the phone. He'd gone back to New Mexico, still gearing up to move to New York without having quite made the decision.

"My lawyer help you with the contract?"

"He was great. I actually have enough money to live for a couple of months."

"And you weren't naked?"

"Covered from head to toe. The photographer was fabulous. It was all sort of tongue-in-cheek for him."

"What's next? How long do you have to be a model?"

"Winfrey's hustling me hard. She's looking for an Essence cover. And Bing Radison—he's the photographer—seems to have some ideas of his own."

"I have an idea too. For a movie—"

"Hold it till next time, Jason. Another call's coming in."

Marisa clicked off and on.

"Are we celebrating?" asked Nelson Clay.

"Looks good," said Marisa, "looks like I'm at least a working girl."

"Save the details for dinner. I want to hear all about it . . ."

The sushi bar off Union Square was done in pinks and blond wood. The place was low-key, crowded with young professionals gossiping over saki. The stereo system played Soul II Soul, soul-styled English funk.

"So you liked the work?" Nelson asked after they sat down.

"More than I thought I would."

"Good. Joan must be pleased too."

"Maybe too pleased."

"What do you mean?"

"I think she's fallen for me."

"Joan?"

"I keep putting her off politely. But I'm uncomfortable. She's persistent. I don't want to hurt her, I don't want to mislead, but at this point I don't want to lose her."

"Look, whatever feelings she might have for you, Joan's a savvy business woman. If you didn't have what it takes professionally, she wouldn't be interested."

"I hope you're right. You know better than I that things aren't always what they seem. Take the photographer. He was exciting, seemed to be excited about me. But he wasn't really seeing *me*. He was seeing my grandmother."

"I don't understand."

Marisa explained Bing Radison's fascination with Georgia.

"Has this happened often?"

"Finding fans of Georgia and Chanel?"

"Having people confuse you with them."

"They say my singing voice is like my mother's."

"And your acting style is like your grandmother's?"

"Who knows?"

"But you don't see them as gifts of inheritance."

"I guess not."

"Where do they stop and you start—isn't that the question?"

"Who knows what the hell the question is."

"Forgive me, Marisa, but it seems to me you're awfully hard on yourself. Look, you've had a good day. Enjoy it for what it is. For yourself. Never mind Mother and Grandmother for a minute. . . . Why don't we go back over to my place? I'd like to show it to you."

She was ready.

His Tenth Street brownstone was very much lived in. There were prints and paintings, pieces of African sculpture, books and journals and scattered papers, piles of magazines, worn Persian rugs, comfortable well-used armchairs, altogether a relaxed and informal feeling.

There were also books on men's issues—male bonding, the men's movement, *Growing Old As a Male in America*, *The African-American Male: A Retrospective in History*.

"Serious stuff," said Marisa, looking over the books.

"I guess I'm interested in people trying to define themselves. No one's doing too good a job of it, or so it seems."

"Not even you?"

"I'm not a husband or a father maybe I have an easier time."

"But with all these books and your practice and your writings, you're a lonely guy, is that it?" She said it with a smile.

"Is that what you sense?"

"You seem sort of shy, and lonely—yes, that's what I sense."

"I haven't heard it put like that before."

"I thought you said you were in therapy."

"That was a while back . . . Want something to drink?"

"Herb tea?"

When he came back with a couple of steaming mugs he sat on a couch next to her. "Well, I still haven't heard a word about your father."

"And you won't."

"Sorry, I'm prying. Bad habit."

"Well," she said quietly, "there's not too much to say. He's long gone. I never ever saw him. He was a soldier, killed in Vietnam. Never married Mom. But she talks about him like he was a combination of James Dean and Jesus Christ . . ."

She sipped the tea, neither said anything. He knew what was happening, she was sure. They were talking about stuff, but what really was happening was definitely physical. The smooth texture of his dark skin made her want to reach out and touch him. When he just touched her cheek she felt warm.

First the kisses were light, then it was tongues and fingertips. For a while they lay on the couch, and they began undressing each other. She saw that his body, while not muscular, was taut, almost boyish. His thin shape excited her. While not aggressive or demanding, he was hardly reluctant or passive. When he slipped off her panties she could hear noises from the street and wondered whether his sheer curtains gave any privacy.

His bedroom was better—at the back of the house, an unmade bed, an exposed brick wall, the FM radio tuned to the classical station. The only words he spoke were the ones she wanted to hear . . . about her body, her passion, the intensity of her eyes. She accepted it all, told him how much she wanted him, urged him on and in, further in, all the way in, harder and harder, feeling freer, free to demand what she wanted, to give it and get it and take it, front and back and on the side, let him slide inside and take his time, hurrying, delaying, now fierce, now with finesse, now just balls-out fucking her with such righteous rhythm that orgasms came in breathtaking succession.

Afterward Brahms played softly on the radio as they relaxed in each other's arms.

"It's better than talking," she finally said.

He kissed her without a word.

"I want to know about your past," she said.

"We're in the present. Besides, I thought you didn't want to talk."

"What do you want, Nelson?"

"Right now I want you to spend the night."

"Maybe another time," she said to him, and *Slow down, girl* to herself.

In the shower, as needles of water washed her tingling skin, she thought about Bing Radison. What other kind of photographs did he have in mind? And what would become of Jason in the big city? And what was Nelson really like? What did he really want?

"At least let me put you in a cab," he said after they had dressed.

Out on Tenth Street a rarity—a big Yellow Checker cab pulled up to the curb before he had a chance to flag it down. A passenger was paying the driver and about to get out. As the door opened Joan Winfrey looked up into the faces of her neighbor and her newest model. No one said a word. What could they say? But Joan's eyes were cold.

"Hi," Marisa finally mumbled.

Joan's words were to Clay. "You dog," was all she told him. Nothing to Marisa, and then she hurried off into her house.

"Look, folks," said the cabbie, "I don't got all night. You going or what?"

Marisa's mind was going a million miles an hour as the taxi sped down to the Lower East Side . . . Had she ruined herself with Joan? Was something happening between Joan and Nelson? Had she been misled by Joan, by Nelson, by her own so-called instincts? Damn it, just when she thought things were going well, things seemed to be falling apart . . .

As the cab pulled up in front of her apartment building a woman was landing a punch on a man's jaw, sending him onto the pavement.

Blood trickled from his cut lip. He looked like one of the characters who hung around Marisa's stoop. And the woman—oh God, was it possible?—the woman was Marisa's mother.

Marisa was out of the cab. "What the hell are you doing here?" she was saying, running toward Chanel.

"This asshole grabbed me," said Mama. "Serves his sorry ass right. Better be glad I didn't use my blade."

Breathing hard, Chanel was dressed in a gold-glitter denim pants suit. Her fake-emerald dome ring, the instrument that cut her assailant's lip, was blood-stained. She stood over him, waiting for him to get up so she could do him again. Either he was out or too smart to risk more from this crazy lady.

"Some neighborhood you live in, honey," said mother to daughter. "Looks like I got here just in time. It could have been you. Boy, do I hate this city."

Marisa looked up at a starless sky and shook her head.

"You didn't tell me you lived in the sure-enough slums, baby," said Chanel once inside Marisa's apartment.

"Well, if you want to live in Manhattan and aren't rich—"

"I hated it when your grandmother and I lived here. Well, at least you've fixed it up nice."

"Why didn't you call? Tell me you were coming?"

"Couldn't say it if I didn't know it . . . I don't see a picture of me around here. None of my records, none of—"

"I got everything, Mama, but they're put away in drawers."

"Nothing on display, nothing anybody can see."

"I've never even seen any pictures of Georgia in *your* house."

"My, my, aren't we in a lovely mood, my darling daughter welcoming her mother . . ."

"You still haven't said what you're doing here."

"Blues festival, in case you care."

"Oh, on such short notice?"

"Someone got sick—Etta James, Koko Taylor, I don't know who— so they took me as a last-minute replacement."

"That's good, Mama."

"Is it? I've been out there busting my tail for the last twenty-five

years and you'd think maybe instead of a substitute I'd get to headline one of these mammajammas. I do headline in Europe—you
know that, don't you?—I headline all over Japan. I can't get arrested
in my own backyard. You'd think by now—"

"You come to get a pep talk from me?" asked Marisa. "Because
that's how it usually works, Mama. You say you're cheering me up
but I'm the one who—"

"Just came to *sing*—that's all."

"When's the concert?"

"Tomorrow night. Somewhere out on Long Island. One of those
Hamptons—east, west, or south, not sure which, but it's no matter,
they're sending a limo for us."

"*Us?*"

"Need a background singer."

"Here we go again."

"Wanda's hoarse and Carolynda can't sing both parts You'll be
singing background—"

"I don't even know the songs."

"It's the blues. Blues don't change. We'll rehearse lyrics and harmonies in the morning. You'll fall into it in a jiffy. With your ear and
your voice there's nothing you can't sing."

"I'm booked up tomorrow."

"Doing what?"

"Modeling . . . I think."

"Be careful. That agent's been getting you work?"

"Well, she was, but tonight—"

"What happened tonight?"

"Don't ask."

"I'm asking."

"Mama, you're here and I understand why and that's fine. But I do
have my own life here and . . . I need to sort out some things—"

"That's why I'm here."

"That's *not* why you're here. You're here because of your career,
not mine."

"Look here, child, that thing out in California messed with my
mind. I know it messed with yours too. That was a bad idea your
grandmother had and I shouldn't have gone along with it. Being
sober is showing me stuff about myself, about Georgia *and* about you
that I never saw before. You might say I'm bursting with truth, child,

with new insights. I'm shaking with the good news. Feel like I'm born again and it's not just the blood of Jesus that's washing me clean but it's clean living that's letting me look into the past to see what happened to us . . . to all of us."

"Mama, you sound like one of those old preachers. This isn't Alabama, it's New York. Now, I'm glad about your insights, your being sober, but please, I've had enough psychology for one day."

"You're going to therapy?"

"Just sort of dating a therapist."

"Jewish?"

Marisa let out one of her large hearty laughs. "No, Mama, you're stereotyping again. This particular shrink's a brother."

"I want to meet him," she said. "We're sure to hit it off."

"I'm not so sure."

"Of him or me?"

"Mama, I'm not very sure of anything right now."

"You got a right, most everything's been unsure your whole life. Georgia did that to you . . ."

"Just Georgia?"

"I could have been more straight-ahead with you, I realize that now. And now I intend to be. I want you to hear some things you've never heard before."

"What things?"

"My story."

"I've heard it, Mama. You've told it, God knows you've told it. And retold it. And told it again."

"But this time, sugar, I'm not sparing myself, I got nothing to hide. I realize secrets are like festering sores."

"We're talking about my father?" asked Marisa, annoyed and impatient at the same time.

"That man was a saint," said Mama, "prettiest white boy I ever did see. I told you he was white—"

"You *told* me, Mama. A white saint. Jesus Christ. Look, Mama, about tomorrow, I'm just not in the mood to sing—"

"I'm in a jam," countered Chanel. "I'm not asking you, girl, I'm telling you. I need a singer and that singer is you—"

"No way."

"I want you to sing something by yourself."

"Is that a bribe?"

"It's a mother wanting to show off her daughter. What's so wrong with that?"

"Because it's not showing me off, it's using me. It's for you and your career. When your career was happening in California, you went to California. When it was happening down South you ran off and left me in California."

"You wanted to stay with Georgia."

"I was a kid. I wanted to say whatever would make you be pleased with me. Not to mention feel good about yourself. I wasn't stupid, Mama. I see it now. I was protecting you from your guilt."

"I'm dealin' with that guilt right now, baby."

"Save it for your shrink, Mama. All I know is that when your career called, you ran—to wherever you thought it would do you the most good."

"I took you whenever I could."

"Whenever it suited you. Like it suits you now to have me singing behind you."

"Look, be practical, it won't hurt you to be heard by those rich show-biz folk. They all go out to those Hamptons for the summer— the big-shot producers, label presidents, even some studio heads. They're always looking—"

"They'll be looking at you, and that's fine, because you're looking for a record deal."

"You think it's so easy, that it feels good being dumped by the record company like I was damaged goods? Think it's fun to still be scuffling?"

"It's your life, Mama, not mine. I think about your life—about Georgia's life—way too much as it is."

"You know something, Marisa, you're the most stubborn of us all. You keep pushing me away—"

"Mama, Mama . . . why can't you just let me be?"

" 'Let It Be'—you always said that was your favorite song, well, you can sing it. I put it in the show because of you and I've been singing it, but I'm gonna let you. How's that for motherly love?"

"Overwhelming."

"Of course. Now get some sleep so you'll be fresh tomorrow. Don't want no tired-ass voices whimpering behind me. Tomorrow night we gonna *burn*."

Marisa shook her head. Mama, in this mood, would not be denied.

Over the phone she had a chance with Chanel, but in person she was just plain emotionally outmuscled. A little girl again.

"You take my bed," she told her mother. "I'll take the couch."

"I don't wanna put you out, baby."

"Sure."

An hour later Marisa still could not sleep. The night's events kept replaying inside her head—Nelson's loving, Joan's anger, Chanel's frustration about her life. What had happened between Nelson and Joan? She had to know, and now called him to ask.

"What was that all about?" she wanted to know.

"I'm sorry," said Nelson. "It wasn't a very pleasant way to end the evening. We caught Joan by surprise."

"She called you a dog. Pretty colorful."

"She was upset."

"Why should she be upset with you?"

"I'm not sure."

"Come *on*, Nelson. You're the shrink."

"Jealousy, maybe."

"Because you and she . . ."

"Only once, and it didn't work out."

"Jesus, couldn't you at least have told me? You knew I was going to work for her. And you also knew it would upset her to find you and me—"

"You knew it too, Marisa. You told me about her interest in you—"

"Yes, but I had no idea about *your* interest in her."

"I told you—it was no more than an evening of too much wine and some unrealistic expectations. Shrinks have those too."

"You still could have warned me."

"About what? Lingering old-fashioned jealousy? Come on, Marisa, you're a big girl."

"I really thought you were so decent. But all that stuff about listening to me, about your big-deal concern for old people . . ."

"It was a minor misunderstanding—"

"Not for me." And she hung up, feeling rotten and stupid.

"Was that your shrink?" asked Mama, standing in the doorway in a red robe.

"I thought you were sleeping."

"I have this long-time habit of hearing conversations behind closed doors. Come tell Mama about it."

"Nothing to tell."

"I heard you say—"

"Goddammit, Mama, *stay out of my business. Please.*"

"I only meant to—"

"Just stay the hell *out*!" And then, without warning or intention, she broke into tears.

Chanel looked at her baby and shook her head. "My my," she said, walking over to cradle Marisa in her arms. "Looks like Mama's right on time after all."

The blues festival was held at seaside in an outdoor arena with a band shell that backed up to the ocean. Marisa got a look at the audience—white folk, little Polo men on cotton shirts and pleated khaki pants, oxblood penny loafers. The late-summer sun was setting and a blues band from Chicago was on stage.

"Don't worry," Chanel assured Marisa, "we'll set 'em on fire."

Chanel had gotten over her resentment of being a last-minute substitute. The sight of the crowd got her up. Crowds always got her up. As ethnic as her music was, she never avoided or rejected white audiences. She'd long claimed that her music was universal—and only the racism of record companies and radio stations kept her music back. Tonight she would give them the works.

She looked outlandish, but outlandish was her style. She was dressed in a glitter-gold pants suit, a matching gold turban on top of her head, gold hoop earrings and gold lamé ballet flats. As soon as she hit the stage, she kicked off her shoes and asked the audience, "You hungry for some soul?"

They said they were. The drummer kicked off a pounding groove; the fat-back bass player popped and slapped; the piano player slid his thumb all the way down the keyboard; the amen girls, Marisa and Carolynda, dressed in simple black, took their place; and the star of the show, Chanel Faith, smiled and hit her first note clean and strong, feeling her opening selection was on the money, the power of her voice pushing the sun down into the sea as she sang:

Everytime the sun sets
I get feelings deep inside
Like a little girl
Looking for a special love
Love lost long ago . . .
Oh no, there ain't nothing like
Your daddy's love

   I'm looking for a man to say that I am his
   Looking for a man to do what's right
   Looking for a man who's gonna claim my soul
   Looking for a man to love tonight

Thought I saw him
In a technicolor dream
Voice like silk
And eyes dark and sweet
A heart that I could feel
But he wasn't real
No, the dream wasn't real

   Still looking for a man to say that I am his
   Looking for a man to do what's right
   Looking for a man who's gonna claim my soul
   Looking for a man to love tonight

Listening to Mama, Marisa felt good all over. Mama was country church, roadshack blues bars, back-alley blues. It didn't matter what you called it, Mama like this was raw and pure—or impure—straight at you, in your face.

They loved it and called out for more. When she sang "Dust My Broom" and "Rock Me Baby," when she tore up "Proud Mary" or "Runnin' Out of Fools," the audience didn't think of Tina Turner or Aretha Franklin. It was Chanel Faith reading them the riot act of soul music—the Gospel According to Faith.

Singing the background parts came naturally to Marisa. It was easy as sliding down a slide, easy as stretching your arms to the sky.

"If you think I'm something," Chanel told the faithful, "wait till you get a load of this. This is my daughter."

Marisa stepped forward, a laugh in her green eyes, her smile wide, her white teeth flashing. The black dress clung to her slim frame. She looked great, she felt great. The night air was cool against her skin. She felt high, free. She sang the first verse of "Let It Be," a song her mother had sung to her when she was a very little girl, a song she had always loved.

The audience could hear she was her mother's child; her voice was rich, powerful, capable of gospel melismatics yet subtly dramatic. Watching, Chanel saw Marisa captivating the crowd and couldn't help but feel proud. She let her sing the chorus alone, but when it came time for the second verse Chanel stepped up to the mike and took over. Naturally.

Marisa was surprised, she thought this was her solo spot, but she also knew Mama—Mama did things on the spur of the moment. They sang the rest of the song in harmony, but at the end when it came time to improvise over a long instrumental vamp Chanel just couldn't help herself, couldn't resist swooping high over her baby's head. Who could follow her? Marisa didn't try. Truth was, on this stage she couldn't keep up with the old lady; she couldn't win back the crowd that now belonged to Chanel.

Marisa stepped back and gave the spotlight over to Mama. When the song was through and the audience exploded with shouts and laughter, Chanel motioned for Marisa to join her, but Marisa only smiled and waved to the crowd. She did not take Mama's hand. How had Marisa so easily forgotten? Chanel had to outdo everyone—even her own daughter.

"She's too much," Marisa was telling Nelson Clay over the phone.
 "Who?"
 "My mother. She's back. She just crashed back into my life."
 "What happened?"
 "I don't want to talk about it."
 "Then why are you calling?"
 "You're the shrink, you tell me."
 "Because you wanted to talk to a friend, I hope."

"Friend? I don't know. What about Joan Winfrey?"

"She said she was sorry."

"Because she's still interested in you."

"No, because she's still interested in *you*, Marisa."

"Then why hasn't she called me?"

"She wanted to make sure I wasn't somehow undermining your professional relationship with her. I assured her I wasn't."

"Well, how about assuring *me*?"

"Marisa, I feel very warmly toward you, I'm fascinated by you—"

"You sound like you're talking about a case study."

"You're complex enough, no question, but I'm talking about *you*, personally. I want to see you again. And I'm hoping you want to see me or you wouldn't be calling."

"You know what, Nelson, if I were honest—if I took a hard look at myself right now—I'd have to say that I probably do need a shrink a lot more than I need a lover."

"Well," he said, his voice lowering, "maybe I can be both."

"You can be anything you want to be," Bing Radison told Marisa.

They were at the opening of his one-man show at a downtown gallery. On display were Bing's art photos, not his commercial material.

Marisa had come with Jason Solomon, who was just in from Santa Fe. It was a Saturday night in early October and the city was finally cooling off from a scorching summer. It had rained that morning and the evening air was clean and cool. Walking through bustling Soho with Marisa, Jason was feeling more confident. He was ready to move to New York. His eccentric documentary *Diners Are Forever* had just won first prize at a Colorado film festival. As a producer, he'd earned his first stripes.

And Marisa had begun to bounce back from her mother's appearance. Talking briefly to her on the phone, she had been able to hold her ground. "You do your thing," she told her, "and I'll do mine."

That same night Joan Winfrey had called and while the agent wasn't exactly apologetic she was at least upbeat. "This sports catalogue," she told Marisa, "is strong stuff. Your personality comes through loud and clear. The calls are already coming in."

Bing Radison's call interested her the most. "We turned a little trick with that catalogue," he told her, "and there's no harm done. It's cute stuff, it'll pay a few bills. But if you come to my opening you'll understand the options that are open to you. You'll understand where I am."

His work was bold, concentrated on the human body, female and male.

"He's a body freak," commented Jason. As he and Marisa scrutinized the photos, a black-and-white rock 'n' roll band began to play.

"He shoots nudes," observed Marisa, "from *every* possible angle."

On swings and tightropes, on motorcycles and skateboards, in bathtubs and on beaches, in formal poses and moments of relaxed candor, Bing had found angles that accentuated body parts—breasts, biceps, elbows, penises—as though they were frozen sculpture. The results were often austere, sometimes dramatic, always on the edge.

"This guy should be directing music videos," Jason was saying.

"Let's do it," said Bing, having overheard the remark.

Marisa introduced the two men, taking in the visual contrast— Bing, with his blond ponytail and electric-green framed glasses; freckled-faced Jason, wanting to look the producer with his tweedy sports coat and Italian loafers.

"We have the star right here," observed Bing, nodding at Marisa. "Now all we need is a song."

Just then the band kicked in—"I'm Ready Right Now"—and Marisa started singing along, as though it were the theme song of her soul. Which in a real way it was.

She *was* ready. She had been ready. And when it all came together— only three weeks later—it happened fast. The band was called Esoterica, a mixed crew of two white male singers, a black female keyboardist and an androgynous Japanese drummer, all wild for Marisa who was wild for their song. They were delighted to back her and appear in the video being shot in the same Soho gallery where the show had been held. The photographs remained in place and, to dramatize the action, Bing brought in the live models to pose before their images. To get the video on MTV full frontal nudity had to be avoided—ever so slightly. Bing would shoot at angles that followed the genital planes and curves but turned from direct exposure. It was daring, the sort of material Marisa knew she needed to get attention, and a deal. "I'm Ready Right Now . . ."

Jason, like Bing, had never made a video, but also like Bing, he had an instinctive belief in Marisa. Convention was out. Extravagant videos were rarely shot without record contracts, but Marisa was tired of making demonstration versions of songs and peddling them to producers. She needed a bolder splash. In the previous six weeks she had made more money than in the previous year, thanks to gigs from the Winfrey Agency. Now Marisa, Jason and Bing were pooling their resources and doing the video together. Jason and Bing were strangely compatible. Jason, favoring out-there avant-garde art, understood Bing's flair, his blend of homo/hetero erotica flash and fashion. Bing needed Jason's production experience.

At the center was Marisa. Bing brought the camera in on her green eyes. They opened the video. From there he pulled back to reveal her face, her funky fly coif, cut close to the scalp—surprisingly like the way her mother had been wearing her hair for years—a simple gold band on every finger, ankhs, African relics symbolizing eternal life, hanging from her ears. Her first outfit consisted of a hand-sewn beaded and pearled black satin baseball cap, mudcloth overalls and red plastic stomp shoes. And that was only the opening shot. Madonna Shmadonna!

Later Marisa's supple body would be highlighted by a leotard custom-created by an artist friend of Bing whose geometric patterns suggested a high-tech futurism.

"I'm ready right now," she sang in a voice that snaked over the rock rhythms. "Wasn't ready yesterday, might not be ready tomorrow, but right now. I'm ready really really ready right now . . ."

The camera too was ready to roam, from male model to female and back again, the vain stances of anatomical superiors who, in contrast to Marisa's vulnerability, stood above mere motion.

Toward the end of the song, as Marisa repeated the chorus, the camera rose over her head, focusing on a photograph from the early fifties, a nude shot of Georgia Faith in Paris taken by Noel Radison. Marisa had not, of course, known the picture was going to be placed there and, after laughing, objected.

"This is *my* video, not my grandmother's."

"It's just a sort of touchstone," Bing told her. "Links our pasts."

*   *   *

"The video's far from perfect," the record executive told Jason, who had been making the rounds with the tape, "but it has possibilities."

HM Records was a hot new label that had enjoyed a bunch of recent dance hits. Its owner was a black man in his early thirties who wore an immaculately cut English tweed suit and conservative blue-checked tie. He had a strong chin, clear dark eyes and a calm sense of organization about him. Jason had the feeling he was on the level.

"I try to balance my musical tastes," the executive told Jason, "with good business sense. It looks like HM will soon be distributed by one of the world's largest record companies. I like to think I know what I'm doing, and I'm certain I could give your artist the sort of attention she'd never find at a larger label. I'd like to meet your artist, Mr. Solomon."

Maybe the man was a little stiff but sincere, self-assured. He came across honest, an unusual quality in the business. He liked this guy, whose name was engraved on a silver plate sitting on his desk:

Herb Montgomery, Jr.

The first time Herb Montgomery, Jr., met Chanel he felt himself falling and did his best to fight the feeling. Among his colleagues he was known as a man who put business first. Serious, earnest, he was determined to have success. He'd been that way as an undergraduate at UCLA. He'd been that way at the Wharton School of Business. He'd been that way even as a child witnessing the unraveling of his parents' marriage. The antagonism between his mother, the former actress Honey Lincoln, and his father, the cinematographer Herb Montgomery, had cut deeply. He loved both, couldn't choose.

Herbie shut down and concentrated on the tangibles. By becoming a perfect student he pleased mother and father, in contrast to his older twin siblings—Marian, who became a religious fanatic like her mother, and brother Randy, who got hooked on dope and disappeared in northern Africa.

"If you want to get somewhere," said Herb, Sr., "you need something of your own. You need to own it and control it."

His father's lack of success saddened and motivated Herbie. Herb, Sr., never talked about his fiascos, those independent films of the forties and fifties. But young Herbie eventually learned the facts and understood how his father had been hurt. Damn it, that would never happen to him. He'd make it, he'd learn to play the game, then to win.

Out of Wharton School of Business in Philadelphia, Herbie went to work for a firm of investment bankers, then real-estate brokers. He could always sell, but he never believed in the product. Only when he entered a training program at Columbia Records did he somehow feel right. The record business—marketing, promotion, evaluation—excited him. All his life he had had an ear for melody and a feel for rhythm. Well, now it was paying off. And it also didn't take long to see the blinkers of corporate life. Even though the major labels had created black music divisions and were hiring more black managers, Herbie understood he could go only so far. He learned the ropes, paid his dues. His parents claimed they were proud, but his father never stopped reminding him that he was working for the white man.

Then he changed all that, and his father was the first one he called with the news. He had discovered a funk-and-rap group in England, Nu Groove, and rather then sign them to Columbia he signed them to *his* own label, HM Records, capitalized through Wall Street contacts. When the first single took off he used the cash to recruit a second group, then a third. Within eighteen months Herbie had put all three HM acts on the dance charts. The trade papers had run features on his quick success. By the time Jason Solomon came to see him, Herb Montgomery, Jr., was hot.

Jason had described him to Marisa, talked about his straight-ahead manner and confidence. The Montgomery name, never having been uttered by either Georgia or Chanel, meant nothing to Marisa. She looked forward to meeting the label boss who had been impressed by her video.

When she entered his office his back was to her—he was speaking on the phone, standing and facing the window that looked out on Broadway, just like in the corny old movies. His shoulders were wide and his waist tapered. Marisa had a thing for broad shoulders. When he turned around and put down the phone he apologized. His smile seemed effortless, his dark eyes were very dark. Not, thank God, movie-star handsome, but there was something solid about him, and that was better.

The Marisa he saw was thin, animated in black tights and loose overblouse. Her body was in motion, her eyes smiled, made Herbie feel he was in the presence of music. Jason was supposed to have come with her but had gotten sick with the flu. Rather than cancel, Marisa came alone.

The video, Herbie felt, had misrepresented her. Too busy, distracting. Just saying "I'm happy to meet you," she knocked him out. What came out of his mouth had nothing to do with what was going on inside.

"I was impressed by your video, I like to think I can recognize real talent."

Marisa could dig that. Why not? At first she worried he was another of those black men desperate to be white, who wore Paul Stuart suits, spoke law-school English. No doubt he was college educated, and no doubt he could talk with any CEO in the land, but this was a man who worked for himself. HM Records was his. Marisa Faith was impressed. He didn't use jargon, he didn't talk Hollywoodeze. He did not call her "baby" or promise to "break" her. He did not refer to her as a "product" or try to impress her with the names of all the stars he knew.

In Herbie's mind Marisa had the brashness of a Madonna, and the vocal punch of a Whitney Houston. She was sexual, theatrical. Herbie had been excited by the other groups he'd signed but they were restricted. Marisa had the variety and ability to go all the way. She could make him rich. But more than money was on his mind. He had, after all, been raised in a comfortable environment; as an executive he'd been earning a good salary for years. What he really wanted was knowing he could do what all the legendary record men had done before him: create a superstar—a Diana Ross, a Streisand, a Bette Midler.

Of course Marisa had heard such talk before. Joan Winfrey was always promising her fame as a model. The work had been coming in, but like Joan herself its attraction had worn thin—in Joan's case, very thin. The first catalogue had been fun but the other jobs were not. Even if Victoria's Secret was the hottest mail-order business in the country, Marisa wasn't exactly thrilled about modeling fancy underwear. "This is the Rolls-Royce of catalogues," Joan had told her.

"The photographers, the art direction, the merchandise—it's all the best. Any model would sell her soul to get the job. And you haven't heard the price yet."

Marisa did take the gig and moved to a nicer apartment in Chelsea, where one night Joan came calling uninvited, claiming, "I just wanted to see my favorite client's new surroundings."

It wasn't easy getting her to leave. Marisa did not want to hurt the woman's feelings, but neither did she want to encourage her.

"Nelson says that you and he are just friends," Joan ventured.

Yes, Marisa thought, we're friends, but also lovers. She wanted Joan to know this, except she also wanted to keep her own privacy. Anyway, after a long evening of chitchat interlaced with innuendos, Joan finally did leave, hugging Marisa goodbye. Marisa didn't feel comfortable. She wasn't even sure she liked the woman, or ever had. But neither was she prepared to alienate her. There was the practical part she couldn't afford to ignore. Not yet.

Marisa was sure, though, that she liked Herb Montgomery, Jr. And when he suggested that they have a drink in a bar on top of an old Art Deco skyscraper, she saw no reason to refuse.

Winter had set in. The sky was overcast and the city seemed bleak. To Marisa, peering out the window, New York was always romantic from on high. She thought of the Cole Porter songs that her grandmother Georgia had taught her as a child. She remembered the records by Mabel Mercer and Sylvia Syms that Georgia loved to play: love lost, love mixed with loneliness, love sought in a world of bittersweet sophistication. She told Herbie what was on her mind.

"You can sing those kinds of songs too," he said. "You can sing your way through a whole range of moods. Once we establish you, anything's possible. It's that breakthrough—"

"A breakthrough based on what?"

"You and your friends were on the right track," Herbie told her. "Dance music is the way. Dance music sells. It's utilitarian, people need it, the clubs feed on it. Dance music has always been the engine that drives pop music."

"That's why I liked the music of Esoterica. I think it's right for me."

"Unfortunately, Marisa, I think it's wrong."

He didn't sound egotistical, merely factual. Which both irritated and intrigued her.

"Why do you say that?"

"Their music is all over the place. I'm sure they're sincere in what they're doing, but they're scattered. We need to target a specific market. Once we sell that market, then we reach to other markets. But the primary market is the first and most important step. The dance-music market is the one I understand best. These days they call it a lot of things, but it's basic rhythm and blues. This country has always danced to basic rhythm and blues."

"My mother is a rhythm-and-blues singer," Marisa said, worried that Herbie wanted to push her in Chanel's direction.

"And a great one," he said. "Also a pure one, an example of someone who still sings in the style of sixties soul. That's beautiful, and, believe me, Marisa, I admire Chanel Faith. I've always thought she deserved wider recognition. I never understood why she never hit big. In her time she was a master. The problem, though, is that the soul era is history and the instrumentation, the rhythm patterns, the grooves, the sounds, the sampling, the way we make records today has undergone huge changes. When I think of your mother, I'm reminded of my father."

"What does your father do?"

"He's another story for another time. He's never understood how to cross over—and I guess the result is frustration."

"I'm still not sure what you mean by rhythm and blues. I hear those words and see my mother."

"When I say rhythm and blues is the way, I'm talking about rhythm and blues as the source, you know, the heart of the matter. I remember my father telling me about Benny Goodman playing 'Let's Dance' back in the thirties. According to Dad, Goodman got his rhythm and sound from a black man named Fletcher Henderson, and Fletcher Henderson, who he said was a genius, understood how to give blues melodies a dance flavor. Today Prince, Bobby Brown or Michael Jackson don't need a Benny Goodman to front for them. Either way, though, it's basic dance rhythms we're after. Some people call it funk."

"So you want me to be *funky?*" she asked with a smile.

"I do!"

"And Esoterica . . ."

"Too esoteric, sorry. I know a couple of gals, two brilliant musicians, who learned the tricks of the trade from Teddy Riley, L.A., Babyface, Jam and Lewis. They call themselves Pop and Fresh. They're not exactly artists—not yet, anyway—but they're trackmeisters. They're laying down burning tracks in their home studio in the Bronx. The room where they work is right off the street, and the street is all over their music. They leave their windows open and the sounds just blow in. I want you to hear their material, Marisa. They're really something. I want you to hear how hard they slam."

"How old are they?

"Sixteen."

"You're kidding."

"Sixteen is about the right age to understand what's happening. They produced a track on one of my rap artists who's now touring England behind it. Have you heard 'Heat'?"

"That's theirs? And you're not worrying about pigeonholing me?"

"I'm worried about marketing you in the most practical way possible. That means finding you a hit song we all can relate to—a black dance hit, pure and simple."

"Well, I have no problems with that."

"Then you think we can work together?"

"I think I do, Herb . . ."

Glancing out the window now, Marisa noticed a light drizzle had begun to fall. Herbie's talk had changed her point of view; from what was no longer a ninetieth-floor perspective, she saw Gene Kelly singing in the rain. Her heart was light; hope tingled along her skin.

As for Herbie, he felt he'd done as well as he could in his pitch to Marisa.

"It won't be easy," he had admitted, "but success in the record business has never been easy."

As a performer Marisa Faith had everything he wanted. But he was worried. He had this nagging feeling that his rule about keeping his business and private life separate was on the edge of collapse.

"You draw people into triangular relationships," Nelson was saying.

"What are you talking about?" asked Marisa.

They had just made love in Clay's bedroom. For several months now their relationship had fallen into a pattern of satisfying sex and open conversation, but tonight something was wrong.

"You grew up in a triangular relationship—you, your mother and your grandmother. It's the only way you can relate."

"Now the true shrink finally comes out. You can't hold back your analysis a single second longer."

"And you can't resist involving me in your relationship with this Montgomery, just as you got involved with both Joan and me at the same time."

"What do you call involvement?"

"Emotional involvement. You know that."

"I just asked for your thoughts about my meeting with Herb Montgomery. Now you turn that into a triangle." She kissed his forehead. "Boy, you're acting so insecure. By the way, your body is adorable."

"Not awesome?"

"Your mind is awesome."

"Seriously, Marisa, you're treating me like your professional counselor—"

"You were the one who said you could be my lover and shrink."

"I wasn't too serious."

"You were on the make."

"If you really want my opinion, Marisa, that's how I read Montgomery. The way you describe him, *he's* on the make."

"He is. If he weren't he wouldn't be of any use."

"So you're using him."

"You're turning into a jealous boy. Your mind's turning to mush. Of course he's using me and of course I'm using him. He's a promoter and I'm an artist. We need each other, we use each other. That's business. That's life, for God's sake."

"You'll be dropping Joan."

"Why did you tell her we were just friends?"

"I didn't think our relationship was any of her business. Joan and I have a special friendship."

Now they were sitting up in bed, talking *at* one another.

"A 'special friendship,' " said Marisa. "What's that supposed to mean?"

"Well, you have a special friendship with Jason Solomon, don't you?"

"Jealousy really is fogging your glasses, Nelson."

"I'm not entitled to normal emotions? Besides, love does pretty strange things to people, and shrinks are people."

"Love? I haven't heard that word out of your mouth before—at least not in reference to me."

"Nor have you used the word *in reference* to me."

"So who's going to use it first?"

Silence. Breathing sounds. Finally he took her in his arms and kissed the nape of her neck, his lips moving to her taut breasts.

And they made love again, the heat they'd generated with words building the sexual urgency. But the word in question—"love"—remained unspoken.

When she put down the script her hands were shaking—and Georgia Faith's hands never shook. But the story was overwhelming. She hadn't a doubt that this was it, the role of a lifetime. The screenplay was called *Pearl*.

All along she'd known that one day it would happen like this: It'd be a typical Southern California morning, sunny and mild. She'd walk into her office next to the garden at Passion Flowers. She'd sit in her flame-stitched Queen Anne chair behind her English Regency desk. Stephen would bring her orange juice, her flaky croissant, her fresh copies of *Variety* and the *Hollywood Reporter*. As she scanned the gossip columns and news reports, underlining with a fourteen-karat gold-tipped Mont Blanc fountain pen the names of people she knew—her friends were always in the news—the phone would ring or a script would arrive by messenger. An agent would tell her that a name director was demanding that she play the lead in his new film. The screenplay would carry a note saying that the central character had been written with only her in mind.

She had lived on such fantasies for three decades. Parts actually had been offered, but slight ones, guest appearances on nighttime soaps. The only ongoing role was for a daytime soap opera but that meant moving to New York. Rather than risk giving up the flower shop, her only financial security, she stayed in L.A. Besides, she considered soaps beneath her.

In truth, it wasn't a call from a powerful agent or prominent director that validated her long years of faith. It was a script from an old friend, a man whose talents she never doubted, no matter how complicated and strained their relationship had become.

No one wrote like Herb Montgomery. No one had his feel for characters, especially black characters. White writers overdid the idiosyncrasies of black speech; they made black people sound either too hokey, slick or silly. Herb's ear was right on pitch. He knew his people. And he knew better than anyone Georgia's abilities.

Theirs was a special and secret relationship. They had fought with and loved one another for over fifty years. The clandestine nature of their occasional rendezvous added to the bond. Nothing, it seemed, could break it. They'd worked well together at the beginning of their careers; now it seemed clear that they would work together at the end. She had given up on him, had sworn never to get involved again with this man but now clearly circumstances had intervened. In Georgia's mind she saw it all falling into place, this master plan, spontaneously unfolding so that the last chapter would end in some personal glory.

Georgia was sixty-eight, Herb Montgomery seventy-three, and now their time, the actress was convinced, had come. All the waiting had been worth it. The incontrovertible proof was in the magnificent script he had written. The audience, she was convinced, would fall in love with Pearl—would fall in love with Georgia. Because finally Herb had quit fooling around. When he was young he had written these message movies with messages directed only to blacks. In middle age he'd stopped making his own movies altogether and worked as a cinematographer. At age sixty he'd begun making documentaries, one of which—on the history of tap dancing—won an Academy Award. But now, if this screenplay was any indication, he was ready to go for it all. He'd meet Hollywood on Hollywood's terms. Who, after all, could resist the fable of a female, a rugged individualist, who fights racism, sexism, abusive men and even cancer to become a Fortune 500 CEO? A former model, Pearl's empire is cosmetics. Georgia read it as an American story of glamor and brains and guts. Horatio Alger—only this time Horatio was black and female.

* * *

"As a kid," said Herb Montgomery, Jr., "I lived mostly in L.A."

Herbie, Jason and Marisa were in the back of a roomy Lincoln Town Car being driven to the Bronx to meet Pop and Fresh.

"We all have at least that in common," Marisa put in, pleased to be sandwiched by these two.

Listening to the chatter, looking at Herbie looking at Marisa, Jason began to have second thoughts. At first he'd seen Herb as an up-front guy. But it was evident, even beyond Montgomery's cool, that his interest in Marisa was more than just professional . . . "He's definitely interested," he had told Marisa, "but there are at least a half dozen labels I want to talk to. He's not going to be the only one impressed with the video." Except he was. The other execs—six men and one woman—all passed, some with mild regrets, most with indifference. "She's too derivative," said one. "Today's market is crowded with these kinds of artists," said another. "A Mariah Carey or Paula Abdul she ain't," claimed a third. "The video looks like an artsy beer commercial," declared an A&R man before sending Jason on his way. Assholes all. Herbie was the only player. And Herbie knew it. Consequently the up-front money was modest and the overall deal far from spectacular. Jason's lawyer and Montgomery's man hammered out the details with a minimum of wrangling. It was agreed that the first order of business was a single, and that Pop and Fresh, Herbie's super-hot female producers, would get first crack.

Jason had worked hard with Bing Radison on the post-production of the video; he had spearheaded the selling effort. Living in a residential hotel on the Upper West Side while looking for an apartment, he was also overcoming his worries about running in the fast lane in New York City. It wasn't a matter of putting his film career on hold— he still thought of himself as a producer—but honing another skill. If anyone could manage Risa, it was Jason, right?

Risa was volatile, unconventional, gorgeous. This particular afternoon she wore a sun-yellow bandanna and beat-up leather bomber jacket. Whenever she greeted Jason, she hugged and squeezed him close to her, which had a predictable effect, but they were close friends and he didn't want to ruin that, and besides, she was in some sort of relationship with Nelson Clay. Why complicate an old friend-ship and a profitable new partnership? If she thought of him as a brother, hadn't it always been that way? They were both raised in the shadows of show business, buddies playing in the same playpen. It wasn't sex that had forged their friendship; it was understanding. Then why was sex on Jason's mind? Ever since he saw Risa at Yan-kee Stadium he had wanted to go to bed with her. Of course, who didn't? The way she smiled and walked and talked she gave the impression that she was available. It just came out of her, not con-trived or affected. But Jason knew it was a false impression. In fact, Risa had never been easy or loose. He'd seen his high school chums mistake her vivaciousness for promiscuity. She was choosy. Jason called it the "asshole detector." She could smell a dog a mile off. "Maybe that's because," she'd once confided to him, "my mother brought so many dogs around."

Driving to the Bronx now with Risa and Herbie, Jason felt a strong link to the past. He was proud and protective of Marisa, although he knew she had also protected him against his self-doubt.

"There's no one I trust more than you," she'd told Jason. "No one understands my life better."

He accepted that, although he had never been quite sure of exactly what she had been through. He had gotten along with Risa, he felt, because he was careful not to probe. He had seen Risa go through all sorts of changes as she came back from her summers with Chanel in Alabama—spunkier, more rebellious, less able to adapt to Beverly Hills. Then as the school year progressed he would watch her react to Georgia's influence, sometimes conforming, often rebelling. It was a merry-go-round, a roller coaster, but somehow through it all they held onto one another.

For all her moods and changes, one day Marisa would light up the sky, no question, Jason felt. Why shouldn't he help her now that it was about to happen? And if that meant putting his feelings for her on hold, well, so be it.

"Are you related to the Herb Montgomery who makes documenta-ries?" he asked Herb, Jr., as the car crossed 125th Street.

"He's my father."

"He made that film on tap dancers, didn't he?"

"It featured my Uncle Harper."

"It was great."

"Dad's good."

"So you were brought up in the film business," said Jason.

"On the edges of it."

"As kids," added Marisa, "seems like we were all on the edge out there."

"What did your father do?" Herbie asked Jason.

"I was raised by my grandfather, Sol Solomon. Ever hear of him? He's a novelist."

"Oh."

"Also a frustrated screenwriter."

"Frustration," said Herbie, "has been my father's middle name."

For a moment no one said anything. It was almost as though the three of them were connected in a way that was at once both clear and mysterious.

"I know you've heard of Risa's mother," Jason told Herbie, "but did you know that her grandmother—"

"Please," Marisa broke in. "I had enough of that with Bing. Let's just forget my family. Let's concentrate on *now*."

Herbie made a mental note to ask about Marisa's grandmother another time. As for the present, they had arrived in the Bronx.

Pop wore overalls and a pink painter's cap; Fresh had dreadlocks and a large mouth. They were sixteen-year-old girls into cutting-edge fashion. Pop had a gap between her two front teeth, and Fresh had a half dozen earrings in each ear. They might not have been beautiful beneath their get-ups but they were sure different. Jason loved them. Their apartment was crowded with keyboards and computers, an eight-track recording apparatus, speakers, headphones, drum machines, mikes, digital this and digital DAT.

"You're gorgeous," Pop said to Risa the moment she saw her.

"Oh, *girl*," added Fresh, "you got it."

"Herbie says y'all have the jam of life," Marisa told them, feeling good from the get-go.

"We got something," said Pop, "that the kids out there like. They're our judge and jury. We lay it down and look outside. If they're moving, we know it's right. If they're not, we start over."

"Well, let's get started," urged Herbie. "Let's hear what you got."

The duo got serious in a hurry. They played their Mac computers like a video game, maneuvering the mouse and making sounds—whistles, bells, synthesized glockenspiels, rim shots, a raunchy sample of King Curtis' tenor, James Jamerson's bass, Slash's heavy-metal guitar—slamming sweetly into Marisa's head. Jason watched her. So did Herbie. She closed her eyes, allowing the music to sink in. Her mouth started moving, though at first the words were indiscernible. They were mere mumbles. But as Pop and Fresh kept at it, as Risa's concentration deepened, the mumbles turned to syllables and the syllables turned to words, one phrase repeating as a refrain or chorus or theme that seemed to be engraved on the back of the notes.

"Got this feeling," Marisa was now singing, "got this good feeling . . . wanna follow this feeling . . ." The more she sang, the more the motif became a full-fledged musical line. "Don't care what you're dealing . . . my heart is reeling . . . gonna follow this feeling . . . gotta follow this feeling . . ."

Jason and Herbie exchanged glances. They didn't have to say it; they had not known each other that long, and they certainly did not completely trust one another. But at that moment they knew they could read each other's mind; they were thinking the same thing. They were witnessing the birth of a hit.

Herbie always faced encounters with his father with ambivalence—curious to see what the old man was up to but never comfortable in his presence. This was the man, after all, who had left Herbie, his twin siblings and his mother when Herbie was five. He had never abandoned the family financially, but emotionally the man was long gone.

Growing up, Herbie was lucky to see his father twice a year, and then only on his own terms and at his own convenience. He was there when Herbie graduated from elementary school, high school and college. In fact, the older and more successful Herbie became, the more frequently he came calling. Resentment set in. Where had the old man been when the kid needed him most? Where was Dad when Herbie wanted advice about girls or when he needed an ally to convince Mom not to drag him to church every Sunday?

For the first twenty-five years of Herbie's life his dad was a dashing figure. He was always arriving from exotic places like Montreal or

Paris, wearing safari jackets, wide-brimmed hats and desert boots. On rare occasions he would take his son to special showings of movies and there'd be talk about black culture, films, poetry, dancing, Duke Ellington and Charlie Parker. The talk, though, was never enough to deflect Herbie's anger. He blamed his mother's unhappiness on his father leaving her. Honey never got over it, grew too fat, took up religion like a fanatic.

By now, though, Herb was in his seventies, Herbie in his thirties. The past was the past, Herbie told himself. Sitting in his office surrounded by full-page advertisements from Billboard and Cash Box for Risa, his hot singing discovery, the head of HM Records was feeling good. "Follow This Feeling," the first single, had been released in April and now on the first of June it had reached number one on the rhythm-and-blues charts. Herbie had already begun to work the stations which, if they added the song to their playlists, could make it a crossover hit. The prospects for big money were there.

Risa had recorded her album, by inventing most of the lyrics and melodies to Pop and Fresh's rhythm tracks. She had proven to be far more talented than Herbie had imagined; the girl could write as well as sing. She was also elusive. Recording the album, she was with Jason Solomon or Nelson Clay. Solomon was her adviser, Clay her lover, and Herbie couldn't help wondering whether those roles were sometimes reversed. Could Risa be managing two lovers at once?

Such thoughts were at night. During the day Herb was back to phone calls, pushing her record, and preparing himself for his one P.M. lunch date with his father. The old man had chosen Sylvia's, a popular eatery up in Harlem. Herb liked to hang around Harlem when he was in New York; Harlem helped him keep in touch. Herbie would have preferred a midtown restaurant closer to the office but what the hell. The A train was still the quickest way to get to Harlem, and a walk across 125th Street was always a kick—the street musicians and merchants out in force selling everything from African robes to fake designer sweatshirts.

Sylvia's was listed in all the Japanese tour books as *the* place to sample soul food, so the place was often crowded with Asian tourists. This day was no exception, two large busses having dropped off a load of Japanese businessmen anxious to brave plates of Sylvia's short-ribs, chitlins, and black-eyed peas. Herbie sat alone in a booth in the back, waiting for his father.

Herbie was always early to meet the old man because, truth to tell, he couldn't wait to see him. It had always been that way. When he was a kid and his dad was due for a visit it was the same. As soon as Herb arrived, though, Herbie started worrying about when he would have to leave—and how long it would be before he'd get to see him again. So the visits were always strained. The old man felt guilty for what he'd done to Honey, for not visiting his children more—and so saw them less. Five years earlier when Honey had died of a heart attack, Herbie finally heard his father say, "I'm sorry," the words said barely loud enough to be understood. After the funeral, though, there was no close talk. Herb Montgomery, Sr., offered his namesake a firm handshake and was on his way. What else was new? . . .

Herbie looked at his watch. Now his father was a half-hour late. He wondered what the old man wanted. Herbie had heard from others how proud his father was of his youngest son's accomplishments— though he'd never heard that from the man himself. Maybe this time was the exception. Don't hold your breath, Herbie told himself.

Yet he did get excited when his father came into the restaurant. For an older man he looked terrific—thin, tall and spry. His beard was groomed, cut close to his skin, gray and white. He wore small silver-framed glasses. He had aged well.

"Good seeing you," said Herb. They shook hands, no hugs. "I see you're still wearing those stuffy suits and ties." Herb was in a denim jacket and white turtleneck.

"Tools of my trade."

"About your trade, seems to me the music's getting worse and worse. What's with this sampling? Isn't sampling just another name for stealing songs?"

"No," the son shot back, "it's using pieces of songs—rhythm tracks, instrumental solos, horn lines, vocal licks—as adornments."

"Adornments? It all comes from a computer, doesn't it?"

"The way a painter's colors come from a palette. The computer helps expand the possibilities, it doesn't limit them."

"It's mechanistic—"

"How about a camera?"

"Cameras need an artistic eye behind the lens. The sounds I'm hearing aren't warm."

"Which sounds?"

"The people you've been talking about for years—Prince, Bobby Brown. You call them rhythm-and-blues artists, but what do they have to do with the great rhythm-and-blues people like Charles Brown, Ruth Brown or Ray Charles?"

"Everything. That's where they come from. If anything, the music's gotten funkier. It's just that the funk has gone high-tech."

"Lightnin' Hopkins didn't need electricity."

"But B. B. King did and used it to create a brilliant sound. You wouldn't call B. B.'s blues diluted, would you?"

"Critics have. They've said he urbanized country blues."

"Critics, Dad? You know that better than anyone. Before Lightnin' Hopkins picked up a guitar to accompany his blues, some guy was hollering through a hollow log. Was the hollow log purer than an acoustic guitar? Was Lightnin' a sell-out for teaching himself the guitar? How pure is pure? The critics' arguments are silly. Things change. Sounds change. Music evolves. Remember what you used to tell me about the Dixieland guys who hated bebop when you were young?"

"That was different."

"Why?"

"Because bebop was the legitimate revolution."

"And how do you know you're not reacting against a legitimate revolution in rhythm and blues?"

"All I know is that I hate what I hear. It's not soulful in the least. It's not about music, it's about money."

"Before we wear out our jaws," said Herbie, "let's order lunch."

Waiting for the food to arrive, the old man took several deep breaths. "Look," he said, "I didn't come to fight."

"Why did you come?"

"First, tell me about your business. How's it going?"

"I have a number-one hit."

"Terrific. Who's the artist?"

"Risa."

"Never heard of her. What's the song?"

" 'Follow This Feeling.' "

"Never heard it."

"Didn't think you had."

"Is it a white hit?"

"No, Dad, it's a *black* hit. Very goddamn black, for your information."

"But you're looking to put her on the white charts?"

"I'm looking to put her on every chart."

"Pretty girl, this Risa?"

"Beautiful."

"No last name?"

"We're just calling her Risa."

"Where'd you find her?"

"She was a model."

"Can she act?"

"She can do anything, she's a natural."

"It sounds like you're involved."

"Professionally, yes."

"Well, I'm glad you're doing so well. I really am."

The food arrived and the conversation stopped until both men ate quickly.

"I still don't know why you wanted to see me," said Herbie.

"Can't I just want to spend some time with my son?"

"You usually have a reason."

"Here's my reason." And the old man handed Herbie a screenplay.

"What's this?"

"My next movie."

"You write it?"

"Come on, Herbie."

"And what am I supposed to do with it?"

"Read it."

"You've never asked me to read anything you've written before."

"This is different."

"Why?"

"I need advice . . ."

"*You* are asking *me* for advice?"

"The story has a black theme, but I want to reach a white audience."

"And I'm the expert in reaching a white audience?"

"The master of crossover, isn't that what you've been working at?"

"You don't want my advice, Dad, you want financing. Isn't that it?"

"The record business has made you cynical."

"You haven't answered me. Don't you want me to help get this funded?"

"All you have to do is read it."

"I want you to be straight with me," said Herbie.

"You have contacts. I've never been good at business."

"Before I agree to read this I want to hear you say it, Dad. I want to hear the words, 'I need your help.' "

The old man smiled. "All right, maybe I could use a little help."

When the check came, Herbie grabbed it. "This one's on me," he said, feeling very good indeed.

"The background vocals are off," Chanel declared. "They're out of tune."

"We were going for a certain style," Marisa argued.

"Where'd you get those singers?"

"The producers are also singing background—that's Pop and Fresh."

"Pop and Fresh? How come you didn't get the Pillsbury Doughboy? What is this crap, some kind of joke?"

"Pop and Fresh are serious, the single has gone number one."

"I know. Why do you think I'm calling?"

"Where are you?"

"Canada. But I'm on my way to New York. I'll be there tomorrow. Looks like I got a recording contract down there."

"That's great." If true.

"It's been four years since I've cut an album."

"I'm happy for you, Mama." And she meant it.

"The first session is Tuesday at noon. That'll give us lots of time to learn the song."

"What do you mean *us*?"

"My producer wants us to sing together."

"What are you talking about?"

"Just because you didn't see fit to use me on your record doesn't mean I have to be that way with you. I intend to use you on my record."

"I'm under contract—"

"There are ways around those things. Believe me, I'm an expert with contracts."

"You don't understand, this thing's taken off—"

"Goddammit, girl, where do you think you got that voice of yours? I schooled you on singing. I brought you up. It's *my* blood that flows through your veins."

"You got a contract because of my hit. Is that it? This producer thinks he can cash in."

"You got your contract because of *my* history in the business—at least partly. You ain't gonna tell me that *your* producer never heard of Chanel Faith?"

"Yes, he heard of you."

"And what did he say?"

"He admires you."

"There you go."

"Last time you asked me to sing, Mama, you blew me off stage. Are you forgetting that?"

"You're too sensitive, I was waiting for you to stand up and fight back, to blow *me* off stage. You could have if you'd wanted to. I don't want you to sing background on my record. Girl, I want you to *sing*."

"I can't handle this."

"There's nothing to handle. I'm handling it all. You'll see when I get to New York. Your mama knows just what she's doing."

And she hung up before Marisa could answer back.

"Just when I was feeling great, this has to happen," Marisa was saying to Nelson Clay, who was reading in an easy chair across from the bed. They were in his place on Tenth Street.

"*What* has to happen?" asked Clay.

"Mama's on her way. Now that things are rolling along she's jumping on my bandwagon."

"I'd like to meet her."

"What?"

"I just said I'd like to meet your mother."

"Here she is, invading my life again and—"

"She hasn't invaded yet. She called to ask—"

"Why in hell should you be taking her part? You don't know her."

"Of course I don't. But I'd like to. Why is that a problem?"

"Every time you dig into my relationships with my mother and grandmother it feels like you're preparing a damn paper."

"And if I don't ask I'm guilty of not caring."

"It's *when* you ask," said Marisa. "It's your timing. Right now's a lousy time."

"Right now should be a great time for you. You have two men crazy about you, doing all they can to help your career—"

"And I have nothing to do with any of it? I didn't sing my ass off? I didn't write the lyrics? That wasn't me dancing in the video?"

"Who said you weren't—"

"You. You were talking like I was a puppet being manipulated by men."

"Speaking of manipulation . . . when you need an in-house therapist I'm your boy, Marisa. When you feel like talking about your long-lost father—"

"We've never discussed my father . . ."

"You've told me your dreams about him. He's somewhere in nearly every conversation you have about men."

"Please, don't give me your analysis, not now."

"You asked for it, you ask for it all the time. The truth is that you're fascinated by analysis, more, I suspect, than by me."

"And with all your great training and experience you've never approached me about my father."

"It's been clear he abandoned you. You have all the traits of an abandoned child—"

"Oh, is that right? And if I told you that he's dead, that he died during the Vietnam War—"

"You've told me that and I've told you that death to a child can be a form of abandonment."

"All these wonderful clichés . . ."

"Look, Marisa, all I said was I was looking forward to meeting your mother—"

"Then let me give you her number. Call her and have a fascinating conversation. Tell her you're writing a book. Tell her you need her for your case study. Then call Grandmama Georgia in California so you can frame the picture nice and neat and square. While you're doing all that, *I'm* going out."

*   *   *

It was a sticky summer night. Thunder rumbled in the distance. Rain was a threat. It had rained that night, over a year ago, when Marisa had met Joan and Nelson. Maybe Nelson was right, maybe Marisa *was* manipulative. But walking past Joan's brownstone, she had to laugh. No one was a bigger schemer than the agent. And what about Nelson? Had he smooth-talked her into this affair or had she used him because of her need, as he called it, for an in-house therapist? Who the hell knew? All Marisa knew was she should be feeling better than she had ever felt before. She had her contract, she had her hit, she'd gotten to the top of at least one record chart—the black chart—and was aiming for the white. Nothing wrong with that. Nelson Clay didn't understand the business. Could it be he was threatened by her success? When she was still grasping at straws, vulnerable and in big need of reassurance, he'd been there. But as soon as Jason and Herbie had stepped into the picture he seemed to change . . . "It was you and your mother and grandmother," he had told her more than once. "Now it's you and Solomon and Montgomery. You have this need to triangulate . . ."

Triangulate. Hell, she felt like *strangulating* Nelson. Walking up lower Fifth Avenue, thinking over his talk, Marisa was furious. She was tired of his analysis. She didn't want to think anymore. Part of her felt that she was no longer Marisa. Now she was *Risa*—the name Jason had always called her, someone apart and different from her family. Now she simply wanted to enjoy the fact that after one hell of a struggle she'd begun to make it and it was going to be better. That's what she believed. No more psychobabble. How about a little celebration? No one would understand better than Jason. She hailed a cab as rain started falling. "Central Park West and Eighty-sixth Street," she told the driver.

He was excited to see her. He had been wondering where their relationship, if that's what it was, was going. There were days when she would call him ten times asking his advice. And there were a lot of days when he wouldn't hear from her at all. She alternately needed and didn't need him. Musically she counted heavily on Herbie Montgomery, but Jason knew she considered Herbie a square, although a brilliant business guy. Then there was this Nelson Clay, a nice guy but too academic for Risa. Recently it seemed He and Risa were fighting. Jason sensed, hoped, they wouldn't last. Changes were in the wind. Hooray for change.

When he took Risa around to radio stations in New York, Philadelphia and Boston on the first leg of her promotional tour, Jason felt her leaning on him, counting on him, trusting him. She was pleased with her growing celebrity, the approval and the early money coming in. But it was also clear that the faster she moved, the more she needed a friend.

Well, she couldn't move too fast for Jason. He thought in terms of feature films—and in featuring Risa in one—but that was a ways off. Meanwhile, juggling a half-dozen balls in the air had given him fresh confidence. And Risa, he understood, was the source of the confidence.

Risa liked being in Jason's apartment. The major objects weren't books—like in Nelson's place—but pictures, posters and paintings Jason had bought from street artists, cartoonists he had found working in the park. "Available art," he called it. Pop and Fresh were in that category.

"I'm glad you're here," said a smiling Jason, "but it's midnight. I guess you don't want to be alone. You had a fight with your shrink?"

"You think you know me so damn well."

He took her by the hand and brought her into his kitchen, where he put on water for tea, then put on a tape, "Ask the Ages," by Sonny Sharrock, the free-spirited guitarist who had played with Olatunji and Pharoah Sanders. Risa liked its fierceness.

Jason poured the spiced yogi tea and sat across from her. "Take off your raincoat, stay awhile."

Underneath she was wearing cut-off jeans and a yellow tank top. She had wonderful legs and beautiful shoulders, and Jason had to fight back an urge to caress her.

"So . . ." he said.

"It's not Nelson."

"Fine."

"It's Chanel."

"Here we go . . ."

"Right, you know the routine."

"She wants in."

"You got it."

"And what did you say?"

"She didn't give me a chance to say much of anything. She'll be in the city tomorrow. She got a record contract . . ."

"Playing off you."

"Maybe . . ."

"Great. So let her make a record."

"She wants *me* on her record."

Jason laughed. "You know, that reminds me a lot of Grandpa Sol. He hears I'm doing okay and the next thing he's doing is hiring me as his publicist."

"You told him no?"

"I didn't tell him anything. I won't call him and argue."

"Chanel won't call, she'll come by, she'll move in."

"And you won't be home," he said abruptly, surprising himself. "You'll move in here."

Maybe it was the hour, maybe just the fact that Risa had come to his place, maybe the outline of her small nipples against the ribbed cotton of her skin-tight shirt. Maybe, too, because he knew her. She was a gutsy lady. She'd been handling rejections left and right in bad-ass New York City while he had played the dilettante in New Mexico. At the same time she was intimidated—she'd always been intimidated by her mother and grandmother, who were also gutsy. Had been at it longer than the third-generation Risa. She needed some protection, and because he understood her he was the one to give her what she needed.

"To hell with Chanel," he said, "let her go looking for you. Let her do whatever she needs to do. At the end of the week we go to Atlanta for more promo. Before that we have to prep the second video. You can't afford distractions, Risa. Not now."

"I'm supposed to hide out from my own mother?"

"Just live your own life. To hell with her."

"You make it sound so easy."

"It's a matter of focus."

He got up, walked over to Risa and began to massage her shoulders.

She didn't want to think. She wanted to be comforted, feel easy. He knew when to start and when to stop. Tonight he didn't stop because he felt her need for him to go on. He kept talking, kept telling her that it was going to be all right, that it was *her*—not her grandmother, not her mother—it was *her* talent that had taken her this far. Her instincts were superb; she had the most beautiful shoulders, the most beautiful back, the most beautiful legs, the most beautiful face he had ever seen . . .

Risa knew he was laying it on thick, knew Jason as well as he knew her. He was horny and probably thinking the same thing she was thinking—how it had been seven or eight years since they had made love. She had felt safe with Jason. He had never hurt her, never bragged to the boys about what he had done, never said a thing to anyone. He seemed to know how to balance her. Tonight he understood the pressure she was under. And the good pressure he was applying to her shoulders, the way he massaged her neck, slow, steady, had her wondering why she'd ever gotten into this complicated relationship with the psychiatrist. Jason's fingers were untying the knots from her neck. Jason's appreciation felt so *un*complicated. Friendship pure and simple, passionate friendship that didn't look for or demand control. Nelson Clay's specialty was the psychology of old folks. What was that really all about? Why couldn't he deal with people his own age? Did *his* need to control others have something to do with his specialty? And why was he having such a hard time getting used to her success? Jason helped bring on that success. He had gotten her the video shot, brought her to HM Records, worked single-mindedly to further her career. Who else could say that? Chanel and Georgia had their own agendas—hidden agendas, thought Marisa; they had always hidden secrets from her and each other. Jason's talk had always been out-front and honest.

"I think we're thinking the same thing," he said as his hand slid up the back of her tank top so he could caress her spine. "What I'm thinking is that we've been thinking too damn much, you and I always think too much, and the only way to stop it is to start feeling, which is why you came over here and why you want to stay and why I can't keep my hands from making you feel better . . . are you feeling better?"

Her half-moan was her answer.

His bedspread was covered with sketches for a poster of Risa. He swept them to the floor as Risa lay on the bed, face down, for a more serious massage. This time he slipped off her top and applied his lips to her back. When she turned over and their mouths met, she was ready. She remembered his red pubic hair and liked the way he tasted in her mouth. She liked the way he licked her, liked his persistence and wondered why this hadn't happened sooner because it felt so natural and right, this man working to bring her to the good place where mind turned off and body turned on . . . high and hard, higher, harder, positioned so she had everything she wanted without worry or stress. No one ever worked harder to bring her—"Come on, baby," he urged, "come on, come on, come *on*." And when she came she smiled and he smiled and knew not to say another word, not to make another sound.

Herbie Montgomery spent the next morning, a Saturday, reading his father's script. When he put it down he found himself reaching for the phone. He needed to talk to Risa.

At her apartment her answering machine was on. He tried her at Nelson Clay's, got another machine. Jason Solomon was the only one to pick up the phone.

"You wouldn't know where Risa is, would you?" asked Herbie.

Risa was lying next to Jason, naked and sound asleep.

"I should be talking to her soon," said Jason. "What's up?"

"Have her call me," said Herbie. "It's important."

"Something I should know about?"

"Yes. It's important. But first I want to speak with Risa."

There was something about the urgency in Herbie's voice that Jason didn't like.

"If you can't get the financing for *Pearl*," said Georgia, seated behind her desk at Passion Flowers, "this once I'm prepared to help you."

"That won't be necessary," Herb Montgomery, Sr., assured her over the telephone.

"I won't allow this project to fail, Herb. We're too old. We've run out of time."

"No one knows that better than me."

"You work your money people," she told him, glancing at the current bestseller list from the Los Angeles *Times Book Review*, "and I'll work mine." Her eyes stopped at the title, *Hit and Run*, and its author, Sol Solomon.

"There's a Chanel Faith here to see you," Nelson Clay's secretary said over the intercom.

Chanel Faith? What in hell was Marisa's mother doing here?

"She says you'll want to see her."

Well, she was right about that. "Have her come in."

A wide, dark-skinned woman with gold eye shadow, gold chain bracelets and rouge came through the door with a huge smile and steady, determined eyes. She wore a cherry-red leather jacket over black leggings.

"You look just like a psychology man," she said, "with your teacher's glasses and your tweedy suit. Why do you guys always wear tweedy suits? You're surprised to see me, Dr. Clay."

"I am, Ms. Faith."

"Chanel. Wasn't too easy finding you."

"I work out of a couple of offices," he said, "and see patients at two hospitals—"

"I know all about it. I go to a psychologist myself. A woman. Been seeing her for a while now. I'm also a card-carrying AA member. Clean and sober. Ain't that something?"

He waited.

"Turning my will over to God. Putting things in the Lord's hands. Now you psychological types, I know you don't always believe in the Lord. But that's okay, because you believe in other things. You believe in looking at mama, looking at papa and seeing where we come from."

"Ms. Faith—"

"You want to know why I'm here. I'm living in this city for a spell and I don't know any good therapists and I figure, well, my daughter, she has a good mind, she found herself a good therapist—maybe he's just the man to see."

"I couldn't see you as a patient."

"Because you're her boyfriend?"

"I am not her boyfriend."

"Well, that's news to me, doc."

"Haven't you talked to your daughter?"

"Not since I've been in the city."

"How long has that been?"

"Two weeks."

"It's been that long since I've seen Marisa."

"So she cut us both out—just like that. Can you beat it?"

"The night you called her to say you were coming, that was the last time I saw her."

"I called her at your place. I thought maybe y'all were living together."

"Things have changed between us."

Chanel nodded. "The girl's impossible, always has been. I know she told you all about her childhood."

"Very little."

"It was something, the way she ran back and forth between me and Mother. For a long time I thought she got the best of both worlds. Anyway, that was my plan."

"But it didn't work out."

"Watch it, doc. Nothing works out like you plan. You love her, don't you? I can see it in your eyes."

"I'm very fond of her."

"Listen to how you psychology types talk. Always so careful. But when it comes to Marisa, men are never careful. They fly around her like moths around a flame. And they get burned because they don't realize the girl's a free spirit, just like her mama. Can't pin her down. You saw that, didn't you, doc?"

"Ms. Faith . . ."

"Chanel. . . ."

"I'm not too comfortable with this conversation."

"Relax, hon. You're not charging me for your advice and I'm not charging you for mine. We're just talking about someone we're both crazy about, in spite of ourselves. We're just chatting. She's a real strong one, isn't she?"

"Very motivated, yes."

"She gets that from me."

"And your mother?"

"Georgia? Georgia's in another world altogether. She's the Grand Duchess. She's expecting to win the Academy Award next year, if only the right role comes along. She's been waiting for that role for fifty years. That's my mother. Above it all. Georgia doesn't understand no rock 'n' roll. Georgia doesn't understand Marisa. Me and Marisa, we're more like sisters than mother and daughter."

"Sisters who aren't speaking."

"My Marisa's edgy, that's all. She's got herself a hit and she doesn't know what to do next. Doesn't realize the people who love her most, people like her mama and a good man like you, doc—she doesn't know she needs us now more than ever."

"I'm flattered by your confidence, but I'm not sure how I've earned it."

"Oh, she's talked about you. Yes, she has. She's told me how intelligent you are. She couldn't do any better than a psychology man. And a brother to boot. Someone who understands the heart and the brain. I see you really care for her. But I also know my daughter. She tends to mix up her business life and her love life. She thinks good business depends on good love. Got that silly idea from her grandmother. See, that's how Georgia does. Right now Marisa is thinking that Jason Solomon is the big key to her success, just like Georgia thought Sol Solomon was the key to hers. Like grandfather, like grandson. They're both full of shit."

"You don't like Jason."

"What's he ever done? What does he know about the record business? The boy's soaking wet behind the ears."

"Marisa seems pretty dependent on him."

"*Co*dependent—that's what they're calling it these days, aren't they, doc? That's when you're afraid to stand alone. Now that's something that's never scared me."

So you say. "To be honest, I never understood your daughter's relationship with Jason. It began when they were children, didn't it?"

"It began on account of my mother—that's how it began."

He kept his mouth shut.

"Georgia has been Sol Solomon's mistress for as long as anyone can remember. That's Jason's grandfather. The writer. You've heard of him?"

"I think so."

"From Marisa?"

"Marisa doesn't like to talk about these things. At least not with me."

"Hey, no woman likes to think of her grandmother as a kept woman. But that Jewish money—Georgia couldn't stay away from it. Now when Jason's parents died, old man Sol took over. And that's when Georgia set up my Marisa with Jason. Georgia could never get Sol to marry her so she figured maybe her granddaughter would have better luck with Jason."

"And you didn't approve." To hell with restraint. He needed to know. He wanted her to keep talking.

"The kid was a space cadet. But you couldn't tell Georgia that. She saw him as educated, so polite, so sophisticated, so *white*. Meanwhile, all he wanted was to get into Marisa's panties."

"One thing," he said, "has always made me wonder about your daughter."

"What's that?"

"Why she'll never discuss her father."

The question hit its mark. Chanel closed her eyes, glittery gold makeup heavy on her lids.

"That's a long story, doc. Maybe we should save it for the next time we get together."

"You've done a masterful job," Georgia told Jason over the phone. She was at Passion Flowers, he was in his New York apartment.

"You've heard the record?" he asked, surprised to be hearing from Marisa's grandmother.

"I don't understand that music but I trust you do. You have taste, contemporary taste. I know that's important. And I'm proud of you, Jason, I truly am."

"Have you talked to Risa?"

"I wrote a letter telling her I know she's in very competent hands. Your grandfather tells me that you've also produced some wonderful documentary movies. You were always so talented, Jason. None of this news surprises me . . . You and Marisa have a special rapport, don't you?"

"Well, things seem to be working out," he said. He was glad to hear from Georgia. Ever since he was a kid she had gone out of her way to treat him kindly. He understood the special relationship between Sol and Georgia, and he knew it was something Risa never wanted to talk about. In his own mind, though, Jason considered Georgia a feather in Sol's cap. The old man was a hopeless square but he did have, even if only on the side, one hell of a woman—a knockout beauty, a black woman with real class. Moreover, during his high school years when encouragement was in short supply, Georgia had been a steady supporter. "He'll get over this time of rebellion," he once overheard her tell Sol. "He's smart and imaginative. Believe me, that boy will make something of himself."

"You must be interested in feature films," Georgia was now saying.

"I sure am."

"And film opportunities for Marisa?"

"Of course."

"You must know that I receive dozens of scripts every month. Over the years I've literally read thousands. But, Jason, something's come across my desk that demands attention. Close attention. It's a wonderful story with a marvelous part for Marisa. In fact, the screenplay reads as though it was written specifically *for* Marisa."

"My grandfather didn't write it, did he?"

"No, no, as a matter of fact I wouldn't say anything to him about it. Sol's always been a little bit jealous of other writers."

"Who is the writer?"

"A man named Herb Montgomery. Have you heard of him?"

"You're talking about Herb Montgomery who makes films?"

"Yes."

"His son is the man who owns HM Records."

"HM Records?"

"The label that records Risa. Herbie's the man who gave us the deal."

"You're joking."

"I'm dead serious."

"Have you and Marisa met his father? Does his father know about Marisa's record?"

"I don't know."

"Well, that's certainly very interesting," said Georgia as she flashed back over thirty years to the day she served as midwife to Honey Lincoln Montgomery. And to the night she conceived Herb Montgomery's daughter—Chanel.

Risa was talking to the late-night talk-show host.

She thought he was a wiseguy but liked being on national television with a national hit. Thanks to the efforts of Herbie Montgomery, her album had crossed over, breaking into the top ten. She was becoming a pop star. To the host, though, she was a manufactured media creation he could goof on.

His questions tried to throw her off balance, poking fun at the "superficial" dance culture he thought she represented. As he sat there with his blazer, khaki pants and tennis shoes—almost a David Letterman, except he had no gap-toothed grin—he was nonetheless taken with Risa's unorthodox look: fake-fur top and silver sweatpants covered with paisley-shaped sequins.

"Weren't you a model?" he asked.

"For a while. Not long."

"Isn't that a prerequisite for becoming a singer these days—being a model or, better yet, a Laker girl?"

"Well, at least that gives some talk-show hosts something to yak about."

"Hey, touché. How do you feel about talk-show hosts?"

"I believe in them. Like I believe in other necessary evils like lawyers, laxatives . . ."

He cracked up. "Are you having digestive problems?"

"My stomach's doing fine, and I'm happy to be here. I really am. I'm ready to shout out some good news."

"Hold on," said the host. "I know a plug when I hear one coming. This card says 'Follow This Feeling' is the name of your hit song."

"I'd like to dedicate it to you."

"Even though I'm a talk-show host?"

"*Because* of it. You've forever changed my attitude about talk-show hosts."

"And you'll never belittle them again?"

"Not as long as they're as sensitive as you."

"I couldn't ask for anything more—except to ask you to sing."

"I'm ready," said Risa, springing out of her chair.

Watching her on a monitor in the green room, Herbie Montgomery was excited. At first he worried about her sarcasm, but she came off finally as a feisty chick who could take it as well as dish it out. Herbie would have preferred Jay Leno or Arsenio Hall or Letterman, but when those shows passed he had, somewhat reluctantly, booked her here. The producer had insisted Risa sing with the house band. Herbie agreed, stipulating, however, that Pop and Fresh be included. Watching Risa and her two producers—who sang backup and played synthesizers—he felt good about his decision. It took guts for Risa to interpret a high-energy dance tune backed only by a small band. Yet even without the full instrumentation that had enhanced the hit record, Risa pulled it off. Her musical personality was that strong. This was her national debut and she wasn't about to blow it. The groove was up in her body; her limbs were loose and free; she swayed and smiled with neither pretense nor effort. Her movements were never clichéd but rather unpredictable—a snap of the head, a flick of the wrist. Her choreography was strictly her own, natural and free. Influenced by the spontaneity of Pop and Fresh—whose outfits were straight off the mean streets of the Bronx—Risa changed her vocal reading every time she sang the song. Tonight she knew she had read it right.

When the taping was complete and she came back to the green room, she was elated. She'd survived the host's caustic wit, and more important, she had sung her ass off.

Herbie confirmed her own instincts. "You were great."

"Where's Jason?" she asked. "What did Jason think?"

"He called from the airport, there's an emergency. He had to fly out to California."

"What happened?" asked Risa, thinking of Georgia.

"His grandfather had a heart attack."

"Jesus. What's his condition now?"

"I don't know."

"I'll call Georgia."

"While you do, I'll get my father."

"Your father?"

"He's in the studio audience."

"You didn't tell me anything about your father coming."

"Well, he's been wanting to meet you. He'll be back here in a minute."

The three of them sat in a Chinese restaurant on the Upper East Side—father, son, and Risa. She was still high from her performance. In spite of her concern for Jason's grandfather, she felt this night was the highlight of her life. She was also intrigued by Herbie's father. He mentioned that he'd been to China three times during his film-making career. His conversation drew on decades of Hollywood tales. She found herself hanging on his every word, and thinking, What a wonderful man. I'd love to have a grandfather this cool . . .

Two weeks earlier, when Herb had learned that Risa was really Marisa Faith, daughter of Chanel and granddaughter of Georgia, he'd been understandably stunned. He thought it best not to say anything to Herbie. For nearly fifty years he'd gone along with Georgia's tall tale about Chanel's father. To suddenly tell his son that Risa was actually his granddaughter would serve no purpose. On the other hand, he had to meet the girl, especially when she was the one who according to Herbie would be perfect for his script, perfect to play Pearl as a young woman. The fact that his son had signed her, re-corded her and promoted her was also amazing. It was Georgia, after she'd learned about HM Records from Jason, who revealed that in-formation to him. What Georgia hadn't revealed to her long-time lover was that Jason Solomon, Sol's grandson, was Marisa's manager.

Everyone's head was swimming: Herb for being in this position; Herbie, for the first time in his life having his old man soliciting *him*, openly acknowledging his success, and obviously nuts about Marisa. Herbie had also delivered on his promise to Risa—her debut album was a runaway hit.

While waiting for the sweet-and-sour soup to arrive, Marisa could hardly wait for the airing time when she, and millions of Americans, would be watching herself on television. Everything she had worked for was happening. Earlier that day she had even spoken to Chanel,

who was living in a midtown hotel while cutting her new album. She
told her mother about the TV show.

"When are you doing it?"

"Today."

"I'll be there."

"Don't. Please. You'll just make me nervous."

"That's a hell of a thing to say. I've been here three weeks and
you've had time to see me for one lousy cup of coffee."

One cup of coffee had been enough, especially since it was when
she learned that Chanel had gone to see Nelson Clay. But she did
want Chanel to watch her on TV, and also had called Georgia about
the show.

"I spoke with my grandmother," Marisa was saying to Herb Montgomery and his son over mu-shu pork. "She just got back from the
hospital. Sol's going to be okay, the heart attack wasn't awful."

"Sol?" asked Herb, Sr.

"Sol Solomon," Risa said. "Do you know him?"

The filmmaker kept his composure. "In fact, I do know Sol Solomon. I know him *and* your grandmother."

"You know Risa's grandmother?" Herbie was surprised.

"I've worked with her, yes."

"I'd like to hear about that," Risa said.

"Not much to tell. A few pictures in the old days. Back then I
worked with every black actor and actress in Hollywood. There
weren't that many of us."

"And what about Risa's mother?" Herbie wanted to know. "Have
you met her?"

"Heard her sing once. In church. Wonderful voice. You come from
a family rich in talent," he told Risa with a straight face.

"When I read your screenplay," she said, "I actually saw my
grandmother as Pearl in her later years."

"Funny," said Herb, allowing a slight smile, "I did too."

Herb excused himself after dinner, having made a strong impression
on his son's star. And his secret granddaughter. It was obvious to him
that Herbie's interest in Risa was more than professional. In Herbie
he saw himself as a young man chasing after Georgia, except Herbie

was a businessman who understood money. He was already doing for Risa what Herb had never been able to do for Risa's grandmother. Well, now his script would soon do it for everyone. His son deserved a Risa just as, after fifty long years, he deserved Georgia.

After Herb said goodnight, kissing Risa on the cheek before catching a cab, Risa and Herbie went off together to a late-night party for friends to watch the show. She had never been in Herbie's Lexington Avenue apartment.

Unlike Jason, Herbie was meticulous. The posh gray carpets were obviously well-vacuumed; the dark glass coffee table shone; the Jacob Lawrence and Archibald Motley prints were framed and hung with precision; the catered food was spread out on the dark wood dining room table. The company, a mostly black crowd of record-business yuppies on the rise, gave Risa star attention. When the show came on and Risa was introduced, they cheered. Watching herself, Risa sat next to Herbie on the gray suede couch. She held his hand and squeezed it a little as she heard herself play with the talk-show host. The invited guests approved. "Go on, girl," they said as she started to sing and dance. When it was over the compliments flowed: "You tore it up, baby." "You threw down." "You killed."

Risa was on top of the world. She was tempted to call her mother and Georgia, but that could wait until tomorrow. Actually, she was afraid they'd be critical—her attitude, outfit, performance—and didn't want to risk anything spoiling her mood. She also wanted to phone Jason but didn't know where to reach him.

"You gotta get this lady in pictures," said one program director before he left at two A.M.

Herbie answered with a small wink.

Risa liked Herbie . . . no, tonight she *loved* Herbie, not to mention his father and his screenplay, *Pearl*; being on national television; being on the inside of the music business; rising on the charts; thinking about the tour Herbie was planning and the appearances she'd be making next week in Atlanta and Houston and San Francisco, hoping Herbie would come along because when he did things were so organized, no detail unattended.

At first she had thought he was too reserved, remote, but now she saw that business meant people *buying* her records. For the first time in the history of the Faith family a Faith woman was a bona fide across-the-board star. And damn it, she was the one who had done it.

She was proud and also grateful, and when all the guests were gone and she let Herbie hold her and kiss her, she wasn't surprised, wasn't hesitant when he took her into his bedroom and the climax of the evening, of her long time of struggle, came over her with breathtaking force.

He was different than she had imagined, hungry for everything she offered. She smelled it on his skin and inside his moist body that wanted more . . . *Give everything to him that he gave to me, Herbie's strength, Herbie's sincerity, Herbie doing it doing it doing it . . .*

Herbie at last got what he wanted. From the moment he saw her, Risa had been what he wanted. He had always been jealous of her other men, always wanted to know what she had with Jason Solomon and Nelson Clay. Now that it was happening for him, he didn't need to imagine. He had never known loving like this, never cared so much, never wanted to please like this and just watch her beneath him and above him and so open that he understood where to go and how to touch, staying with her until, exhausted, she had to ask him to stop while he said, and clearly meant it, "I love you, you don't know how much . . ."

Nelson Clay was going a little crazy. It had started with the visits from Marisa's mother, and now it involved Marisa herself. He felt control slipping away.

His head said forget her. His head said she was gone and there was nothing he could or should do. He understood the forces pulling at her, the demands on her, the drive pushing her on. But when he saw the huge poster of her at Sam Goody's on Sixth Avenue, when he heard her voice on the radio, when he read about her in the New York *Post* and People magazine, he felt he had to have her back. So against his better instincts he would casually meet with her mother from time to time—for a sweet roll at Chock Full o'Nuts or a hot dog at Nathan's just to maintain some sort of contact. Besides, he liked hearing Chanel say how, in spite or everything, he was the one Marisa loved, not Jason. Chanel obviously despised Jason, saw him as a link to Georgia, and it was Georgia, Chanel was still convinced, who wanted to control Marisa's career.

"Through Jason," Chanel told Nelson, "my mother is keeping my child away from me."

If that were so, the plan was working, he thought.

"She won't listen to me, she won't even see me. But when my record comes out and hits bigger than hers she'll come running. Oh yes, she will. I know my baby. She'll come to Mama."

Nelson saw Mama as one of the world's pushiest women, but certainly not without charm. Moreover, to her credit, she had managed to stay clean. Going to one and sometimes two AA meetings a day, concentrating on her career, singing, as she claimed, "better than I've ever sung in my whole goddamn life," staying clear of sexual entanglements, she was feeling strong and straight.

"It's crazy, my daughter's making it this big and not even letting me share the good shit with her," Chanel told Nelson, "but I'm turning it over to God. Two years ago I'd use it as an excuse to go out and burn through a bag of smoke or a mountain of coke. Not now. Now I got a Higher Power and, believe you me, Chanel's gonna be *all right.*"

Nelson wished he could be so confident about himself. Seeing patients, making hospital rounds, reading professional papers, his mind wandered. Every time he turned on the radio he seemed to hear Marisa. Every time he walked down the street he seemed to see her on a bus or taxi poster. Once late at night, going past an electronics store, he did see her on television. That same night she called to him in his dream, and when the following morning she actually did call him, he wasn't sure where he was.

"I'm in California," she told him. "They got me out here for meetings . . . Jason and Herbie have me going to a million damn meetings."

He rubbed sleep from his eyes. He wanted to say that he'd been dreaming about her but didn't, trying to affect a detached tone.

"I was asleep."

"I'm sorry . . . it's just that I needed to hear your voice. I need to hear a calm voice. You're always so calm."

"I'm surprised to hear from you. I thought things were going so well."

"Too well."

"What does that mean?"

"Too much happening too quickly."

"Wasn't action what you wanted?"

"I miss you."

He fought himself but said it anyway. "I miss you too." She had on her needy-little-girl air he couldn't resist.

"It's so crazy," she went on, "and I'm caught in between. I'm here and I'm there, I'm everywhere and I'm nowhere and everyone around me has his own thing—make this new record, make this new movie. I'm not sure where I come in, I'm not sure of anything right now except I have to get away, I really do, Nelson. I'm going plain nuts."

"It sounds like you need to be alone for a while."

"Or with a friend."

"We went beyond that."

"But at least you were never interested in the business side of me. Now I can appreciate that. I need someone like you."

"I don't think so, Marisa." Did *that* ever take an effort to say.

"You're the great listener."

"Marisa, I'm really not. You take off, then suddenly you come back into my life—"

"My mother said you ask about me all the time."

"You've talked to her?"

"She told me how much you care. She thinks you're good for me. She says I never appreciated what was there right in front of me."

Three cheers for Chanel, he thought.

"She's stayed clean, you've helped her."

"I've had nothing to do with it. I—"

"Look, listen to me, Nelson. I have to get away. I'm going to the desert for a couple of days. No one will know where I am. Meet me. Spend the weekend with me. It's ninety degrees in Palm Springs."

"Fly out to California just like that?"

"Right now."

"I can't."

He did.

He knew not to go. He understood what was happening. She was sweet, sensuous, irresistible, *and* she got what she needed, whom she needed, when she needed them. Right now what she needed was a shrink for the weekend—and he got the call. Refuse. Stay in New York. Keep a distance between himself and this lady. Easier thought than done.

Here he was on an airplane speeding for the Coast. He tried to laugh at himself, but knew this was no laughing matter. At thirty-one he had never even been engaged. He could honestly say that he had never been in love. Until now. The old restraint had crumbled. Even though he was flying to California, he knew he'd fly to Outer Mongolia if that meant seeing Marisa. Compulsion was setting the pace. To hell with cool deliberation. Screw reason. To the elderly woman sitting next to him on the plane he may have seemed an easy-mannered college professor quietly reading professional papers, but inside he was churning, burning for that moment when he'd find himself in Marisa's arms.

From Los Angeles International Airport he took a prop into Palm Springs. It was dark, the desert night still. Nelson looked about the airport and, at first, didn't see her. When a young woman with wraparound sunglasses and an Oakland Raiders baseball cap turned beakback on her head said hello, he wasn't even sure it was Marisa. She was wearing baggy workout pants and an oversized sweatshirt that said in big black letters: "I'm Centered." She took off the sunglasses, hugged him. The feel of her body against his made him realize he was still flying.

She drove a rented Saab deep into the desert to a remote hotel whose rambling two-bedroom suites overlooked a golf course. The sliding glass doors were open. The night was clear, the temperature cooled to seventy degrees. Nelson was still in his traveling clothes, still in shock. He took off his jacket, walked out onto the green to where Marisa stood examining the stars. In Manhattan he had forgotten about stars.

"Isn't this better?" she asked.

"Much."

She smelled of perfume and flowers. She took his hand and led him back to the patio outside her suite, where she sat on a cushioned bench, her face lit by moonlight. He could do nothing but look at her and listen.

"You were always the best listener," she said. "Everyone else wants to talk but you actually want to listen."

"I've been trained." As though he had a choice.

"Mama says you're sincere."

"I see you're reconciled with your mama."

"We've been talking for the first time in years. I realized how I underestimated her. She has a wisdom. I was afraid of her, I guess. Because I was afraid of her power. For sure I was threatened by her talent—her voice, I never felt as though I could match her voice. And then there's her personality. You know how she takes over any situation. I also realized I'm afraid of her mood swings. I really never knew her straight—not until now. As a little girl it didn't take me long to understand what she was doing to herself. When I'd visit her in Muscle Shoals I knew what kind of day we were going to have, based on which drugs were in the house. If there was coke, watch out. Mama would be wild. If there was pot, things would be more mellow. Vodka made her loud and 'ludes put her to sleep. I'd have to tiptoe around the moods, and that was exhausting. So when I got back to Beverly Hills and Georgia it was a relief. At least Georgia was always the same. I trusted that, but maybe my trust was misplaced."

"What happened to independence? When I first met you that's all you were talking about."

"The pasts of my mother and grandmother have a weird way of becoming my present. You know about Jason. Georgia might as well be his mother. Georgia, for your information, has been his grandfather's mistress for fifty years."

"Interesting . . ."

"I knew you'd like the story. I'm still a great case study, right?"

"You're great—period."

"Jason's terrific," she said. "He's always been there for me. He's helped me in so many ways I tended to forget about his ties to Georgia. Georgia is the most fabulously controlling woman in the world."

"More so than your mother?"

"Remember, Nelson, Georgia was my mother's teacher. Georgia is the original. Herbie Montgomery, it turns out, is working for Georgia."

"What are you talking about?"

"His father and Georgia are friends. That means they're probably old lovers. Maybe they're still at it. I have a feeling she can't live without juggling at least two men at once—Jason's grandfather, Herbie's father."

Nelson was about to draw a comparison between grandmother and granddaughter but stopped himself. "What exactly has Georgia been doing?" he asked.

"Planning her great triumph—a plan, by the way, that's been in the works for a good half-century."

"And it involves you?"

"It sure does. It's a movie, a big-budget movie in which she's the central character. Her plan is to manipulate all her marionettes—me, Jason, Herbie and Herbie's father. Herbie's father wrote the script, Herbie and Jason will co-produce, Jason's grandfather will help interest a studio and get financing, and I'll play Grandmama Georgia as a young woman. A perfect plan—except I'm not playing her game."

"You've told her this?"

"I've told her nothing. I'm just realizing what's happening. That's when I called you. I knew I had to think out loud. Chanel made me see things more clearly but there's no time. Jason and Herbie are pushing me in twelve different directions."

From another suite on another part of the green the sound of some old Broadway musical on someone's stereo spilled over the golf course. Nelson felt foolish. What was he doing in a retirement community in the California desert? He had traveled across the country knowing that this woman was having her way with him. She was mixed up by two mothers, mixed up by two lovers, mixed up by a stalled career that had suddenly taken off. She was reaching for him, he understood, not because she loved him but because she needed him. Every ounce of reason in his head told him to kiss her and take off. To become mixed up in her mixed-up life was dumb. But Nelson was not in his office, not in control. He was nothing but a man smitten. Nothing mattered except to be with Marisa, to stay with her tonight.

The real truth was that Nelson no longer cared what had happened among Marisa and Jason and Herbie. All he knew was that *he* was with her now, they weren't, no one knew where he and Marisa were, no one had the number, the curtains were drawn, the lights dimmed, and when she stood in front of him in her panties and lace bra, when he took her in his arms and covered her with his love, the world was outside, he was inside her, and she was calling out his name. All the discipline of his training was gone, all meaningless. What had meaning were the sounds of delight coming from her, the smell of her, and how when she climaxed and shuddered she called him back for more.

Johnny Dodd Huggins was in his dressing room waiting for rehearsals to begin. Female fans had filled the room with flowers and notes offering their eternal love and available bodies. At forty-seven, after twenty-five years in the business, Johnny Dodd had become a sex symbol. Country music had exploded, and he, along with singers like Garth Brooks and Billy Ray Cyrus, had profited from the sound's widespread popularity. His lucrative market was middle-aged ladies intrigued by his lean six-foot-six frame, ruggedly handsome face and molasses-smooth voice. He had made a transition from a rhythm-and-blues guitarist working East Coast studios to a full-fledged national star singing country songs of his own making.

The key was Nashville.

After ten years of New York City, Johnny Dodd had been ready for a change. Close to home without being home, Nashville was the mecca of the kind of music Johnny had grown up with. He had always favored blues, but country was in his blood. He could handle a country guitar—acoustic, slide, you name it—with the best of them. So he settled in Tennessee, where he played behind Waylon Jennings, Charley Pride and David Allan Coe. The more he listened to these singers the more his confidence grew, the more he considered stepping up from the background into the spotlight. That took some years, but finally he found a producer who put some money in Johnny Dodd Huggins demos. His first few albums flopped. Forced to return to work as a sideman and studio musician, he still didn't give up. He found other producers, wrote other songs until in the wake of the mushrooming popularity of country music, labels started looking for singers to groom into stars.

In the last few months Johnny Dodd had become a star. He was wearing three-hundred-dollar black Stetson hats and thousand-dollar green lizard-skin boots. He looked good on TV. With his penetrating green eyes, there was a mysterious allure in his quiet, laid-back manner. The few words he did speak were coated with the syrupy slang of the South.

He was a woman's man.

Among his friends Johnny Dodd's womanizing was legendary. He was especially fond of ladies of color, an indulgence he had decided to give up now that he had become a celebrity in the white world of country music. He had never married, never thought twice about Chanel and the child he had fathered.

Not until now.

Here he was about to headline on "Country Nights," a network television program. Taping was due to start in an hour. He was relaxing, reading over the Billboard charts, which showed his album *Magnolia Highway* the fifth-ranking entry. Sales had passed platinum. It was just a matter of crossing over into the lucrative pop market, which should happen any time. In fact, he was mentioned in an article about records that had sold a million or more in the past year. As he noted the other artists—Color Me Badd, Hammer, Michael Bolton—he stopped at the name of Risa. There was a picture of the stunning young woman whose eyes stared at him with a strange familiarity. He read on: "Risa," said the story, "is the daughter of veteran r&b singer Chanel Faith."

"Well, I'll be goddamned," he muttered to himself. "Looks like I sired me a winner."

"I think this is the strongest photograph in the series," Joan Winfrey told Chanel Faith. They were seated across from one another in Joan's Madison Avenue office. Chanel was looking at a smiling photograph of herself wearing a denim jacket from the Gap, the chain of clothing stores.

"This poster will be plastered at bus stops all over the country," said Joan. "The Gap will be using this shot in ads—full-page ads, no less—in Rolling Stone, Vanity Fair and Vogue. As you know, their ads have featured Betty Carter, Dizzy Gillespie, Queen Latifah, to mention a few—all hip personalities. They're saying we're with it and we're basic, classic but contemporary, and, believe me, Chanel, no one is more with it or basic than you."

"The timing's perfect," said Chanel, her smile even wider than the one in the photo. "I'm shooting my first video tomorrow. My new record's already on the streets. It's straight-ahead rhythm-and-blues, but they tell me straight-ahead is stronger than ever. They're looking to make money on me. I love it. After waiting all this time my attitude is—hey, the more money the merrier. Shit's happening, and far as I'm concerned it can't be happening fast enough. I like you, Joan. I like you 'cause you move fast and pay good."

Chanel had become Joan's brainchild. It had happened one night when Winfrey was watching a local talk show on late-night television. The host had invited a number of blues artists enjoying a renaissance. Of the assembled artists, Chanel was easily the most flamboyant, wearing a spangled wraparound outfit of purple and silver, a sparkling headband and thigh-high silver boots. Joan dug the look. The Gap's ad agency had already approached the Winfrey Agency about another unconventional celebrity, and this woman seemed perfect. Learning, then, that Chanel was the mother of Marisa, Joan stormed into action. She remembered Marisa talking about the mother/daughter competition. Now that Marisa refused to return her calls—much less even consider modeling for her agency—what better way to reinsert herself into Marisa's life than by promoting her ambitious mother? She was delighted with her plan—it served her agency, served the client and served Chanel, all the while feeding Joan's fascination with all things concerning Risa.

As she walked into Passion Flowers Marisa had all her conflicting feelings about seeing her grandmother.

She'd been with Nelson Clay for a week in Palm Springs, a week when no one knew her whereabouts. She'd simply called Herbie and Jason and told them she needed time off. They were crazy with questions but there was nothing they could do.

It had been a good decision. Nelson, as friend and lover, brought her back to earth, settled her. Jason and Herbie had practical grounds for their affection. Nelson had no motive. He just plain loved her. Hard to beat that.

When Nelson's plane took off and she was left alone in Palm Springs she had felt an understandable letdown. All the pressures came rolling in. Herbie and Jason were in Los Angeles, where they wanted her to attend meetings about the film script. Herb Montgomery, Sr. and Georgia would be there. Back in New York, Chanel was waiting for her. Her mother had urged her to come back to Manhattan with Nelson, to boycott the meetings, which, claimed Chanel, just served Georgia's and Georgia's minions' interests.

Marisa tended to believe her mother. Georgia was an expert at juggling the lives of others to suit her own. Except she knew Georgia also loved her. And no doubt *Pearl* was something special. Plus the idea of playing her grandmother as a young woman intrigued Marisa. Well, even if she had decided against the project, the least she could do was see Georgia. Yes, before she left for New York, she had to face Georgia. Besides, it had been over a year since she had seen Grandmama. Truth was, she actually missed the old lady . . .

The old lady did not look old. Marisa often wondered whether there had been facelifts but could never detect any telltale lines or tucks. No, it was sheer natural beauty and it wouldn't quit. This morning it was also natural light that poured through the windows of Georgia's study, where she sat behind her English Regency desk. Her silver hair was coiffed simply but elegantly. Her burgundy dress had been designed in Paris. She was talking on the phone when Marisa came into her office and smiled and waved, as though she were expecting her granddaughter all along.

When she put down the receiver she stood up, came around her desk and took Marisa in her arms. It was the embrace of a woman who was happy to see her granddaughter but who also held a tight rein on her feelings.

"I'm glad to see you look rested," said Georgia, inspecting Marisa in her tailored black linen suit and high heels. She was pleased that her granddaughter had dressed up to see her. It showed respect. "You're looking like a star, Marisa. Now tell me where you've been hiding. Your friends are frantic." Georgia walked back behind her desk and sat in the Queen Anne chair.

"I needed time to think."

"I can appreciate that, sweetheart. Things are developing quickly. It's easy to feel as though you're losing control. There are times—I remember this was true in my own career—when events seem to sweep us up. It can be frightening."

"I'm not frightened," said Marisa, trying to steel herself to say what she thought she had to say. "I'm . . . annoyed."

"At what, dear?"

"At how you've been playing me."

Georgia sighed, not surprised by the accusation. She understood who was behind this. "I know your mother isn't happy—"

"This has nothing to do with Mama."

"Oh, I don't believe that, child. I don't believe that your mother hasn't been whispering in your ear—warning you about my so-called manipulations. She's been saying such things all her life, so why would she stop now? Chanel is Chanel. She's never been able to deal with me, not as a small child, not as a teenager, not as an adult. I love her. I'm proud of her talent, whether she believes it or not. And God knows I realized she hasn't had it easy. No daughter without a father ever has it easy. We all have that in common. But where her mean streak comes in . . . I confess I don't know. It's as if she won't allow herself to love, to be loved. As if she doesn't feel worthy—"

"I've heard your theories about Mama before. Anyway, I'm not talking about Mama. I'm talking about *me*. You've stepped right into the middle of my career. Just like that, you got Jason working for you, you got Herbie, you even got Herbie's father to write this script."

"Herbie's father will tell you that I only inspired the script. I did not *get him* to write anything. Herb Montgomery is the most independent mind I've ever encountered. He's a director and a writer—"

"And your long-time lover."

Georgia collected herself, stood and walked to the front of her desk to stand directly in front of Marisa. "My lover," she told her granddaughter, "has been my work, my passion for acting. As a black American woman in a world ruled by white men, I've done what I can. I've faced up to prejudice and never stopped trying to realize my potential. Now as far as my personal relationships are concerned, those have been private. Discreet. I've always understood that distinct boundaries must exist between family members."

"What?" For a while Marisa had been nearly mesmerized by the lilting pattern of her grandmother's speech. But this business of boundaries? "You've wanted to pick my boyfriends, my clothes, my schools, my college, my career—and now my first film. What *boundaries*?"

"The ones, dear, that separate you from whatever private life I have chosen for myself."

"Like Herbie's father and Sol Solomon?"

"Mr. Solomon and Mr. Montgomery are dear friends. Our friendships have lasted a lifetime. I consider that an accomplishment. These are gentlemen . . ."

"Dangling on your string . . ."

Georgia shook her head and smiled. If only this child knew, if only she could understand. Still, the angrier Marisa grew, the more control Georgia felt.

"You'll have to live a bit longer to appreciate just what such friendships can mean to a woman."

"And now you're cashing in on those friendships. Montgomery writes the script and Solomon gets you the financing and the studio—"

"I wish you wouldn't try topping your mother, Marisa. The style isn't becoming to you. It goes against your nature. You're far more sensible than Chanel. You always were. Your mother rants and raves and winds up nowhere. You've always been more realistic. Wasn't that what your decision to move to New York was all about? You've inherited that quality from me. We're very much alike, you and I. I really do respect your privacy, my dear, but that doesn't blind me to seeing that your relationships with Jason and Herbie have been extremely important in all the wonderful things that have happened in your career this past year. You've made a wise choice of collaborators—"

"But *I've* made that choice—not you."

"I'm not disagreeing with you, Marisa. I'm applauding you. I just hope you've learned something from me—"

"I am *not* you." Marisa's voice had gone up several decibels. "I think you see your life being relived by me. *That's* what frightens me. It frightens me because I think you set it up that way. Jason, Herbie . . ."

"Aren't they genuinely fond of you? Aren't they interested in helping you in every way they can?" Her tone changed. "Look here, Marisa, let's be frank with each other. Say what you want, feel however you feel. But understand that this group of individuals we have brought together—these four men—represent real power for you. You're every bit as savvy as I am, so there's no need to tell you the odds we face when it comes to feature films. You can read scripts forever and not find a part this powerful. Herb Montgomery has put a lifetime of insight and wisdom into this story. The story is your struggle and it's mine. It's the struggle of all independent-minded black women in modern America. The fact that the movie may actually be made through a major studio is a major victory, as I see it. When I came here in the forties as a naïve girl I believed talent and ambition were enough. I was wrong I became a star in Europe. I was featured on Broadway. But Hollywood, my dear, Hollywood has been mostly beyond the reach of black actresses. Doing something about that has been, I admit it, a near-obsession. I've learned a lot. Now I want to share it with you. Is that anything to be criticized for? We either win or lose. And at this point in my life, there's no way in hell I'm willing to lose. Or see you lose. You've made a strong first step. But believe me, the next one is far trickier. For Barbra Streisand or Liza Minnelli or Madonna the road from music to movies might be relatively smooth, but not for you, my dear. All I'm saying is let me help you down that road."

In spite of her doubts, Marisa was beginning to feel the way she had often felt as a little girl—calmed by Grandmama's powerful persuasion and good sense.

"Now then," said Georgia, smiling, "let's read over the script together. Herb Montgomery writes like an angel, and I'm especially anxious to hear how you read his lines. I know you'll do them just beautifully . . ."

"If you want to understand Risa," Sol Solomon was telling his grandson Jason, "you gotta understand her grandmother."

They were sitting out by the pool on a sun-filtered Bel Air afternoon. Below them the view of the Los Angeles basin was blocked by a thick curtain of golden-brown smog. Sol was wearing a swimsuit with matching sports shirt he'd bought in Jamaica while recuperating from his heart attack. He'd lost twenty pounds and spent his mornings briskly walking through his hilly neighborhood, intent on getting back on track. He was, in fact, feeling much better.

Jason wasn't. He was certain he was losing Risa.

"I've known her my whole life," said Jason. "She's nothing like her grandmother."

"Says who?"

"Should you be smoking a cigar?" Jason said as he watched Sol light up, then lean back in the low reclining chair, his face shiny with tanning cream.

"I don't inhale. Besides, I eat grapefruits. The acid in grapefruits cuts right through the smoke. We were talking about Georgia. A piece of work, that lady. When I was a kid and I was all hot to trot, Georgia Faith made me crazy. At one point I even thought I wanted to marry her. This was sex like the gods have sex. Do you know what I'm saying?"

Jason was thinking of Risa. He thought he knew.

"But who am I kidding? I asked myself. I ain't marrying a colored woman. Love her, yes. Keep her, of course. Spoil her, why not? But marry her . . . no, I'm not a crusader and I'm not one of those guys on the picket lines. I'm a man who sits all day and makes up stories. So Georgia realizes this, see, and she goes off with another white man she thinks will marry her, but this guy, I know this guy, he loves her body, he appreciates her mind, he sees her talent, but he ain't marrying her either. That was Miss Georgia Faith's introduction to the wonderful world of white men. So she develops an attitude, but not what you'd think. This woman is a class act, so the attitude isn't 'Fuck you, I'll take my marbles and go home.' It's 'Okay, you guys, I see what's what and what's not. Let's us be friends. How can we help each other?'

"Sounds simple, doesn't it, kid, but ninety-nine out of a hundred broads don't have such smarts. She's got a superior mind. She also has this take on Jewish men. I know how she thinks. She thinks we control Hollywood, for chrissake. Still thinks it's like one big poker party of rich Jews getting together on a Tuesday night at the country club and making all the decisions—make this movie, don't make that movie, let's make this one a star, let's ruin this other one's career. I tried to tell her that we're fighting each other, we're all in competition, but it don't sink in and anyways it don't really matter. Let her think that way. What it means, though, is that she ain't really falling for anyone. She don't really trust anyone 'cause of what happened when she first came out here."

"What about Herb Montgomery?"

"Herb Montgomery? I'll tell you about Herb Montgomery. I've known Herb for over fifty years. Nice man, smart man. Good director, good writer. This is the one man Georgia really wanted to love and live happily ever after with, but Herb Montgomery didn't come through for Georgia. You could say he was ahead of his time but his time had no use for him. Today you got your Spike Lees and all your boys in the hood, or whatever the hell it is. Today they'll get big money from the studios to make their movies, but not in 1949, not in 1952, not in 1965. In the seventies there was that run of black cops-and-robbers movies. They were pimp-and-whore flicks. Maybe you remember *Shaft*. But Shaft got shafted and so did all the other black artists trying to write and direct, real talented people too. That was something Georgia learned early in her career, something she never forgot. She'd never attach herself to Herb Montgomery, at least not permanently. She was too smart for that."

Sol puffed on his cigar and blew out the smoke. He picked up the portable phone and asked someone in the kitchen to bring him a grapefruit. "Don't forget to put a little brown sugar around the rim." He took a deep breath. "Georgia Faith. Herb Montgomery. Two tough ones, Jason. I respect that. Sometimes I've seen how some colored blame everyone in the world for their problems. My mother, may she rest in peace, did the same thing. I don't like that, it gets you nowhere. Now Georgia and Herb, they're workers. They never gave up. Maybe they didn't get rich but they got self-respect, that's what they got, and they sure as hell got my friendship. I think this *Pearl* script's terrific, and if I can make a call and get them a meeting, why not?"

"What about putting up money?"

"Are you crazy? In this town no one puts up money for movies. That's for banks. That's what studios are—banks. You go to a bank for money. If I taught you anything I should have taught you that."

"Herbie thinks you're willing—"

"I never even met Herbie, so how can he know what I think? With his father, though, I was very honest. I said, 'Herb, because of Georgia, and because I think you've written a terrific story, I'll get you some meetings with important people.' He was glad to hear it."

"He and Herbie have also been trying to raise the money privately. They think the studios will compromise their style."

"If they get it, more power to them. Personally I think they're nuts. At this point they can't afford an attitude. They got to take whatever money they can get, private, public, who gives a shit?"

"Well," said Jason, "the only way a studio will even consider the project is if Risa is in. Risa's album is super hot. Georgia Faith means nothing."

"And Georgia is more aware of that than anyone. That's why she's cooked up this combination."

"But Risa's furious with Georgia. She refuses to act in the same movie with her."

"Georgia will bring her around. The girl's confused."

"She is about men, anyway. She's seeing another guy. Maybe two."

Sol smiled. "She's her grandmother. I'm *telling* you, she's her grandmother. The other guy is Herbie, isn't it?"

"I don't know . . . I think so."

"And you're going nuts."

"I love her, Sol. I always have."

"Jason, my handsome grandson, apple of my eye, pull your chair closer to me. Look at my eyes. They're old and tired, aren't they? Look at the bags under my eyes. Worry. Heartache. It ain't easy, I know it ain't easy, but for God's sake try to learn from my past. This is a beautiful colored girl you've fallen for. Beautiful heart, beautiful tushy, beautiful voice, beautiful everything. But for you and her it ain't gonna be no white picket fence around some house in the suburbs. She wasn't raised that way. She don't have it in her blood. She has her grandmother in her blood. And her grandmother is all about finding work and building her career and never stopping, not for anyone or anything. I don't mean Risa doesn't like you. Maybe she even loves you. Sure. You're her buddy. But you're not the most important thing in her life. And neither is this Herbie. You and him, you're part of her career. You're the help, just like I'm Georgia's help. That's a fact. And you know what? For me it's been a real pleasure to help a broad like that."

The Watts Jazz Festival, hard by the famous Watts Towers, was in full swing. Herb Montgomery and his son Herbie were seated in the first row listening to Don Cherry play his pocket trumpet, sounding all the world like Miles Davis of the fifties. Only this was now and the almost all-black crowd, well-heeled and hip, was outfitted in Malcolm X baseball caps, Billie Holiday T-shirts, Public Enemy sweatpants and Nike Air Structure jogging shoes. Many drove to the Watts section of the city this afternoon from their Baldwin Hills homes in German sports sedans and Swedish convertibles. Others, less fashionable, wandered in from down the street. Herb had suggested the outdoor festival as a place to meet his son, who said he wanted to talk.

The stage was set up in a makeshift tent. Cherry was joined by pianist Cedar Walton, saxist Joe Henderson, bassist Charlie Haden, drummer Billy Higgins and guitarist Kenny Burrell, mainstream masters in a postmodern mode, the sort of style Herb most appreciated. His son got restless. He liked jazz but didn't love it. Herbie's specialty was black pop, commercial sounds that appealed to a much broader audience than the complexities of a music he recognized was important but difficult art.

"Jazz is our genius," Herb was saying after a blistering Joe Henderson tenor solo.

Herbie was not prepared to argue. Besides, his father was probably right. Jazz was the product of a proud culture, but jazz didn't make money. Risa's music made money. Risa's music was making a lot of money. HM Records was enjoying a very positive cash flow. Herbie had the number-one selling artist in the United States and England, and the last thing in the world he wanted to think about was jazz. But he knew if he was going to relate to his father it would have to be on his father's terms.

Afterward the two of them walked around the festival, visiting a few of the booths selling African garb, African-American literature, sculpture, wall hangings and masks. Herb was greeted by several of his contemporaries, painters, poets, aging hipsters with bushy beards, beaded necklaces, tiny earrings of mother of pearl and onyx.

Father and son bought a few ears of corn on the cob and sat on a bench facing the eccentric Watts Towers. The sun was setting behind the fabulous 107–foot structure, the work of an obsessed Italian immigrant, a helter-skelter concoction of Coke bottles, ceramic tiles, broken china plates and seventy thousand seashells.

"There's something especially bold about these towers," said Herb. "Think about the old guy who built it. He had no plan, just this passion. He had no real education, just his instincts. He never read an art book or took an art lesson. This thing was built on a dream. Look at the design and you can feel his optimism. Isn't it grand? Just keep pouring it on, just get out there every morning and use whatever you can, whatever's around. Guts—that's what this guy had. Guts and spirit. Can't you feel his spirit?"

What Herbie was feeling was impatience with his father's ramblings. To him the Watts Towers looked more like a mess than a miracle. Besides, he was anxious to get to the subject that had been haunting him.

"Risa's still out of pocket," he told his father. "I don't feel like I can control her any longer."

"Whatever made you think you could?" said Herb, half-remembering his distant past with Risa's grandmother.

"I signed her, I produced her album, I broke her on the charts. She depended on me—"

"Only in *your* mind. In reality she was free as a bird. That's the gift she inherited from her grandmother."

"It's her mother who can sing, not her grandmother. You don't know anything about her mother, do you?"

Herb looked at his son and was tempted, once and for all, to say the words: *Her mother is my daughter. Chanel is the child I had with Georgia. Chanel is your half-sister.* It would be so liberating finally to let loose a secret nearly fifty years old. The secret had been smoldering, especially in these past months when the Faith women had again played such a prominent role in his life. His life and theirs were permanently interwoven. Sometimes it seemed downright crazy that he didn't let the news out. Why not broadcast it to the world? But because Herb Montgomery was a responsible man, he always wound up doing the responsible thing. He had no desire to hurt his children, and even less desire to alienate Georgia, with whom he hoped, finally, to achieve a cinematic triumph. Besides, there was the complication of Herbie's involvement with Risa—the daughter of his daughter, for God's sake. How much more complicated could you get?

When Herb first learned about the liaison he had to think twice about the relationship between his son and granddaughter. What were they to one another? Half-uncle and niece. But what would be gained by letting Herbie know the truth? What harm would be done by saying nothing? He had talked to Georgia about the situation, and she had agreed: just leave it alone, it'll work itself out.

Yet it was becoming clear that Herbie's love for Risa was as obsessive as his own love for Georgia. Herbie was convinced that he could change her life, make her career, guarantee her success. In fact, he had done a hell of a better job than his father—another reason why Herb was reluctant to disclose the secret.

"What I know about Risa's mother," Herb finally answered, "is that like Georgia and Risa, she's an individual. These aren't ordinary women, Herbie."

"Risa's treating me like . . . like a throwaway—the guy who made the decisions that got her where she is, and now—"

"You're also the man who fell in love with her. That changed everything."

"It's her manager . . . he's working behind my back . . . he wants to kill this film deal . . ."

"Are you sure?"

"I'm sure. He resents—"

"Georgia says he's very much in favor of the deal. He's even gotten his grandfather Sol Solomon to arrange meetings with some studio heads."

"I already told you, I don't want those meetings, I don't need them. We can get our own meetings—that money has strings attached. It's script-control money. When you came to me I thought you wanted *me* to handle the financing. Well, I have. I've tapped into resources I've been cultivating for years—a black-controlled bank in Atlanta, a black insurance company in Chicago."

"Look, son, all my life I've been fighting the studios. You know what? The studios *are* Hollywood, and all the so-called independent producers know it. For years I made movies now gathering dust on the shelves of warehouses. My movies never made a cent. So I did what any reasonable man would do—I punted. I became a cameraman. I found work and I survived out here. But I never stopped writing. Now I've written a movie I'm determined to get made. Say what you want, but the studios are still the quickest and surest way to do it."

"Dad, that's old-fashioned thinking. The studios have been fucking you around your entire life. Can't you see that? Things have changed. I thought that's why you came to me in the first place. Give me a chance. There's a way to raise ten million without—"

"It's going to take twice that."

"If I can get ten, the other ten will come. But now it may all be academic because Risa isn't talking to anyone about any of this. She's backing out—that's what I've been trying to tell you—backing out of this movie and backing away from me. I'm losing her, and it's driving me crazy."

"No need to go crazy, son," said Herb, gazing at the Watts Towers against a darkening purple sky. "The man who built these towers understood improvisation. It's all one big jazz solo. We never know what's coming next."

Herbie exploded. "What in *hell* are you talking about? You're talking jazz and I'm talking numbers, reality. I'm telling you that I have an artist, a very hot artist, and I don't even know where she is, much less what she'll agree to do next. It's crazy and it's dangerous for her."

"Not as dangerous as you think. I'm telling you, I know her grandmother as well as your own mother."

Suddenly Herbie thought he saw the light. "You really love her, don't you?"

"In a way . . ."

"Not in a way . . . you plain love the woman. She's the reason you left Mom. She's the goddamn love of your life, isn't she?"

"It's not that simple—"

"Simple? Look, I'm a businessman, Dad. I was trained in business and I'm damn good at it. Business is developing the right product and selling it. I don't have your wonderful artistic temperament, or Risa's." He was revving up, working off his anger at Risa, his fear of losing her. "I'm treating this as a straightaway business deal. I have Risa's name on a contract. I have her where I want her. If she decides to dump me, if she violates one tiny paragraph of our agreement, I'll sue her ass. That's what I'll do. And you can sit here and be mellow, you can listen to your jazz and contemplate the beauty of our black culture, you can hope the studios are finally going to reward you for your life of patience. You can hope that the scheme will finally bring your love to your side and give you the happy ending you've been trying to write for fifty years. But, goddammit, *not me*. I have an investment to protect, and you better believe I'm going to protect it."

Herb knew it was no use talking to his son. Hell hath no fury, he thought, like a *man* scorned.

* * *

Chanel's album was selling. The release of "It's My Time" coincided with a revival of sixties soul music. Suddenly the Golden Era of Soul was the subject of documentaries and feature films. Kids in Wales, Scotland, Ireland, Germany, Japan and Italy were rediscovering the sexy, riveting sounds by which their parents conceived them. James Brown, Wilson Pickett, Otis Redding, Aretha Franklin—their names were revered, their records re-released and sold as though they were new.

Sitting in the Lexington Avenue residential hotel which had been her home for the past three months, watching the nightly news's four-minute segment on this phenomenon—the resurrection of soul music, the rise of The Commitments—Chanel couldn't help but think of her past. She'd been there the first time the music had taken off; she'd been in the perfect place, Muscle Shoals, with the right musicians, producers, and songs. And yet she had missed out. The big-time had eluded her. Her payoff had been tiny. Why? Maybe it was the partying, maybe her attitude, certainly the men with whom she surrounded herself. But times had changed. Yes, Lord, she told herself. She was no longer living stoned. This time she was dead-set determined to take full advantage of the explosion of the musical genre that was her meat and potatoes. Opportunity was knocking twice, and this time she was opening the door wide. Hell, this time she was kicking in the jamb. She was nearly fifty and it wasn't likely that opportunity would come calling again.

Chanel was thrilled for her daughter. She was proud as could be. Risa had achieved what Chanel had missed. But that didn't mean Chanel was any less focused on her own career. She saw it all as some kind of mystical meeting of minds, some mysterious justification for all the pain she had inflicted and endured. Her Alcoholics Anonymous program spoke of promises that would come true if sobriety were kept. Those promises were being fulfilled. Her dream—for herself and her daughter—was being realized. Years of frustration had not been in vain, not by a long shot. The long shot, in fact, had come in. Chanel remembered the first morning she had sung at the Full Gospel Church of the Living Christ on Central Avenue. That was thirty-seven years ago, but she recalled the moment vividly, the thrill of discovering the power of her voice and the response it could evoke in others. That, too, took the form of a promise—God's promise that praise brings joy. No matter that she switched from sacred to secular, no matter that she had spent decades soused on booze and whacked out on weed, she still felt God in her heart, God directing her decisions, God letting her know that at least He would never abandon her or her daughter. After so long a struggle, thank God things between her and her daughter had finally been set right.

Marisa had made the calls from the limousine. Nelson Clay was by her side. She was back in Manhattan, living in a suite at the Carlyle Hotel and finally figuring out what she wanted. She wanted Nelson. He was the one who could listen, really listen. He was with her every night. He seemed stable; he had nothing to push.

Herbie and Jason were jumping out of their skins. She had avoided them now for weeks. Something had to be said. She and Nelson were being driven down to the Village—she was going to stay at his place this night—when she decided to call California.

"I'm doing the 'Today' show," she told Herbie. "And I'm doing the Rolling Stone interview."

"Of course you're doing it," said Herbie. "It's the cover."

"But that's it for now."

"And *Pearl?*"

"I'll let you know about that later."

"I thought you talked to your grandmother when you were out here."

"I did. We had a good talk and I'm still thinking."

"Look, Risa . . ."

"I know how you feel, Herbie, but I need time."

"I'll be in New York tomorrow. I'll be there for the 'Today' interview."

"Fine. Jason's also coming in."

"You talked to him?"

"Briefly," said Risa. "I'm resurfacing. I'm feeling a lot stronger. I told Jason what I'm telling you—I refuse to go running after something I'm not sure is right."

"Who says differently? You don't have to run after anything . . . it's running after you."

"Well, I just don't want to be another bimbo with a hit record who loses all perspective."

"We'll talk about this when we're all in New York," said Herbie, relieved that at least she had called.

Outside, the last winter snowfall was melting on Madison Avenue. March had started on a mild note. Sitting next to her in the limo, Nelson helped quiet her. He had urged her to call her mother when she returned to the city, and thought it was good that the two women had managed a relatively calm conversation.

"I know Georgia makes it sound like Hollywood is dying for you," said Chanel, "but it's never that easy. You're a singer, honey, not an actress. Sure, you can act, but you want to get another two or three albums out there. You want to take your time and call your shots. Play your own game—not your grandmother's."

Georgia and Chanel. Georgia vs. Chanel. Well, at least something had changed. Chanel's new record was clear. It was straight-ahead soul singing and pleased Risa to no end. It was an honest statement —no frills or bullshit. Her mother might be coarse to some people but she was what she was. Watching her sing on television the previous week, Risa was reminded of what she loved about the woman's style. Mama did a version of the great soul ballad, Sam Cooke's "A Change Is Gonna Come," with riveting conviction, her eyes shut tight, her vibrato now fluttering, never losing control of the lyric or the soaring melody, adding nuance and flavor to a song that with all its heartache and hope seemed autobiographical. Risa could accept her with all her flamboyance and excesses. And the acceptance came at just the right time, when in the midst of the hoopla over her own success she needed an anchor.

"What in the world is that?" she asked Nelson as she pointed to a huge poster dominating the window of a Gap store on Madison Avenue. She had the driver stop so she could get out of the car and take a closer look.

"You haven't seen your mother's poster before?"

"What's my mother doing on that poster?"

"She's modeling a denim jacket."

"Modeling? How did *that* happen?"

"I didn't tell you that Joan Winfrey called me looking for Chanel's number? Joan thought Chanel would be perfect as a Gap model."

"Joan Winfrey? You're talking to Joan Winfrey?"

"She's still my neighbor."

"But what are you doing, involved with my mother?"

"Wait a minute, Marisa. You're blowing this thing out of proportion."

"Joan and my mother," Risa mumbled to herself. "*You*, Joan and my mother. My grandmother, my manager, my manager's grandfather, my record executive's father. Jesus. And by the style of the picture the photographer had to be Bing Radison. Too damn much. I'm going back to the hotel. You can take a cab home, Nelson. You can go next door and tell Joan she's done a terrific job with Mama. And when you're done telling Joan, call Mama for me and tell her the same thing. Tell her she did a great job with you and a great job with me, tell her I'm coming along just fine, and my next record will be duets, just me and her, and the record after that she'll have to herself. I'll just sing background like old times. Or maybe I'll just hum. She's clean and sober and she deserves everything she can get. Isn't that right, Nelson? Aren't you the one who's been telling me what a wonderful woman she is? So go home and call her and tell her everything's arranged, everything's fine, and if she's lonesome and needs company, why you can hippety-hop right over and fuck her if that's what she needs, because you're that kind of guy, you're a wonderful guy and she's a wonderful mother who's worried about nothing but her darling baby Marisa."

Chanel wanted a drink, a smoke, a hit of coke. She looked in the directory of Alcoholics Anonymous and found a meeting due to start in an hour. Outside it was drizzly and nasty, not a cab to be found. She wanted the peace and comfort of Muscle Shoals but she wasn't about to give up. No, not this time. She had to break the pattern of her past. This time she was out to win and winning meant staying sober. Looking for a cab, she noticed that she was standing right in front of a bar. She could taste the bite of straight bourbon, feel it burning her throat, imagine that boozy afterglow warming her body. One drink. That's all it would take.

An empty cab finally pulled up and she slid in. Ten minutes later she got out on Seventeenth Street just off Fifth Avenue. The meeting was in a restored office building, the room already crowded with forty or fifty people, men and women in business suits, others in torn jeans, some teenagers, a few so-called bums.

Hell, she could face any audience. She missed her old sessions, but now AA was her therapy. It was even better than going to a private shrink because it gave her an audience. She raised her hand, was called on and laid it on the line:

"I'm pissed," she said, "and I feel like a drink. I feel like a snort and I feel like a joint and I feel like breaking up someone's happy home—that's what I feel like doing. I hope I'm not offending any of you locals but I also gotta say I hate this city and I'm trapped in this city, I gotta deal with this city and I also gotta deal with a mother who's a bitch on wheels and a daughter who won't talk to me, who just shut me out of her life. Now this is my baby, my only baby, the only person in the world I'd take two bullets for. I'm a singer and I taught her to sing and she's singing her ass off, she's making it big and everyone in this room has probably heard of her and maybe you've even bought her record or maybe you've bought mine, it doesn't matter, because we shouldn't be fighting now, me and her, we should be getting along better than we ever have in our lives since we're getting what we always wanted. So I got me a little money and now I want me a little buzz. That's my addictive mind talking. Just a little buzz. One line. One taste. One toke. Then I'll leave the shit alone, except I know I won't because I never have. When I was out there using I'd use till it was all used up. And I'd wind up using people, sleeping with people, living with people I shouldn't even be drinking coffee with, much less screwing. I know I'm nuts. That's the one advantage I have. I know. I know I'm angry about my daughter and the way my mother messes with her mind. I'd love to space out on it all, to have a couple of belts to kill the tension because there's other tension I haven't even mentioned to you which would blow your mind except my time is running out so I just want to say I'm grateful for this opportunity to speak my peace. Staying sober's not easy but nothing worthwhile is easy. The only easy thing is praise. You all praise your Higher Power, I praise Jesus, but it don't matter. I praise *anything* that keeps me sober. I even praise this goddamn meeting."

*   *   *

On the ride back uptown Chanel was starting to relax, relieved of much of the anxiety that had been boiling inside. When the cab drove past Radio City Music Hall her eyes were half-closed. She had almost drifted off but the letters on the marquee startled her full-awake. She bolted up and rolled down the window so she could get a better view.

Tonight Only! JOHNNY DODD HUGGINS
Special Guest Star—RISA
Sorry, sold out

It was Friday afternoon, and Georgia drove her new teal-blue Lexus through Beverly Hills at a leisurely pace. She was reflecting, burning with low-flame anger. She was not about to let Sol Solomon get her down. She'd been counting on him to provide major development money for *Pearl*—to cough up $100,000 of his money or at least find the money for them. All he'd done, though, was arrange a few meetings. That hadn't panned out. The studios had too many reservations. Like always. Herb and Herbie had also run into financial stone walls. The script was strong but the script alone couldn't guarantee a green light. Something had to be done—and quickly. Georgia had to take matters into her own hands.

When she walked into the Bistro Gardens heads turned. She was wearing a dramatic white turban fastened in the center by an exquisite cameo, a silhouette of an aristocratic Roman woman delicately carved from yellow-white shell. Her robin's-egg-blue dress designed by St. John was gathered at the waist by a thin sash of green. Her suede Joan and David shoes picked up the lavender of her amethyst earrings. She had settled on her scent, Joy, because the fragrance was neither new nor trendy; it was a classic, the image Georgia herself projected.

When people noticed the actress, as they did today, there was often a moment of discomfort for Georgia. She saw them asking themselves: *Who is she?* "She *looks* like someone," Georgia once heard someone say. Once in a while someone would identify her, usually from one of her TV appearances, but such instances were rare. Mostly the observers couldn't place the face.

"Georgia!" Brenda Cohen called out, "you look ravishing, I'm so glad to see you."

Brenda was seated at a choice table up front. As the Hollywood *Daily News'* most senior writer, Brenda wielded considerable power in the community. A high-strung woman in her mid-fifties, she wore too much makeup and favored colors—gaudy yellows and reds—that reflected her personality but hardly flattered her ample frame. She had known Georgia for years and respected her spunk, admired her acting, loved her fancy flower shop and appreciated the fact that Georgia never never said die. As a reporter Brenda thought of herself in much the same way. Two tough ladies, two outsiders managing in an insider's town. Whenever Brenda could help Georgia she did. A decade ago, when Georgia had appeared on "Dynasty," Brenda had written a piece that brought the actress additional work. For her part, Georgia was quick to supply Brenda with whatever news she picked up from her Passion Flowers patrons.

"This must be important," Brenda said, sipping on a pre-lunch glass of burgundy. "You sounded so serious on the phone."

"It's serious," Georgia told her friend.

"Well, make it juicy, darling. I'm ending a week that's been drier than the Sahara. Hollywood's turned into one big AA meeting. And sobriety is about as interesting as my dead Uncle Saul who kept books for a button factory. May he rest in peace."

She took a long gulp of wine as Georgia began speaking slowly, deliberately, allowing her story to build.

"We've certainly been through a lot together, haven't we, Brenda?"

"You're an inspiration, Georgia. No kidding. Not to mention a fabulous source. No one in this town networks better."

"Why thank you, Brenda, but this is beyond networking. This is a piece of providence, perhaps *the* piece of providence I've been waiting for all my life."

"Do tell."

"Now you know that my Marisa's record has been the bestselling album in the country for weeks."

"Risa. Of course. We talked about her on the phone. She's incredible. You must be dying, you must be so proud. I'd love to do a profile on her. I've been trying to break into Vanity Fair. Maybe—"

"No, believe me, Brenda, I have a bigger story for you."

"About Risa?"

"About a grandmother and granddaughter about to launch a major motion picture portraying two aspects of a single character—her youth and her maturity. This character, of course, is a black woman, a highly successful black woman. *Not* a nanny, a maid, or a prostitute. Not a singer or a dancer but an internationally renowned businesswoman who's created a cosmetics empire. The story goes from Mississippi to Paris, with all the stops in between."

"It sounds great. I love the granddaughter-grandmother angle."

"There's more. The man who's written the script and is directing the film is Herb Montgomery."

"Your old flame?"

"After fifty years my old flame has proposed marriage."

"Georgia—you're joking!"

"What's more, his son Herb Montgomery, Jr., is the president of the record label responsible for Marisa's spectacular success. He and Risa will also be announcing their engagement. You have this exclusive, Brenda, and the source is strictly confidential."

"My God, I do love it. When can I run with it?"

"After dessert. You must have your chocolate first. I know how much you adore chocolate."

"You son of a bitch," Chanel was saying to Johnny Dodd Huggins, runaway father of her daughter. "You bloodsuckin' pig . . ."

Johnny Dodd, always a man of few words, looked up and offered his lazy half-smile. The after-the-concert well-wishers had left his dressing room. The place was filled with bouquets of flowers, platters of half-eaten food and bottles of wine. Johnny Dodd slumped in an easy chair, pulled off his green lizard boots and lit a joint. He offered Chanel a toke. "I'd rather stick it up your ass than stick that shit in my mouth."

"If I remember right," Johnny Dodd drawled, "you once would kill for this shit."

"No more."

"Well, good for you, babe."

"Fuck *you*, babe. You'd like to see me back on dope, wouldn't you?"

His half-smile elongated. "Precious angel, you're looking good, you really are. Lost some weight, I see. Right becoming, too."

"Stuff it, Johnny. I'm here about my daughter. Why you'd book her on the bill, and what did you tell her?"

"I never realized you had a daughter, baby," he said, slowly exhaling the sickly-sweet-smelling smoke. "Funny, when I asked her about you she sounded like she was pissed off at you. All I told her was that Chanel's always fightin' and fussin' at someone."

"That's all you told her?"

"She was surprised I knew you. Told her back in Muscle Shoals we were all real friendly, so to speak. Far as her appearing with me, total accident. Didn't even know it was happening. It was my manager and her manager who hooked it up. You figure right now country's a lot hotter than R&B, and her manager wants to sell her white."

"Bullshit."

"She put on a hell of a show. You see it?"

Chanel had thought it was a little too flashy—too many smoke bombs, fancy lights and slick dancers. It looked overchoreographed, Chanel wanted more emphasis on Risa's voice. But it was clear the audience loved the high-tech show and its special effects. They sang along when she went into "Follow This Feeling" and "Flame," the two megahit dance numbers off the album. No doubt, the girl could move. But it was her voice that gave Chanel satisfaction. When the house went dark and Risa stood at center stage in a blue spotlight and sang the ballad "Inside of Me," sang it with a mature and mellow sense of timing—slow, relaxed, bittersweet—Chanel felt really proud. She also wanted to join her daughter during her moment of glory.

"Yes, I saw her tonight," Chanel told Johnny Dodd. "She was dynamite. She's her mother's daughter."

Johnny Dodd took another long toke. "And mine."

"You never knew you had a girl—you just said so. You never bothered to check 'cause you never gave a shit."

"Look, woman, you never gave me a chance to give a shit. You never told me."

"And if I had told you, you'd come running back to Alabama to marry the colored lady of your dreams? Oh sure, I can see you taking our black baby to brunch every Sunday at the Sheffield Holiday Inn."

"My life changed. And right now the changes are all for the good."

"I don't want you getting involved with Marisa, you understand me? I don't want you near her."

"Wait a minute, you think I'd—"

"I don't know what you'd do or what you'd say. I don't want her to know a damn thing."

"No problem. That ain't the kind of publicity that makes country fans too happy anyway."

"And *you* sure wouldn't want to do anything to make your white fans unhappy."

"Wouldn't wanna do nothing to make *you* unhappy, baby," said Johnny Dodd, up from his chair, the smoldering joint hanging out of his mouth. As he came over and put his arm around Chanel, she just stood there, her mind moving back in time, remembering what it was like with long-legged Johnny Dodd. It had been good. Beforehand, they always smoked strong reefer; the reefer had him loving for days. She closed her eyes for a second and she was back in those days. She wanted a taste of the pot, maybe a taste of Johnny Dodd—her old man, her old patterns.

"Get that shit out of my face," she told him, surprised by her own conviction. "I'm going to see my daughter now and tell her we're just old friends."

"Cool," said Johnny Dodd, putting his fingers to his lips and blowing her a goodbye kiss. "At least our stories are together."

In his Central Park West apartment Jason put down the copy of the Hollywood *Daily News* and called his grandfather Sol in L.A.

"I'm out," said Jason. "I'm washing my hands of her. If she wants to marry him, let her. If she doesn't have the decency to tell me in person, if she's happy to have me read this in the trades, to hell with it."

It was eight A.M. in Bel Air and Sol Solomon had been sleeping.

"I don't know what you're talking about."

"The paper says she's marrying Herbie. They're *engaged*, for God's sake. In fact it's a double engagement. Herb's father and Risa's grandmother. You'd think it was the British royal family or something . . . the making of two marriages, father-son, grandmother-grand-daughter."

"All that's in the paper?" Sol said, coming full awake.

"It goes on and on. It's crazy."

"Look," said Sol, not too concerned, "let me ask Georgia about this and I'll get back to you."

Sol turned to Georgia, lying next to him, her smooth-skinned body remarkably toned for a woman her age.

"What's this b.s. about you marrying Herb?"

She smiled and kissed his nose. "Well, Sol," she said, "don't you think it's about time I settled down?"

"I've never heard you talk this way," said Dr. James Bell, the sixty-five-year-old white-haired black man who had been Nelson Clay's medical school professor fifteen years earlier. He had also been Nelson's mentor and surrogate father, a prominent psychoanalyst who took special interest in his black students, among whom Nelson had been a favorite.

"I've never acted like this," Nelson said. "I've never *felt* like this. I could diagnose my condition but I can't change it."

They were in Bell's office on the campus of Yale University in New Haven. Nelson had come to see his old professor out of desperation.

"My practice is in shambles," said Clay, his eyes bloodshot from a long series of sleepless nights. "I've lost half my patients. They're tired of me cancelling their sessions and I can't blame them. The hospital is about to replace me. I can't even finish an article for Psychiatric Journal that was due six months ago."

"Nelson," said Dr. Bell, "is it drugs?"

"I wish it were, I could deal with that. I could check into a rehab center. There's no rehab center for what's been eating me."

"Go ahead," urged Bell.

"A woman."

Bell was good enough not to say he thought so.

There was a strange feeling in the air. Both men were professionals. Both could analyze behavior, utilizing systems of complexity. Yet
here was the distinguished professor sitting across from one of his
brightest graduates discussing what seemed to be a high-school
heartache.

"Tell me about this woman."

"I'm about to give up my life for her."

"That sounds a bit . . . unbalanced, not to mention melodra-
matic."

"I *am* unbalanced, Dr. Bell. I've lost the center."

"Tell me about this woman . . ."

"She's an entertainer, a star."

"And beautiful?"

"More than that, she's enchanting, effervescent, also emotionally
very needy."

"And she needs you."

"Yes, she does . . ."

"I understand the intensity of such feeling, Nelson, but why does
it have to restrict your work?"

"She wants me to travel with her, to be with her every day. That's
how much she needs me."

"Go on . . ."

"At first I dismissed the notion. As you know, I've spent a lot of
time and energy building my practice. Granted, I might have ignored
my emotional life for too long. Maybe I've worked too hard and lost
perspective about relationships with women."

"It happens."

"But this is crazy . . ."

"Like an obsession?"

"A neurosis, a . . . it doesn't matter what I call it or how well I
understand it, I still can't stay away from her."

"And she's controlling . . ."

"That's a fair way of putting it. Yes, she's controlling my nights,
my days. . . . Now she's talking about going to Europe, getting
away from all the pressures. She's achieved phenomenal success and
everyone's looking for a piece of her. For the first time she has
money of her own but she doesn't know what to do next. There's this
long-time struggle for her between her mother and grandmother, the
real controlling forces in her life . . ."

"And you're involved in that struggle?"

"I know the mother."

"And?"

Nelson shook his head. "She's one of a kind. She's estranged from her daughter and doesn't see why. She'd like me to help bridge the gap."

"Triangulation."

"Triangulations, plural. The family can't relate any other way."

"And you're caught in it."

"I realize—"

"Look, Nelson, let me tell you a story. When I was young and growing up in rural Louisiana I thought I was immune to matters of the heart because of my seriousness. Nothing was going to distract me from my education, my career-to-be. In fact, I didn't even date until I was in my mid-twenties. One time I went to a movie, a colored-only theater, of course. In those days there were some all-colored films and one called *Jenny* featured a Negro actress who took my breath away. I actually sat down and wrote her a letter, which was hardly typical behavior for me. I declared my eternal love for her, and if she had so much as written me one line saying 'Meet me in California' or 'Meet me on the moon' I would have been on my way. Thank God I never heard a word, but for several months I was a kid obsessed. Her image on the screen had knocked me way off course."

"Do you remember her name?"

"I surely do. Georgia Faith."

Risa looked at the Rolling Stone reporter, who was jotting down phrases like "high energy" and "creative spirit."

"No, I'm *not* marrying the president of my record label," she told him. "I don't know where that came from. I'm marrying my shrink, I think."

In red tights and an oversized black sweatshirt with a large white "X" across the front, she was seated cross-legged on a couch in a loft she had just leased in trendy Soho. She had just had her hair cut scalp-short in a style described by her hairdresser as "Sinead O'Connor meets Nina Simone." On anyone else it might have seemed severe. On Risa seemed right. Actually, most anything did.

She was doing it her way, was saying whatever she felt like saying, doing whatever she wanted to do—or at least doing what her grandmother had done . . . playing the press the way she pleased.

"What about the reports in the trades?" the reporter wanted to know.

"Daydreams of Hollywood publicists."

"*Your* publicists?"

"I don't have publicists."

"Then whose publicists are they?"

"Mysterious sources, unnamed mouthpieces. I don't know, don't care."

"So you won't be making a movie?"

"In a few hours I'll be making dinner—that's my immediate project. After that I'm not really sure of anything."

"What about your grandmother? It's been said she's controlling your career. What about Georgia Faith?"

"Terrific actress."

"And?"

"How do you feel about your grandmother?"

"I love her."

"There you go. We all love our grandmothers."

"What's your psychiatrist's name?"

"I don't want to give him a complex, I'm protecting his privacy."

"Tell me about your father."

"Killed in Vietnam, never knew the man."

"Your mother told Spin magazine that your next album will be a duet with her."

"My mother's a singer, a great one. Maybe she's right, maybe my next album will be a trio with my mother and grandmother. We'll be the new Supremes." She said it deadpan.

"You grew up in Los Angeles?"

"And Muscle Shoals."

"And went to college at Barnsdale. Tell me about that."

"Musicals, plays, a few crushes on a few boys, the usual."

"But it was Herbie Montgomery who actually discovered you, wasn't it?"

"Actually it was my grandmother and my mother."

"I want to go back to them. Tell me about those relationships."

"One big happy family." Her smile was wide.

"I feel like you're putting me on," said the reporter.

Risa laughed easily. "Hey, whatever I have to say about my family, I'm saying it to my shrink."

"So there were problems."

"Ours is a typical American family. Like the Simpsons."

"Funny," said the writer, "but I need some straight stuff. Our readers want to know who you are."

"So do I. That's why I'm marrying my shrink."

"Seriously . . ."

"Okay, try this. I busted my ass in New York looking for work—acting, singing, any kind of work—and didn't get anywhere until a modeling agency took me on. I did a little modeling, then cut a video and a demo and two guys—Jason Solomon, a buddy from L.A., and Herbie Montgomery, a new buddy, helped put me over. That's the story."

"There's more to it than that."

"Say that two single parents, both strong black women—Georgia Faith and Chanel Faith—fought the good fight for me until I was strong enough to fight the fight myself."

"Why won't you let me inside your head?" asked the reporter, showing his frustration.

"Hey," said Risa, "I let you inside my apartment."

When the writer left, Marisa reviewed what she had said and thought it was okay. She wasn't about to bad-mouth her family. She also felt good about some decisions she had recently made . . . she was not going to let Jason Solomon manage her; and she would not let Herbie Montgomery run her career. Both of them were too involved with Georgia and Georgia's schemes. In announcing her granddaughter's alleged engagement plans, Georgia had finally gone too far. Now, several weeks after the fact, Risa could almost laugh at the ludicrous notion. Nelson was her one link to sanity, especially since he had cut off all contact with Chanel. Marisa was starting to feel like she finally could stand alone, on her own.

Chanel knew who was to blame. Nothing had changed. Her mother, her goddamn meddling mother. Georgia was undermining her relationship with her daughter, just like she had always done. She couldn't let it alone, had to get in the middle, had to take it over, had to run everything her way. Now she'd done the ultimate. Georgia had completely alienated Marisa from her mother—at least that was how Chanel saw it as she packed her bags to head out to California to promote her album, which, unlike her daughter's, had stopped selling. While she was there, she wasn't going to ignore her mother. The truce was off, the gloves were off. She was hanging tough. Even if her daughter wouldn't talk to her, even if her daughter's shrink wouldn't talk to her, even if she didn't know what the hell was going on in her only child's life, she wasn't going to lose it. She wasn't going to think of a man who lived uptown and specialized in mellow herb. He had been her supplier and lover only three years ago. He owned a fleet of cabs and called himself a "mama freak," liked his ladies large. Chanel needed to feel appreciated. Uptown Man made her feel appreciated. Call him up. Get him over here. Cancel the California trip. Get laid and get high. Stay high for days, weeks. Kick back and get a perspective on things.

No. No Mr. Mellow. No Dr. Feelgood. Stay on track. Keep the faith. Deep down Chanel knew her daughter loved her. After all, didn't Marisa have her voice, her spunk? She had all her best qualities, she had to see that. . . .

"You're still sleeping with her," Jason was saying to his grandfather. They were in the paneled den of Sol's home in Bel Air. Sol sprawled on a brown leather couch, Jason was pacing.

"You're still too young to appreciate the situation," said Sol. "I shouldn't have told you. I shouldn't have opened my big trap. By now, though, I thought you'd understand—"

"I understand that she's marrying a man who's making a movie with her . . . a movie that now has absolutely nothing to do with us. And I understand that Risa is marrying—"

"Marriage schmarriage. These are trade-press reports, Jason. You know those. They're like tip sheets from the nags. Put too much faith in them and you'll lose your ass. I told you Georgia's a piece of work. She raised her granddaughter all by herself, didn't she? Well, naturally granddaughter Risa's a piece of work herself."

"I'm cut off from her."

"For years I was cut off from Georgia. But she came back. You know why?"

"To make Herb Montgomery jealous. How else is she going to get him to marry her?"

"Maybe. And if that works for her, fine and dandy. My compliments. But I think the real reason she came back is because she recognizes a friend—"

"Bullshit."

"I'm telling you, Jason, you still think because you stick your dick in someone that means love and devotion for a lifetime. Well, I'm telling you that sometimes that's just old-fashioned friendship between people who understand each other. That's beautiful stuff. It's what Georgia and I have."

Jason shook his head. Sol was out of it. He'd been hung up on the same pussy for a hundred years and was now too rich and old to care any more whether he was being used. Well, he, Jason, *had* been used. The least Risa could do was hear him out. At the same time, knowing her as well as he did, he understood her paranoia about Georgia. She figured Georgia was behind the whole thing. Maybe the old dame was. Well, he knew his mind. He was in love with Risa—always had been—and got into this thing because he felt she needed him. After all, he had other stuff going, he was busy producing and directing videos for rappers and rockers. He was making good money. Now he was a discard? A reject? Would he have to sue Herbie Montgomery, who claimed that he too had been cut off by Risa? Did Jason believe that? The trade mag said she was marrying him . . .

For a few years now Herb and Herbie had balanced their once-estranged relationship. Now all bets were off. Herbie had flown in from New York, where his inability to reach Risa was driving him up the wall. He had signed other acts and had a few hits, but nothing affected his label like Risa. She was the cornerstone. Damn it, he had pushed her into stardom, and now he couldn't even get her on the phone.

Herbie knew he'd fallen hard for Risa. Maybe that was the problem. He'd broken his code and mixed business with pleasure. Maybe that had mixed her up . . . it had sure as hell mixed *him* up. The answer to her cutting him off must be in California with his father and his father's friend, Georgia Faith. They were the ones, with their crazy press reports of fictitious engagements, who had sent Risa into a tailspin. If Risa would listen to him, if only she would realize he had nothing to do with the article in the Hollywood *Daily News*, if only she'd let him explain . . .

He had tried to work through Jason, but Jason was no use. Jason was furious with him, convinced the press reports were true and claiming that he too had been cut off. Herbie didn't believe him. Trust between the two had collapsed.

Arriving at his father's apartment in the El Royale, a vintage Spanish-style apartment house on Rossmore Avenue, Herbie could barely hold in his anger. The long plane ride had him jet-lagged. The old man had been working on still another rewrite of his screenplay on an antique Underwood manual typewriter. "I don't like electricity going through me when I'm working," Herb had told his son years ago. "It's not natural." The apartment looked something like Herb— well-preserved, old-fashioned. Scripts and books were everywhere, black-and-white photographs of black dancers, including action shots of Herb's brother Harper, who in his early eighties could still do a passable soft-shoe. There were stills of black musicians, black actors and actresses. There were no photographs of Herbie, no photograph of Herbie's mother, and the most prominent photograph of all, the one that hung in the place of honor over the fireplace in the spacious living room, was of Georgia Faith. Which was all Herbie needed to see.

"It's like you worship her, for God's sake."

Herb wasn't quick to reply. His mind had been on the screenplay and ways to develop the character of Pearl. Georgia, in fact, had been on his mind. For the first time in his life he was certain that he wanted her. Permanently. He guessed he always had, but the timing was never right and his instincts were slow. Other men moved quickly, men like Peter Gold and Sol Solomon. That she still slept with Solomon had made him crazy, so crazy that he had proposed to the woman who was a girl when he first met her in Hollywood. For all that time, for all the changes, for all they had gone through, including having a daughter, he had never gotten over her. This time he was not going to lose her—not to Sol Solomon, not to anyone. He needed to do what he should have done fifty years ago—make a commitment, say the words. Maybe it was crazy—at this late date—but it made no difference. He had tried to be detached about this screen-play and Georgia . . . see her as an actress . . . but when he learned she was sleeping with Sol Solomon, his old feelings for her took over. The next night Herb and Georgia made love, and for those moments an energy that should long ago have drained away returned. "We're screwing like a couple of kids," Herb had said to her after-ward. She smiled, things were going her way, as planned. The next night they made love again. Herb was so intoxicated—with his own renewed powers, with his old feelings for this woman—that he pro-posed marriage and she accepted.

"I don't worship Georgia," he was now telling his son. "But I admire her. I also love her very much."

"And you're *really* going to marry her? This is a woman who plants a story that wrecks—"

"Wait a minute. I told you on the phone, Georgia mentioned only that she and I were engaged. The reporter invented that part about you and Risa to improve the story. Hollywood gossip is something—"

"And you believe Georgia?"

"Why shouldn't I?"

"Because she's a conniver—that's why. She's got you by the balls. She's the reason you left Mama, the reason you deserted your fam-ily—"

"Now wait just a minute, young man. I never deserted my family. I always provided—*always*. And as far as Georgia and I are concerned, don't pretend to understand something you don't."

"I understand what an old snatch can do to your brain."

Herb's arm was raised, ready to strike, but stopped. Herbie didn't flinch. His expression said, Go ahead, old man. Maybe it'll help bring you to your senses.

"This is a woman I've loved seriously for fifty years," Herb said slowly, getting back some of his composure.

"Fucked for fifty years . . ."

"*Enough*, damn it. You don't know what you're talking about. You don't understand this kind of love. Your generation doesn't—"

"Bullshit. She's your backdoor bitch—"

"Shut your mouth. I had a *child* with this woman."

He said it before he could stop himself. For years he had wanted to speak the words, and now that they were out of his mouth he felt

. . . what? Enormous relief. The huge burden of his secret was finally lifted.

"A child . . . ?" Herbie repeated.

"A daughter. Georgia and I had a daughter."

"And my mother never knew?"

"No, she'd been through enough. I didn't want to hurt her, I didn't want to hurt you. But now you need to know. You have a half-sister . . ."

"*Who?*"

Herb Montgomery sighed deeply before he allowed the words to leave his mouth. Once they were out, he knew nothing would ever be the same. "Risa's mother," he told his astonished son. "Chanel Faith is my daughter."

When Risa suggested to Nelson that they fly to Jamaica for a week he agreed—no arguments, no excuses. He couldn't complain . . . how could he be sure she wouldn't suddenly decide to turn her life over again to Herbie Montgomery, Jason Solomon, her grandmother or her mother?

Reality—at least for now—was unreal. He and Risa were suspended in time. His stomach might have been churning, his mind reminding him of all the things he should be doing and wasn't, but it didn't matter. He couldn't escape like his old professor had from Risa's grandmother.

For Marisa, her anxieties couldn't compare with the sensuously mild weather, the flower-perfumed breezes. Their rented villa had its own private beach, where Risa could bathe nude.

Watching her dive through the waves, Nelson wondered how it had come to this, how he was being led by this lady. But of course he knew. He just didn't know what to do about it.

Marisa came out of the water and saw him sitting on the sand. She sensed his feelings and reassured him that hers about him were real. She wanted him, hell, she wanted him right then and there. Making love under the noonday sun, under the theater of a cloudless sky, the sounds of gentle waves, the ocean washing off sweat and semen, Nelson Clay was lost in the arms of a woman who held him in absolute thrall. And who could blame him? Except maybe himself. The warmth of her thighs against his thighs, the feel of her hand on his buttocks, the need to be with her were overwhelming. Even when his mind strayed back to the practical concerns he had left behind, those concerns didn't last—not while she was stroking his forehead, not while she was kissing his lips, his nipples, his cock.

"Has a woman ever proposed to you before?" she asked.

"Never."

"Well, get ready, doc. I'm proposing." And she laughed her big, spontaneous laugh.

And he answered without thinking: "I'm accepting."

"Good, darling. Because the announcement's being made in next week's Rolling Stone."

Georgia Faith put down Rolling Stone. She was in her Beverly Hills apartment, and she was smiling. She was not upset by what she had just read. She understood that her granddaughter was sending her a message, using the press just as Georgia had used it earlier. The cross-claims could only create more publicity. Good. Marisa was flexing her muscles, using the media.

"I don't think she said it as a joke," said Herb Montgomery, who had heard about the article from son Herbie, who was more angry and confused than ever. Herb bought the magazine on this Sunday afternoon and took it over to Georgia's, where he had been spending most of his nights.

"You really don't know my Marisa," said Georgia, cool as cool could be. "She's just having fun. She realizes this movie is the best move for her. How could she possibly come to any other conclusion? She wants to toy with us for a while. It's only natural. If I were in her position I suspect I would be acting the same way."

"Herbie's devastated," his father said. "He's worried she's having a breakdown—"

"Breakdown? Herb, *please*. Faith women do not have breakdowns. We have neither the time nor patience for such self-indulgence. Nervous breakdowns are for rich white women."

"He has a lot of money tied up in that girl. I can understand—"

"That *girl* is making *him* a great deal of money."

"Georgia, I don't want a fight," he said, sipping his cup of coffee.

"It's just that your Hollywood *Daily News* story has been a sort of bombshell. At least one heavy-hitter is ready to finance the film based on casting you and Risa. I don't want to hurt his interest."

"Then don't."

"I'm not going to promise him something I can't deliver."

"You're not doing the delivering," Georgia reminded him. "I am."

"I have my credibility—"

"Herb, you're an artist, you're full of credibility. You were when I met you and you haven't changed. But damn it, Herb, there are times when the truth needs to be stretched a little—especially in *this* town. If you haven't learned that by now . . ."

"Georgia, marrying you is part of my pledge to myself to be true to *all* my feelings, even if it might be a little late in life for such grandiose gestures. Writing *Pearl* is another gesture. And telling my son Herbie about you and me and Chanel is the third—"

"You *wouldn't* . . ."

"I have."

"Why? For what possible purpose?"

"Like you, baby, I'm interested in finally getting things straight."

"My God, you've done just the opposite. This only confuses everything."

"I don't see why."

"Some secrets are supposed to be kept. Don't you understand that? Some secrets are secrets out of consideration and kindness to other people. That was something between us, our bond—"

"A lie."

"A lifetime bond, Herb. Why ruin it now? For God's sake . . ." Georgia felt her hands shaking, her life unraveling. Herb started to walk over to put his arm around her and comfort her, but the sound of the doorbell stopped him.

Georgia opened the door. In a black-and-white-striped jumpsuit too tight for her bulky frame, her makeup too heavy and her wig tinged with streaks of blond, Chanel Faith stood there.

"You're not going to say hello?" said Chanel.

"I'm surprised," said Georgia, feeling for perhaps the first time that she was losing control.

Chanel walked inside and saw Mr. Herb Montgomery. She remembered him, of course, as the husband of the choir director, Honey Montgomery, who had given her the first chance to sing solo in church. Over thirty years ago, but the memory was still intact. Later she knew him as one of her mother's friends in the movie business, a man who made movies of his own. Of course, she had thought about him again when Marisa had signed with his son's record company, a move, Chanel assumed, engineered by Georgia. In these past few days she had thought about Herb even more. The Hollywood *Daily News* article had done that. She wondered about the truth of the story, which was another reason she had to see her mother. A phone call wouldn't do. She wanted to look Georgia in the eye. She wanted to find out whether her mother was tricking or telling the truth. But somehow she wasn't looking at her mother at this moment. She was looking at Herb Montgomery, this gray-haired gentleman dressed in a denim workshirt and freshly pressed khaki pants. There was something about this man, something about the vibes in the room, the way he walked over to her, the words he seemed to speak, not with his mouth but with his eyes. They looked at one another—Herb Montgomery and Chanel Faith—for a very long time. Georgia wanted to say something, wanted to step between them because she understood too well what was being communicated. But Georgia couldn't. They were on their own.

Chanel had arrived with an angry heart, prepared for a long overdue, all-out confrontation with her mother about her daughter. But her anger had evaporated, time had stopped. The way she was looking at this man, the way he was looking at her . . .

"It's him," Chanel finally said, turning to her mother, who understood that the drama of the moment could not be avoided. She kept silent. "He's my father, isn't he?" said Chanel.

It was the first of May. Sunshine was pouring through the windows of Marisa's Soho loft, and in a few minutes Herbie Montgomery and Jason Solomon would be arriving. Nelson had advised her that it would be best to tell them together. That way there could be no doubts. Nelson couldn't be there. He was seeing patients, but he promised Risa that he would call after the meeting; he knew it wouldn't be easy. She wasn't worried. She had a handle on her life now. With Nelson's help she thought she finally understood what she had to do and how to do it. She was dressed in baggy jeans, a loose white silk shirt with tiny pearl buttons and a blue Keith Haring baseball cap to cover her hair still damp from a long shower. She applied bright red lipstick, made a pot of strong coffee and by eleven was ready to meet Jason and Herbie.

Jason arrived first. She kissed him on the cheek. She knew she had injured him but there was nothing she could say—not yet—except that she was sorry and that she had to figure this out on her own.

Herbie arrived with an attitude. He looked stiff, uptight. Jason was in sports clothes, Herbie in a three-piece suit, carrying a leather attache case. "Let's get started, Risa, I have a busy day."

Risa sat on a couch, the men in easy chairs facing her.

"Okay," she began, "I know how much both of you have helped me. You've believed in me and in a way that's been the most important thing. I'm going to honor our agreements for at least another year. But I have to get other representation. What's professional and what's personal among us has gotten blurred. I'm not saying I didn't contribute to it. I did. But it's got to stop, it's no good anymore for any of us—"

"That's going to be difficult," Herbie broke in. He'd been waiting for this moment.

"I know that."

"No, you don't, Risa. You haven't a clue . . . "

"What are you talking about?"

"My father, your grandmother, their little secret." Herbie was speaking slowly, savoring the best till last.

"*What* little secret?"

The moment had arrived. "Fifty years ago Georgia Faith and my father had a child. Her name was Chanel."

Chanel was sitting in a motel in West Hollywood a few hours after the cataclysmic news, wondering what to do, checking out her feelings as though they belonged to someone else. She felt empty, cheated. She thought about a lifetime of wishing for a father, someone to look up to, someone to handle Georgia, to set things right like fathers were supposed to do. She blamed Georgia, and she blamed Herb. She couldn't stay there in Georgia's apartment, she couldn't stand to look at Georgia. The idea that this man who seemed so kind and understanding had deserted her a lifetime ago was too much. In a way she'd been better off in the dark, she figured. It was too late to find out now. She didn't want to talk about it, didn't want to be here, didn't want to look at *him* or *her* for another minute . . .

Now that she was alone in the motel she felt like a victim. It was cruel of Georgia to invent a lie, even though Chanel had never believed it. She had said so to the shrink she had seen last year in Alabama. But she also remembered the shrink asking her, "Is there a relationship between the story your mother told you about your father and what you've told your daughter about hers?" Chanel didn't want to think about that. Herb Montgomery was a dog. Chanel had been dogged. What else was new? And how was she supposed to resolve all this with Marisa? "Yes," Herb had told her before she left Georgia's apartment, "Georgia and I are getting married." Hilarious, when you thought about it, she muttered to herself. Getting married all these years after the fact. The questions were weird . . . Did that mean she would be acknowledged as their daughter? Would she be a member of the wedding? Wild, crazy. The whole goddamn thing was beyond weird. Life made more sense when she was getting looped. Which was just what she badly wanted to do—get wrecked. This was too much, too much. Her hand trembling slightly, she picked up the phone and called an old connection. Minutes later she left the motel, took a walk and ended up at a liquor store where she bought a bottle of bourbon. By the time she returned to her room, her connection had arrived with a bag of fresh weed and a packet of cocaine.

So much for the truth shall set you free. Free for what?

Marisa knew Herbie had told the truth. When the words came out she actually had felt her breath shorten and her heartbeat quicken.

"That's just what I'm talking about," she told Herbie and Jason. "It's all about my grandmother and your father Herb, my grandmother and your grandfather Sol. That's why I just can't handle working with either of you. It's too crazy."

"I didn't know," said Herbie. "If I had I would have said something to you."

"You knew when we were in high school," Jason reminded her,

"that Georgia and Sol were screwing. We didn't like talking about it but we both knew what was going on. To tell you the truth, sometimes I wondered whether Sol was your grandfather as well as mine."

"Look," Risa said, "you're making my point. No more. I'm going to separate myself as far from all this as I can."

"It's not going to work," Herbie said. "You can't."

"The *hell* I can't." Now Risa was up from the couch and on the edge of losing control.

Interestingly, Jason agreed with Herbie. "Risa, sorry, but we're in this together. It's like a web, and whether you like it or not, Risa, you're stuck in it too."

Now that she had the drugs, Chanel didn't know what to do. She didn't want to throw them away. She didn't want to wipe out her years of sobriety. She didn't want to stay in Los Angeles, didn't want to go back to New York. She had stared at the bottle of booze and packets of dope for so long, her eyes clouded over. Only the ring of the phone brought her back. It was her publicist saying that the only way to jazz up her album's sales was to have a dual interview with her and Risa. People magazine was interested. Could she get her daughter to agree? Are you kidding, she thought. "I'm going home to Muscle Shoals," she told the woman. "I'll call you from there."

She took a deep breath, went to the bathroom and flushed the drugs down the toilet. The day was overcast. She cried in the cab to the airport, and barely held back the tears on the plane.

Back in her small house that overlooked the Tennessee River, the great Wilson Dam in the distance, she looked out the window and saw that the clouds still hadn't lifted.

Why? Why now? Why did she have to learn this now? *It's My Time* was the name of her album. Like hell. She wanted to talk to someone and thought of Georgia, but what would Georgia have to say? Clever rationalizations for what she'd held back for so long. Her mother would be composed, always the actress. She'd be reassuring. It made Chanel sick to think about it.

In the middle of the night Chanel woke up soaked in sweat. She felt feverish but it wasn't the flu, it was the dream. She couldn't remember the details, but they were all there—her father Herb

Montgomery, her mother and her daughter, Johnny Dodd Huggins, they were all after her with guns and razor blades, or was it her daughter they were after? Or her poor dead son . . . ? Well, at least she understood what had to be done. Call Marisa. Tell her—not about Herb, by now she must know—but about her real father, Johnny Dodd. At most her daughter wouldn't have to wait another quarter century to learn the truth. The sooner she found out, the better. Let her at least be free of the lie. Break the damned pattern of the Faith women. Don't wait. Do it now.

Marisa was in bed, Nelson next to her, when she heard the phone ring. The answering machine was on but for a reason she would never know the ring had her up and into the next room listening to the caller's message.

"If you're there," said her mother, "pick up. It's important."

Risa picked up.

"Are you sick?" asked Marisa.

"Yes, but not the way you mean."

"Look, Mama, it's four in the morning, I don't really want to hear—"

"I know you already heard about my father . . ."

"I don't want to talk about it, not now—"

"Now *listen*, girl—for months you've shut me out and I just accepted it, but that ain't gonna work no more . . ."

"You know, Mama, Georgia called yesterday talkin' the same way you're talkin' now. And I told her what I'm telling you—I don't want to hear it. I don't want to hear any more excuses or lies—"

"Good. Because this time I'm telling you the truth."

"That's what you said last time."

"Something's changed."

"*Nothing's* changed, except I'm not having any more. Forget it, forget me. I mean it." She hung up.

In Muscle Shoals, the dark night yielding to murky gray outside her window, Chanel just sat there staring, as though transfixed, the dial tone sounding in her ear like an ultimate rejection. Marisa hadn't even given her a chance. Her daughter had turned into her mother. The door was closed.

She couldn't go back to sleep. She sat at her kitchen table smoking cigarettes, drinking coffee and watching morning light fall over the river. Anger boiled up. She had the truth but Marisa wouldn't hear it. All right, she'd waited too long, but now that she was willing, was able to face the truth and tell it, no matter the hurt or consequences, Marisa had slapped her in the face. Well, she wasn't going to get bombed, lose her grip. She wasn't going to hurt herself anymore. She was going to tell the truth, one way or the other. At nine-thirty she called Joan Winfrey in New York.

"Tell the publicist that we can do that People story now."

"Risa has agreed?"

Chanel ignored the question. "You're going to have to make me up real nice and pretty and get that photographer Bing to shoot my picture, 'cause with what I'm going to say they're going to put me on the cover."

FIVE MONTHS LATER

After the People cover story—"JOHNNY DODD HUGGINS IS THE FATHER OF MY CHILD . . . AND HER NAME IS RISA" —Chanel Faith was a nationwide celebrity. Oprah, Geraldo and Joan had her on their shows. Because of her flat-out frankness she was admired by viewers. She talked about her addiction and was candid about her relationship with Johnny Dodd. "He was my dope man," she told a national television audience, "and my backdoor lover too." She talked about her recovery—she'd been clean for nearly three years. Her message was uplifting. Her album sales soared—*It's My Time* sold over 250,000 units and she had two years of bookings at blues festivals at home and abroad.

For Johnny Dodd Huggins the fallout was something else. Unprepared for Chanel going public, at first he tried to deny everything, then changed his story, saying that Risa might, after all, be his daughter and he was proud of her. But he wound up cancelling a national tour because of the negative publicity, and his album fell from the top of the country charts into the half-price bins within a matter of weeks.

After the sensational round of publicity that focused on Chanel, Georgia, through old friends in Hollywood, approached the number-one interview personality. Would she be interested in the true story of the Faith women? She would be.

In a prime-time segment Georgia Faith held the national TV spotlight— held it, played with it, controlled it. The interview took place at Passion Flowers among displays of yellow roses that matched

Georgia's yellow silk dress. Her green eyes bright as ever, she spoke of her great pride in both her daughter Chanel and granddaughter Marisa, of the courage it took for her daughter Chanel to reveal such private matters for the good of her family. She told of how her prior revelation—that director Herb Montgomery was the father of her daughter—had apparently encouraged Chanel to speak out herself, and she was grateful for that. She went on to say there was a new dawn of unabashed candor for women everywhere, especially black women. She reminisced over highlights of her own career—her hard times in the forties, her years in Europe, on Broadway, in television . . . her "challenge to a system that was designed to exclude me and women like me. They didn't count on our spirit." The interviewer adored her, respected her. Georgia also mentioned her impending marriage to Herb Montgomery—"up to now, an unsung hero of African-American culture"—and Paramounts green light to *Pearl*, project of a lifetime. "My fairy tale," she told the fascinated interviewer, "is finally coming true."

Marisa watched the tape of the Georgia Faith television interview from Switzerland. She and Nelson had rented a villa in the hills above Montreux, glittering Lake Geneva and the imposing Alps visible from their living-room window. She remembered as a child hearing her mother rave about the beauty of this spot, the place where Chanel had gone to sing shortly after Marisa was born.

Marisa had been out of the country ever since Chanel's People story hit the newsstands. She could not possibly speak to either her mother or grandmother, not now, probably not for years. The shock of the deception was still too acute. Her dreams, though, wouldn't leave her alone, filled with perverse images of Herb Montgomery and Johnny Dodd Huggins. All right, it was her fault that she had to hear about Huggins being her father the way she did. She had hung up on Chanel, after all, before her mother could get it out. But there had been all her life to tell her the truth, and neither Chanel nor Georgia had been able or willing to do it. God, what a pair. What a *threesome* . . . Nelson had pegged it right with his fancy term "triangulation."

Nelson had advised that she not try to face her newly discovered grandfather and father—at least not yet. "Deal with them first as mythic material," he said. "If you can handle them in your dreams, you'll stand a better chance of coping with them in reality."

As for Nelson, he put his own practice on hold for a year, turning over his patients to several colleagues. Marisa was more than enough to take up all his time and talents. Maybe she was his obsession, but it did no good to deny it. Besides, he was enjoying himself in ways he never had before. He didn't crack a medical or psychoanalytic journal. It was a wonderful release, this obsession.

Of all the Faith women, Risa had, ironically, benefited most from the publicity. At least financially. The more intense the firestorm surrounding her mother and grandmother, the more attention focused on Marisa. And the more reticent Marisa became, the greater the interest in her music. By now her debut album had surpassed eight million copies in America and was starting to show big numbers in Europe. She planned to center herself in Switzerland, make her follow-up record in the state-of-the-art Montreux recording studios and keep her distance from both Los Angeles and Muscle Shoals. Her English lawyers had worked out a more-or-less amicable buy-out with Herbie and Jason, who privately said they'd never get over her, though the money helped ease the pain. Besides, Herbie was producing *Pearl*, his father's first mainstream film, and Jason had changed directions and convinced his grandfather to let him direct *Hit and Run*, the film version of Sol Solomon's novel about the fifties, when the Dodgers were in Brooklyn and the Giants at the Polo Grounds.

All in all, Marisa thought as she stood on the balcony of the old Swiss villa on an October afternoon, regarding the mighty Alps with wonder, things seemed to be working out. What a hoot, as Chanel might say. Who in the whole wide world would ever have thought it?

And then, unbidden, from the very depths of her came that whooping laugh that echoed like a shout across the valley, bringing Nelson out to the balcony on the run.

"Risa, is anything wrong. Are you all right?"

"Honey," she said, "nothing is wrong, and yes, I surely am all right. Now go and figure *that* . . ."